Born in Detroit in 1945, **Woody Haut** grew up in Pasadena, California, attended San Francisco State University, and has lived in Britain since the early 1970s. Presently a London-based journalist, he has worked as a college lecturer, taxi-cab driver, record-shop assistant, cinema programmer and freelance journalist. His earlier books, *Pulp Culture: Hardboiled Fiction and the Cold War* and *Neon Noir: Contemporary American Crime Fiction* were both published by Serpent's Tail.

**Also by Woody Haut and
published by Serpent's Tail**

*Pulp Culture: Hardboiled Fiction and the Cold War
Neon Noir: Contemporary American Crime Fiction*

HEARTBREAK AND VINE

The Fate of Hardboiled Writers in Hollywood

WOODY HAUT

Library of Congress Catalog Card Number: 2002101378

A catalogue record for this book is available from the British
Library on request

The right of Woody Haut to be identified as the author of this
work has been asserted by him in accordance with the Copyright,
Designs and Patents Act 1988

Website: www.serpentstail.com

Set in 10pt Baskerville by Intype London Ltd

Printed in Great Britain by Mackays of Chatham, plc

10 9 8 7 6 5 4 3 2 1

Contents

Acknowledgements

Thanks to the following: Mike Hart, John Williams and Philippe Garnier for pointing me in the right direction; Pete Ayrton for unknowingly suggesting the subject of *Heartbreak and Vine*; Mavis Haut for reading the book in manuscript; Emma Waghorn for her astute copy editing; A.I. Bezzerides, Edward Bunker, James Lee Burke, Michael Connelly, James Crumley, James Ellroy, Barry Gifford, James Hall, Dennis Lehane, Elmore Leonard, George Pelecanos, Gerald Petievich, Joseph Wambaugh and Donald Westlake for kindly answering my questions; and to the many novelists–scriptwriters who, for lack of space, have gone unmentioned.

Heartbreak and Vine is dedicated to Caroline S. Haut, with whom I watched my first movie, lost in the light, Pasadena, California, 1949; and to the memory of poet and cultural critic Edward Dorn, 1929–1999.

INTRODUCTION: THE BIG NOWHERE

For the past 75 years there has been an uneasy fit between the movie-made HOLLYWOOD! image and the actual Hollywood district. Indeed, at any level, 'Hollywood' is a difficult concept to come to grips with, elusive and elastic at the same time. First of all, there is maximum official disagreement about where Hollywood is even located. Each Los Angeles city and county agency has a service unit called 'Hollywood,' yet no two share the same boundaries and only one is identical to the city limits of the short-lived city of Hollywood (1903–10).

Mike Davis, *Ecology of Fear*

As a dream-suburb of Los Angeles, Hollywood is as imaginary as it is real.

Though its location is open to debate, its name, narrative-exploiting reality and function – the manufacturing of dreams and modern-day myths – is undeniable.

With the ability to turn anything – emotion, event, person, place or literary artefact – into a commodity, Hollywood can destroy as well as create. Those not meeting its primary criterion – profit, at any cost – are quickly replaced by the next in a long line of Tinseltown hopefuls.

Making up a substantial section of the *entertainment industry*, Hollywood is, above all, a corporate enterprise, and its presence looms large in the directory of conglomerates. An economic driving force, it underwrites production companies and employs casts of thousands, whether writers, directors, actors, camera operators, carpenters or caterers.

But it is the writers that concern this study – specifically novelists, particularly of the hardboiled variety, who have decided to become scriptwriters. Many of these writers would turn to that most subversive of Hollywood genres, film noir – subversive because anyone who writes noir film, or for that matter noir fiction, must question the culture, and so treads on dangerous ground. Up against the studios and the culture, few would escape unscathed.

Most successful writers of American hardboiled fiction, at one time or another, would try their hand at writing screenplays. Likewise, Hollywood has always been willing to invite noirists – Raymond Chandler, Horace McCoy, James M. Cain, Elmore Leonard or Donald Westlake – into their midst, co-opting their talent in the hope of enhancing studio profits. Some hardboilers have been able to adapt to the strictures of scriptwriting and the Hollywood lifestyle, while others have been destroyed by it.

For being a successful writer of noir fiction does not mean that one will be a successful writer of film noir. True, both activities are dependent on an ability to establish a convincing narrative and a willingness to investigate the culture. But the two forms depend on different factors. By looking at the careers of those writers who have engaged in both activities, some of these factors will become apparent.

In earlier days those best able to adapt to the industry's demands often came from the deadline-oriented world of journalism (Ben Hecht, John Bright, James M. Cain, Niven Busch). Not surprisingly, creativity and literary ability were, in Hollywood, often less important than the ability to write quickly and to order (the sign in one writers' building was said to have read: WRITE FASTER). Writers also had to be adept at adapting the work of others. Significantly, the original film script-story, which has since become a Hollywood staple, was only to become a full-fledged commodity after World War II when low-budget B features reflected a more economical approach, and studios were in need of scripts written quickly and on the cheap. With the exception of work by Elmore Leonard, James Ellroy and Jim Thompson, recent film noir, from Robert Towne's *Chinatown* to Scott Rosenberg's *Things to Do in Denver When You're Dead*, is as likely to derive from original screenplays. Accordingly, many present-day scriptwriters have no experience of writing fiction, nor a background in journalism, but are film-school products whose only thought is to succeed in Hollywood's competitive marketplace.

Though there have been numerous books on film noir, the careers of those who wrote the screenplays of such movies have rarely been investigated. Equally, even though hard-boilers from Chandler to Ellroy have been a staple of postwar cinema, the relationship between writing noir fiction and film has been largely ignored. This is ironical, since hardboiled fiction has enjoyed a special relationship with film noir, a genre as dominated by dialogue as by camerawork and the signature of individual directors. All successful film noir has been the product of a particular chemistry between writers and directors, whether Polanski and Towne in *Chinatown*, Bezzerides and Aldrich in *Kiss Me, Deadly*, or Scorsese and Shrader in *Taxi Driver*.

Hollywood's hostile treatment of screenwriters is legendary. Because they were in a position to disseminate ideas, screenwriters were distrusted, not allowed to control their product, and constantly fired by studios. Their status was damaged further during the 1960s with the rise of *auteur* criticism, a theory insisting that the director is responsible for the cinematic totality, including the script. Nevertheless, noir screenwriters have recently gained a more respectable position, some becoming, at least in the imagination of film aficionados, figures of romance. This is partly because writers, once in Hollywood, have often had to reject the world of literature and embrace the role of literary worker.

The cynical scriptwriter in Billy Wilder's *Sunset Boulevard* might have been right when he said, 'Audiences don't know anyone writes a picture. They think actors make it up as they go along.' But scripts, without which few Hollywood pictures would ever have been made, are essential to the film-making process.

These days, some suggest scriptwriters themselves are the real *auteurs* (Gerald Horne in *Class Struggle in Hollywood* maintains that bankers have an equal right to the term *auteur*). In reality, movies remain the province of producers and directors, whose perspectives supersede that of the writer. As William Goldman puts it in *Adventures in the Screen Trade*, 'In terms of authority, screenwriters rank somewhere between the man who guards the studio gate and the man who runs the studio (this week).' Their demotion in the studio hierarchy, and, by contrast, promoting the position of the director, would become particularly noticeable in the late 1940s, coincident with the gradual erosion of the negotiating power of writers. Today, the screenwriter's popular image is as someone cynical, money-oriented and melodramatic (*Sunset Boulevard*); a romantic hack (Wim Wenders's *Hammett*) or comic naif (the Coen brothers' *Barton Fink*).

The truth lies in between these perceptions. Yet however one regards the process, screenwriting remains an art that many novelists are unable to execute, and that many producers and directors are unable to appreciate. At the same time, some turn to the form only because they cannot abide the artistic and financial insecurity associated with the life of a novelist. Robert Towne may be a formidable screenwriter, but he is not a formidable novelist. In fact, he is not a novelist at all. Likewise, Raymond Chandler and Dashiell Hammett, whatever their worth as novelists, were not great screenwriters. No wonder Ernest Hemingway and, for many years, James Ellroy, would have nothing to do with Hollywood. In the hierarchy of writers, the novelist is considered the superior creature, but that quickly changes when he or she begins to work in an industry that caters to the lowest common denominator.

Though some (Nathaniel West, William Faulkner, F. Scott Fitzgerald) produced little if anything in the way of fiction while working in Hollywood, others, like W.R. Burnett and James M. Cain, were able to produce their best fiction while working there. On the other hand, Chandler's career as a novelist was by and large over by the time he began working on Billy Wilder's *Double Indemnity*, a film that marked the beginning of his tenure in Tinseltown.

The image of screenwriters as grovelling hacks willing to sell themselves at any price was always a convenient one for Hollywood to perpetuate. But in 1939, prior to the formation of the Writers Guild, studios were hiring junior writers for $35 a week or less and also had them write scripts on speculation. Such was the degree of penny-pinching regarding salaries that Republic once fired their writers on Thanksgiving, only to rehire them the following Monday, thus avoiding holiday pay. Later, studios would take advantage of industrial action to clear their decks of unwanted scripts and reduce the wages of their writers. As John Gregory Dunne points out in *Monster*, screenwriters have measured their success in financial terms because they have no power, nor means to measure themselves and their writing skills.

Some, like Fitzgerald, Faulkner, West and John O'Hara looked to Hollywood during low points in their careers as novelists, while the careers of others reached their nadir only when they decided to seek work in Hollywood. Yet writers went all the same. Some sought fame; others sought money. Some sought fame *and* money. Some went out of curiosity, or to tame the great beast languishing in the land of philistines. For Hollywood – in contrast to New York, a city of playwrights, novelists and high culture – represented plebeian tastes. East-coast writers may have thumbed their noses at screenwriters, but most, at some point, would join their ranks. For 'doing Hollywood' was *de rigeur* for novelists, particularly during the 1930s. As Pauline Kael puts it in *Raising Kane and Other Essays,* 'expatriates without leaving the country . . . adapted each other's out-of-date plays and novels, and rewrote each other's scripts . . . and within a few years were rewriting the rewrites of their own or somebody else's rewrites'.

These days, when much of Tinseltown proper is a semi-slum, and the famous Hollywood sign is guarded by state-of-the-art motion detectors, infrared cameras on computer disk and city park rangers who use loudspeakers to warn away trespassers, writers are likely to be freelancers who, as in Bruce Wagner's novel *Force Majeure,* spend their time hustling to get someone even to read their scripts, let alone to produce them.

So competitive has screenwriting become that not only do university film departments offer screenwriting courses but expensive, weekend courses also beckon aspiring writers to hone their skills. A scriptwriter need not have a novel under his or her belt, though there might be an unpublished one lurking under his or her bed. Likewise, few writers are tied to studio payrolls. This is partly to keep writers on a short leash, and partly because, compared to earlier eras, fewer Hollywood films are being made – 477 films were made in 1940, but, with the growing popularity of TV, the number dropped to 154 in 1960, rising again with the advent of the video age in the early 1990s. With Hollywood not quite so desperate for stories and original material, Tinseltown remains a fool's paradise, in which the market dictates taste, and monetary reward has become greater than ever.

The chapters that follow recount the careers of an assortment of noirists. Some succeeded as screenwriters, some failed, and some were merely run-of-the-mill. Though 'doing Hollywood' is no longer obligatory, the attraction remains. Meanwhile, writers continue to arrive in Hollywood with great expectations only to find that working in the industry will eventually take its toll. As Goldman puts it, '[If] you are the kind of weird person who has a *need* to bring something into being, and all you do with your life is turn out screenplays, I may covet your bank account, but I wouldn't give two bits for your soul.' No matter how much the film industry has changed, it still represents a specific aspect of transnational corporate power, part American Dream and part American Nightmare. As A.P. Giannini of the Bank of America, one of the industry's prime founders, prophetically observed during the early days of Hollywood, 'Those who control the cinema can control the thought of the world.' Writers should be forewarned: engage with Hollywood at your peril.

I

UNDER THE SIGN OF HOLLYWOOD

Dashiell Hammett and Raymond Chandler

Dashiell Hammett and Raymond Chandler may not have been the only noirists to seek fame and fortune in Hollywood, but they are the best known and most widely read to have done so. Together they represent the two faces of noir. A former Pinkerton detective, Hammett virtually created the modern hardboiled novel. The more realistic of the two, he produced five genre-defining novels – each a subtle leftist critique of American society – within six years. The more opaque Chandler, who often acknowledged his debt to Hammett, sought to parody the genre, using a camera eye that ruthlessly observed and commented upon the manners and mores of Southern California life. An American raised in England and educated in an English public school, Chandler was, above all, a stylist. With an English middle-class perspective of Los Angeles, his protagonist, Philip Marlowe, had a ready-made witticism for every occasion.

Neither's career in Hollywood could be called successful. Yet both speak volumes about the role of the hardboiled writer in Hollywood, and the relationship between such writers and the movie industry. It's a moot point whether Hollywood wrecked them as writers, or whether their careers were wrecked by the time they arrived. In any case, working in the studios would earn them substantial amounts of money and increase the negotiability of their names, while their protagonists, Philip Marlowe and Sam Spade, would become icons whose styles, comments and critiques would be widely emulated.

Dashiell Hammett

> For many years it has been . . . impossible to steal from the rich.
>
> (Dashiell Hammett, 'How to Live in the United States')

Seeking work in the studios was, in the 1930s, the domestic version of travelling to Paris, a process that enabled the real 'lost generation' to buy time before getting down to more serious work. In practice, it did not necessarily work like that. Certainly not for Dashiell Hammett. An existential Marxist who defined the political wing of the hardboiled movement, he was the first personality to emerge from noir fiction, and the first noirist to move into the film industry. Seeking to exploit the industry, Hammett would pay a high price for his audacity, earning power and political critique.

What Hammett offered Hollywood was authenticity. Not only acquainted with the world of literature, this former gumshoe was well-versed in the language and psychology of the private eye and the criminal class. Born into a working-class Baltimore family, and raised a few blocks from a young H.L. Mencken, Hammett was by nature a man of the streets, who would always demonstrate a fondness for the accoutrements of privilege and wealth. By the time he arrived in Hollywood, Hammett had not only written four best-selling hardboiled novels, but as a Pinkerton agent had also, to his embarrassment, helped break strikes and contributed to the decimation of the Wobblies (Industrial Workers of the World). Combining an eye for detail with an ability to create wonderfully memorable characters, he wrote stories that were eminently filmable. From the studio's perspective, the hard-drinking, larger-than-life Hammett, who, to W.R. Burnett, looked like a university professor, was the ideal commodity.

Though there were pulp investigators prior to Sam Spade, Hammett's protagonist kick-started the public's fascination with the private eye. Turning the private-eye-as-pulp-hero inside-out, Hammett would create protagonists, only to eventually trash them. Before Sam Spade there had been the hardcore and streetwise Continental Op, while after Spade there would be Nick Charles, a retired private eye who, in an alcoholic haze, vanished into the literary ether accompanied by wife Nora and dog Asta. Taken together, these protagonists represent different sides of Hammett's personality: the toughguy, the hard-bitten humanitarian, and the *bon vivant*.

Even before 1931, the year when his career in Tinseltown began in earnest, Hammett had been to Hollywood on at least two occasions. The first was in April 1928, to negotiate with Fox the film rights for *Red Harvest*, at which time he was to come away empty-handed, unable even to sell episodes of what would become *The Dain Curse*. Then, in the summer of 1930, having published *The Maltese Falcon*, Hammett was again searching for a Hollywood deal. During these early visits, he was to learn something about negotiating with the studios. It also illustrates an often overlooked side of the author: namely, that Hammett, at that time, was quite willing to hustle his work. This in contrast to the notion of a laidback writer, unconcerned about selling himself to Hollywood. On the contrary, Hammett was constantly pitching ideas to the studios. At that point he didn't have the luxury of a highpowered agent to represent him, but he had spent considerable time writing advertising copy for Samuel's Jewellery in San Francisco, he knew the art of salesmanship, and was adept at talking up his work.

Initially, Hammett considered himself a cut above other screenwriters. This was a view studios actively encouraged. They liked to have writers divide themselves according to how much they made and where they worked. According to Otto Friedrich in *City of Nets*, 'Survivors of the 1940's . . . recall that Paramount writers talked only to other Paramount writers, and that a $500-per-week writer would not be welcome at a party given by a $1,500-per-week writer.' So Hammett gravitated not to pulpists and screenwriting hacks but to literary refugees like S.J. Perelman, Dorothy Parker, Budd Schulberg, Ira Gershwin and Ben Hecht. Soon he was immersed in the Hollywood lifestyle, which revolved around eating at expensive restaurants, partying and, more than ever, as these were the last days of Prohibition, drinking. Once settled in Tinseltown, Hammett hired a black cook and chauffeur, while David O. Selznick hired Hammett.

Having come west from New York four years earlier, Selznick would soon quit Paramount to become studio boss at RKO, where he would produce *Gone with the Wind*. He considered Hammett would be a good name to add to his list of writers, and someone he could substantially underpay. 'Hammett is unspoilt as to money,' said Selznick, who was about to offer the author $400 a week, even though this was half the amount Hammett claimed he was making from books and magazine articles. If Hammett was making $800 a week in 1931, it was, at today's prices, a staggering sum for a crime writer. The author of *Red Harvest*, *The Maltese Falcon* and *The Dain Curse* could not have known, however, that by the time he began working for Selznick his best work was behind him.

At Paramount, Hammett's first film was Rouben Mamoulian's *City Streets*, starring Gary Cooper and Sylvia Sidney. Based on a short story, 'After School', Hammett purportedly wrote it in one weekend, though *Halliwell's Film Guide* maintains that Mamoulian's film was adapted from 'Ladies of the Mob' by the ex-convict and professional thief Ernest Booth. In any case, the film's snappy dialogue is typical of Hammett. Marked by an overly stylised expressionism and overt symbolism, the film concerns a gangster's daughter recently released from jail, having been sentenced for a murder she did not commit. Fortunately for Hammett, the film was a moderate box-office success.

While at Paramount, Hammett was also working through the proofs of *The Glass Key*, and trying to finish *The Thin Man*. It was not just a case, as some have reported, of postponing the latter's completion because he did not want its publication to coincide with that of *The Glass Key*. Already tiring of the detective format, Hammett was attempting with *The Thin Man*, which parodied his new Hollywood lifestyle, to move outside the genre of hardboiled fiction. It would be Hammett's only novel written while in Hollywood, and the last novel he would ever complete.

In November 1930, while working at Paramount, Hammett began an affair with the precocious Lillian Hellman Kober. At the time, Hellman, a twenty-five-year-old MGM script-reader, was married to the playwright and screenwriter Arthur Kober. Hammett was also married. Jose, his former nurse, lived in Los Angeles with their two daughters. Despite, or because of, his disrespect for the institution of matrimony, Hammett had agreed to become Jose's husband when she told him that she was pregnant. Although Hammett was not the child's father, he had felt indebted to Jose for nursing him back to health and had realised the guilt she must have felt as a Catholic woman about to bear an illegitimate child. So the anything but monogamous Hammett felt little compunction about taking up with Hellman. The two, though seldom sharing the same quarters, would remain a couple for the rest of Hammett's life. *The Thin Man* would be a tribute to the early stages of their relationship.

Like *The Thin Man*'s Nick Charles, Hammett could be both charming and belligerent. Within months of arriving in Hollywood, he was bickering with his publisher, Alfred Knopf, who had voiced reservations about the title *The Maltese Falcon*. Knopf thought *Falcon* too difficult for book buyers to pronounce. He also felt the same about the name *Hammett*. Fortunately, the person responsible for Hammett at Knopf was neither Alfred nor his wife, Blanche, but Bernard Smith, who would edit Hammett, as well as Chandler, James M. Cain and B. Traven. Hired in 1928, Smith worked at Knopf's for twenty years, before moving to Hollywood where, despite his leftwing politics, he befriended John Ford and produced *Elmer*

Gantry and *Cheyenne Autumn*. But Knopf would bear the brunt of Hammett's counter-complaints. Eventually, amicable resolutions were reached and the novel appeared later in the year. Within months, Hammett had sold the film rights for $25,000. He hoped *The Thin Man*, which he was seeking to finish by the end of year, would prove even more lucrative.

Initially, Hammett was able to couple a writing career with a frenetic social life. But before long his writing was to become a secondary concern. A frequent visitor to the Brown Derby and the Clover Club, he had a taste for the high life, and differed from Wim Wenders's portrayal of a solitary and dedicated writer in the film *Hammett*, a depiction more applicable to the years Hammett spent as a struggling author. Furthermore, by the time of Wenders's film, attempts to portray Hammett had been tempered by Hellman's recalcitrance regarding material contradicting her version of events. Though a highly paid screenwriter, Hammett, who liked nothing more than hopping from one club to another, was often in need of cash and regularly cabled Knopf to deposit money into his dwindling bank account.

Rather than finish *The Thin Man*, Hammett, when he wasn't socialising, worked on whatever scripts the studio threw his way. His job was to adjust story-lines, add scenes, write additional dialogue and do redrafts. Much of his work at this time would go uncredited. As his biographer Diane Johnson says, Hammett had become a kind of Pinkerton of film, secretly investigating films that others had already corrupted.

When *The Glass Key* was published in 1931, it sold 11,000 copies within three weeks, and was soon set to be filmed. However, plans were scuppered when the Motion Picture Producers and Distributors of America – which censored films and devised the Motion Picture Production Code, otherwise known as the Hays Office after its first president Will Hays, or the Breen office, after Joseph Breen was appointed head of the Production Code Administration in 1934 – raised objections to the way the novel portrayed public officials. Despite the success of the novel, and although filming would not begin for another four years (when the first version, starring George Raft, appeared, director Frank Tuttle made sure the politics of the novel were toned down), Hammett sought wider recognition. He was now hoping *The Thin Man* would be his last detective novel.

Though it had only been a matter of months since he had arrived in Hollywood, Hammett already wanted to leave. Not only did he want to join Lillian in New York, but his debts were beginning to pile up, and Warner Brothers was demanding that he return their advance for a rejected story, 'On the Make'. Needing money, Hammett wired Knopf for $2,500. He even tried to stop drinking. Knopf dutifully sent the money, and Hammett promptly tumbled from the wagon.

In September 1931, a year after his arrival, Hammett was stuck on the studio treadmill. He was suffering from severe headaches and his tuberculosis symptoms, dormant for some years, had returned. He spent his time reading. He had begun Faulkner's *Sanctuary* but thought it overrated (he had even less regard for Hemingway, saying the latter 'saw himself as Hercules astride a woman'). It could have been, however, that Hammett was envious because Faulkner could write so well *and* drink so much.

Hammett's novelty in and around Hollywood was beginning to wear thin. He was even becoming something of a social embarrassment. Once more he tried to stop drinking, only to settle into a suicidal gloom. When Hellman arrived from New York, she found Hammett at a low ebb. 'I'm a clown,' he said, knowing that Hollywood had already eaten into his soul.

He and Lillian left for New York in the autumn of 1931. They booked rooms at the Elyseé. Faulkner arrived in town. Despite Hammett's reservations regarding *Sanctuary*, the two became drinking partners. In their matching tweeds, they looked like English gentlemen on a pub crawl. They crashed a cocktail party at Knopf's. At another party, Dorothy Parker fell to her knees, kissed Hammett's hand, and confessed her love for Sam Spade. Hammett was bemused, but Hellman was furious.

Back in Hollywood, the studios considered Hammett unreliable. They also knew he was too valuable a commodity to let go. So they did what studios do when they want to reign in recalcitrant talents: they threw money at him. Even before *The Thin Man* was published, MGM had purchased the rights for $21,000. Knopf published the novel in January 1934, some months after an expurgated version appeared in *Redbook* magazine. Though Hammett had virtually stopped writing, MGM was offering him a further $2,000 for a screenplay sequel to *The Thin Man*. Hammett accepted and in October 1934 returned to Hollywood, where he took up residence at the Beverly Wilshire Hotel. The studio supplied him with a comfortable office where Hammett tried to hammer out *The Return of the Thin Man* (there would be other *Thin Man* films – *After the Thin Man, Another Thin Man, Shadow of the Thin Man, The Thin Man Goes Home, Song of the Thin Man* – but Hammett wrote none of them). He stayed at the task until boredom set in, whereupon he got drunk. Once inebriated, Hammett would remain so for days on end.

With Hellman in New York for the opening of her play, *The Children's Hour*, Hammett moved into a spacious house on Bel Air Road. Feeling like an overpaid wage slave – his 1934 income came to approximately $80,000 – Hammett hired a butler, who, in turn, brought his male lover, while MGM supplied a secretary. Not that Mildred Lewis was much of a secretary; she was merely the cousin of a high-ranking studio executive. During working hours Hammett would call her upstairs and ask her to lie on the bed with him. Mildred had heard stories about Hammett's womanising. But her employer had no intention of adding her to his string of conquests. Though her horizontal proximity gave her no particular pleasure, Lewis grew to like Hammett and would accompany him to the Clover Club, where her boss would imbibe with

Dorothy Parker and the Marx brothers and, with scant regard for money, gamble the night away. She observed that Hammett would get up late and spend most of the day reading, had a penchant for black and oriental prostitutes – sent by the famous Los Angeles madam, Lee Francis – and liked playing Lucienne Boyer's 'Parlez-moi d'amour' on the Victrola. In turn, Hammett grew fond of Lewis and, on several occasions, had his chauffeur deliver flowers to her apartment, much to her husband's consternation.

As Hammett's drinking increased, his behaviour became more unpredictable. At one of his parties, Hammett humiliated Nathaniel West, who made the mistake of asking Hammett about a job. Said West, '[He] called out in a loud voice so that everyone could hear, "I haven't any money to lend you now, but call me next week and I'll lend you some." ' In all likelihood, however, Hammett's aggression was the result of hearing about Hellman and West's brief affair in New York a couple of years earlier.

A friend of Hammett's, Albert Hackett, who, along with his wife Frances Goodrich, wrote scripts for *The Thin Man*, *Father of the Bride* and *It's a Wonderful Life*, witnessed another example of Dash's humour. This time the recipient was Marx Brothers' scriptwriter S.J. Perelman. Having excused himself to go the bathroom, Perelman had been gone for an inordinate amount of time. His wife, Laura, went to see what had become of her husband, only to find him in the bathroom with a naked prostitute that Hammett had hired for the evening. Before Perelman could disentangle himself, Hammett and Laura had left the party together, headed for San Francisco, where they remained for a number of days. Another woman who had had an affair with Hammett said she ended the relationship because she couldn't take all the prostitutes traipsing through Hammett's house. Regarding Hammett's lifestyle and his ill health, scriptwriter Nunnally Johnson said that Hammett's 'behaviour could be accounted for only by an assumption that he had no expectation of being alive much beyond Thursday'.

Admitting he wrote purely for the money, Hammett declared he was wealthy enough, so had no reason to continue writing. Doing as little as possible, he refused to ingratiate himself with others and played the role of Hollywood iconoclast to the hilt. When not at one of his watering holes, he lounged around his house dressed like Nick Charles in silk dressing-gown and scarf. Perhaps Chandler had been right when he said that Hammett was 'one of the many guys who couldn't take Hollywood without trying to push God out of the high seat'.

Not that Chandler knew Hammett. The two men would meet only once: at a 1930s *Black Mask* writers' dinner, after which Chandler commented that his hero had '[A] fearful capacity for Scotch' but 'seemed quite unspoilt'. Chandler would admit that it was from Hammett, six years his junior, that he learned how to turn a 'physical observation into something that reveals character'. Equally, Chandler would say that Hammett – who had learned the art of the detective novel from reading Henry James and Dostoevsky – had taken murder away from the 'upper classes, the week-end house party and the vicar's rose garden' and given it back to 'people who commit it for reasons, not just to provide a corpse'.

Though he briefly returned to New York, Hammett was still negotiating with MGM over a treatment for the Nick and Nora sequel. Back in Hollywood, he took up residence in a six-room suite in the Beverly Wilshire. Regularly giving parties and getting drunk, Hammett began to suffer from headaches and sexual impotence. Despite attempts to go on the wagon, he could not stop making a spectacle of himself.

However, Hammett's life was to change. Two events prompted this: the maritime strike in San Francisco and the formation of the Screen Writers Guild. The former occurred in 1934, when longshoremen, supported by teamsters, fought a pitched battle with the police in the city's streets, followed by a short-lived general strike. The event exploded like a bombshell in Hammett's otherwise sheltered Hollywood existence, rekindling political opinions he had held while living in San Francisco. Those opinions had partially been formed in the wake of World War I, when Hammett had tried to collect disability pay and a war pension after contracting tuberculosis brought on by Spanish influenza and bronchial pneumonia. Since he had never before received benefits, Hammett's attempt to collect disability pay would result in government harassment.

The maritime strike coincided with Hammett's involvement in the Screen Writers Guild, which had its origins in the first months of 1933, when studio writers were told that they would have to take a pay cut. Contrary to the popular belief that screenwriters of that period were overpaid, 30 per cent were earning less than $2,000 a year, while 10 per cent made more than $10,000. This, as well as the conditions in which they had to work, prompted the formation, in April, of the Screen Writers Guild. The movie moguls – Mayer, Thalberg, Warner and Harry Cohn – objected to the Guild's formation. (During the war, Warner would refuse to hire a young Chester Himes as a studio reader, saying, 'We don't want no niggers on this lot,' and Cohn was so enamoured of Mussolini that he designed his office in the style of Il Duce, placing his desk on a raised platform and putting a photograph of Mussolini on the wall.) Backed by President Roosevelt's National Reconstruction Act, the Guild presented a series of demands to the studios that ranged from ending the practice of lending writers from one studio to another to stopping writers having to write 'on spec'. Negotiations stretched into 1935. Hammett, despite his individualistic nature, took a leading role in the Guild and in the leftwing League of American Writers (formerly known as the John Reed Club).

His role in the Screen Writers Guild may not have done much for his writing, but it did give Hammett a platform from which he could vent his spleen. According to biographer

Joan Mellen, Hammett, since establishing himself in Hollywood, had been plagued by 'the emptiness of a life devoid of
convictions', which contributed to his alcoholism and, as early
as 1931, thoughts of suicide. His lifestyle also helped him
blank out his political convictions. But Hammett knew he had
been in political arrears since, as a Pinkerton agent, he helped
break up the Anaconda miners' strike of 1922, and reduce
the power of the Industrial Workers of the World. During
his final days, he would even ask Hellman to bring him a
copy of Allan Pinkerton's autobiography, *Strikers, Communists,
Tramps, and Detectives*, a book that producer Ben Schulberg
would later give to John Bright and Robert Tasker to adapt
for the screen. But the latter two – leftwing members of the
Screen Writers Guild – turned it down. One wonders if they,
or Hammett, realised that Pinkerton was a former Chartist,
forced to leave Scotland after being named by an informer,
only to end up turning against his class.

In line with his repoliticalisation, Hammett became an
active member of the Communist Party, the Hollywood
branch of which is said to have begun in his living room
(though leftwing screenwriter Ring Lardner Jr. claims the first
meeting was held at the home of fellow screenwriter and
future informer, Martin Berkeley, and neither Hammett nor
Hellman was present). In 1938, a sober Hammett was elected
chairman of the Motion Picture Artists Committee. Committed to the Party, Hammett wanted to fight General Franco
in the Spanish Civil War. To his disappointment, he was told
by the Party hierarchy to remain in Hollywood. Instead, it
would be the less political Hellman who would travel to Spain.

With Hellman in Europe, Hammett, ten months without a
drink, was still trying to complete the sequel to *The Thin Man.*
He was sick of Nick and Nora Charles. In a letter to Hellman,
he wrote, 'Nobody ever invented a more insufferably smug
pair of characters.' As a story, *The Thin Man* carried none
of the innovative qualities that marked his Continental Op
narratives, nor did it have anything in common with the

kind of literary and socially significant novels that Hammett envisioned writing. Apart from the never-to-be-finished novel *Tulip*, Hammett would soon be writing by proxy. For as his literary prowess declined, Hellman's began to grow. As it did, Hammett centred his attention on her plays, giving her what advice he could regarding structure, dialogue and character development.

In February 1938, Hammett was instrumental in the Screen Writers Guild winning their fight to incorporate as a union. However, his political work and drinking had taken their toll. After fourteen months without a drink, Hammett was lonely, weary and losing weight. Worried about his impotence and a long-standing venereal disease, he took to the bottle again. As a thinly disguised Hammett says in *Tulip*, 'I drank a lot in those days, partly because I was still confused by the fact that people's feelings and talk and actions didn't have much to do with one another.' While Hammett, one of highest paid screenwriters in Hollywood, drank to fill the void, his decline as a writer would progress in proportion to his increasing involvement with the Communist Party. But this time his drinking was nearly fatal. Collapsing in his hotel room, Hammett was rescued by screenwriters Albert Hackett and Philip Dunne, who put him on an aeroplane and sent him to Hellman in New York.

Watch on the Rhine was to be Hammett's final screen credit. Directed by Herman Shumlin at Warner Brothers and starring Paul Lukas and Bette Davis, the 1943 film, based on Hellman's play, sought to persuade Americans of the inevitability of the war. Adhering to the party line and the remnants of the Hitler-Stalin pact, Hammett had originally objected to the play, but once the war began his objections were lost in the play's Popular Front ideology. Though he had not written anything of substance for over nine years, Hammett was paid $30,000 for a script, which came with a stipulation from Hal Wallis that Hellman and Shumlin be responsible for Hammett's contribution.

However, even though Hammett had watered down the politics and removed any reference to Karl Marx and communism, the script would run into problems with the Hays Office. Joseph Breen, who headed up the Production Code Administration office and was formerly a PR man for Peabody Coal Company, expressed concern that the film's protagonist commits a murder – the victim is, in fact, a Nazi – that goes unpunished. He also objected to what he thought was suggestive dialogue between husband and wife, as well as to the 'display of liquor and drinking'. And in a note to Jack Warner, Breen said, 'Please avoid any showing of, or reference to, a toilet.' Fortunately, Hellman, now a major playwright, went on the attack, threatening to write a piece about censorship and the Hays Office. Believing Hellman would take her case to the newspapers, the Hays Office backed down.

But it was still necessary for Hellman to rewrite Hammett's script. Finding it self-indulgent, loose and lacking narrative drive, Hellman spent a week redrafting the eighty-page script. With the credits reading 'Screen Play by Dashiell Hammett . . . Additional Scenes and Dialogue by Lillian Hellman', the film received an Academy Award nomination, losing out to Howard Koch, and Julius and Philip Epstein's screenplay for *Casablanca*.

In September 1942, after finishing his draft of *Watch on the Rhine*, Hammett wrote to Bennett Cerf at Random House informing him that he should no longer be considered a writer. A few days later Hammett joined the army. He was forty-six years old, ill, underweight, with lesions on his lungs. The Secretary of the League of American Writers, Franklin Folsom, said Hammett must have bribed the army doctor to overlook his physical condition.

Serving in the Signal Corps, Hammett was moved from one US base to another before being posted in 1943 to the Aleutian Islands, where he edited a newspaper for the troops in the region. Discharged from the armed forces in 1945, Hammett immediately set to work on *Tulip*, a novel that he would never finish, owing to his drinking and ill health. What's more, he had returned from the war against fascism only to find that anti-fascists were being persecuted at home. With the House Un-American Activities Committee out to cleanse Tinseltown of leftwing influence, and the Party hopelessly split, Hammett seemed more disillusioned than ever. He was now dividing his time between his new apartment in New York and Hellman's country retreat. As well as teaching a course in mystery writing at the Jefferson School for Social Science, he joined the Joint Anti-Fascist Refugee Committee and was elected president of the New York Civil Rights Congress, the main role of which was to support those under rightwing attack. Not surprisingly, Hammett's name was cropping up on everyone's list of subversives. After he was hospitalised in 1948 – his drinking had once again nearly killed him – Hammett spent the next year recuperating. As he did so, he gave money to various causes, invested in Arthur Miller's *Death of a Salesman*, hoped to get *The Maltese Falcon* staged and joined the American Labor Party.

Hammett returned to Hollywood in 1950 to work on a screenplay for Sidney Kingsley's Broadway play *Detective Story*, which William Wyler would direct. Though he worked on it for six weeks and enjoyed dining with actress Patricia Neal, who at the time was cast in the film, Hammett realised that he wasn't up to writing the script and returned his $10,000 advance, after which the project was handed on to the ubiquitous Philip Yordan. The following year Hammett was again in Hollywood, this time to see his daughters and grandchild, and to begin legal proceedings against Warner Brothers for their use of *The Maltese Falcon*. Hammett had no great love for any of the films based on that novel, including John Huston's 1941 effort with Humphrey Bogart. Having made three versions of *The Maltese Falcon*, including a 1931 film of the same name and a 1936 version entitled *Satan Met a Lady*, Warner Brothers insisted that they owned the story and the character Sam Spade. They claimed that Hammett, by using the name Sam Spade for a radio series, had himself infringed the copyright law. For his part, Hammett insisted that, as the author, the name was his property. The appellate court eventually ruled in his favour.

With Hammett's health fading, the government closed in on him, sentencing him to six months in prison. His crime was that, as President of the New York Civil Rights Congress and trustee of its bail fund, he was personally responsible for a group of communists who, having been accused of attempting to overthrow the government, had become fugitives from justice. A few days after the gaunt, toothless and tubercular Hammett was dispatched to prison, the Treasury Department filed an income tax lien against him for $100,629.03. Though Hammett had often worked to get others out of prison, only an anonymous donor, whose anonymity made her money unacceptable to the court, was willing to put up his bail or pay his debt.

After spending three months in prison, Hammett was released. But he was never to regain his health. As the media vilified him, he sought refuge in the rural confines of Katonah, New York, where he hoped to work on his unfinished novel, *Tulip*. But in 1953, when Senator Joseph McCarthy found that Hammett's books were on the shelves of overseas US libraries, the writer was subpoenaed to appear in front of McCarthy's subcommittee. Two years later, Hammett was made to testify once again, this time before the New York State Joint Legislative Committee investigating the Civil Rights Congress over which he once presided. In 1957, Hammett, more ill than ever, was being pursued by a Federal Court for non-payment of back taxes. Relapse followed relapse, until 31 December 1960, when Hammett, still under FBI investigation, entered Lenox Hill Hospital. On 8 January 1961 he slipped into a coma, and died two days later.

Following his death, Hellman purchased the copyright to Hammett's work from the US government for a mere $5,000. She claimed that her former partner's work had fallen out of favour with the public, and was worth no more than that. Despite Hammett's stipulation that his estate be divided between Hellman, his stepdaughter Jo, and half to his daughter Mary, the royalties from Hammett's fiction are, to this day, the province of the Hellman estate.

Soon Hammett's life, thanks to Hellman, would be sanitised for public consumption. When Mike Nichols tried to film the story of Lillian and Dash in the mid-1970s, Hellman demanded $450,000 and 6 per cent gross. She also made various stipulations. The film could contain no approval or disapproval by others of the way Hellman and Hammett conducted their lives; it had to be based on Hellman's memoirs; it could contain no lies or half-truths, as determined by Hellman, including the question of whether Hammett was a Communist; it could not treat Hammett or Hellman as lost, loose, redeemed, sad or comic; it was to make no mention of Soviet prison camps, nor adversely comment on Hammett's political beliefs. Moreover, Hellman would retain the right to the 'final cut'. In the end, Nichols gave her final script approval, but, even so, the deal collapsed. The rights were then sold to Warner Brothers for $400,000, with Hellman receiving $75,000 on signing, to which she added a new stipulation: Hammett should not be portrayed as someone with leftwing convictions.

In the end, Hollywood brought out Hammett's worst habits; it turned him into a public spectacle and assisted in the destruction of his writing career. Though Hollywood might have been a perfect setting for his nouveau-Marxism, presenting the writer with the conditions in which he could rediscover himself politically, it ended up buying and selling Hammett as it would any other product. One can only speculate on what Hammett might have become had he not gone to Hollywood. An embittered ex-writer, or a novelist of even greater stature?

Raymond Chandler

Following in Hammett's footsteps, Chandler would fare only slightly better in Hollywood. The further he travelled, the more he would disintegrate as a writer and as a person, eventually moving, as Kevin Starr says in *The Dream Endures*, to the edge of nothingness. Making increasingly outrageous demands, Chandler, like Hammett, attempted to take on an industry, but on terms more personal than political.

A failed poet, alcoholic and snob, Chandler was no match for Hammett in the charm department. Born in Chicago in 1888, and descended from sixteenth-century Quaker colonists, Chandler came to England as a boy, attended Dulwich College – a London public school where one of his classmates would be Boris Karloff (Marlowe meets Count Dracula on the playing fields of south London!) – and received the balance of his education in France and from a private tutor in Germany.

Arriving in Southern California in 1913, Chandler found employment as an accountant with the Los Angeles Creamery. At the time, LA was renowned for its oddball churches and morality-imposing ordinances. Said historian Carey McWilliams, 'Migration is the basic explanation for the growth of cults in Southern California.' He noted that, out of 1,833 churches in Los Angeles, only a thousand belonged to orthodox religions. Interested in Madame Blavatsky and Ouija boards, Chandler gravitated towards a small group of artistically inclined but insignificant dilettantes, and, with his friend Warren Lloyd, earned a reputation as a practical joker, ever ready to pull assorted pranks on the bourgeoisie, a class to which Chandler was more than precariously tied. They would, for instance, find a cinema where a well-advertised melodrama was playing, sit on separate sides of the theatre and laugh loudly to make the audience reverse its perception of the film.

In 1919, Chandler fell in love with Cissy Pascal, a twice-divorced former artist's model, the stepmother of Chandler's best friend, and seventeen years his senior. Though in love with Cissy, Chandler refused to marry her until his own mother passed away, an event that did not occur until 1924. Cissy and Chandler would remain together for four decades. Rarely socialising as a couple, they lived like urban gypsies, changing addresses up to three times a year.

Chandler was able to find work as a junior accountant for the Dabney Oil Syndicate, later renamed the South Basin Oil Company. Soon the company had moved to Signal Hill in Long Beach. Within two years, Signal Hill and its neighbouring oil fields were producing 20 per cent of the world's oil. After Chandler discovered that the chief accountant had been embezzling money, the company promoted him to head accountant. His salary would rise from $1,000 a month to $3,000 a month, more than adequate for the early 1920s. However, when the Depression cut into the company's profits, Chandler was laid off. Fortunately, he managed to secure a stipend of $100 a month in exchange for assisting in a lawsuit against his former company.

Even before losing his job, Chandler had acquired two bad habits: binge drinking and reading *Black Mask*. Still considering himself a poet, he decided to try his hand at writing a story that would fit the magazine's format. It took five months to produce the 18,000 word 'Blackmailers Don't Shoot'. The story was accepted by *Black Mask* in 1933, and Chandler, at the age of forty-four, had a new career. His first novel, *The Big Sleep* ('What did it matter when you were dead . . . You just slept the big sleep, not caring about the nastiness of how you died or where you fell'), followed six years later. Written in his Santa Monica apartment during the summer of 1938, the novel introduced Philip Marlowe, destined to become the template for future fictional private eyes.

To publicise *The Big Sleep*, Knopf published the following advertisement:

In 1929 Dashiell Hammett
In 1934 James M. Cain
In 1939 Raymond Chandler

Thus *The Big Sleep* was touted as another *Red Harvest* or *The Postman Always Rings Twice*. More to the point, Cain had yet to publish a book that equalled *The Postman* in popularity, and it had been five years since Hammett's *The Thin Man* had appeared. Consequently, the field was open for a new voice. Chandler's novel fitted the bill perfectly. Cynical, wise-cracking, perceptive and hardboiled, *The Big Sleep* initially sold 18,000 copies, earning Chandler $2,000 – not quite as successful as Hammett's last novel, *The Thin Man*, which had, within three weeks of its 1934 publication, sold 20,000 copies, and was bought by MGM for $21,000. It was not just that Chandler wanted to surpass his predecessor financially. About Hammett, he said, 'What he did, he did superbly, but there was a lot he could not do.'

Chandler followed *The Big Sleep* with *Farewell, My Lovely*. Published in 1940, and written, like his previous novel, in the style with which Chandler would forever be associated, it was largely ignored by the critics. It earned the author another $2,000. Chandler's third novel, published in 1942, was *The High Window*, followed a year later by *The Lady in the Lake*. Chandler was producing books at a staggering pace – four superb novels in four years. But Chandler was growing tired of the genre, and, having failed to make a Hammett-like splash, opted to ply his trade in Hollywood.

At the time, the Production Code Administration office had become Hollywood's de facto censoring body. With its strictures about punishment, guilt, sex and politics, the Production Code, influenced by the Catholic Legion of Decency, made it difficult for many books, particularly of the hard-boiled variety, to find their way to the screen. This might explain the low prices Chandler's novels fetched from the studios. For instance, *Farewell, My Lovely* was bought by RKO for $2,000, while *The High Window* was purchased by Twentieth Century Fox for $3,500. If compared to what Hammett was earning ten years earlier – selling the rights to *The Glass Key* for $25,000 – one gets an idea of how the studios regarded Chandler's work.

Initially, the studios purchased Chandler's fiction just to appropriate his plots. With Hammett's *Maltese Falcon* casting its short shadow over Hollywood, *Farewell, My Lovely* was to become, in the hands of RKO executives, *The Falcon Takes Over.* Twentieth Century Fox, meanwhile, took the plot of *The High Window* and, in 1941, turned it into *Time to Kill,* featuring Michael Shayne, a private eye created by pulp novelist Brett Halliday. Regarding the former film, the Production Code office, unperturbed whether the falcon was Maltese or Dulwich-bred, demanded changes in the script. Though innocuous sounding these days, the following lines had to be cut: 'Sorry, I live with my mother', 'It ain't that kind of place', and single words like 'tramp', 'broad', 'can' and 'lousy'. The Production Code office also thought that one of the male characters was too effeminate – 'We assume that there will be nothing even remotely suggestive of a "pansy" ' – and were concerned that the film contained too much violence and drinking.

Paramount hired a nearly broke Chandler in 1943. When the studio's paycheques began to arrive, he and Cissy moved to a Spanish-style house on Drexel Avenue in West Hollywood. Initially, Chandler liked working at Paramount. At fifty-five, he was older than most of his colleagues, and, with four novels under his belt, reasonably comfortable in Hollywood's anti-intellectual climate. Also, as a former pulp writer, businessman and accountant, Chandler was unperturbed by the studios' lack of artistic integrity, nor bothered that he was in a profit-driven industry. Though his view of Hollywood would change, Chandler would always hit back at armchair critics, saying, 'Hollywood is easy to hate, easy to sneer at, easy to lampoon.'

Jumping in at the deep end, Chandler's first assignment was working with Billy Wilder at Paramount on James M. Cain's *Double Indemnity*. Wilder had wanted to hire Cain, but the latter at the time was under contract at Twentieth Century Fox and working on a treatment for Fritz Lang's *Western Union*. Wilder then approached Charles Brackett, who would collaborate with Wilder on movies like *Sunset Boulevard* and *The Lost Weekend* and would be Wilder's main writing partner until the emergence of I.A.L. Diamond. Brackett thought *Double Indemnity* disgusting, but in turning it down merely said, 'It's too grim for me.' In fact, Brackett was known to stay clear of any film likely to offend the Production Code office. Even so, two years later he would be writing *The Lost Weekend*, perhaps the bleakest of Wilder's films. (Gangster Frank Costello, on behalf of the liquor industry, offered $5 million for the negative in order to rid the world of this paean to alcoholism.)

It was Paramount producer Joseph Sistrom who suggested to Wilder that he hire Chandler, even though the latter had never written a screenplay. When Chandler demanded $150 a week, Sistrom told him the studio had intended to offer him $750. To protect Chandler from himself, Sistrom asked an agent, H.N. Swanson, to represent the writer. 'Swanie' – or, as Chandler called him, 'Swede' – was already one of Hollywood's best agents, representing the town's most prominent writers (Fitzgerald, Faulkner, James M. Cain, Horace McCoy, John Fante), most of them confirmed alcoholics. Years later, Swanson would represent Elmore Leonard: 'I climbed the stairs of the Swanson Building to Swanie's second-floor office of dark wood, wall scenes, venetian blinds, and a thousand books. A silver-haired gentleman in a double-breasted, pin-stripe suit, a carnation in the buttonhole, said, "Well, kiddo, welcome to Hollywood." '

Prior to *Double Indemnity*, Wilder had never heard of Chandler. But Wilder, who had been working in the shadow of Fritz Lang ('Look for good shooters,' was Lang's advice), was impressed by Chandler's *The High Window:* 'How often do you a read a description of a character that says he had hair growing out of his ear long enough to catch a moth?' One wonders if Wilder, a Jew who left Berlin after the burning of the Reichstag, was also aware of Chandler's anti-Semitic tendencies, expressed in the following: '[The] Jew is a distinct racial type, that you can pick him up by his face, by the tone-quality of his voice, and far too often by his manners. In short, Jews are to some extent still foreigners . . . I've lived in a Jewish neighborhood, and I've watched one become Jewish, and it's pretty awful.'

Their relationship was to quickly sour. Chandler had never collaborated with anyone, while the mischievous and competitive Wilder (critic Andrew Sarris said that Wilder, after arriving in the US, wrote his mother in Europe that he was doing well, but circumstances had forced him to change his name to *Thornton*) was certain that Chandler hated him. For his part, Chandler should have realised what was coming when, at an early story conference at which Cain was present, Wilder criticised Chandler for not including more of the author's dialogue in the script. Years later, Wilder would half-humorously remark, '[There] was a lot of Hitler in Chandler.'

Working with Wilder affected Chandler as well. Whenever the director went to the bathroom – which he often did just to escape from Chandler – the writer would reach into his desk and pull out a bottle. However, Wilder realised that Chandler was a talented scriptwriter, and 'one of the greatest creative minds I've ever worked with', though also 'more trouble than any other writer I've ever worked with'. It was Chandler's use of language that most impressed Wilder: '[From him] I learned . . . what real dialogue is. Because that's all he could write. That and descriptions.' As for Chandler, he was to comment that working with Wilder 'shortened my life'.

Brackett was right, *Double Indemnity* did run into problems with the Production Code office, who considered the film an instruction manual for potential criminals. They were less concerned about the sexual content, an aspect that Chandler had toned down as much as possible, for he had always thought the novel contained too much sex. In fact, Chandler would say, '[Cain] is the kind of writer I detest, a faux naif, a Proust in greasy overalls, a dirty little boy with a piece of chalk and a board fence and nobody looking. Such people are the offal of literature, not because they write about dirty things, but because they do it in a dirty way.' So the more prudish Chandler tried to create a sexually charged atmosphere without portraying anything that might cause offence.

Wilder and Chandler worked together on the script for five months, each day tenser than the day before. When Wilder asked Chandler to fix the venetian blinds to stop the sun shining through, Chandler walked out of the room and off the lot. He would not return until Wilder apologised, promised not to issue arbitrary orders nor point his walking stick in Chandler's direction. Eventually, Wilder bullied and cajoled Chandler into creating a magnificent script, one markedly different from the novel. This blend of two distinct but equally perceptive and creative personalities helped make *Double Indemnity* a critical and financial success. Nevertheless, the Academy Award for best script that year would go to Frank Butler and Frank Cavett for their contribution to the light-hearted Bing Crosby vehicle, *Going My Way.*

In the aftermath of *Double Indemnity,* Paramount offered Chandler $1,250 a week. Chandler accepted and was given the New England love story, *And Now Tomorrow,* starring Alan Ladd and Loretta Young, to fix. Ironically, for someone possessing a larger-than-life ego, the overpaid and under-employed Chandler enjoyed being a script doctor, and this was one of the few occasions in his Hollywood career he would admit as much. He even liked his fellow scriptwriters – many of them, in his view, mere hacks. Later he would look back and say, 'The only employer I got on with in Hollywood was Paramount.' Chandler's next effort, the melodramatic horror film, *The Unseen*, lived up to its name, a pedestrian affair lacking any discernible sign that the writer of *Farewell, My Lovely* had contributed to it. Perhaps that was the point.

In 1944, Jack Warner, looking for a Bogart–Bacall follow-up to the successful *To Have and Have Not*, gave Howard Hawks $50,000 to buy the rights to *The Big Sleep*. Hawks paid Chandler $5,000 and pocketed the remaining $45,000 (some say Chandler received $10,000 for the rights). Chandler had always thought Cary Grant would be the perfect Marlowe. It was easy to understand why, since Chandler saw Marlowe as a sardonic down-at-heel transplanted Englishman. If not in fact, then in spirit. An established star, Grant had the necessary ingredients: good looks, sophistication, charm and cynicism. Chandler's second choice was Humphrey Bogart. Said Chandler, 'Bogart can be tough without a gun [and] has a sense of humor that contains that grating undertone of contempt.' Light years from Grant in terms of style and temperament, Bogart, who, three years earlier, had given a near flawless performance as Sam Spade in *The Maltese Falcon*, would land the role and come as close as anyone to putting a personal stamp on Chandler's protagonist.

RKO owned the rights to *Farewell, My Lovely*, and hoped to cast John Garfield as Marlowe, but eventually opted for former Missouri hog farmer Dick Powell. It was a controversial choice. But according to the film's director, Edward Dmytryk, 'He fit the character . . . After all, what is Marlowe? He's no Sam Spade.' Powell's portrayal would turn out to be surprisingly subtle, leaving one to speculate on how Garfield, had he played Marlowe, might have changed our perception of Chandler's protagonist. True, Garfield was the superior actor, but with his aura of class consciousness he could not have conveyed so effectively Marlowe's nondescript view of the world.

The film would be retitled *Murder, My Sweet* because RKO thought that *Farewell, My Lovely* sounded less like a tough-guy film than a happy-go-lucky musical. In the wake of the film's

1944 success, Pocket Books' paperback sales shot up to over two million. Within two years, Chandler was paying over $50,000 in income tax. But his greater earning power came at a price. He would say that the writer in Hollywood is 'revealed in his ultimate corruption . . . [and praised] in the form of a salary check'. But that came with the territory, and Chandler was not about to turn his back on such an obvious, if crude, form of praise.

When news that one of Hollywood's highest paid stars, Alan Ladd, was about to be inducted into the armed forces (though apparently there is no evidence of him having served his country at this point of the war), Chandler offered his half-finished script, *The Blue Dahlia*, to fellow Englishman and public-school product, John Houseman. Chandler was paid $25,000 for it. Ladd had been brilliant in both *The Glass Key* (1942) and Frank Tuttle's *This Gun for Hire*. As well as Ladd, *The Blue Dahlia* stars Veronica Lake, whom Chandler would dub 'Moronica' Lake. The problem was, Chandler had yet to figure out the ending. When Chandler was unable to keep up with the shooting schedule, Houseman said he would give the writer a $5,000 bonus if he could finish the script on time. Chandler pretended to be insulted by the financial inducement, and threatened to quit. But not before telling Houseman that the only way he could complete the job was if he was drunk, a state in which Chandler claimed he hadn't found himself for a number of years – in fact, he actually had gone some months without a drink. He told the producer that, to keep him on the job and away from alcohol, he would have to agree to his demands: that he be allowed to work at home; that he be given an open telephone line to the studio switchboard and Houseman's office; that six secretaries work for him; and that two Cadillac limousines be put at his disposal, to fetch a doctor if necessary, drive his script to the studio or take the maid to the market. It was an audacious set of demands, but Houseman, on Sistrom's instructions ('If the picture closed down, we'd all be fired anyway'), agreed.

Forty-two days later, a perpetually drunk Chandler handed in the script.

In truth, Chandler really had become an alcoholic wreck. It's hard to believe that Houseman had not known that Chandler's life revolved around alcohol. Not only did his writer have a reputation as a heavy drinker, but the half-finished script that Houseman had seen had been filled with alcoholic imagery and vocabulary. According to Wilder's biographer, Maurice Zolotow, Chandler's list of demands had simply been a means of exerting power, and to secure the right to work from home, which few writers at the time were allowed to do. Said Chandler, 'I've pulled off the sweetest deal in town . . . No writer has ever been able to wrangle a contract like this.' Because the film was so successful at the box office, Swanson was able to obtain a $4,000 a week contract for Chandler.

Despite his new contract, Chandler announced that he was quitting Hollywood. Either he had grown weary of the place, had realised he had hit the creative or financial apogee of his screenwriting career, or he was trying to squeeze even more money out of the studio. In any case, he had once again raised the ante, which meant putting any future novels on the back burner.

In July 1945, Chandler decided to go to Big Bear in the Southern California mountains, where, since 1940, he and Cissy had gone to find peace and quiet. MGM had just paid him $35,000 for the rights to *The Lady in the Lake*, and he needed some mountain seclusion if he was going to write the script. But, as usual, he grew bored with the project, and the script was given to fellow hardboiler Steve Fisher. *Lady in the Lake* would star Robert Montgomery, who also directed the film. Noted for its subjective camerawork, a good portion of the movie is filmed through Marlowe's eyes. It was a bold technique that Delmer Daves would also deploy less than a year later in his adaptation of David Goodis's *Dark Passage*.

When Chandler told the studio he intended to stay in Big

Bear, Paramount pleaded with him to return, saying that if he came back they would let him produce and direct his own films. When Chandler didn't take them up on the offer, the studio, in January 1946, suspended him, only to lure him back with the promise of $1,500 a week and the chance to adapt a novel of his choice. So Chandler began working on a script for Elizabeth Sanxay Holding's *The Innocent Mrs. Duff*. At first sight this was a bizarre choice for Chandler, who seemed to once again be trying to undermine Hollywood's expectations. However, Chandler believed Holding to be 'the top suspense writer of them all'. Three years later Max Ophuls would adapt Holding's *The Blank Wall*, retitling it *The Restless Moment*, only for Holding to become another lost writer of the 1940s. Regardless of her standing, Chandler soon grew bored with his project. In the end, his lack of interest cost Paramount $53,000, of which $18,000 had been paid to Chandler over a period of seventy-two days.

Next, it was Samuel Goldwyn who tried to lure Chandler. But instead of working at MGM, Chandler and Cissy packed their bags and moved to La Jolla, some two hundred miles south. They would remain there for the next nine years. In a 1945 article in *Atlantic*, Chandler reflected on the state of the writer in Tinseltown: 'What Hollywood seems to want is a writer who is ready to commit suicide at every story conference. What it actually gets is a fellow who screams like a stallion in heat and then cuts his throat with a banana.' For some reason, writer Charles Brackett found it necessary to criticise the article, saying that Chandler's books were not good enough to merit his criticism of Hollywood. Finding such verbal lobs exceedingly easy to return, Chandler said, 'Had my books been any worse I would not have been invited to Hollywood and if they had been any better I would not have come.'

The year Chandler moved to La Jolla also saw the release of *The Big Sleep*, starring Bogart and Bacall and directed by Howard Hawks. The film was universally acclaimed. Not that

Chandler had anything to do with it, for the script had been written by William Faulkner and Leigh Brackett (no relation to Charles). The film only reminded Chandler of how much he wanted to get back to writing fiction. Unfortunately, after leaving Hollywood, he would complete only two novels: the mediocre Hollywood-set *The Little Sister* (1949) and one of his best books, *The Long Goodbye* (1953), which Leigh Brackett would adapt in 1973 for director Robert Altman.

The more recalcitrant Chandler became, the more the studios hoped to tempt him back. Each offer was met by another refusal, and each refusal was countered by a more lucrative offer. Finally, in February 1947, Universal made an offer that he could not refuse: a one-off deal for an original screenplay, for which he would be paid $4,000 per week and given a share in the film's profits. Not only would Chandler be allowed to work at home, but the studio also agreed to accept the script sight unseen. It would be one of the most profitable deals ever secured by Swanson and, up to that time, one of the best deals offered to a scriptwriter. Chandler countered with an idea for a story entitled *Playback*, about a girl living in an apartment under an assumed name, who leaps to her death. In accepting it, the studio agreed to pay Chandler $140,000 for the script. But the money did not make the job any easier. Regarding its writing, Chandler said, 'I have hated it more than anything I ever did.'

Unfortunately, the postwar boom was over. Universal was on the verge of bankruptcy. Faced with a series of expensive location shots, they were forced to write off *Playback* as a tax loss. Chandler insisted that he really was finished with Hollywood. To him, it had come to signify ignorance, stupidity and pettiness. He cited MGM deputy boss and ex-bouncer Edgar Mannix's deciding that writers could do more work if there were no couches on which to relax – suddenly there wasn't a couch to be found in any studio office. Then there was Paramount's Y. Frank Freeman, who had a special dog-run built so he could exercise his prize boxers. In the years to come Chandler liked to regale his friends with such stories, some of which would find their way into his fiction. Chandler remained above all an iconoclast. When it came to the blacklist and the Hollywood Ten, Chandler, hardly a leftist, said he reserved his real contempt for movie moguls who wanted to expel the Ten from the industry.

Though he wrote about Los Angeles, Chandler tried to stay clear of writing about Hollywood. He had always said that life in Tinseltown so resembled a piece of fiction that writing a novel about it was unnecessary. Though *The Little Sister* would be as close as he would come to writing a Hollywood novel, he found the going difficult. With Cissy seriously ill, Chandler said that he wrote the novel while in a prolonged depression. *The Little Sister* is only average, but it represents Marlowe at his bleakest, and is filled with doubt and despair. It received lacklustre reviews when it appeared in October 1949.

Still Hollywood pursued Chandler. There was now a deal on the cards for a *Marlowe* television series. Before he would agree, Chandler insisted on a veto over scripts and the right to choose who would play his detective. Realising that times had changed and that TV would soon become a dominant medium, Chandler commented that, if he were a young man, he would have chosen to write for television rather than for films.

In July 1950, Warner Brothers offered him $2,500 a week to adapt Patricia Highsmith's *Strangers on a Train* for Alfred Hitchcock. The great director had originally wanted Hammett to write the screenplay, but the latter was beyond writing much of anything. Hitchcock was optimistic about working with Chandler. In turn, Chandler thought that teaming up with Hitchcock, who had already made thrillers such as *The Lady Vanishes*, *Spellbound* and *Notorious*, might be interesting. Indicative of Hollywood's pecking order, it was Hitchcock who had to travel to La Jolla for story meetings. It would not turn out to be the happiest of collaborations – 'Look at that fat bastard trying to get out of his car,' said Chandler of

Hitchcock when the latter first arrived. The director hated the way Chandler would dismiss his suggestions, while Chandler, never one to kowtow to Hollywood, was disappointed that Hitchcock – 'as nice as can be to argue with' – had a fixed idea of the film. Within two months, Chandler, some ten years older than the British director, had again become bored. After he insulted Hitchcock, Chandler, to his relief, was fired. Though Hitchcock wanted Ben Hecht to finish the script, he had to settle for his assistant, Czenzi Ormonde, who was paid $40,000 for the final rewrite. Said Chandler of the finished product, 'The picture has no guts, no plausibility, no characters, and no dialogue.'

It was another case of Chandler flexing his muscles before corporate power, and seeing how far those representing the industry were willing to go to appease him. Book publishers had never thrown that kind of money at him. While he could make $2,500 a week for film work, Chandler, from 1939 to 1950, had received only $56,000 in royalties.

When Cissy died in 1954, Chandler took it badly and never got over it. A year later, drunk and depressed, he took a loaded gun into the bathroom of his La Jolla home, phoned the police and tried to kill himself. The shots were, whether intentionally or not, wide of the mark. Still, the pain and cry for help were obvious.

A loner who distrusted women, other than his wife and mother, and whose books were filled with misogyny and middle-class prejudices, Chandler, though not from California, was a typical Southern California product. While his work provides a snapshot history of Los Angeles and its inhabitants, his critique concerns manners rather than politics. Yet about his hero, Chandler never says much, except that he was 'a lonely man, a poor man, a dangerous man . . . I think he will always have a shabby office, a lonely house, a number of affairs, but no permanent connection. I think he will always be awakened at some inconvenient hour by some inconvenient person to do some inconvenient job . . . I see him always in a lonely street, in lonely rooms, puzzled but never quite defeated.' One of the few physical descriptions appears in a letter to an English reader, in which one learns that Marlowe is 'slightly over six feet with brown eyes and dark brown hair. Smokes Camels. Lights them with kitchen matches. Drinks anything so long as it's not sweet. His date of birth is uncertain – a kind of perpetual late thirties . . . And . . . reminds us of Cary Grant.'

In trying to make sense of the world, and his isolation from it, Marlowe might be said to personify the modern condition. And so he has come to have many faces: William Powell, Robert Montgomery, James Garner, Elliott Gould, Alan Ladd, Robert Mitchum, Humphrey Bogart and Danny Glover. A number of years ago, Leigh Brackett conceded that one had to be careful when adapting Marlowe because the 'private eye has become a cliché'. That is now truer than ever. These days Marlowe-type perceptions and witticisms have become standard and all too easy to make. Though he might have any number of faces, his ubiquity, like his observations regarding the human condition, is a weakness as well as a strength.

Not surprisingly, Chandler, no less than Marlowe, was the consummate outsider, an impenetrable and formal individual who never went out without a tie and jacket, a man without a country, neither a full-fledged American nor an Englishman. Meanwhile, a skin condition required Chandler to constantly wear a pair of white gloves. One might conclude that he wore white gloves (why *white*?) because he didn't want to leave his metaphorical fingerprints in a culture foreign to him. Ironically, it was this sense of alienation that provided Chandler a marginal position from which he could make comments and criticisms about the culture. He called California 'the department-store state. The most of everything and the best of nothing.' Writing about Hollywood with intelligence, Chandler understood that film was '*not* a transplanted literary or dramatic art . . . it is . . . closer to music, in the sense that its finest effects can be independent of precise meaning, that its transitions can be more eloquent than its high-lit scenes, and that its dissolves and camera movements, which cannot be censored, are often far more emotionally effective than its plots, which can.'

Chandler also understood the effect that writing screen-plays can have on a novelist, that working for the studios can 'destroy the link between a writer and his subconscious. After that what he does is merely a performance.' The comment goes some way to explaining Chandler's career in an industry based on 'some male idol' who has 'the build of a lifeguard and the mentality of a chicken-strangler.' In the end, not even the studios' money made screenwriting tolerable. Said Chandler, 'I don't care how much they pay me, unless they can also give me delight in the work.' Chandler had travelled a long way since his first contribution to *Black Mask*: '[There] comes a time when that which I write has to belong to me, has to be written in silence, with no one looking over my shoulder, no one telling me a better way to write it. It doesn't have to be great writing, it doesn't even have to be terribly good. It just has to be mine.'

One reason Hollywood chased after the likes of Chandler and Hammett was that, by the 1930s, movies had become the world's most lucrative form of entertainment. Between 1930 and 1939 some five thousand films were produced and released in the United States. Between 1940 and 1949 the figure fell to around four thousand films. In 1939, it was the fourteenth most profitable business in America, and the biggest money-spinner in the greater Los Angeles area. Cinema, as William Goldman has pointed out, is a gold-rush industry, and, in the era of Hammett and Chandler, studios had struck a lucrative vein, particularly so for the majors like RKO, Twentieth Century Fox, MGM, Warner Brothers and Paramount, which also owned chains of movie houses. Thus they were able to control the production, distribution, mar-keting and exhibition of their films. In fact, studios were making more money from their theatres than from films. This was halted in 1948 when the Supreme Court decided that such vertically controlled businesses violated antitrust laws and the studios were made to sell their theatres. Nevertheless, it took five years before the studios totally divested themselves of their theatres.

With few other distractions, more people than ever were flocking to the cinema. By the end of the 1930s, 75 million Americans watched films every week. By 1946, that number had increased to 100 million (compared to 20 million in the 1960s and 1970s) – two-thirds of the total population. No wonder studios were willing to invest money to attract and maintain a stable of writers.

Hammett and Chandler were among the first to be cast into the role of writer-as-personality. For a short time they believed they could, and did, dictate their own terms, confronting Hollywood, while making precise and sometimes perceptive investigations of the culture. Their desire to make money was more a case of ego and politics than greed, more an attempt to squeeze the studios and exercise what little power they had.

The commodification and co-option of the writer, previously limited to the world of publishing, was now firmly established. Both Chandler and Hammett were to push Hollywood to an unprecedented degree. For Chandler, it was a case of making ever-more ludicrous demands on the studios. Pushing movie moguls and their underlings as far as he could, he made them appear ridiculous in their pursuit of profit. Hammett, trading on his notoriety, also sought to take on corporate America. He too failed, but, owing to the exigencies of history, Hammett was at least able to repoliticise himself, his perspective hardening as his experience of corporate Hollywood gained clarity. Though both writers wanted to leave Tinseltown, they would be repeatedly enticed back into its world. Despite their fate, Hammett and Chandler raised interesting questions: Can a hardboiled writer succeed in

Hollywood? Can such a writer escape unscathed? Such questions are still being asked. As for Hammett and Chandler, their reputations continue to grow, while their investigations remain nearly as relevant as when they were first written.

2

OUTSIDE STRAIGHT, INSIDE FLUSH

Horace McCoy and W.R. Burnett

Some writers, unlike Hammett and Chandler, were able to negotiate careers as screenwriters *and* hardboiled novelists. Such was the case with Horace McCoy and W.R. Burnett, both of whom, thanks to their workmanlike attitudes and perspectives, would exert a considerable influence on noir fiction and film. While Burnett remained relatively placid about his relationship with the industry, McCoy, wracked by doubts, rode Hollywood as though it were a roller-coaster, bumpily moving between literary highs and studio lows. Though neither sought to provoke the studios, both would bear the scars associated with a long and lucrative screen-writing career.

Horace McCoy

A willing creature of Hollywood, Horace McCoy, in his twenty-year career, wrote some forty screenplays (some say closer to a hundred), including *Texas* (George Marshall, 1941), *Gentleman Jim* (Raoul Walsh, 1942), *The Lusty Men* (Nicholas Ray, 1952) and *The World in His Arms* (Raoul Walsh, 1952). Though these might have been among his better efforts, McCoy, the most literary of hardboilers, was, in a studio context, rarely more than a hack. Yet his tenure in Hollywood did serve the purpose of providing him with material for his fiction. It could be said that McCoy's success as a novelist was, in part, the result of his ability to transfer his negative feelings about the film world into his fiction. Unquestionably of greater merit than his films, McCoy's novels would, in their portrayal of lost and disillusioned losers, become emblematic of an era. Functioning as psychological autobiography, McCoy's fiction stands the test of time and has been emulated over the years by numerous writers.

Born in 1897 in Pegram, Tennessee, to 'book-rich and money-poor' parents, McCoy quit his Nashville high school at sixteen to become a car mechanic. He went on to work as a travelling salesman and taxi-cab driver, before becoming a journalist. During World War I, McCoy spent eighteen months in the US Air Corps in France, becoming a decorated pilot. Wounded in action and discharged, McCoy lived briefly in Paris, where he led a bohemian existence and contributed to fly-by-night magazines run by expatriate Americans, and toured Europe with a song-and-dance review, *The Romeo Follies of 1919.*

Returning to Dallas, McCoy worked as a reporter, first for the *Dispatch*, then, a year later, in 1920, for the *Journal*. It was in Dallas that McCoy, to supplement his newspaper income, began to write fiction. Soon he was contributing to pulp magazines like *Black Mask, Detective Dragnet, Detective Action Stories, Battle Aces* and *Western Trail*. Selling his first story to *Black Mask* in 1927, McCoy would contribute to the pulps throughout the Depression, up until the time he was firmly established in Hollywood. *Black Mask* editor Joseph T. Shaw commented that McCoy was one of a handful of 'older writers who helped establish the *Black Mask* standard'.

His departure from the *Journal* had less to do with Depression cutbacks than with the reaction in certain quarters to a series of articles he'd penned on city corruption and the local chapter of the Ku Klux Klan. At the time, the Dallas Klan, with its more than 100,000 members, controlled local government. Thanks partly to McCoy's articles, the Klan's political power began to wane. Besides the anti-Klan articles, there were other reasons for McCoy's hasty departure: namely, impatient creditors and the parents of a young society woman whom McCoy, with his tendency towards social climbing, had secretly married. The parents fought to have the marriage annulled, a situation that McCoy would later describe in his novel *Kiss Tomorrow Goodbye*.

America was in the midst of the Depression when McCoy, having lost his job at the Dallas *Journal*, arrived in Hollywood. It was 1931, the same year that Dashiell Hammett came to town. Unlike Hammett's, McCoy's arrival was unfêted. Initially confident and ambitious, the unknown McCoy would have to fight to make his mark in the studios, just as he would when it came to his fiction. In the end, McCoy would become a more integral and established studio player than Hammett. In fact, apart from the five years from 1944 to 1949, he would work for the studios for the remainder of his life.

On his way west, McCoy had picked fruit and was briefly a professional boxer and wrestler. Unlike Hammett and Chandler, on his arrival in Tinseltown he had yet to write a novel, much less a successful one. With his eye on stardom, McCoy chose to join the ranks of the town's 20,000 movie extras, working, when the opportunity arose, for the standard salary of $17.50 per role. When extras were not needed, McCoy found employment as a soda jerk, union picketer, bodyguard to a politician, press agent to golf champion Walter Hagen and a bouncer at a dance marathon contest in Santa Monica. The latter would form the backdrop to McCoy's *They Shoot Horses, Don't They?* At the time, dance marathons were common in Santa Monica and Venice. They had begun as a jazz age fad during the 1920s – 'The marathon dance hall on Ocean Pier,' says Mike Davis in *City of Quartz*, 'became virtually a death camp for the Depression's lost souls' – but quickly turned into a Depression racket.

Eventually, McCoy secured a place at MGM's talent school, where his fellow students were Clark Gable, Robert Young and Robert Taylor, and did a screen test for Walter Huston. But the studio decided against giving McCoy a contract.

McCoy's thoughts were probably similar to those of his protagonist, a failed actor, in *I Should Have Stayed Home*, who spots Robert Taylor in the Macambo night club accompanied by Barbara Stanwyck, and wonders to himself, What does he have that I don't have?

At least McCoy looked like a Hollywood personality. At six foot four, athletic and good-looking, he was one of Hollywood's more proficient tennis players, who could have been a professional if he had not, years earlier, injured his knee playing football. Across the street from the El Rey apartments on Rossmore, where he first lived, McCoy could see the tennis courts of the Wilshire Country Club, an establishment he would soon join.

McCoy's break came when H.N. Swanson, who had recently set himself up as a Hollywood agent, learned that McCoy had been a journalist. Swanson secured a place for him in his brainchild, the RKO junior writers' pool. The latter was meant to school screenwriters and to provide the studios with a ready source for original stories. Having graduated from the writers' pool, McCoy, in 1932, became a junior writer at Columbia, at a salary of $50 per week. Working in a bungalow in Beachwood Canyon, his first scripts were for films like *Dangerous Crossroads*, *Man of Action* (uncredited), *Hold the Press* and *Speed Wings*. He also rewrote dialogue for *Soldiers of the Storm*. Seeing the possibilities inherent in his new career, McCoy stopped contributing to the pulps and concentrated on screenwriting.

The following November, McCoy married Helen Vinmont, much to the consternation of the young woman's well-to-do Los Feliz family. It seems that McCoy was not the only person interested in her. Dashiell Hammett inscribed McCoy's copy of *The Thin Man* in the following way: 'To Horace McCoy, who married my dream woman.' Though it should be said that, for Hammett, there was no shortage of *dream women* in Hollywood.

The couple stayed together until McCoy's death in 1955. Helen may have been wealthy, but that did not stop McCoy from going bankrupt in July 1934, after which the couple moved to the Montecito on Franklin just behind the Musso and Frank Grill. It was the same residential hotel where James M. Cain, in similar circumstances, had moved the year before. Not long afterwards, McCoy's agent sold some stories he had written for *Black Mask* and *Battle Aces* to Harry O. Hoyt at Columbia. When Hoyt announced a delay in his production schedule, he hired McCoy as an assistant. At this time, McCoy was also working on a novel, an amplification of a short story he had written the year before. By November he had finished a draft of *They Shoot Horses, Don't They?*, which drew upon his experiences at the marathon dance contests.

They Shoot Horses, Don't They? was McCoy's first and best-known novel. After going through numerous revisions, and having been reduced from 90,000 to 45,000 words, making it little more than a novella, it was published by Simon & Schuster in 1935. *They Shoot Horses* was hardly a best-seller, though it did go through two quick printings at 3,000 copies each. Though Simon & Schuster wanted to market the novel as a hardboiler in the tradition of Cain's *The Postman Always Rings Twice*, McCoy took exception and persuaded the company to drop any mention of 'hardboiled' from their promotional material.

Not a directly political novel, *They Shoot Horses* possesses a social outrage and radical edge that much noir fiction lacks. In 1937, McCoy said regarding it, 'There [was] decadence and evil in the old walkathons – and violence. The evil . . . fascinated the customer and the violence possessed a peculiar lyricism that elevated the thing into the realm of high art.' The murder in the novel is understandable and inevitable, but remains incidental to the narrative's overall emphasis, which, as in the best *Black Mask* stories, is on character and human behaviour. Like McCoy's subsequent novels, *They Shoot Horses* is more a work of social commentary than a crime novel. Though in an unequal society there is often only a flicker of an eyelid separating the two genres.

Months after the book's publication, McCoy was put under contract by Walter Wanger at Paramount, while *Esquire* magazine commissioned an article entitled 'The Grandstand Complex'. At Paramount, McCoy worked on *Prince of Rhythm*, a story destined for Fred Astaire that would eventually be shelved, then on a larger production, *The Trail of the Lonesome Pine* by Henry Hathaway, followed by *Spendthrift* (uncredited), a Raoul Walsh film starring Henry Fonda; *Postal Inspector*, an Otto Brower film starring Ricardo Cortez; as well as *Parole* and *Fatal Lady*.

In 1937, McCoy worked on a watered-down adaptation of *They Shoot Horses, Don't They?*, called *Life is a Marathon*. The 'trades' announced it as a forthcoming Associated Artists' production. Dudley Murphy, known for his version of *Emperor Jones*, was set to direct the picture. It was even said that Bette Davis wanted to star in the film. But no adaptation of *They Shoot Horses* would be forthcoming until Sydney Pollack's 1969 version (some years before, Swanson had been able to negotiate a deal for the author, despite the fact that McCoy had sold the theatrical rights of the novel for $250). Filmed at the Aragon Ballroom in Venice, and starring Jane Fonda, Pollack's film, though passable, lacks the despair, nihilism and hopelessness of the novel.

McCoy's next novel, *No Pockets in a Shroud*, was written in fits and starts during 1935 and 1936. Published in 1937, it is partly based on McCoy's experiences as a Dallas journalist. Though McCoy found it difficult to find an American publisher, Arthur Barker in England offered to bring out the novel if McCoy would get rid of the 'pornographical elements'. Convinced the book would do well, 'assuming we don't go to gaol on it and in spite of having to cut a certain amount', Barker finally published what would be McCoy's story of a crusading journalist's fatal battle against crime, corruption and Klan-like activities. Though it would be McCoy's most translated work, the first US edition did not appear until 1948, and even then only after it had been considerably rewritten. New American Library (NAL) had insisted on changing the book's emphasis, turning, most notably, the novel's communist into a sexual pervert. While McCoy's book resembles proletarian novels of the 1930s, its protagonist, Michael Dolan, adheres to no specific ideology – though that does not make him any less angry. As for Myra, she is certainly a communist, but thinly drawn and of secondary importance. Though NAL demanded the revisions, it was McCoy who changed Myra from a person who takes orders from Moscow to 'a goddamn sex-maniac'. Now minus some 35,000 words, the revised version was, for McCoy, a vast improvement on the original.

McCoy's next effort was *I Should Have Stayed Home* (1938). Rejected by Simon & Schuster, the novel was bought by Knopf. The Knopfs said they liked the novel but wanted to rename it. They suggested *Looks Like They'll Never Learn*. But that was too literal for McCoy, who insisted on retaining the original title. Like much of his work, *I Should Have Stayed Home* concerns the relationship between failure and success. The plot focuses on two movie extras, Mona Matthews and Ralph Carston. To Carston, Hollywood is 'the most terrifying town in the world', a place populated by lonely and marginal personalities, opportunists, confidence men, racketeers, bookies, race-track touts and people desperately on the make. *Saturday Review*, on the novel's publication, would note that 'McCoy hates Hollywood, not enough to stay away from it, but enough to get all the bile out of his system in a short, bitter, name-calling novel.'

Less autobiographical than his previous book, *I Should Have Stayed Home* centres on studio publicist, budding writer and McCoy *doppelgänger*, Johnny Hill. When his studio acquiesces to demands made by the German Embassy – this prior to World War II, but prophetic of the politics behind future studio negotiations of world rights (60 per cent of all prewar films in Germany were American imports) – Hill resigns. It's not a question of politics, but of expediency, for Hill desires to write a novel about Hollywood, specifically the world of the extra: 'That side of Hollywood's never been told.'

McCoy's attitude regarding successful writers like Hammett and Ben Hecht is revealed in Hill's critique: '[They] move to Malibu beach and into mansions at Bel Air and run around with Mr. and Mrs. Richbitch's society and get to see the wrong side of it.' One cannot help but note McCoy's envy, his feelings of failure and desire to fit into movie culture, no matter how distasteful it might be.

After the publication of *They Shoot Horses, Don't They?*, McCoy landed his first major Hollywood writing assignments. At Paramount he was put to work alongside William Lipman on films like *Hunted Men, King of the News Boys* and *Dangerous to Know.* Then in 1939, at Republic, he contributed scripts for *Persons in Hiding, Undercover Doctor* and *Island of Lost Men.* He was back at Paramount in 1940, working on *Queen of the Mob, Parole Fixer* and *Women Without Names.* In 1941 he was at Columbia for *Texas Rangers Ride Again, Wild Geese Calling* and George Marshall's *Texas.*

At Warner Brothers in 1942, McCoy and Vincent Lawrence – the latter having been James M. Cain's scriptwriting mentor – slogged away on Raoul Walsh's *Gentleman Jim* starring Errol Flynn. McCoy was now earning $750 per week. When he finished working for Walsh, McCoy insisted that Warner Brothers give him a seven-year contract starting at $850 per week, and that he be allowed to work at home. McCoy maintained that he found it difficult to apply himself to the discipline of studio writing, and did his best work at night. He even maintained that Jack Warner had agreed to his proposal. Of course, Jack Warner knew nothing about it. When the studio turned him down, McCoy cut his ties with Warner Brothers, and did not return there until August 1954, when he worked on *Bimini Run*, a film that would never see the light of day.

Now living in a large house on Alpine Drive in Beverly Hills, McCoy was journeying each day to RKO to work on

George Marshall's *Valley of the Sun* (1942) and, a year later, to Columbia to work on *Appointment in Berlin* (1943). It was in their home on Alpine Drive that Helen, in 1945, gave birth to their first son Peter (Nancy Reagan's future White House press officer). Though McCoy would not work for most of that year, he was by no means starving; he dined at Chasen's, wore expensive clothes and purchased a Lincoln, one of the first such cars to be bought in Beverly Hills. By September he was working on what would be his most ambitious novel, *Kiss Tomorrow Goodbye*, and talking about moving to Connecticut, where he could do some 'serious' writing. But McCoy was destined to remain in Hollywood.

It was at this time that he began to hear about his success in France, where the intellectual left – Camus, Sartre and de Beauvoir – were saying that McCoy was 'the first American existentialist', and the greatest exponent of the American nihilist novel. For a man who thought of himself as teetering on the edge of failure, their opinion was important. McCoy could now consider himself an artist unappreciated in his own country. As Geoffrey O'Brien says in *Hardboiled America*, 'The postwar philosophers were inclined to see what no American critic . . . had noticed – that McCoy had penetrated deeper than anyone into the zero state at the heart of the hardboiled novel. He had produced a sharp, dry, arbitrary kind of book . . . poised so precisely at the edge of the real that it seems to cancel itself out.'

Not your typical Hollywood hardboiled tragic figure, 'Horses' McCoy did his utmost to fit into Tinseltown culture. He frequently could be found dining with Dorothy Parker and Alan Campbell at Musso and Frank's, and joined the Wilshire and Hillcrest Country Clubs, as well as various tennis clubs in and around Hollywood. The Hillcrest was known as a meeting place for the Jewish elite, new and old. Neither Jewish nor part of the Hollywood elite, McCoy thought it important to be where deals were made. While it is hard to imagine Hammett or Chandler schmoozing on the golf course or networking between sets of tennis, McCoy knew the importance of being in the right place. (He even kept a scrapbook in which his old golf scores stood alongside articles written about him by various French intellectuals.)

Having received such adulation, McCoy felt he was in a position to devote himself full-time to writing fiction. *Kiss Tomorrow Goodbye* (Random House, 1948), which had been brewing in McCoy's consciousness for some time, would be a hardboiled stream-of-consciousness novel about the rise and fall of a Phi Beta Kappa gangster. Its origins went back to his final *Black Mask* story, which was published in 1934 under the same title. Influenced by the years McCoy spent writing B features, and based on a handful of FBI cases, *Kiss Tomorrow Goodbye* is concerned with states of awareness, death, the quest for self-identity and, once again, the thin line separating success and failure. The killer's story, told in the first person, is marked by a mood of imminent disintegration. Reflecting the ups and downs of McCoy's life, and emblematic of his regeneration as a writer, the novel is remarkable for its lyrical and poetic style, and its pathological gangster, Ralph Cotter/Paul Murphy, who, as the most brutal of hardboiled fictional characters, can be placed alongside Jim Thompson's twisted but intelligent protagonists.

Kiss Tomorrow Goodbye would also spark an internecine war between Knopf and Bennett Cerf at Random House. With Knopf holding an option on McCoy's next two novels, Cerf appeared at McCoy's Alpine Drive door urging the writer to sign with his company. Clearly, McCoy was, for some, a hot property. Yet reviews of *Kiss Tomorrow Goodbye* were mixed. Nelson Algren was scathing about the novel; others were offended that McCoy would have the temerity to marry hardboiled fiction and literature. It looked like McCoy's fear of failure had become self-fulfilling. It was only when New American Library editors Victor Weybright and Don Desmaret entered the picture that, through their series of Signet paperback editions, McCoy's career would be resuscitated. With an initial print run of 300,000, Signet paperback sales of *Kiss Tomorrow Goodbye* had, within a few years, exceeded 1,600,000 copies. Impressive numbers even if they paled when compared to the 35 million sold by Signet writers like Erskine Caldwell and James M. Cain. Of course, the lurid cover illustrations by artists James Avati and Stanley Zuckerberg helped boost sales of Signet paperbacks in general. For instance, Avati's cover illustration for *Kiss Tomorrow Goodbye* depicts a cigarette-smoking man sitting on a bed, watching a semi-clad woman, who, with her back to him, assumes a provocative pose. The blurb reads: 'Love as hot as a blow-torch. Crime as vicious as the jungle.' Signet's authors received advances of between $1,500 and $2,500, and were paid one and a half cents in royalties on each twenty-five cent paperback. Even if *Kiss Tomorrow Goodbye* had been more successful, the money, a fraction of what he received from the studios, would not have been enough to support McCoy in the manner to which he had grown accustomed.

Despite his reputation in France, McCoy still wondered if he might be a failure, some kind of studio fugitive-slave. His feelings were mirrored in *Kiss Tomorrow Goodbye*'s protagonist, Ralph, who escapes from prison to begin a new life manipulating the police, exploiting government corruption and marrying a wealthy society woman. *Kiss Tomorrow Goodbye* would be McCoy's final declaration of independence from the hardboiled school of writing and, in particular, from the work of James M. Cain, to whom he was still compared. Said McCoy, 'I do not care for Cain's work, although there may be much he can teach me. I know this though – continued labelling of me as of "the Cain school" . . . and I shall slit either his throat or mine.'

However, McCoy, as much as any other writer, picked up the gauntlet thrown down by Raymond Chandler when, in 1945, the latter said, 'the possibilities of objective writing are very great and they have scarcely been explored'. Twenty years later, critic Philip Durham would say that *Kiss Tomorrow Goodbye* had taken objective writing 'to its furthest development'. McCoy had hoped that the book would deliver him from Hollywood 'whoring', but its moderate success meant that he was once again back in the studios, even if at a considerably higher salary, what McCoy described as a 'brass check'. In 1949, as well as writing a defence of Hollywood in *Esquire,* McCoy managed to sell an abridged edition of *Kiss Tomorrow Goodbye* to Hollywood.

In poor health, he had, by this time, resigned himself to remaining in Tinseltown. In 1950, making $1,000 a week, McCoy churned out a script for *The Fireball,* directed by Tay Garnett and starring Mickey Rooney. That same year also saw the release of Gordon Douglas's adaption of *Kiss Tomorrow Goodbye,* starring James Cagney and Barbara Payton (whose memoirs, *I Am Not Ashamed,* published some years later, read like an ersatz McCoy novel). With a script by McCoy and Harry Brown, the result was a watered-down version of the book. The following year McCoy was at RKO, where he worked for Jerry Wald, writing a script for Nick Ray's *The Lusty Men,* with Robert Mitchum and Susan Hayward. At the same time, he sold an original treatment of a medical yarn, *Scalpel,* to Hal Wallis for between $50,000 and $100,000.

McCoy was excited about the prospect of working with Ray. 'I used to do fifteen to twenty scripts a year for Universal,' he told the director, hoping to impress Ray or just relieved that he was finally working on a project of some substance. In a Los Angeles *Daily News* article, McCoy said, 'For once I have a chance to do a script exactly as I want, with no interference from the front office.' It didn't work out quite like that. McCoy delivered a script entitled *Cowpoke,* which contained a number of scenes that would remain in Ray's final cut. But the original writer, Claude Stanush, claimed that McCoy had written the script in a southern Negro dialect rather than in cowboy-speak. Relations between McCoy, who had researched the script by putting in five months on the rodeo circuit, and the production team grew tense. On Howard Hughes's urging, the film began to tilt towards the Susan Hayward character. This annoyed McCoy, whose script had a different emphasis, and he was soon off the project, returning later to write the newspaper headlines and commentaries used by the radio announcers in the film.

The year 1952 saw the release of three films with script contributions by McCoy: Budd Boetticher's *Bronco Busters* (Universal-International), Raoul Walsh's *The World in His Arms* (Universal) and Allen Dwan's *Montana Belle* (RKO). Two years later, McCoy's *Scalpel* treatment had mutated into Hal Wallis's *Bad for Each Other*. Directed by Irving Rapper at Columbia, with a script by McCoy and Irving Wallace, it starred Charlton Heston and Lizabeth Scott, who was to sue *Confidential* magazine in 1953 over allegations regarding her sexual proclivities. The following year, McCoy scripted *Dangerous Mission* for RKO, with Victor Mature and William Bendix. When the script was handed on to W.R. Burnett, the latter took one look at it, and, regarding McCoy's contribution, said, 'He must have been drunk.' Though he and McCoy would remain close friends – they shared an interest in cars, sports and jazz 78s – Burnett was to criticise not only McCoy's script but also, in a *Saturday Review* article, the Dell edition of *Scalpel*, now titled *Corruption City*.

Yet by this time, McCoy's four previous novels had earned him a reputation as the poet of tabloid crime fiction. Though his ultimate goal was to be taken seriously as a novelist, McCoy also considered himself an actor, producer, documentary maker, art collector, athlete and painter. Ironically, he did not include scriptwriting among his talents, even though this was the medium by which McCoy supported himself and his family. Convinced he had failed as a writer, in 1955 McCoy was working on a hardboiled novel, *The Hard Rock Man*, for which he had received a $7,500 advance. He was also about to form a production company with the actor William Bendix, and begin work on a film, to be directed and scripted by McCoy, called *Night Cry*, about professional wrestling, when a heart attack cut short his career. He died on 5 December, aged fifty-eight.

After his death, to pay back his various advances, Helen had to sell her husband's immense record collection and library, for which she received a grand total of $750. Among the books was a first edition of *The Great Gatsby* inscribed by Fitzgerald:

> From Scott Fitzgerald
> of doom a herald
> For Horace McCoy
> no harbinger of joy

In the screenwriters' file kept by William Fadiman, who was head of the literary department for Howard Hughes, McCoy's name could be found under the heading 'masculine relationships'. It seems a sad and simplistic category in which to file a writer of such talent. In the final analysis, McCoy was a great hardboiled novelist and a hack screenwriter. Ironically, the novel that would become McCoy's only best seller, *Corruption City*, would be his worst book. Appropriately for McCoy, the novel ends with the words, 'God was in His Heaven and all was right with the script writer.'

Like Chandler and Hammett, McCoy would influence the direction of hardboiled novels and films. While his scripts varied in quality, his four novels were original and influential. Yet they have never been adequately adapted for the screen. In the end, McCoy's story causes one to consider, on the one hand, what price a writer must pay for his art, and, on the other hand, the relationship between writing and financial success. For better or worse, all roads for the likes of McCoy lead to Hollywood. Though he called it 'A cheap town filled with cheap stores and cheap people', McCoy knew it was also filled with possibilities, 'where miracles are happening all around you'. It was the space between the cheapness and the miracle that McCoy examined in his fiction. His success as a novelist was based not only on the quality of his writing but also on his ability to turn his studio work into fodder for his fiction. For McCoy was a creature of Hollywood, a man who gave up a lot to create so little and so much.

W.R. Burnett

My work doesn't exude liberalism. It's not anti-liberal, it's not anything – it's the way I see the world.

Unlike those of many writers in Hollywood, William Riley Burnett's forty-year career was an unmitigated success. Though he had reservations about living and working in Tinseltown, he would remain relatively content doing so. With a realistic notion of the writer's place within the studio hierarchy, Burnett regarded screenwriting as a way of financing his fiction. But once in Hollywood, the money, he said, simply fell from the sky.

When he died, aged eighty-two, in 1982, Burnett had garnered over sixty screenwriting credits, more than half relating to films in the crime genre. He had also published thirty-six novels, fifteen serialised stories, a hundred songs, twenty plays, and some twenty short stories. As well as crime novels, Burnett wrote political westerns – *Saint Johnson*, for instance, tells the story of the gunfight at OK Corral, and would be adapted for the screen on four occasions – and narratives about dog-racing, boxing, music and art.

Born on 25 October 1899 in Springfield, Ohio, Burnett was a large but gentle person. At Ohio State University he excelled at sports. His grandfather had been mayor of Columbus, Ohio, his father Governor James Cox's right-hand man. In 1920, Burnett helped with Cox's presidential campaign. At the age of twenty-one, he married Marjorie Louise Barlow, and landed a job in a factory, then in an insurance company, before becoming a statistician at Ohio's Bureau of Labor

Statistics. Initially wanting to write plays and musicals, Burnett would go to the library during his lunch break and spend his nights reading fiction, particularly French writers like Maupassant and Balzac. Soon he was devoting whatever spare time he had to writing. Dissatisfied with his all too settled existence, Burnett escaped to Chicago where, in 1927, he found employment as a desk clerk in the Northmere Hotel. By this time he had written five novels and a hundred short stories, but had sold none of them.

It was the era of the Chicago gangster, one of whom, upon hearing that Burnett was a budding writer, decided to show him the city from his perspective. In the company of a news reporter, Burnett would be one of the first to arrive on the scene of the Saint Valentine's Day Massacre. Though the job of desk clerk seems to have been a popular job for such aspiring writers as Burnett, Jim Thompson, Chester Himes and Nathaniel West, it would be another two years before Burnett, now living in Chicago's Hazelcrest Hotel, would write his classic crime novel, *Little Caesar.*

Within weeks of its 1929 publication, the novel had sold more than 100,000 copies. Based on the rise of Al Capone, it struck a chord with readers, and influenced writers like McCoy, Faulkner (*Sanctuary*) and Graham Greene (*Brighton Rock*). According to critic George Grella, *Little Caesar* fails to be a great novel but 'remains the classic gangster story', the greatest achievement of which lies in its depiction of Rico, which would inspire countless imitations in both fiction and film. Grella maintains that there is also a political dimension to such characters: 'The tough guy . . . , a totally disinterested killer who cares about nothing but power . . . in a world where slaughter and corruption dominate, where cops and judges and lawmakers can all be fixed . . . is the perfect symbol of society.'

Little Caesar was quickly bought by Jack Warner in Hollywood, who paid Burnett $15,000 for the film rights. He also gave him a contract worth $1,000 a week and the opportunity to collaborate with John Monk Saunders on *The Finger Points*. Warner would maintain that he bought the book simply because its protagonist came from Youngstown, Ohio, the home town of the Warner brothers. But Warner must have sensed that the novel would prove a lucrative acquisition.

By the time *Little Caesar* was published, Burnett had completed a second novel, *Iron Man*, a boxing story, and was working on *Saint Johnson*, which, prior to his arrival in Hollywood, he had been researching in Tombstone, Arizona. Once in Los Angeles, Burnett took up residence in South Saint Andrews Place. The following year, he won the O'Henry Prize for a short story, 'Dressing Up' (one of the few Burnett stories not to be bought by the studios), and sold a treatment of *Iron Man* to Carl Laemmle Jr., who, on his twenty-first birthday, had recently become head of Universal. *Iron Man* would be filmed twice, in 1937 under the title *Some Blondes Are Dangerous*, and in 1951.

Once settled in Los Angeles, Burnett cultivated an interest in greyhounds and racehorses. Both would figure in a number of his films and stories. Something of a displaced person, Burnett could often be found at Santa Anita in nearby Arcadia, a racetrack constructed three decades earlier by railway baron Lucky Baldwin. Though friendly with a number of people in the industry, Burnett would never become a full-fledged member of the film community.

Because his primary goal was to establish himself as a novelist, Burnett had hoped to steer clear of scriptwriting, preferring to sell stories and ideas to Hollywood. But his weakness for betting on the horses eventually became a contributing factor to his 1941 bankruptcy, which forced him to turn to the more lucrative but less rewarding profession of screenwriting. Even so, Burnett would never forsake his preferred career.

Released in 1930, the movie version of *Little Caesar* was as successful as the novel had been. Regarding the character of Rico, Burnett told Ken Mate and Pat McGilligan, 'I was reaching for a gutter Macbeth . . . Nobody understood what I meant by the quotation from Machiavelli at the front of *Little Caesar*: "The first law of every being is to preserve itself and live. You sow hemlock and expect to see ears of corn ripen." It meant, if you have this type of society, it will produce such men.'

Stylistically, Burnett sought to write a novel consisting of natural speech, and to portray the world as seen through the eyes of someone outside society, who has created his own rules and therefore turned the social order upside-down. Cliché-ridden though that might sound today, it was an electrifying approach in the era when *Little Caesar* was first published and filmed.

Given the production team, the film might have been the *Reservoir Dogs* of its day. For it marked the coming of age of a new generation of film people. At the time, director Mervyn LeRoy was only twenty-eight, producer Hal Wallis was thirty-one and Darryl Zanuck, the executive producer, was only twenty-seven. Burnett himself was twenty-eight, and actor Edward G. Robinson was thirty. An easy film to make, the script, written by Francis Faragoh and Robert N. Lee, came directly from the book, with the exception that, in the novel, the Irish detective does not apprehend Rico, and Rico does not die in a flophouse, which, according to Burnett, is 'the last place he'd ever be'.

As far as Burnett was concerned, it wasn't the script – he never thought much of the adaptation – that made the film successful, but Robinson's portrayal of Rico. However, it rankled Burnett that, while the crooks were supposed to be Italian, there was hardly an Italian accent to be heard. This is hardly unusual in Hollywood, where special interests are not to be offended and foreign rights not to be endangered. So casting incongruities prevail – biblical characters have Brooklyn accents, Native Americans are played by Jews or Italian Americans, and Spanish Civil War Loyalists can be played by Swedes and Russians. Studio executive Samuel

Goldwyn would even say, 'You can't have a Jew play a Jew. It wouldn't work on the screen,' while his counterpart at Columbia, Harry Cohn, once boasted that the only Jews he had under contract played Indians.

There was such public interest in *Little Caesar* that, when it opened at the Strand Theater in New York, mounted police were called to control the crowd, and the film had to be screened twenty-four hours a day. Back in Hollywood, Burnett was to get a whiff of how writers are regarded when, at the premier, everyone connected with the film assembled onstage. As an afterthought, someone asked about the writer. 'Oh, yes, the writer,' said the emcee. 'There always has to be a *writer.*' An insulted Burnett refused to join his colleagues.

Thanks partly to Burnett, the gangster, born out of Prohibition, the Big Crash and the Depression, was to become a cultural icon. The likes of Capone, Dutch Schultz and Legs Diamond had become household names, their warped anarchism indicative of an ambivalence regarding law and order, and capitalism at its most extreme. Edward G. Robinson and George Raft, whose screen personalities epitomised gangsterism, played characters that understood and defined urban America's language and landscape. Interestingly, gangsters only became cinema icons with the advent of the 'talkies'. It was not until such characters could speak that they were able to comment on society, intone the rhythms and argot of the streets and become emblematic of the culture. 'Mother of God, is this the end of Rico?' says Little Caesar after he's been shot, his vernacularism denoting that, though his time has come, gangsterism would outlive the geography of Rico's world as well as the Depression, to seep into the fabric of American culture.

Among Burnett's early screenplays was *The Beast of the City* (though future rightwing president of the company union, John Lee Mahin, received credit for writing the picture), directed by Charles Brabin, starring Walter Huston, Jean Harlow and Jean Hersholt. An early film noir, its protagonist modelled on Al Capone, *The Beast of the City* focuses on the political, social and law-enforcement problems coincident with Prohibition and the Depression. Originally entitled *City Sentinel*, it was conceived in 1930 when Irving Thalberg sought to make a Warner-style underworld movie. Burnett forged a screenplay from his experiences in Chicago, elements of his novel *Saint Johnson*, and Mahin's unpublished story. MGM never quite came to terms with the movie and held up its release for a year. When it finally went out in 1932, its name was changed to *The Beast of the City* and, with its J. Edgar Hoover prologue, was shown only in second-run movie houses. Nevertheless, Burnett considered it one of the best films about Capone, and one of the best crime pictures ever. Certainly it prefigures contemporary films like *The Enforcer* and *Dirty Harry*, while Hersholt's portrayal of the gangster was, according to Burnett, 'greasy and offensive' – a commendation in Burnett-speak. Despite his opinion of the film, Burnett did not have much regard for Brabin as a director, maintaining that the transplanted Englishman did not know his subject, and showed his lack of enthusiasm for the project by sleeping through story conferences.

The most influential gangster film of the 1930s, for which Burnett did earn a screenwriting credit, was *Scarface* (1932). Because the film contained forty-three murders, the Motion Picture Production Code demanded that the film be subtitled *The Shame of the Nation* – though, given the rise of gangsterism during the Depression, it could equally have been called *The State of the Nation*. *Scarface* was produced by Howard Hughes, who paid Burnett $2,000 a week to work on the picture. Twelve writers had worked on the film before Burnett, who would have to rewrite the entire screenplay. However, Hawks was still not entirely satisfied, and asked Hughes to hire Ben Hecht to add some finishing touches to it.

To secure the rights to *Scarface*, Hughes had to pay the novel's author, Armitage Trail, $25,000. He purchased the narrative not so that he could adapt the plot but simply so that he could use the title. Hughes, with his bizarre business acumen, retained elements of the story, specifically its incest theme. According to Burnett, who had a low opinion of the novel, Trail – real name, Maurice Coons – cut a pathetic figure: 'He was lucky to have four dollars in his pocket at any given time.' Trail, whose only other novel would be *The Thirteenth Guest* (1929), would be fatally struck down by a heart attack a few years later while watching a film at Grauman's Chinese Theater.

Though at loggerheads with Hawks, Burnett had nothing but respect for Hecht, who said he would produce a shootable script if Hughes would pay him $1,000 a day. Hughes agreed and, according to Burnett, received a finished script forty days later (David Thomson, in *A Biographical Dictionary of Film*, says Hecht wrote it in eleven days). Burnett considered Hecht the best writer in Hollywood. But what makes the film memorable, for Burnett, is not the script but George Raft's coin trick. It had been the actor's idea, and Burnett considered it a wonderful ploy. When asked about the 1932 film, Burnett merely replied, 'They paid every Wednesday.'

No discussion of screenwriter-novelists would be complete without commenting upon Hecht's career. Born in Chicago in 1893, this ex-journalist arrived in Hollywood from New York after his friend, fellow writer Herman Mankiewicz, cabled him – 'Millions are to be grabbed out here and your only competition is idiots.' Though more skilful at banter than plot construction, Hecht became one of Hollywood's highest paid writers, averaging between $50,000 and $125,000 for scripts he usually completed within a fortnight. Heaping scorn on an industry that paid so well for so little, and bemoaning the effect of film on American cultural life, Hecht, in his forty-year career, worked with such directors as Josef von Sternberg, Alfred Hitchcock and Howard Hawks – and writers like Charles MacArthur and I.A.L. Diamond. Credited with over seventy films, Hecht could write in an assortment of genres, from gangster films like *Underworld*, for which, in 1927, he received $10,000 for a week's work, to films noirs like *Kiss of Death* and *Where the Sidewalk Ends*, and comedies like *Front Page*, *It's a Wonderful World* and *Monkey Business*.

To bring the discussion back to *Scarface*, Hecht, in his autobiography, recollects that, during the shooting of the film, two henchmen employed by the real Scarface came to his hotel to find out if the movie was really about Capone. Hecht said to them, 'If we call the movie *Scarface* everyone will want to see it, figuring it's about Al. That's part of the racket we call showmanship.' Hecht's dealings with the mobsters underlines what actor Marc Lawrence, in an interview with Lee Server, had to say about the way gangsters viewed their screen portrayals: 'They . . . copied the gestures, the clothes.' Gangsters have always had an intimate relationship with Hollywood. When Lawrence met Lucky Luciano in Italy, he realised that the famous gangster was imitating the way he, Lawrence, played tough guys on the screen. And when Bugsy Siegel met George Raft, he not only studied the actor's mannerisms but asked for the name of his tailor. Clearly examples of life imitating art imitating life.

Another emblematic screen gangster created by Burnett was *High Sierra*'s Roy Earle. Prior to writing the novel, Burnett had been working with a reporter, Charley Blake, who had done considerable research on John Dillinger, and had even accompanied the gangster's body to the morgue after his fatal shooting outside Chicago's Biograph Theater. After the release of *Little Caesar*, Blake and Burnett had planned to write a screenplay about Dillinger, but, because of pressure from the press and public, Warner Brothers backed out of the deal. Still, Burnett kept the material at hand. He got the idea for *High Sierra* at June Lake. As well as realising that the place would make an excellent hideout, he met an elderly black man whose dog, he said, brought bad luck to anyone who came in contact with it. So Burnett took those elements and built the plot to *High Sierra* around them.

After the book's publication in March 1940, Warner

Brothers, competing for the rights with Paramount, purchased the novel for $12,500. The film adaptation would be directed by Raoul Walsh, with Burnett and John Huston sharing screenwriting credits. Full of praise for the novel, Huston wanted to follow the book as closely as possible, just as he had with Hammett's *Maltese Falcon*.

Sensing trouble, Huston warned Hal Wallis that sanitising the story would be disastrous. Nevertheless, when elements of the press heard that Warner Brothers was planning a film based on Dillinger, the studio came under fire for glorifying a criminal. It prompted the Production Code office to maintain a presence on the set for most of the film's shooting. Eventually Hollywood's *de facto* censor sent Warner forty-three objections to the film in a report spanning twenty-seven pages. Consequently, Burnett and Huston had to rewrite the script and resubmit it. To their surprise, what they had considered the most contentious element, that the script depicted a woman living with two men, received the green light, probably because Huston and Burnett had insisted that it was integral to the plot. Eventually they managed to get most of their script past the Production Code office, and *High Sierra* became another quintessential Burnett gangster film.

When it came to working together, Burnett and Huston got on well, though Burnett, like Ben Maddow nine years later, would complain about the way Huston went about writing a screenplay. It irked Burnett that Huston found it necessary to talk out each scene, then dictate it to someone at a typewriter. It was a time-consuming process. One scene might take two days for Huston to write. Burnett, banging away on his Underwood, could write the same scene in a matter of hours.

George Raft might have turned down the part of Roy Earle because he did not want to again play someone who dies on screen, but it was Paul Muni, one of the era's biggest stars, who had originally been offered the role. However, some years previously Huston had insulted Muni at a Hollywood party, and Muni, seeing Huston's name on the script, turned down the film to exact revenge. When Jack Warner heard about Muni's rejection, he said to Huston, 'Get Burnett and let him work on the script with you, and if Muni comes up with any objections, we'll say, "For chrissakes, what do you want? We got the author on it." ' When Muni turned it down again, Warner's reaction surprised everyone: he simply fired Muni, who at the time was making $5,000 a week. Only then was the part offered to Raft, who was talked out of the role by Bogart, presumably because he wanted to play the part himself. Interestingly, Raft also turned down the role of Sam Spade in Huston's *The Maltese Falcon*, as well as the lead in Sidney Kingsley's *Dead End* (1937). Both parts would go to Bogart. Dissatisfied with the roles offered by Warner Brothers, Raft would pay Jack Warner $10,000 to get out of his contract. 'I was never very good with money,' said Raft. He might have added that neither was he very good at standing up to Bogart.

Bogie's snarling determination fitted perfectly with Burnett's notion that Earle, like Dillinger, was a person with a Midwest mentality stranded in an alien landscape, that of the Sierras. A different breed from Rico, Earle was a reversion to the type of bandit who once inhabited the West. Resembling Arky in Burnett's novel *Little Men, Big World* and Dix in *Asphalt Jungle*, Earle exemplified the growing urbanisation of America at a time when there was still a rural culture seemingly prelapsarian in its isolation from the rest of the world. Influenced by literature of the American West, *High Sierra* illustrates Burnett's ability to combine the ethos of the western with the gangster novel, much as Elmore Leonard would do three decades later.

Apart from the Production Code, Huston and Burnett's biggest problem was producer Mark Hellinger, who could not understand what motivated the lame girl in the film to turn against Earle. So Burnett and Huston had to sweeten that part of the script, something that Burnett would correct when he wrote the 1956 remake, *I Died a Thousand Times*, starring Jack Palance and Shelley Winters and directed by Stuart

Heisler. A more claustrophobic film, Burnett believed it to be the better picture. In between those two movies there was another version of *High Sierra*, a mediocre western entitled *Colorado Territory* (1949), directed by Raoul Walsh and starring Joel McCrea and Virginia Mayo.

High Sierra had turned Burnett into one of the highest paid screenwriters in Hollywood. Knowing that they had too valuable a commodity to let loose on the open market, Warner Brothers sought to hold on to him at any cost. After all, here was someone who not only could provide the studio with ideas and scripts but also was willing to collaborate with others, work without credit, and salvage substandard scripts. Occasionally, Burnett even acted as a conciliator between actors like Bogart and Raft and the studio. In the five years he worked at Warner, Burnett's pay rose from $750 per week to $1,500. So integral had he become to the studio that a car would pick him up each morning and take him home each evening. The only other scriptwriter to have this luxury lavished upon him was Julius Epstein.

In 1941, Warner paid Burnett an additional $8,000 for the rights to a story entitled 'Nobody Lives Forever', about a Chicago gangster married to a nightclub singer. The studio allowed Burnett to retain literary and theatrical rights. Though nothing was to come of that particular project, two years later Burnett sold a story, 'I Wasn't Born Yesterday', to Warners for $10,000. The plot concerned a New York gambler who returns from the service to find his girlfriend and gambling operation have been taken over. Burnett suggested to Hellinger that the title of the latter story should be changed to the aforementioned 'Nobody Lives Forever'. Hellinger agreed, and hired Jean Negulesco to direct. Starring John Garfield as the ex-serviceman and gambler (originally it had been announced that Bogart, following the completion of *To Have and Have Not*, would land the role), the film, by exploiting the usual noir trappings, articulates postwar disorientation and alienation. Burnett would capitalise on the title once again, having turned *Nobody Lives Forever* into a novel, which Knopf would publish two years later.

Burnett could have made more money elsewhere, but Warner Brothers had become, for him, a secure and not unpleasant place to work. However, in September 1945, Burnett asked to be released from his contract. He had ear-marked Joan Crawford for the lead in the adaptation of his novel, *Romelle*, which he wanted to sell to the highest bidder. So Burnett eventually moved to MGM. His version of *Romelle* would never be made.

In 1950, MGM's Dore Schary, seeking to make a picture about 'shooting and fucking', acquired the rights to *The Asphalt Jungle*, which had been published a year earlier, for $100,000. John Huston and Ben Maddow – with an uncredited contribution from Burnett – would stick close to the book. The script, which portrays straight society to be as crooked as its criminal counterpart, made one departure from the novel, however: it did away with the police lieutenant as narrator. As Maddow told Pat McGilligan, 'The crime is simply normal endeavour, another form of business; therefore the concentration on the characters of the criminals makes you like them ... and sympathise with them.' Over the years, *The Asphalt Jungle* would be remade as *The Badlanders* (1953), a western starring Alan Ladd, *Cairo* (1963) with George Sanders, and the blaxploitation film *Cool Breeze* (1972) with Raymond St Jacques (there was also an ABC television series entitled *The Asphalt Jungle*, which ran from April to September 1961, with Jack Warden and Arch Johnson). Yet Huston's version remains by far the most memorable and artistically satisfying.

When *The Asphalt Jungle* was released in 1950, the congressional investigation into the influence of communism in Hollywood was reaching its peak, and the role of the studio writer was being reassessed. Fewer studios were employing large numbers of writers. While movie theatres were in decline, the number of drive-in theatres was increasing (300 in 1946, 1,200 in 1949 and 2,200 in 1950). Many studios had stopped making B movies, while some, like RKO, stopped making movies altogether. Burnett would begin to refer to Warner Brothers' studio at Burbank as Death Valley.

As far as Burnett was concerned, Huston was, like himself, a rebel: 'A revolutionary is a politician who is out of office. A rebel is a guy who is suspicious of all authority, left or right.' While Burnett had little time for Hollywood politics, he had nothing against Huston's casting of leftists in *The Asphalt Jungle*. Those in the cast considered to be members, at one time or another, of the Communist Party were Sterling Hayden, Marc Lawrence and Sam Jaffe. Burnett believed that Huston's casting – which helped launch the careers of Sterling Hayden, James Whitmore and Marilyn Monroe – only served to strengthen the story. Co-writer Ben Maddow was also a leftist who would fall victim to the blacklist, only to be exonerated when, at the last moment, he supplied names to the McCarthyites.

Just as he hadn't any problems regarding the leftists in Huston's *Asphalt Jungle*, so Burnett, despite his aversion to Hollywood Communists, worked amicably alongside Party members like Albert Maltz (*This Gun For Hire*) and the first president of the Screen Writers Guild, John Howard Lawson (*Action in the North Atlantic*). Some have suggested that the pairing of Communists and anti-Communists was a case of Hollywood hoping to halt the Party's propaganda machine. Having said that, Maltz would maintain that Burnett's input on the noir classic *This Gun For Hire* was negligible. He claimed that he, Maltz, had written the script on his own, and had simply sent it upstairs to Burnett's office. According to Maltz, Burnett merely returned it with his stamp of approval.

Despite his willingness to work with leftists, Burnett refused to participate in the formation of the Screen Writers Guild, and even balked at becoming a member. His view was that, by the time the Guild was formed, he was already financially secure. Burnett would later maintain that he had nothing against unions, but had always been opposed to the closed shop. Despite his views, screenwriter John Wexley (*Angels with Dirty Faces, The Long Night, Hangmen Also Die*), whom the House Un-American Activities Committee named as a communist, fondly recalled conversations he had had with Burnett while working at Paramount. Likewise, Burnett had enjoyed collaborating with Maltz. The same could not be said, however, for the more doctrinaire Lawson, though this might have had less to do with the latter's politics than with the fact that he had received top screenwriting credit for *Action in the North Atlantic*. Burnett would not only claim that he, not Lawson, had written most of that movie's action scenes, but that Lawson had done little more than read the script. Though he avoided political pigeonholes, Burnett, regarding blacklisted writers, would say, 'I am not exactly in favour of people who advocate the overthrow of the government by violence.' Nevertheless, there are moments in the novel *High Sierra* in which Roy Earle speaks sympathetically about communism. As does Arky in *Little Men, Big World*.

In 1950, almost twenty years after *Scarface*, Burnett would again work with Howard Hughes, when RKO contracted him to write *The Racket*, followed by *Vendetta*. Starring Robert Mitchum, Lizabeth Scott and Robert Ryan and directed by John Cromwell, who, despite turning down the chance to direct *I Married a Communist*, was viewed favourably by Hughes, *The Racket* concerns a struggle between a cop and a mobster in a Midwestern city against the backdrop of a local election. Portraying corruption as an integral part of urban life, the film makes no moral distinctions, nor depicts criminals as more dangerous than anyone else. Based on Bartlett Cormack's play, which Hughes had bought in 1927 and, under Lewis Milestone's direction, filmed the following year, Burnett's version would be one of the first projects announced by Hughes's newly controlled RKO. Samuel Fuller had originally been hired to write the screenplay, followed by a stream of other writers. Halfway through production, and after

$500,000 worth of retakes, Hughes asked Burnett to work on the film. Even with his script, *The Racket*, though containing a political edge that even *The Asphalt Jungle* lacks, remains a pedestrian effort.

Vendetta was even less successful. Concerning revenge and incest (again) in Corsica, the film was originally to be directed by the once brilliant Preston Sturges. In Burnett's opinion, the movie was so bad as to be laughable. With Hughes's approval, the project, despite more than a million dollars' worth of film in the can, was scrapped. While Burnett was rewriting it, Hughes would phone him late at night to go through the film line by line. At one point, he spent several hours trying to convince Burnett that a colon should replace a semicolon. The eccentric producer was also writing memoranda that spiralled into nowhere, and 'Notes on Notes' which dealt at great length with the punctuation in his latest will. Having told Burnett and Stuart Heisler, who was at that time directing the film, to meet him at his Sunset Towers apartment at two in the morning, the producer arrived in a beat-up car, wearing tennis shoes, a dirty shirt and a pair of old trousers. Nor could Hughes decide on a director. Besides Sturges and Heisler, he would hire the renowned Max Ophuls, and even attempt to direct the film himself. Eventually, *Vendetta* would be handed on to Mel Ferrer, to whom the film was finally credited, and released in 1950 to no great acclaim.

Burnett also worked for RKO on *Dangerous Mission*, a film on which Horace McCoy had been employed. Three writers would be credited with the screenplay: Burnett, McCoy and Hitchcock's favoured screenwriter, Charles Bennett (*Thirty-nine Steps*, *Sabotage*, *Secret Agent*). Unfortunately, such combinations of writers rarely augur well for a film. With shooting having come to a standstill, Burnett read McCoy's script and junked it. After four weeks of writing, Burnett was finally able to come up with something shootable.

Burnett would always have a soft spot for Hughes, and

would recall how the producer once shyly approached him to ask if he would sign his copy of his novel *Goodbye to the Past*. 'He didn't mismanage RKO,' said Burnett. 'He didn't manage it at all.' In the 1950s, Burnett would briefly return to Warner Brothers. But with only a handful of writers still doing contract work, Burnett said the studio was like a ghost town. The only person left from the old days was McCoy, who didn't seem to mind that Burnett had panned his novel, *Corruption City*, in the *Saturday Review*.

During all this time, Burnett continued producing novels like *Little Men, Big World* and *Vanity Row*, which, along with *The Asphalt Jungle*, comprise a trilogy regarding corruption, each book representing a different aspect of the relationship between crime and society: the status quo (*The Asphalt Jungle*), imbalance (*Little Men, Big World*) and anarchy (*Vanity Row*). Concerned with Watergate-style intrigue, a struggle for control of the wire service, and what happens when government goes out of control, *Vanity Row* was, according to Burnett, ahead of its time. Republic bought the novel, and paid Burnett to do the script. Eventually the studio decided to alter the plot and retitle the film *Accused of Murder* (1957). Their reason for doing so had less to do with artistic considerations than the fact that Vera Ralston, the wife of the studio head, had been cast in the lead role, and it was deemed unseemly for her to commit a murder. The film's alteration was, in Burnett's opinion, the most senseless decision he had encountered in his Hollywood career.

By this time, Burnett was married to Whitney Forbes Johnstone, having met her in 1943 when she was working as a secretary at Twentieth Century Fox, and when he was still married to Marjorie Louise Barlow. It was a situation Burnett would write about in his novel *Nobody Lives Forever* (dedicated to Whitney), in which the protagonist must choose between two women. Burnett chose Whitney, and, two years later, they were married. One of the first places Burnett took his new wife was Santa Anita racetrack. Over the years the couple would have two children and they stayed together for the remainder of Burnett's life.

When, in 1964, their Bel Air house burned down, Burnett and Whitney escaped with the clothes they were wearing, their five dogs and children. After the fire, Burnett's career altered. It was the 1960s and the studios were interested in another kind of story. Though Burnett turned to television, the medium was not to his liking. He hated the gossip and the meetings. Around this time Burnett began having problems with his vision, which made writing difficult. In addition, a new generation of editors was taking over, and it was harder for Burnett to get his novels published. So he began publishing with paperback companies like Gold Medal, often writing under a *nom de plume*. Most of the books were good; some were better than his earlier novels. Though he still harboured a desire to be the American Balzac, Burnett realised that his work was slowly disappearing from bookstores and the collective literary memory. Soon his novels would be better known to collectors than to the general reading public. As for films, Michael Cimino's 1974 excellent *Thunderbolt and Lightfoot* was the final movie on which Burnett would work. True to form, his contribution was to go uncredited.

Besides Hecht, Burnett's favourite screenwriter was Dudley Nichols (*The Informer, Bringing Up Baby, Man Hunt*), who had penned scripts for Lang, Cukor, Renoir and Hawks. As directors go, Hawks was his favourite, followed by Wilder ('eccentric') and Preston Sturges ('crazy'). When it came to novelists working in Hollywood, Burnett liked Faulkner personally – he would have cast him to play Edgar Allan Poe – but had never been able to read his books. Surprisingly, he would never meet Raymond Chandler, whom he rated below Simenon as a writer, and came across Hammett ('he looked like a university professor') only once. But he occasionally saw James M. Cain ('weird'), with whom he was on friendly terms, in H.N. Swanson's office.

As far as Burnett was concerned, none of the studios valued

writers. Nevertheless, Warner Brothers was 'the best place to be'. Metro, he said, was like being in 'the middle of the desert – no one knew you were there'. Paramount was a bit better, though not as well run as Columbia under Harry Cohn, or Twentieth Century Fox under Zanuck. Like Sam Fuller, Burnett had a certain respect for Zanuck, who appreciated writers, being something of a writer himself.

So how did Burnett manage to combine fiction and films? According to Whitney, Burnett would allow his novels to gestate before writing them. Once he started, the writing came quick and easy. He would work through the night and never revised anything. Nor would Burnett allow his editors to do so. He simply sent his manuscripts off and expected them to be published as they were. More than that, Burnett, to his credit, never took films too seriously, nor considered them an artistic endeavour. Yet he always made sure he did the best he could. Said Burnett, '[The] circumstances are mostly poor, because writers have no control whatsoever. Screenwriting consists of rewriting and I don't rewrite.' In the end, Burnett was smart enough to regard scriptwriting and Hollywood as part of the cultural mix, even commenting that the degeneration of narrative structure was a sign of a degenerating social framework. 'There's no doubt about it,' said Burnett, 'everything is falling apart.'

Yet it was ironical that this writer of stories depicting outlaws and amoral protagonists would fall out of favour in the 1960s, when outlaws and criminals had again become cultural icons. To Burnett, the screenwriters of that era had little feel for film. 'They're writing stories, they're plays, they're not writing for film. There's far too much dialogue written.' Burnett believed his own strong point was his sense of structure. 'Once you've got structure,' he said, 'you've got the whole picture.' As for others adapting his work, Burnett would maintain that all anyone had to do was use the dialogue and the script would form itself. In the end, it was Burnett's perspective that kept him going. 'I have a pretty good grip on reality,' he said, 'so I pretty much know the limitations of humanity and the possibilities in life, which aren't very great for anybody. You're born, you're gonna have trouble, and you're gonna die.'

3

THE POSTMAN RINGS TWICE BUT THE ICEMAN WALKS RIGHT IN

Paul Cain and James M. Cain

Other than their biblical surname and the fact that both wrote culinary articles and resided, during the same year, at the Hotel Montecito in Hollywood, all that connects Paul Cain and James M. Cain is that both, while working in the studios, produced fiction powerful enough to influence future noir novels and films. Stylistically speaking they were at opposite ends of the hardboiled spectrum. While Paul Cain's writing – hard-edged and visual – epitomised tough-guy fiction, James M. Cain sought a more circuitous and, in comparison, softboiled route, veering in the direction of steamy middle-class sleaze. While his career might be an open book, little is known about Paul Cain's life, nor do we have a clear idea of the films he worked on. In the end, both writers would seek refugee status in Hollywood, even at the risk of sacrificing the context in which their best work had been produced.

Paul Cain

The mystery man of hardboiled fiction, Paul Cain remains a reminder of how Hollywood can so easily drive writers to extremes. Though for a short period of time Cain was able to get away from Hollywood and get his life in order, he would be lured back, unable to resist the money that working in Tinseltown offered.

The most hardboiled of writers, Cain helped define the genre, taking it, in terms of style, to what was up to then its furthest point. Hardboiled writing may have existed before Paul Cain, but nothing before or since has matched his matter-of-fact attitude and stripped-down style. Deploying an objective voice that allowed him to write scenes of extreme violence with a high degree of detachment, Cain's cinematic writing could at times turn into something akin to hardboiled poetry.

When it came to screenwriting, however, Cain was indistinguishable from countless other writers. He is yet another example of the gulf separating the two occupations, one solitary and artful, the other collaborative and money-oriented. Sometimes one can only conclude that the two media have nothing in common other than they both use words and tell stories; or perhaps it is a case of collaboration killing art. Whichever, success in one medium does not guarantee success in the other.

Like Hammett and Chandler, Paul Cain began his hardboiled career in *Black Mask*. In fact, that was practically the only magazine in which Cain would publish his stories, though from 1935 to 1936 he did place a narrative in *Detective Fiction Weekly* and another in *Star Detective Magazine*. But unlike others, Cain began publishing stories only after moving to Hollywood and establishing himself as a screenwriter.

About Cain's physical appearance, we know, thanks to hardboiled historian William F. Nolan in *The Black Mask Boys*, that he was slender, blond and bearded. Among the other facts are these: Cain's real name was George Carrol Sims; he was born in 1902 in Iowa; grew up in a grim Chicago neighbourhood; moved to Los Angeles in 1918; and five years later entered the film industry, though the exact nature of his work is unclear. In 1933, Cain, with some films under his belt, took up residence in Hollywood's Montecito Hotel, which had just opened on Franklin Street. It would prove a popular spot for writers. The following year, both James M. Cain and Horace McCoy would live there.

With a career in Hollywood ahead of him, Cain, at thirty-one, published *Fast One*. It is a novel whose camera eye depicts a world of gamblers and assorted tough guys. Unwilling to pass judgement on the characters or the violence that ensues, Cain's narrative voice is not so much cynical as alienated. Hardboiled expert Philip Durham described the novel's plot in the following way: 'Having acquired in the East two thousand dollars and a reputation for knowing how to play "rough," Gerry Kells arrived in Southern California. His reputation made it possible for him to begin taking over the Los Angeles rackets, which he proceeded to do by playing off one racketeer against another and by eliminating a few himself. Double-crossing, smashing, shooting and ice-picking were all in the act.'

When it came to Hollywood screen credits, Cain preferred the name Peter Ruric, occasionally changing it to George Ruric. However he would use the name Paul Cain for both *Fast One* and his collection of short stories, *Seven Slayers*. The stories comprising the latter volume had almost all been published in *Black Mask* from 1932 to 1936. *Fast One* was also, in fact, a compendium of short stories – 'Fast One', 'Lead Party', 'Velvet', The Heat' and 'The Dark' – which Cain had thrown together and packaged as a novel. They too had been published in *Black Mask* between March and September 1932. These, plus the two stories in *Detective Fiction Weekly* and *Star Detective Magazine*, constitute Cain's entire literary output.

Fast One was one of the first hardboiled crime novels to be set in Los Angeles. Though Cain accurately depicts the city, his perspective and style differ from that other LA chronicler, Raymond Chandler. Not only is Cain's world more localised than Chandler's but, unlike the latter, he feels the need to prove neither his protagonist's wit nor his geographical acumen. When it comes to the backdrop for his fiction, Cain, like Chandler, depicts such landmarks as The Lido apartments on Yucca at Wilcox, the Musso and Frank Grill on Hollywood Boulevard, the Brown Derby on Vine, the Knickerbocker on Ivar, and the Hollywood Division Police Station. But Cain's descriptions become part and parcel of the narrative. Here he describes Bunker Hill: 'Ansel's turned out to be a dark, three-story business block set flush with the sidewalk. There were big For Rent signs in the plate-glass windows and there was a dark stairway to one side.' Cain is not interested in cataloguing the city's sites, or deploying these sites as signifiers containing arguable amounts of meaning. Rather he simply uses them as settings that help move his story from one point to another.

Before writing screenplays, Cain worked as a production assistant on Josef von Sternberg's *The Salvation Hunters* (1927), a silent film set amid the mud flats of San Pedro, in which a young man wins the girl otherwise destined for her brutish suitor. Produced by Academy Photoplays, a production company begun by von Sternberg and George K. Arthur, *The Salvation Hunters* was lauded by Charlie Chaplin, only for the comedian later to add a disclaimer, saying, 'I thought I'd praise a bad film and see what happened.'

By the early 1930s Cain had graduated to scriptwriting. His first writing credit would be for Edgar G. Ulmer's *The Black Cat* (1934). Made for Universal and influenced by the Bauhaus, it is, according to critic Clive Hirschhorn, 'A truly bizarre concoction of mayhem, necrophilia, sadism and satanism.' The film was the first to pair Boris Karloff and Bela Lugosi (Cain and Lugosi met on the set and became friends), and concerns a doctor who seeks out an Austrian architect and devil-worshipper who betrayed his country during World War I. According to Ulmer, who is best known for directing that noir exercise in paranoia, *Detour*, the film bears little relationship to the Edgar Allan Poe story from which it is taken. Yet the film stands as a fascinating, if somewhat disappointing, collaboration between one of the great hardboiled writers and arguably the greatest B film-maker.

Cain/Ruric also helped write Robert Wise's *Mademoiselle Fifi* (1943) for Val Lewton at RKO. Based on a story by Maupassant, and starring Simone Simon and Kurt Kreuger, it is about a prostitute who refuses to sleep with a Prussian officer. When she finally gives in, the woman is shunned by society and ends up killing the officer. Robert Wise, who had recently edited *Citizen Kane*, would go on to make a number of excellent films in the noir tradition, such as *Born to Kill* (1947), *The Set-Up* (1949) and *Odds Against Tomorrow* (1959). *Mademoiselle Fifi* would be praised by none other than the critic James Agee, who, writing in *The Nation*, said, 'There is a gallant, fervent quality about the whole picture, faults and all, which gives it a peculiar kind of life and likeableness, and which signifies that there is a group of men in Hollywood who have neither lost nor taken care to conceal the purity of their hope and intention.'

Cain also contributed to the screenplays for *Affairs of a Gentleman* (1934), starring Paul Lukas and directed by Edwin Marin, about a novelist who, having depicted his affairs in his books, holds a reunion; *Jericho* (1937), co-scripted with Frances Marion and George Barraud and starring Paul Robeson – a court-martialled officer crosses Africa in search of a deserter (it was purportedly Robeson's favourite starring role); *Twelve Crowded Hours* (1939) – a reporter gets the goods on a racketeer; *The Night of January 16th* (1941), from Ayn Rand's play – a secretary is arrested for a murder that may not have occurred; S. Sylvan Simon's *Grand Central Murder* (1942), for MGM, starring Van Heflin and Cecilia Parker; and *Alias a Gentleman* (1947), also for MGM, starring Wallace Beery – an ex-convict tries to find his daughter and go straight. *Grand Central Murder*, adapted from Sue McVeigh's novel, concerns a train station slaying, and was one in a series of McVeigh novels that combine a structure similar to that of *The Thin Man* with the 'had I but known' school of writing.

Cain's contribution was to toughen up the script by disposing of the husband and wife investigatory team and turning Van Heflin into a lone private eye.

Some critics maintain that Ruric wrote other films, either uncredited or under other pseudonyms, but they are difficult to track down. Meanwhile, Max Marcin, a year before *Affairs of a Gentleman,* adapted Cain's *Fast One* for Paramount, retitling it *Gambling Ship.* Released in 1933, it stars Cary Grant and Benita Hume. Though, like the novel, it focuses on offshore gambling, the film has none of the book's pace, impact or hardboiled minimalism.

A letter from Cain to *Black Mask* editor Joseph T. Shaw only adds to the myth. In it, Cain states that, prior to establishing himself in Hollywood, he had travelled from South America and North Africa to the Near East, during which time he had worked as a tramp-steamer boatswain's mate. Cain also claims to have been a Dadaist painter and a professional gambler. While these alleged biographical details sound like a series of Hollywood clichés, they could have some truth to them. While Cain, in his fiction, never made much use of any experience he might have gained from the world of art, he did demonstrate, in *Fast One*, an insider's view of the subculture of gambling.

One of the few times Cain revealed anything about himself was on the backcover of a 1946 edition of *Seven Slayers*, where he listed his likes and dislikes. He claimed to hanker after Mercedes automobiles, peanut butter, Scotch whisky, Garbo, Richebourg 1904, and some of de Chirico's paintings. Among his dislikes were parsnips, the colour pink, sopranos, white nylon, cigars and a great many women and children.

In New York, Cain carried on a stormy relationship with cult actress Gertrude Michael. Like Cain, she was a heavy drinker, and was the inspiration for Kelly's dipsomaniac lover, Granquist, in *Fast One*. Cain also dedicated the novel to her. From Talladega, Alabama, Michael was born in 1911, and left home at eighteen to become a Hollywood star. Though she found some success, her career would be blighted by alcoholism, mental breakdown, road accidents, bad timing and embarrassing publicity. Her first movie appearance was in 1931, but the bulk of her acting career was sandwiched between 1938 and 1945, during which time she appeared in twelve films, most of them poverty-row exploitation dramas and comedies. She specialised in 'tough broads', and was best known for her role as the heroine in *The Notorious Sophie Lang* (1934). Michael was last seen on screen in 1962, when she indulged in some mid-street twisting with trumpeter and Las Vegas veteran Louis Prima (*Twisting the Night Away*). She died two years later. Her drunken exploits are unflatteringly immortalised in Kenneth Anger's *Hollywood Babylon*.

Série Noire creator Marcel Duhamel, in his memoirs, mentions meeting Cain in 1948, when the latter sought Duhamel's help during his three-week stay in France. According to Duhamel, who published *Fast One* the following year, Cain was suffering from depression and, most of all, wanted to stop drinking. It had been his intention to get as far away as possible from Hollywood, a town he thought lay at the root of all his problems. Cain told Duhamel he despised the work he had done for the film industry. Fortunately, Duhamel helped Cain relocate to the Balearics. A year later he saw Cain once again and found that he had totally recovered his health and had restarted his life with a young woman from Alicante.

Not only was Duhamel about to publish Cain, but it could be said that Série Noire fiction derived from his work. At the end of the 1950s, Duhamel was telling Chester Himes to write in a similar style:

'Start with action . . . – a man reaches out a hand and opens a door, light shines in his eyes, a body lies on the floor, he turns, looks up and down the hall . . . Always action in detail. Make pictures. Like motion pictures . . . No stream of consciousness at all. We don't give a damn who's thinking

what – only what they're doing. Always doing something.
From one scene to another. Don't worry about it making
sense. That's for the end.' (Chester Himes, *My Life of
Absurdity*)

In 1951, Cain was once again publishing his work. But this
time it would not be crime fiction. Instead, Cain, an enthusiastic cook, was writing a series of culinary articles for *Gourmet*
magazine.

All the mystery surrounding Cain would only add to his
legend. Even his limited output contributes to his notoriety.
For Cain personifies the romantic notion of the hardboiled
writer as someone of limited but influential output, at odds
with the world, who moves into films only to be fatally
wounded by the experience.

After the Balearics, Cain, unable to stay away, returned to
Los Angeles, wrote some undistinguished TV scripts, such as
The Lady in Yellow for Screen Gems in 1960, and died a few
years later, at the age of 64.

Not many writers can claim to have made their reputation
on the back of one novel and a collection of short stories.
But Cain apparently had no need to write anything else. What
he did, he did to perfection. This was anything but the case,
however, when it came to his screenplays. After spending all
those years writing screenplays of monumentally mundane
proportions, Cain ended up just another writer laid low by
Hollywood. Still, as Raymond Chandler once said of *Fast One*,
Cain's writing was 'as murderous and at the same time as
poignant as anything in that manner that has ever been
written'.

James M. Cain

Coming from the world of journalism, James M. Cain made
good use of his time in Hollywood, even if it was to drag him

into the murkier depths of the industry. Of course, it would not be his screenplays for which Cain achieved Tinseltown notoriety, but the novels he wrote during the years when he was writing screenplays. Ironically, Cain, who might be said to have invented the modern psychological crime novel, never considered himself a hardboiled writer, but just a writer of tragic tales.

True, Cain's novels are not in the *Black Mask* tradition, and bear little resemblance to previous hardboiled stylisations. In fact, Cain claimed that he had only read ten pages of Chandler, and nothing of McCoy. As for Hammett, Cain could only recall leafing through the first twenty pages of *The Glass Key*, when, as managing editor at *The New Yorker* in 1931, he had picked up a copy while waiting at the printers.

Despite Edmund Wilson labelling him 'the poet of tabloid murder', Cain did not consider himself part of any school of writing. In a sense he was right. Certainly Cain had little interest in advancing the typical hardboiled protagonist. Indeed, most of his narratives concern their comeuppance. Applying hardboiled fiction's minimalism to narratives steeped in a Dostoevsky-like mode of criminal psychology, Cain was less influenced by *Black Mask* revisionists than by the naturalism of Theodore Dreiser, the vernacular-oriented stories of Ring Lardner and the cultural criticism of H.L. Mencken. It was a mix that would later influence Rebecca West, André Gide, Albert Camus, Jean-Paul Sartre and Ross MacDonald, as well as future film directors and screenwriters. While few of his scripts reached the screen, fourteen films would be made from Cain's stories and novels.

Born on 2 July 1892 in Annapolis, Maryland, James Mallahan Cain came from an educated, upper middle-class, Irish Catholic family. His father was president of Washington College, and Cain himself had been an exemplary student. Despite a religious upbringing, by the age of thirteen Cain had already cut short his church attendance. Even so, or because of that, his future novels would be filled with a sense of guilt, sin and retribution. Meanwhile, Cain's mother, a coloratura soprano whose marriage halted her career, dissuaded her son from becoming a professional singer. His mother's predicament helps explain why Cain's work is filled with ambitious and vengeful women stuck in unfulfilled marriages.

After the war, Cain found work as a reporter, first for the *Baltimore American*, then *The Sun*, where for a time he was a Labour reporter. It was in Baltimore in 1920 that Cain married his first wife, Mary Rebekah Clough. According to Cain, she was somewhat 'high-brow' for him. Two years later, Cain was cheating on Mary and contributing articles to *The Nation* and *Atlantic Monthly*. Despite his lapsed religious status, Cain would maintain that it had been God's voice that had directed him to pick up the pen, even though he would also claim that he never had much aptitude for writing.

After meeting another Baltimore favourite son, H.L. Mencken, in 1924, Cain began contributing to the *American Mercury*, which Mencken was still editing. Having divorced his wife, Cain moved to New York where he found work on Walter Lippman's newspaper, *The World*, and embarked on an affair with a Finnish woman, Elina Sjosted Tyszecka. A mother of two, Elina was, according to Cain, the 'great love of my life'. But by the time they married in 1927, the passion had already been expunged from their relationship. A year after their marriage, Cain published his first story in the *American Mercury*. Appearing a year before Hammett's *Red Harvest*, 'Pastorale' was a grotesque and comic tale of murder in the Appalachians.

Knopf published Cain's first book, *Our Government*, in 1930. Comprising satirical pieces, sketches and dialogues between imaginary politicians regarding the inanities of government policy as they affect a poorhouse in Baltimore, which Cain had written for the *American Mercury* and *The World*, it remains one of the few books by Cain that, despite its historical importance, has never been reprinted. A year after the book's publication, Cain would lose his job at *The World*, and become managing editor of *The New Yorker*.

Cain would go on to publish eight novels, three novellas and numerous stories about crime, illicit sex, death and violence set in a middle-class milieu. More often than not, he utilised the same fatalistic hook: a man falls for a woman, they join forces to commit a crime, the man is betrayed by the woman. Meanwhile, Cain's females, like Mildred Pierce or Cora in *The Postman Always Rings Twice*, are invariably tougher, smarter and more acquisitive than their male counterparts, who, motivated by lust, unwisely put their faith in them.

There is a brutal simplicity about Cain's prose, giving it and his themes a timeless quality, even though he was writing about a particular era and people, the sort that Mencken described as 'morons who pour [into Los Angeles] from the prairies and deserts'. Writing with a detachment worthy of Flaubert, Cain made their destinies appear universal. He would describe his writing as a 'type of American tragedy' that deals with 'the force of circumstances that leads a person to committing or commissioning a dreadful act'.

Not that Cain, who had cultivated the habit of speaking in sharp tones from the corner of his mouth, could be mistaken as anything other than a former journalist. At the time, studios looked favourably on his ilk, who on the whole were faring better in Hollywood than playwrights like Clifford Odets, who would go from writing *Deadline at Dawn* to penning *Wild in the Country* for Elvis, or novelists like Faulkner, who, other than *The Big Sleep*, could barely write a screenplay. Under few illusions, journalists were willing to write to order and unlikely to complain if their work was rewritten – as long as they were paid. Nor were they likely to moan about Hollywood causing them to lose their artistic integrity.

Having said that, Cain did not immediately take to his new profession and was reticent about learning its subtleties. This was because Cain never really liked the movies. He was more interested in opera and gourmet food – he wrote culinary articles for *Esquire*. The only films for which he would express admiration were *Girl Shy*, a 1924 silent movie starring Harold Lloyd, and *The Exorcist* (1973), though his appreciation of the latter had less to do with its plot, which he dismissed as trivial, than with its lighting, which he said was incomparable. 'Most pictures aren't worth seeing,' said Cain when Peter Brunette and Gerald Peary interviewed him. 'Pictures don't go deep. If a girl has a pretty face, that's as far as the camera can look.'

Though Cain might have come to Hollywood during what has been called its golden age, the Los Angeles that lay outside the studio gates was, according to Carey McWilliams, a place of 'lonely, insecure . . . marginal personalities . . . barely able to make ends meet; . . . of opportunists and confidence men, petty chiselers and racketeers, bookies and race-track touts; of people desperately on the make'. With more than two thousand jobless and homeless individuals arriving in the area each day, LA was rife with vice and corruption. Organised crime had moved into various industries, including motion pictures, while a 1937 Federal Grand Jury declared that there were 600 brothels and 18,000 unlicensed bars in the city. It would be in this environment that Cain would set his passionate melodramas.

Arriving in Hollywood in November 1931, in the midst of a torrential rainstorm, Cain found temporary accommodation for himself and his family at the Knickerbocker Hotel. By 1932, he was briefly employed at Columbia while at the same time contributing editorials to Hearst periodicals and publishing stories like 'The Baby in the Icebox' in Mencken's *American Mercury*. The latter, retitled *She Made Her Bed*, would in 1933 be Cain's first narrative to reach the screen.

Cain moved to Paramount, where his initial assignment was a remake of *The Ten Commandments*. Unless it was intended as a satire, the film seemed ill-suited for a writer like Cain, even considering his obsession with guilt, sin and betrayal. Neither he nor his co-writer, Sam Mintz, had any idea how to approach the subject. When they met with the production team for a story conference, Cain assumed a brave face and assured studio executives that everything was fine. He was roundly cheered. But when the studio realised he had written next to nothing, Cain was promptly fired.

For the next five months, with the studio unwilling to give him another picture, Cain could only sit in his office and collect his pay. Finally, with three weeks remaining on his contract, he was assigned to work on *Hot Saturday* by Harvey Fergusson – small-town gossip causes girl to lose job – starring Nancy Carroll and two young actors, Cary Grant and Randolph Scott. When Cain's contract ran out, the studio was not keen on renewing it, and he was replaced on *Hot Saturday* by the more professional Seton I. Miller, who had written for Howard Hawks and Fritz Lang. It looked like Cain's Hollywood career had come to an abrupt end.

Rather than packing their bags and returning to the East Coast, Cain, his wife and her children moved to the Montecito, a residential hotel on Franklin just behind Musso and Frank's. Since Paul Cain was also living there at the time, one wonders if the two Cains ever crossed paths, or, for that matter received each other's post. James M. Cain and family took two apartments, which cost the writer $300 a month. Though Cain, not yet forty, was having health problems, he and Elina were determined to stay. Elina, who had lived through the Russian Revolution, liked Los Angeles, while Cain, having quit *The New Yorker* without giving notice, had burnt his East Coast bridges.

After his Paramount contract expired, Cain survived by freelancing. To economise, he and his family moved to Burbank. One of his first dinner guests in his new home was Niven Busch, whose contract at Warner Brothers had also expired. Cain had been Busch's boss at *The New Yorker*, where the latter had been employed as a sports writer. Before he left for Hollywood, Busch had visited Cain's office to tell him about his new job. Cain had simply stuck out his hand and congratulated him. A couple of weeks later, Busch spotted Cain dining at Musso and Frank's. Cain immediately apologised for his terseness, saying he had been unable to mention that he too was going to Hollywood because he, unlike Busch, hadn't told anyone about his departure. Back in Burbank, as they ate duck, which Cain invariably prepared for guests, Busch asked his host what he had been doing since leaving Paramount. Cain said he was writing something about the insurance business. He said that his father had been in insurance (he was a director for US Fidelity Guaranty Co.), and he knew something about it. Cain told Busch the plot, adding that he had cut the novel from 200,000 words down to 60,000. Whether this was simply another canard or not, Busch said the book sounded like a best seller.

Nevertheless, Knopf initially rejected the novel. It was only when Cain's old newspaper editor, Walter Lippman, intervened that they changed their minds. Responsible for so many of the era's hardboiled and proletarian novels, Knopf ended up paying Cain an advance of $500. At the time, Cain was calling the book *Bar-B-Q*. When Knopf asked for another title, Cain suggested *Black Puma* followed by *The Devil's Cookbook*. Knopf didn't like those either, and proposed *For Love or Money*. Cain said it made the book sound like a musical, and countered with what he thought was a great title, *The Postman Always Rings Twice*. Knopf didn't like it and insisted on his original suggestion. Cain offered *Hell on High Water* and then *Hold Everything*. Fed up, Knopf finally let Cain have his way.

Busch had been right. *The Postman Always Rings Twice* would, upon publication in 1934, spend several weeks on the *New York Times* best-seller list. Written between May and September 1932, the novel was based on the case of Ruth Snyder, who in 1927 had murdered her husband and tried to poison her lover-accomplice. Yet before settling on the waif-like Cora, Cain had envisaged a 'bosomy-looking thing' who pumped gas at a local filling station: 'Commonplace but sexy, the kind you have ideas about.' At the time, the book's style was powerful enough to shock many readers. For Cain staked out his pulp modernist ground in a bold first-person narrative that left out the customary 'I said' and 'she said', thus allowing the reader to infer, much as they would with a radio play, who was speaking.

While negotiations regarding *The Postman Always Rings Twice* were taking place, Cain, on the back of his story, 'The Baby in the Icebox', secured a contract at Columbia for $300 a week. Despite his shortcomings as a screenwriter, Cain managed to impress Columbia producer Harry Cohn. Cain would maintain that Cohn – the model for Rod Steiger's portrayal of the studio head in Robert Aldrich's critique of Hollywood, *The Big Knife*, written by Clifford Odets and James Poe – was elegant and gracious, and his brutish side was merely an act. If accurate, this contradicts reports portraying Cohn as a megalomaniac who humiliated and bullied those working for him, luxuriated in power, wiretapped his sound stage and called in sexual favours. Yet Cohn understood the industry as well as anyone and, working with directors like Frank Capra, Howard Hawks, Fritz Lang and George Cukor, produced scores of excellent movies.

Cain soon got the hang of scriptwriting and became adept at writing good dialogue. In 1935 he was back at Paramount, working on William Dieterle's *Dr. Socrates*, based on a story by W.R. Burnett. In 1938 Cain was sold to Metro – a common practice following the 1933–35 Screen Writers Guild dispute, which ended the practice of trading writers between studios and turned them into ordinary chattel. On his first day at Metro, Cain sat behind his desk and proudly surveyed his surroundings. He was interrupted by a knock on the door. It was F. Scott Fitzgerald dropping by to welcome the new writer. Cain thanked him and Fitzgerald quickly disappeared. To show his appreciation, Cain went to Fitzgerald's office and asked if he would have lunch with him. As they left the studio, Cain realised Fitzgerald had hardly said a word. They ate together and still Fitzgerald was silent. Unable to understand why Fitzgerald was not speaking, Cain picked up the bill and walked out. Later, writer John O'Hara said that Fitzgerald, now a spent literary force and, though earning a princely $1,000 a week, reduced to writing films like *A Yank in Oxford*, *Marie Antoinette* and *Three Comrades*, thought Cain was taking him to lunch out of pity.

Fitzgerald's Pat Hobby stories are arguably the best fictional portrayal of 1930s Hollywood. (In 'Homes of the Stars,' Hobby tells a tourist that he is not writing because he is on strike for 'free pencils and paper'. 'If you're on strike, who writes the movies?' asks the tourist. 'The producers,' says Hobby. 'That's why they're so lousy.') Cain must have given some thought to the other writer's predicament and concluded that, in comparison to Fitzgerald, he had not nearly so far to fall. Nor was Cain beneath taking on a film like *Algiers*, which would be his first screenwriting credit. A remake of the French classic *Pépé le Moko*, it marked Hedy Lamarr's debut. Lamarr, née Hedwig Keisler, had recently arrived from Europe, having escaped from her husband, Fritz Mandl, a munitions manufacturer who bankrolled the Austrian Nazi party. *Algiers* also starred Charles Boyer as Pépé le Moko, who, though it has often been attributed to him, never said, 'Come with me to the Casbah.' However, the Casbah does figure heavily in the first reel, which was the part of the film for which Cain was responsible. Though Lamarr's purported autobiography, *Ecstasy and Me: My Life as a Woman*, tells it differently (Lamarr tried to prevent its publication, filing suit that the book, based on interviews with her, was 'false, vulgar, scandalous, libelous, and obscene'), Cain wrote none of the leading lady's dialogue. When Cain, who was credited for additional dialogue, was closed out of the film, the studio hired John Howard Lawson, whom Cain considered talented but humourless. Consequently, the movie contains a sharp change of mood, which disrupts an otherwise entertaining, if mediocre, film.

In 1939 Cain, along with Jane Murfin and Harvey

Fergusson, received a credit at MGM for *Stand Up and Fight*. Taking place in nineteenth-century Maryland, it stars Wallace Beery and Robert Taylor. It was on this film that Cain, thanks to producer Jack Rubin, learned the art of scriptwriting. The following year, Cain left Elina, whom he eventually divorced, and moved back to the Knickerbocker, where he began to drink heavily and put on weight. With his health declining, Cain underwent an operation for ulcers and kidney stones in 1941. In the same year he worked uncredited for five weeks on von Sternberg's *The Shanghai Gesture* – the proprietress of a gambling casino belittles her ex-husband by showing him his daughter in a state of degradation, only to learn that the girl is also *her* daughter, whom she thought was dead. In the same year, Knopf published *Mildred Pierce*, followed in 1942 by *Love's Lovely Counterfeit*, which would be adapted for the screen in 1956 by Alan Dwan, and retitled *Slightly Scarlet*. Starring Arlene Dahl and John Payne, it is best remembered for its cynicism, violence, and depiction of nymphomania and kleptomania, as well as John Alton's colour photography and lighting.

Having guaranteed Cain two weeks' work, in 1944 Universal assigned him to write dialogue for Maria Montez in *Gypsy Wildcat* – a Gypsy girl discovers she is really a countess (Pauline Kael called it 'an *opéra bouffe* without music'). Cain read the original script and found it impossible to follow. Now conversant with the medium, he set out to simplify the story. When his contract ran out he went to the producer's office and saw that his script had been rewritten. When he asked about it, the producer, former B-movie director, George Waggner, told him that he had liked Cain's script, but Montez was unable to read his lines, so he had transposed what Cain had written into a kind of baby talk, which was the only type of dialogue the queen of camp, Montez, could handle. *Gypsy Wildcat* would be Cain's only other screen credit.

It was RKO producer Warren Duff who, in 1946, asked Cain to adapt Daniel Mainwaring's novel, *Build My Gallows High* (also known as *Out of the Past*). Cain would junk Mainwaring's original script, for which the latter had already been paid between $20,000 and $30,000, and write an entirely new screenplay. Unfortunately, Cain's draft, set exclusively in the city, strayed too far from the novel. Dissatisfied, Duff asked Mainwaring to rewrite the screenplay Cain had written based on Mainwaring's original script adapted from his own novel.

Not that Cain was bothered by such occurrences, nor discouraged that his screenwriting career was not working out as planned. For Cain, now married to actress and Mencken acquaintance Aileen Pringle, was gaining a reputation for his fiction, particularly in Europe. Uninterested in Tinseltown notoriety, Cain thought himself fortunate to be making so much money in exchange for doing very little work. As long as he was interested in the story, he was willing to work anonymously. As he said in the interview with Brunette and Peary, 'If you start grieving over that kind of money, you'd go nuts . . . Some people did, and that would account for some of the . . . weird things out there in Hollywood.'

Though Cain, a lifelong Democrat, supported the formation of the Screen Writers Guild, he could not understand why, as well-paid workers, the Hollywood Ten had cause to join the Communist Party. Friendly with a number of studio leftists, he remained adamantly opposed to anyone being thrown out of Hollywood for their political beliefs. Cain himself would enter politics in 1946, when, after noting that writers were constantly forced into disadvantageous contracts by unscrupulous publishers, he attempted to form an American Authors' Authority. The project received the lukewarm backing of the Screen Writers Guild – they called Cain's effort to gain more rights and royalties 'capitalism naked and simple. But it is capitalism for writers.' Nevertheless, the plan was mercilessly red-baited. Journalists like Dorothy Thompson asserted that Cain's intention was to control what people wrote. Meanwhile, Louis B. Mayer, normally a trite, bigoted and vulgar individual, supported Cain's plan, probably to stave off more radical proposals.

Cain and Mayer, however, had a good working relationship. As did Cain and Eddie Mannix, the MGM executive so despised by Chandler. Yet Cain had no such praise for MGM's second-in-command and head of production, Irving Thalberg. What particularly irked Cain was that, when the Screen Writers Guild was forming, Thalberg had called his writers together and declared the Guild off limits. As for the egotistical and opinionated Samuel Goldwyn (formerly Shmuel Gelbfisz, then Samuel Goldfish, he founded Goldwyn Picture Corporation in 1916 with the Selwyn brothers, changing his name to Goldwyn to make the company sound like it belonged exclusively to him), Cain found him to be intelligent and perceptive. It amused Cain that, when he spoke to Goldwyn, the latter showed no sign of his famous Polish accent, but when an agent phoned to negotiate a deal, Goldwyn would immediately revert to his old-world dialect.

Of the many Cain narratives adapted for the screen, only a few survived the transition with any distinction. *When Tomorrow Comes*, the 1939 movie version of Cain's *The Root of His Evil*, which in turn came from his 1937 serialisation, 'The Modern Cinderella', ended up bearing little resemblance to the original story. About a Harvard graduate who marries a waitress, it stars Charles Boyer – certainly not the person who springs to mind as someone upholding the lofty traditions of Harvard – and Irene Dunne, who unfortunately had a clause in her contract to the effect that she be allowed to sing at least one song per picture. To accommodate Dunne, the studio found it necessary to turn Boyer into a French pianist. The film was also the subject of an unusual lawsuit. When Cain saw that there was a scene in which the couple spends the night in a church, he knew it had been taken from his novel *Serenade*. Later the film's scriptwriter, Dwight Taylor, apologised to Cain for using the scene, saying that he had done so on the instructions of the director, John Stahl. To protect other writers from this practice, Cain sued. In court, Stahl said that he could not remember whose idea it was to include the church scene but, if it helped, he would take responsibility for it. While the court ruled against Cain, one can only surmise that Taylor preferred it not to be known that he had read Cain's novel, which concerns homosexuality, a subject that at the time was a no-go area in the world of Hollywood film-making.

Despite its subject, *Serenade*, which had been published in 1937, was bought by Warner Brothers in 1942 for approximately $35,000. When the studio deemed Cain's original treatment too long and complicated, a series of other writers was hired – including hardboilers Cleve Adams, James Gunn and Margaret Millar, whose contributions would go uncredited. Warner, too, would be troubled by the novel's homosexual angle (interestingly, Gunn was one of the few openly gay hardboiled writers in Hollywood). On Cain's hasty advice, they changed the homosexual angle to a woman who has a taste for wine, as opposed to the male lead's preference for liquor. So absurd was the alteration that Cain, after suggesting it to studio executive Jerry Wald, realised that it was not going to work. Directed by Anthony Mann in 1956, the film stars an overweight Mario Lanza, who, according to Cain, was on a crash diet, bad-tempered and interested only in his song cues. Indicative of the fact that the novel was ahead of its time, several directors and screenwriters during the 1980s, including Coppola and Robert Towne, would seek to option the novel.

The only adaptation that Cain would praise would be Wilder's *Double Indemnity*. He considered Wilder's ending more successful than his own, and it was the only movie made from his books that contained elements – for example, using the dictation machine as a means of telling the story – that he wished he had thought of. When he wrote the novella in 1935, Cain had no idea how popular it or any subsequent film adaptation would be. He had written the story quickly and without much enthusiasm, getting the idea from a newspaper item about a printer who, in setting the type for an advertisement for women's underwear that read, 'If these sizes are too big, take a tuck in them', substituted the word *fuck* for *tuck*. When interrogated, the printer said, 'You do nothing your whole life but watch for something like that happening . . . and then you catch yourself watching for chances to do it.'

'Double Indemnity' concerns not a typesetter but an insurance salesman who yearns to commit the very type of crime he is responsible for preventing, and who, upon meeting a woman who wants to murder her husband, uses his knowledge to corrupt the social contract that accompanies his job. Cain had originally said to his publisher, Alfred Knopf, that the story was a 'piece of tripe [that] will never go between covers'. While he might well have been referring to the fact that 'Double Indemnity' was his attempt to cash in on the success of *The Postman Always Rings Twice*, Cain had always considered the story the least likely of the three novellas that comprised his 1943 publication *Three of a Kind* to be sold to the studios (by the time *Three of a Kind* appeared, the other two stories – 'The Embezzler' and 'Career in C Major' – had already been adapted for the screen). After all, written in 1935 and serialised the following year in *Liberty* magazine, for which Cain received $5,000, 'Double Indemnity' had already made the rounds of the studios. All five of the major studios were interested in the story and were willing to pay $25,000 for the rights, but not until it received clearance from the Production Code office, which had declared the story unfilmable. One of the first narratives to successfully exploit the language of the emerging Southern California middle class, 'Double Indemnity' was, in the view of the Hays Office, little more than a crime manual for would-be crooks. Eight years after the story's initial publication, Cain, in need of money to cover the cost of his divorce (he had recently separated from his wife Elina), had hired the ubiquitous H.N. Swanson to take over his literary interests. Swanson was not only able to negotiate the sale of *Three of a Kind*, but, on the back of that deal, he was also finally able to sell 'Double Indemnity' to Paramount.

Cain and Raymond Chandler – also represented by Swanson – finally crossed paths at a story conference for the film. Chandler, who was adapting the novel, not only disliked the way Cain dealt with sex, he disliked Cain's writing altogether. Wilder, however, admired the language of 'Double Indemnity' and wanted Chandler to use more of the story's dialogue in the script. But when Wilder read Cain's dialogue out loud he realised that it wasn't going to work on the screen. For his part, Cain was put off by Chandler because the latter kept calling him by his first name – ironical that the cultured but sometimes gruff Cain should be insulted by a middle-class quasi-Englishman. Said Chandler, 'Jim, that dialogue of yours is to the *eye*.' Cain responded by saying that he knew his dialogue was to the eye, but he could also write for the *ear*.

At that story conference was a bespectacled Paramount producer with jet-black hair. Joe Sistrom was part of a younger breed of Hollywood producer, the kind who believes a producer is someone who knows everything but does next to nothing. Sistrom, whom Frank Capra considered a brilliant intellectual and self-styled rebel, said it bothered him that the protagonist had hit on the murder scheme so quickly. When Cain told him that it must be understood that he had been thinking about it for some time, Sistrom said, 'Characters in B movies are always too smart.' His words impressed Cain, who concluded that when a character gets too smart, the story invariably becomes overly slick. Cain would make sure he applied Sistrom's observation to his future fiction and film writing.

Double Indemnity was one of the first films to detail the means by which a murder is committed. The couple are punished, but not before throwing away their lives in an effort to make their oppressive middle-class existence bearable. Few could have known that *Double Indemnity* would be a primer for future film noir directors. In fact, Billy Wilder was only made aware of the novella when he walked into his office one day to ask after his secretary. He was told that she had gone to the ladies' room where she was reading 'that story'. Just as Wilder began to ask what story could keep her away for so long, the secretary emerged clutching the book with 'a gaga look on her face'. Wilder took the book home with him and the next day offered $15,000 for the rights, $10,000 less than the amount Cain had been offered eight years earlier. But, according to Robert Portfirio's 1975 interview with Wilder, which appears in *Film Noir Reader 3*, it was Joe Sistrom who brought the story to the director, who said, 'Terrific. It's not as good as *Postman*, but let's do it. So we bought it.'

The film would be a success, despite the efforts of Kate Smith, a Hayes Office propagandist whose rendition of 'God Bless America' would become a hit on three separate occasions, to persuade audiences to boycott the film.

But Cain would not be so fulsome in his praise for Michael Curtiz's 1945 adaptation of *Mildred Pierce*. While he admired Joan Crawford's Oscar-winning performance, he thought the movie was cashing in on the success of *Double Indemnity*, which is why, according to Cain, it begins with a murder and relies on flashbacks to tell the story. The idea for the novel *Mildred Pierce* had come to Cain after a Columbia producer, holding forth on the subject of stories, remarked that narratives regarding women who use men to get what they want never fail to be successful in Hollywood. Concluding that a sure-fire success should not be passed up, Cain set to work on it. He first envisioned Mildred as an airline stewardess, then as a girl who comes to Hollywood after winning a beauty contest, then as a housewife. Finally, he hit upon the idea of a woman who uses her children to control men.

The film would be Catherine Turney's first screenplay. Best known as a writer of 'women's pictures' (*The Man I Love, A Stolen Life, Cry Wolf, Of Human Bondage*), Turney put a different spin on *Mildred Pierce*. 'The property remained on the shelves . . . because nobody wanted to do a movie about a housewife who made pies. It wasn't very glamorous . . . to people at the studio. No actress wanted to play it, no director wanted to do it . . . Then Wald wanted to turn the thing into a murder mystery.' When it was decided that *Mildred Pierce* should be less a 'woman's film' than a straight melodrama, and that the plot be altered to accommodate the flashbacks, which, in turn, meant adding the opening murder, Turney quit the film, replaced by a former president of the Screen Writers Guild, Ranald MacDougall, whose writing credits included *Possessed* and *We're No Angels*.

Despite the success of *Mildred Pierce*, *The Postman Always Rings Twice* remains the novel and film for which Cain is best known. It would also be his best-selling paperback. By 1950, Pocket Books had sold over a million copies. (Cain's best-selling hardback was the more pedestrian historical novel of 1946, *Past All Dishonor*, which Cain believed to be his best book, even though at the time it was his only novel not to be bought by Hollywood.) It was only after the Production Code office gave the script the go-ahead that Metro bought the rights. When Cain saw a rough cut of the film at a preview in Glendale in 1946, he thought it unremarkable, and it would be thirty years before he would see it again. Yet *The Postman Always Rings Twice* would become another classic Cain film noir, remade on four other occasions: in 1939 in France by Pierre Chenal, entitled *Le Dernier Tournant*; in 1942 in Italy by Luchino Visconti, entitled *Ossessione* (because Visconti did not obtain the rights to the novel, its world distribution would be blocked by MGM and producers of the French version); in the US in 1981 by Bob Rafelson; and in 1998 in Hungary by György Fehér, entitled *Szenvedély*.

Originally, Niven Busch had been hired to write the script for the 1946 version, directed by Tay Garnett and starring John Garfield and Lana Turner. At the time Busch, who had been Samuel Goldwyn's story editor and had just finished working on a script based on his novel *Duel in the Sun*, was a sought-after screenwriter. Because he knew Cain, he agreed to take less than his usual fee, though with the usual successful proviso that he be allowed to work at home. After Busch finished the script, MGM called in gag-man Harry Ruskin to add a few telling lines. Busch complained when Ruskin received a credit for co-writing the film, but the Screen Writers Guild ruled in Ruskin's favour. Like Cain, Busch was dissatisfied with the final script, and annoyed that the sexual aspect of the novel had been watered down. Busch made the same complaint the following year when King Vidor's adaptation of *Duel in the Sun*, with a script by David O. Selznick, was released. But it wasn't only the steamy quality of *The Postman* that MGM had wanted to alter. They also decided to turn Nick, a Greek of slovenly proportions, into an equally unkempt Englishman. This had less to do with artistic considerations than with the fact that the studio did not want to be denied an export licence in Greece. Presumably the British were considered sophisticated enough not to take such unflattering portrayals as an affront to their culture.

Despite the success of his novels, Cain had grown weary of Hollywood. He had only remained there because he had been able to sell his work to the studios. Yet Hollywood had given him the space and economic conditions in which to write his best novels. Unappreciative of the effect the film industry had on his fiction, Cain would leave Tinseltown embittered. In a 1933 essay, 'Paradise', published in *American Mercury*, he attacks Southern California for its car fetishism, bad food and lack of an organic culture, yet admits that there are more talented people there than in other parts of the country, and that 'some sort of destiny awaits this place'.

Perhaps he was burnt out, or maybe he simply wanted to return home. Back in Hyattsville, Maryland, Cain continued to write, but none of his novels equalled those he had written while living in Southern California. No longer was he interested in that terse, hardboiled style that he had developed on the cheap in Hollywood. Besides, the studios were now doing Cain better than Cain was able to do. Even *Slightly Scarlet* (RKO, 1956) was an improvement on Cain's novella *Love's Lovely Counterfeit* (1942). Though the studios steered clear of the sexual aspect of Cain's stories, they were producing films with *femmes fatales* – portrayed by the likes of Lana Turner and Joan Crawford – who were ripped straight from the pages of Cain's fiction. But his literary style had become a cliché. Not only were hardboiled writers imitating him, but he had become the subject of parody, both in song – 'The Postman Always Rings Twice, the Iceman Walks Right In' – and humorous fiction – James Thurber's 'Hell Only Breaks Loose Once'.

Cain died in 1977, aged eighty-five. Though he would never have acknowledged it, Hollywood suited him as a writer. Having done his best work under such restrictive conditions, one can hardly say: if only Cain had not been tainted by the industry, he would have produced more, and better, novels. The fact is, Cain's best efforts were written quickly and carried a literary populism that spilled into the world of film and beyond. What that says about the writer in Hollywood is something few have had the nerve to consider. For if some writers are able to produce their best work under such conditions, perhaps there is something to be said for the exigencies of corporate power, and those tarnished enough to flourish in the mean streets of Tinseltown.

4

DEADLINES AT DAWN

Cornell Woolrich

According to his biographer, Francis M. Nevins, Cornell George Hopley-Woolrich led 'the most wretched life of any American writer since Poe'. Steve Fisher, in his novel *I Wake Up Screaming*, describes his Woolrich-based homicide detective in the following way: 'He had red hair and thin white skin and red eyebrows and blue eyes. He looked sick. He looked like a corpse. His clothes didn't fit him . . . He was a misfit . . . He was frail, grey-faced and bitter . . . His voice was nasal. You'd think he was crying. He might have had T.B. He looked like he couldn't stand up in a wind.'

Whatever his personal deficiencies, Woolrich wrote twenty-two novels and some 350 stories. More than thirty films were made from his narratives. However, Woolrich would adapt none of them. With a presence in Hollywood conspicuous by his absence, it might be said that Woolrich's output and the quality of his writing can be attributed to his having had so little to do with the film industry.

Though his somewhat bizarre autobiography, *Blues of a Lifetime*, barely mentions Hollywood, Woolrich made a trip west in 1928, travelling from New York by train, to observe First National Picture's adaptation of his second novel, *Children of the Ritz*. Written in the style of F. Scott Fitzgerald, the novel had been bought by the studio after its serialisation in the August to November 1927 issues of *College Humor*, edited by the author's future agent H.N. Swanson. Woolrich ended up staying in Los Angeles for three years. During this time he continued to write and publish novels, stories and magazine articles. While his film contributions were minimal, Nevins says, 'Exposure to the film world ... helped develop his already evident talent for writing visually and taught him lessons in narrative drive and pace.'

There would be two film versions of *Children of the Ritz*, one silent and one with sound. The critics treated neither kindly. And unless an observer's presence can alter what is observed, Woolrich made no discernible contribution to either film. Nor would he ever receive a screenwriting credit under his own name, though he did garner three credits – *The Haunted House* (1928), *Seven Footprints to Satan* (1929) and *The House of Horror* (1929) – under the name William Irish, a *nom de plume* he later used for numerous stories, and would adopt as his legal name in 1961. All three films credited to Irish were made at First National and directed by Benjamin Christensen, a Danish-born former opera singer who, in Sweden, made the infamous *Häxan*, or *Witchcraft Through the Ages* (1922), a film subsequently banned in many countries for its scenes of cruelty and nudism. Irish would be credited for writing dialogue for *The House of Horror* and the titles for *The Haunted House* and *Seven Footprints to Satan*, based on a novel by the popular fantasist Abraham Merritt. If nothing else, working for Christensen gave Woolrich an appreciation for the macabre, which he would later exploit in his fiction.

In Hollywood, Woolrich married Gloria Blackton, daughter of pioneering director, producer, screenwriter and actor J. Stuart Blackton, who had once so impressed Thomas Edison with his drawings that the inventor suggested he photograph them with his Kinograph camera, resulting in the 1896 film, *Blackton, The Evening World Cartoonist*. Blackton made his first film on the roof of the Morse Building in Nassau Street, New York, in 1897. His last film, *The Passionate Quest*, would be made in 1926.

Just three months into the Woolrich–Blackton marriage, Cornell suddenly disappeared. During her husband's absence, Gloria discovered Woolrich's diaries, in which he recorded his homosexual encounters. She also found, tucked away in the closet, a neatly folded sailor's suit that Woolrich would wear on his evening trysts. One imagines a sailor-suited Woolrich seeking out male companionship on the Santa Monica pier, a quest echoed almost four decades later when Dennis Hopper, playing a sailor, searches for a mermaid beneath that same pier in Curtis Harrington's Woolrich-inspired *Night Tide* (1963). Most hurtful to Gloria was that Woolrich indicated in his diary that his marriage was a cover for his homosexuality.

The supposedly unconsummated marriage was annulled, after which Woolrich returned to the New York hotel where, for the next twenty-five years, he lived with his mother and his typewriter. While he had a love-hate relationship with his mother, his love for his typewriter was apparently unconditional. So attached was he to his machine that he dedicated his novel, *The Bride Wore Black*, to it, and amorously addressed it – 'This was a mating if there ever was one' – in the first chapter of his autobiography, entitled 'Remington Portable NC69411'.

One reason Woolrich never returned to Hollywood was his belief that his novel *I Love You, Paris*, as it made the rounds of publishers, had been stolen by Paramount and turned into the 1934 film *Bolero* (Paramount, 1934), starring Carole Lombard and George Raft. In reality, Woolrich, settled in his Harlem hotel and unable to break away from his mother for any great length of time, was living such an insular life that any disruption, such as travelling to the West Coast, much less residing there, would have been difficult, if not impossible.

Woolrich was born in New York on 4 December 1903. His father was an engineer, his mother a pianist. Like Hammett and James M. Cain, he was raised a Catholic. Like Cain, his lapsed beliefs would influence his fiction, particularly regarding such themes as guilt, redemption and sin. After his parents divorced, Woolrich was taken to Mexico by his father, who was administering construction projects there. The Mexican Revolution had impressed the young Woolrich, but not nearly so much as a production of *Madame Butterfly* that he had witnessed in Mexico City. It was during that performance that Woolrich resolved that he would compose dramatic stories. Meanwhile, his doom-laden perspective also seems to have been formed in Mexico when, as an eleven-year-old, he looked up at the stars hanging over the Valley of Anahuac (Mexico City) and concluded that 'I would surely die finally, or something worse . . . I had that trapped feeling, like some sort of poor insect that you've put inside a downturned glass.'

Back in the United States, Woolrich attended Columbia University. Though he never graduated, it was at college, after a foot injury prevented him from leaving his rooms, that he wrote his first story. In 1926, a twenty-three year old Woolrich published his first novel, *Cover Charge*. This was followed by *Children of the Ritz* in 1927. Both were influenced by Fitzgerald. Although at the time Woolrich could not understand the lukewarm reception that greeted both books, he later admitted that he only learned the art of writing during the 1930s, when he began publishing stories in various pulp magazines.

In 1934 there were some 150 such magazines in which Woolrich could have placed his fiction. Out of these he chose *Detective Story*, *The Shadow*, *Argosy*, Mencken's *The Smart Set*, Foley and Burnett's *Story*, and *Black Mask*. By 1936 Woolrich was already making $6,000 a year from his writing. Soon he would be one of America's highest paid pulp writers. Woolrich's primary publishing platform, *Black Mask*, was now edited by Fanny Ellsworth, who had taken over from Joseph T. Shaw, who had been fired because he hadn't wanted to cut the rates paid to his authors. Ellsworth, the magazine's second female editor and a former editor of magazines specialising in romantic fiction, immediately recognised Woolrich's talent and published nearly everything he sent to her.

Regarding mood and literary quality, Woolrich's stories were unlike anything previously published in Ellsworth's magazine. Part of *Black Mask*'s second wave of writers,

Woolrich avoided the clichés associated with the genre. Not really a hardboiled writer, Woolrich invested his stories with an identifiable darkness and real emotions. As Mark Bassett points out, in his preface to *Blues of a Lifetime*, Woolrich's world is more romantic than most hardboilers. Though plotting was never his strong point, Woolrich, uninterested in private eyes and ordinary denizens of the mean streets, populated his fiction with inept cops, sadistic detectives and obsessed and psychotic individuals, each capable of being both victim and tormentor. Meanwhile, his protagonists are struggling solitary figures who ache for love but are destined to die alone. According to critic Donald Phelps, writing in *Film Comment*, Woolrich's 'low income heroes and heroines' are 'white-collar scramblers, dancehall hostesses, watch repairers . . . *determined amateurs*; committed . . . to salvaging their negligible yet threatened worlds'. Subject to the malign indifference of the universe, these 'amateurs', in their 'pilgrimages of detection', often disappear into thin air. While Woolrich's protagonists, invariably male, are frail, effete or primitively poetic, his women are fired with devotion and maternal passion. Unusual for the genre, Woolrich's female characters are believable and affecting, despite the fact that Woolrich was a homosexual who found dealing with women difficult.

Gradually, in stories from 'Speak to Me of Death', which appeared in 1937 but was expanded in 1945 to become the novel *Night Has a Thousand Eyes*, to 'They Call Me Patrice', first published in 1943 but transformed into the 1948 novel *I Married a Dead Man*, Woolrich ceased being a precocious pulpist and became an authentic poet of the shadows. Few have been his equal at portraying the destruction of innocent lives by a tightly knit pattern of events so dependent on multiple coincidences that some sadistic power must surely be behind it all; or at depicting situations in which there are only two possibilities open to the protagonist, neither of which makes sense.

According to Nevins, the prevailing economic circumstance of a Woolrich narrative is invariably the Depression; the dominant political reality is one of corruption; the prevailing emotional states are loneliness and fear; and the prevailing time framework is night-time. Nevins also points out that Woolrich relies on basic narrative templates: the Cop story, based around the personality and actions of a sadistic police officer; the Clock story, or the race against time; the Waking Nightmare story; the Oscillation story, in which trust or love is eaten away by suspicion; the Headlong Through the Night story, in which one follows the last hours of a desperate man moving through a dark and deadly city; the Annihilation story, in which a man meets a woman only to discover he needs her to corroborate his story, but cannot find her; and the Doom Ridden story, in which readers share the final hours of a person who is about to meet a terrible death.

Most of Woolrich's noir narratives were written between 1934 and 1948. While his characters are products of the Depression, they reflect the paranoia and anxieties created by World War II, the Cold War, the atomic bomb and McCarthyism. This was the era of 'the Great Fear'. As Geoffrey O'Brien says in *Hardboiled America*, '[For] ten years the key words will be "night" and "dark". The hardboiled wry grimace will be replaced by abject terror, by a sense of ultimate impotence in a world suddenly full of danger.' He could have been describing Woolrich's fiction. Not surprisingly, Woolrich would become the most filmed of noirists. By the end of the 1940s all but four of Woolrich's published novels had been adapted for the screen.

The first noir narrative Woolrich sold to the studios was 'Face Work', which appeared in a 1937 issue of *Black Mask*. Columbia paid him $448.75 for the film rights, before turning it into the film *Convicted*. Shot in British Columbia, the movie is notable for performances by two young actors, Rita Hayworth and Marc Lawrence, in the days before the former became a glamorous star and the latter a film noir hoodlum

(*The Asphalt Jungle, This Gun For Hire* and *Key Largo*). The next Woolrich adaptation, for which he would be paid $2,225, was *Street of Chance* (Paramount, 1942). Adapted from Woolrich's 1941 novel *The Black Curtain*, it was the first film to accurately capture Woolrich's dark perspective. With Burgess Meredith playing an amnesiac – one of the earliest Hollywood films to deal with the subject – who must piece together his life, the movie is noted for its jazz score and Theodor Sparkuhl's cinematography, influenced by German expressionism and French poetic realism.

The next film to be adapted from a Woolrich novel was *The Leopard Man* (1943). Produced by RKO, adapted by Val Lewton, and directed by Jacques Tourneur, it is based on Woolrich's *Black Alibi*, and is set in a Mexican border town where either man or beast is prowling the region, killing people at random. Tourneur's film would be followed in 1944 by Universal's adaptation of another Woolrich novel, *Phantom Lady*, about a husband who picks up a woman in a bar and takes her to a show, then returns home to find his wife has been murdered. The 'phantom lady' is his only alibi. Directed by Robert Siodmak, this classic rendering is visual enough to have come out of the era of German silent films and best remembered for the scene in an after-hours jazz club in which Elisha Cook Jr. plays the drums with orgiastic fervour, the climax of his solo intermixed with shots of Ella Raines's wordless sexual innuendoes. Shot on a sound stage, it gives the appearance of having been made on the sweltering New York streets. As critic James Agee pointed out, much of the dialogue is banal, but the film is redeemed by its *mise-en-scène* and overall style.

Deadline at Dawn (RKO), made in 1946, was also based on a Woolrich novel. The film was Harold Clurman's sole directorial effort. The story revolves around a sailor on leave (the uniform worn by Bill Williams was something that might have appealed to Woolrich), who passes out, waking to find that the woman he has been with has been murdered.

Williams, here a kind of primitive poet, is aided by a philo-sophical taxi-cab driver and a maternal taxi dancer, played by Susan Hayward. Though it was an effective period piece with some touching moments, Clurman and his screenwriting col-laborator, Clifford Odets, jettisoned much of Woolrich's plot, turning a noir thriller into a film celebrating the plight of the common man.

The Chase (1946), based on the novel *The Black Path of Fear*, was adapted by the suspiciously prolific Philip Yordan, and directed by Arthur Ripley. Set in Cuba, it stars Robert Cum-mings as a shell-shocked ex-serviceman who finds a wallet and, after returning it to a Miami gangster, is hired as his chauffeur. The film combines two conditions: malaria and amnesia. While the former – a relatively new cinema malady – leads to hallucinations, which could give rise to a variety of political conditions (the Cold War, McCarthyism), the latter – fast becoming a cliché – enables one to forget recent history (concentration camps, atom bomb). A race against time, the protagonist realises he has from midnight to sunrise to track down the perpetrator of the murder for which he will be charged.

Also made in 1946 by Universal and adapted from a Wool-rich novel, *Black Angel* concerns an alcoholic songwriter who tries to visit his ex-wife. When she is found murdered, the songwriter is the logical suspect. Since he has an alibi, a man visiting the apartment to retrieve some incriminating letters is convicted of the crime. The man's wife asks the songwriter to help her find the murderer. In an alcoholic haze, the songwriter finally realises that he is, in fact, the culprit. The film stars Dan Duryea as the songwriter, June Vincent as the wife of the condemned man, and Peter Lorre as a sadistic underworld figure. Unusual for a film noir, there is little violence. But such is often the case in a Woolrich narrative. Considered in its time an erotic thriller, *Black Angel* is one of the better adaptations of a Woolrich story, and was the final film directed by Roy William Neill. The British-born Neill, best known for his Sherlock Holmes films, ignores the novel's plot, yet remains faithful to the spirit of Woolrich's warped universe. The film's success can partly be attributed to Paul Ivano's lighting and camerawork, which creates the appropriate atmosphere. Yet Woolrich hated the film. In a letter to the poet Mark Van Doren, he wrote, 'Is that what I wasted my whole life at?' Whatever the author's opinion, *Black Angel* contains a nostalgic sensitivity and humanism, qualities hitherto alien to the mood and ethos of film noir.

Fear in the Night, made in 1947 and based on the story 'And So to Death', concerns a man who discovers he has been hypnotised into committing a crime. Directed by Maxwell Shane and produced by 'the Dollar Bills' – William Pine and William Thomas – at Paramount, it is a low-budget affair with a creaking plot. But not as low-budget as *Fall Guy* (1947), based on Woolrich's story 'Cocaine', or, as it was also called, 'C-Jag', which concerns the effect of narcotics on a person's self-determination. In keeping with the country's fear of drugs, the characters in *Fall Guy*, when drugged, commit crimes, suffer from amnesia, have nightmares and experience feelings of entrapment. Made by Monogram, the prototypical Poverty Row studio (their 1940s pictures cost between $16,000 and $75,000), the film almost moves beyond the exploitational aspect of its theme into a territory inhabited by the more lavish *Panic in the Streets*. Made in the same year by Monogram, *The Guilty* (1947), directed by John Reinhardt, is based on a Woolrich story 'He Looked Like Murder' and is another low-budget but convincing example of a Waking Nightmare narrative wherein an apparently innocent man turns out to be guilty.

Night Has a Thousand Eyes, made in 1948, and adapted from Woolrich's novel, focuses on a mentalist who discovers he really can predict the future. The plot may have been suggested to Woolrich after seeing Charles Hutchinson's 1935 *On Probation* (Peerless Pictures). Despite an exemplary performance by Edward G. Robinson, *Night Has a Thousand Eyes* has little connection to Woolrich's novel, which is saturated in death and a ominous sense of destiny. In that same year, *I Wouldn't Be in Your Shoes* would be adapted by Steve Fisher for Monogram. Directed by William Nigh, the plot centres on a man sentenced to the electric chair because, one stifling night, he throws a pair of shoes out of his window at a yowling cat, only to learn later that his shoe prints have been found at a murder scene. It is a Race-Against-the-Clock film, in which a policeman and the man's wife attempt to save the shoe-throwing husband. When Fisher could not resolve the ending, he phoned Woolrich, who told him to turn the homicide cop – based on Woolrich – into the culprit, whose actions are motivated by his lust for the condemned man's wife.

The Window (RKO, 1949) is an adaptation of Woolrich's story 'The Boy Cried Murder'. As a kind of celluloid Aesop's fable, it turns the American dream of freedom – whether of movement or expression – on its head. When a New York slum boy, who cannot help telling tall tales, witnesses a murder, no one believes him. Its claustrophobic setting – when his mother tells her son not to leave the apartment, Tommy replies, 'There's no place for me to go' – is typical of many Woolrich narratives. Though he toned down the original plot, director Ted Tetzlaff was able to create a box-office success, which paved the way for *Rear Window,* with which it is often compared.

When it came to writing, 1947 might have been Woolrich's least productive year, but it would be his most lucrative regarding film adaptations. During that year, Woolrich made some $56,000 – including $36,000 from the sale of movie rights to *Waltz into Darkness.* The following year, Woolrich published no new stories yet made $49,000 from film adaptions. With the 1940s drawing to a close, Woolrich's earnings from Hollywood would start to dwindle, as would the number of film adaptations. From 1949 to 1952, his income from the sale of his work would drop to $14,000.

No Man of Her Own (1950)– a pregnant wanderer, after a

train accident, assumes the identity of the wife of one of the dead passengers – is largely a vehicle for Barbara Stanwyck. Based on Woolrich's 1948 novel *I Married a Dead Man*, which in turn is an extended version of his 1943 story 'I Married a Dead Man', it was made at Paramount and directed by Mitchell Leisen, who specialised in 'women's films'. While Sally Benson and Catherine Turney are credited with the script, Leisen is said to be the film's true author. Unfortunately, the movie lacks the spirit and mood of Woolrich's original narrative. Moreover, Stanwyck is slightly miscast in the role of someone who, having been mistaken for another, begins her new identity in relative innocence.

It would be four years before there would be another Hollywood adaptation of a Woolrich narrative. In the meantime, television was growing in popularity. At the end of the war, there had been only 6,500 television sets in the United States, but by 1950 there were more than 11 million. Soon television would affect the number of movies made. Out of the $14,000 earned by Woolrich between 1949 and 1952, $1,750 would come from television work. Soon Woolrich, whose work over the previous twenty years had been broadcast on the radio (*Escape, Hour of Mystery, Radio City Playhouse, Suspense*), would be selling more stories to television (*Suspense, Mystery Playhouse, Fireside Theatre, Ford Theatre, Playhouse 90, Journey to the Unknown* and *Alfred Hitchcock Presents*) than to the studios.

Woolrich's most famous adaptation is undoubtedly *Rear Window* (1954, Paramount). Directed by Hitchcock from the 1942 short story 'It Had to Be Murder', the plot concerns an incapacitated newspaperman confined to a wheelchair, who witnesses a murder in one of the apartments visible from his window. To pad out the story, Hitchcock added characters and themes not present in the Woolrich narrative. The film, with a subtext that relates to the era's paranoia, voyeurism and political apathy, hit a cultural nerve. Despite its success, Woolrich would receive a mere $600 for the story, which had been one of eight sold by Swanson to the studio. It might have been one of the worst deals that an otherwise shrewd Swanson would make, but what really angered Woolrich was that Hitchcock never consulted him, nor even sent him a ticket to see the film.

Nightmare (1956), directed by Maxwell Shane, is a remake of his 1947 *Fear in the Night*. Starring Kevin McCarthy, it was made in the same year as Don Siegel's *Invasion of the Body Snatchers*, which also stars McCarthy and uses a similar narrative voice-over. *Nightmare* revolves around a young musician hypnotised into committing a murder. With a script by Shane, it would be the final Hollywood film made from a Woolrich narrative.

But it was not the final adaptation made in the author's lifetime. That honour would go to François Truffaut's *La Mariée était en noir* (US title, *The Bride Wore Black*).

The French *nouvelle vague* director had the sense to retain Woolrich's plot, but altered the story's atmosphere. In the end, it was more a homage to Hitchcock than to Woolrich. Published in 1940, *The Bride Wore Black* had been Woolrich's first noir novel. A tale of vengeance concerning a woman widowed on her wedding day, who adopts various disguises and insinuates herself in the lives of her victims, it would influence many writers, including Marc Behm, whose *The Eye of the Beholder* and *Afraid to Death* might well have been written by his predecessor. Ironically, Woolrich never saw Truffaut's film, even though writer Michael Avallone tried to persuade him to do so. By this time, Woolrich, like the protagonist in *Rear Window*, was confined to a wheelchair and reluctant to go out. For *The Bride Wore Black*, Woolrich would receive a mere $250, the standard amount paid at the time for a mystery.

Other Woolrich adaptations include *The Boy Cried Murder* in 1966 and Truffaut's *La Sirène de Mississippi*, made in France in 1969 (US title, *Mississippi Mermaid*). The latter, based on Woolrich's *Waltz into Darkness*, is another Truffaut homage, this time to Renoir, and stars Catherine Deneuve and Jean-

Paul Belmondo. Set on a remote African island, a factory owner sends for a mail-order bride, who fails to live up to his expectations.

Combining the talents of two distinct storytellers, Rainer Werner Fassbinder's *Martha* is one of the more interesting adaptations of a Woolrich narrative to appear over the last thirty years. Made in 1974 for West German television, and based on Woolrich's story 'For the Rest of Her Life', *Martha* concerns a thirty-year-old single woman who accompanies her father on a holiday in Rome, where she falls in love with a man. After her father dies she marries the man, who gradually tries to control her and, ultimately, to break her. The woman has an affair with another man, after which her husband attempts to kill her. Equally unusual is *Union City*. About a man who murders someone over a bottle of milk and stuffs the body into a folding bed, the film is a vehicle for pop star Deborah Harry. It is directed by Dick Reichert, who changes the film's setting from the Depression to the McCarthy era, and extends the story. It is a nicely shot, slow-moving film, which ends up more an evocation of Edward Hopper than a convincing Woolrich adaptation.

From the release of the film *Manhattan Love Song* in 1934 to *Nightmare* in 1956, Woolrich lived with his mother, Claire, in the rundown Hotel Marseilles. Located on 103rd Street in Harlem, the hotel was popular with prostitutes, thieves and various lowlifes. From his room Woolrich could, as in *Rear Window*, survey other apartments, alleys and fire escapes. Though he sometimes disappeared for weeks at a time, Woolrich preferred to stay at home, where he churned out stories he imagined were occurring in the city. Some say Woolrich's delirious output can be attributed to the fact that whenever he heard a siren in the distance – not an infrequence occurrence in Harlem – he would automatically begin pounding the keys of his beloved NC69411.

Though there is no way of knowing if Claire ever saw any of the films made from her son's stories, according to

Woolrich she was not to read a single line of his work. This was not because she hadn't wanted to do so. It was simply that Woolrich would not let her, saying he wanted her to read only his best writing, and his best had yet to be written. After Claire's death in 1957 – like a plot from one of his stories, he believed the nurse caring for his mother had murdered her – life proved difficult. Drinking heavily, he was able to write only a few stories, most of which he would be unable to sell, whether to magazines, publishers or production companies.

However, he did manage to move to the more up-market Franconia, a hotel on 72nd Street near Central Park, and eventually ended up in the semi-luxurious Sheraton-Russell at Park Avenue South and 37th Street. There Woolrich would invite hotel staff to drink and watch television in his room. Eventually he descended into a world of paranoia, guilt, ill health and self-recrimination regarding his homosexuality. His self-loathing is apparent in a story from that era, 'A Story to be Whispered', in which the protagonist picks up a woman in a bar. She takes him back to her apartment, they have sex and, as he is about to reach orgasm, he beats her to death, saying, 'It wasn't as though I had killed another man. Or even . . . as if I had killed a woman. Or yet . . . killed a child. All I had killed was a queer.'

Incapacitated by failing eyesight and diabetes, Woolrich became increasingly reclusive. He grew to hate his books, handing them out to maids, bellboys, elevator operators and anyone who would take them. He rarely left the hotel, but managed a trip to Canada where he stayed for a number of months and wrote *Blues of a Lifetime*. He also attended the 1961 Mystery Writers of America conference in New York. In that same year, on hearing from a half-sister that his father had remarried, Woolrich legally changed his name to William Irish. With a career in which his writing had been an attempt to come to terms with himself and the world, he was now turning into his own fictional creation. When science-fiction writer Barry Malzberg, who would briefly act as Woolrich's agent, once complimented him on *Phantom Lady*, Woolrich said, 'I can't accept your praise. The man who wrote that novel died a long, long time ago.'

Falling apart psychologically as well as physically, Woolrich had become convinced that another Sheraton-Russell resident was sneaking into his room, searching through his belongings and seeking to take over his life. After a pair of ill-fitting shoes led to a foot infection which, untreated, turned gangrenous, Woolrich's leg had to be amputated. It is ironical that it was a foot injury during his college days that prompted an incapacitated Woolrich to write his first story, and now another foot injury, leading to an infection, was to precipitate his demise. Said Malzberg, '[In] the last year, he looked three decades older. The booze had wrecked him, the markets had wrecked him, he had wrecked him; by the time friends dragged him out in April to St. Clare's Hospital . . . he had the stunned aspect of the very old.' On his return, the hotel staff left trays of food outside his door. At the end of his tether, Woolrich rejoined the Church. He told Malzberg that he feared 'the endless obliteration, the knowledge that there will never be anything else. That's what I can't stand, to try so hard and to end in nothing.'

In September 1968, Woolrich suffered a stroke and died. He left $850,000 to Columbia University for a creative-writing graduate programme to be established in his mother's name. Before his death, Woolrich had attempted to describe the theory behind his fiction, saying, 'The path you follow is the path you have to follow; there are no digressions permitted you, even though you think there are.' Following his own path to the very end, Woolrich remains one of the few writers who might have fared better if he had, all those years ago, opted for a Hollywood career. But had he done so, he would not have written so many great stories, nor would there have been so many excellent film adaptations of his work. Yet it begs the question: how much suffering does it take to produce stories of such fear, darkness and self-loathing?

5

COURTING OBLIVION

Jim Thompson and David Goodis

What sets Jim Thompson and David Goodis apart from other
writers of the era is not merely their individuality, but also
their perspective, which was saturated in the paranoia and
alienation that lay beneath the surface of Cold War America.
Having courted a mass readership, both would romantically
look to Hollywood for affirmation or even redemption.
Though neither fared well in Tinseltown, they could not help
but move, like moths to a flame, in its direction. It was an
era when many noirists travelled west, and Hollywood was a
sort of test to discover if a given pulpist could survive where
others had failed, as well as a path to autonomy, and the
possibility of gaining the time and space to embark on more
literary endeavours.

Becoming an anonymous hack might have made economic
sense, but engaging the dream machine would, for the likes
of Thompson and Goodis, bring only nightmares. Their vision
was too extreme and eccentric, their imaginative powers too
warped and romantic, to find a place within the confines of
film noir. Yet they came close to delivering the goods. Despite
their efforts and willingness to compromise, Thompson would
end up a broken man, while Goodis would finish his days in
Philadelphia, burnt out and obsessed by a ludicrous lawsuit.

No matter how extraordinary they were as novelists, their
screenplays only occasionally exceeded the ordinary. The situation might have been different had producers been willing
to use either writer unexpurgated. But film noir, even at its
most extreme, would invariably play it safe, giving audiences

an escape route, be it with a reassuring ending or a hero who lives to tell the tale. Representing the dark, poetic side of noir, Thompson and Goodis were unable to reassure audiences. In the hardnosed and corruptible world of Hollywood, producers – not to mention bankers – to protect their interests were not going to give the writers any degree of input into the running of the well-oiled dream machine. To examine their time in Hollywood is to glimpse how Hollywood regards writers as marginal to the industry, much less the culture.

Jim Thompson

Motion-picture executives prefer to do business with men whose values they understand. It's very easy for these executives – businessmen running an art – to begin to fancy that they are creative artists themselves, because they are indeed very much like the 'artists' who work for them, because the 'artists' who work for them are, or have become, businessmen. Those who aren't businessmen are the Hollywood unreliables – the ones whom, it is always explained to you, the studios can't hire, because they're crazy. (Pauline Kael)

In a perverse way, it is understandable that Jim Thompson's books should be widely read and filmed only after his death. For it was then that Hollywood producers, and to a lesser degree publishers, could breathe a sign of relief, secure in the knowledge that they had finally ridded themselves of this strange man who had pestered them, a drunk who had sharecropped a table at Musso and Frank's, spieling out stories as though he were a jukebox of lost narratives.

Born in Anadarko, Oklahoma, in 1906, James Myers Thompson had long been infatuated by Hollywood, and did what he could to become part of it. Unfortunately, shortsighted producers were unable to figure out how to make money from his wayward stories, while their more far-sighted counterparts would exploit Thompson's talents only to discard him. Not that Thompson's stories are the stuff from which Hollywood dreams are made. In fact, they work to undermine those dreams, shoving the extreme nature of human behaviour back in the faces of those seeking redemptive fables and reassuring interpretations of history. But then screenwriting was never Thompson's forte. He preferred pouring out his soul in the guise of pulp narratives, such as his famous run in the 1950s when, beginning with *The Killer Inside Me* and ending with *A Hell of a Woman*, he churned out twelve pulp classics within the space of eighteen months.

In the end, Thompson's Hollywood sojourn reads like a narrative from one of his books. Eventually, too ill to type or write and with his speech impaired, he became the kind of helpless victim about whom he had often written. If it had been a novel, Thompson would have had to tell it in one of his famous split narratives: a device to let his narrator combine internal subjectivity with external agony – one voice seeking fame and fortune in the studios and another seeking to undermine his *alter ego*'s success.

Thompson's tuberculosis had been acting up again when he set out with his wife and two children, in late 1940, from his native Oklahoma for California. Having been given command of the official Communist Party car – an old black Plymouth that had once belonged to folk singer Woody Guthrie – and told to deliver it to an International Labor Defense lawyer in San Francisco, Thompson stopped off in San Diego, where he deposited Alberta and the children. On his way to San Francisco, he picked up a hitchhiker. As they drove up the Pacific Coast Highway, Thompson bragged about his success as a writer. The hitchhiker responded by robbing Thompson. Viewed with hindsight, the scene seems all too prophetic of the way Thompson would be treated once he arrived in Hollywood.

Taking the train back to Los Angeles, Thompson attempted

to see Donald Ogden Stewart, who had just written *The Philadelphia Story* and, at the time, was head of the League of American Writers. This former member of the Algonquin Round Table, and the model for Bill Gorton in *The Sun Also Rises*, was a friend of George Milburn (author of *Hoboes and Harlots* and *Catalogue*), who had been a major influence on Thompson. A leftist who, though eventually blacklisted, once had to apologise to the Party for writing scripts that were, in an era of social realism, too light-hearted, Stewart did not want – or did not have the time – to see Thompson. With his most promising door closed to him, Thompson sought refuge in a Hollywood Boulevard bar, where he met director Sam Fuller, at the time a reporter for a San Diego newspaper. Fuller dragged Thompson off to a party in National City, where he introduced him to Nathaniel West, just ten days before the latter, while driving on the Calexico road, had his fatal car accident.

With his in-progress proletarian novel, *Always to Be Blessed*, Thompson made the rounds of the studios and agencies, but was unable to generate any interest. Nor was he able to pitch a story idea, 'The Osage Murders', to Warner Brothers. Fawcett Publications suggested Thompson try writing for one of their movie magazines. The idea was for Thompson to become another Jim Tully, the hobo-novelist whose Hollywood reportage had appeared in *Photoplay*. But that was not the sort of writing Thompson had in mind. On the bus back to San Diego, a disillusioned Thompson removed the manuscript of his novel from his knapsack, glanced at it one last time, and threw it out of the window, watching the pages as they scattered across the Pacific Coast Highway.

Not that this ended Thompson's writing career, nor his flirtation with proletarian fiction. He would return to the latter in his 1942 *Now and on Earth*, a novel that, ironically, marked his break with the Communist Party (Thompson remained a socialist throughout his life), then, in a modified form, in his 1967 *South of Heaven*. By the time Thompson junked *Always to Be Blessed*, the era of proletarian fiction was already drawing to a close. Nevertheless, Viking had commissioned the novel three years earlier, coming to an arrangement – the object of which was to mitigate Thompson's inability to deal with relatively large sums of money – whereby each week he would send Viking a 5,000 word instalment and receive, in return, a partial advance on his royalties. With publication scheduled for six months from the time the deal was struck, Thompson found himself working to a tight deadline. In future, to ensure a regular wage, Thompson would suggest a similar arrangement to other publishers. *Always to Be Blessed* was meant to be an account of the Depression from the perspective of a jobless man in Oklahoma, Texas, Kansas and Nebraska. Describing hobo jungles, Hoovervilles and freight-hopping, it was in the tradition of Tully's hobo narratives, Edward Dahlberg's 1929 *Bottom Dogs*, Nelson Algren's 1935 *Somebody in Boots* and Edward Anderson's 1935 *Hungry Men*. From the pages that survive it is clear that Thompson was already using a split narrative, as he would later do in novels such as *A Hell of a Woman*, derived, in part, from reading Faulkner, who referred to the technique as a break between the objective picture and subjective thought transference. Not only had Viking, the company to whom he had been sending instalments, rejected the novel, but so had Simon & Schuster, Vanguard and various other publishers. Now, to make matters worse, even the studios had been unimpressed.

Like Horace McCoy, Thompson was wondering if he was destined to be just another literary failure. Despite some critical acclaim, *Now and on Earth*, his first published novel, had sold poorly. Needing to support his family, Thompson returned to Los Angeles in September 1948 for an interview at the *Los Angeles Mirror*. Recently launched by Norman Chandler, the *Mirror* was meant to be a working-class companion to the *Los Angeles Times*, and rightwing competition for the liberal, pro-union *Daily News*. On the train to LA,

Thompson ran into Raymond Chandler, now living in La
Jolla. They spent the journey talking. At the time, Chandler,
still peripherally connected to Hollywood, was working on the
ill-fated *Playback*.

Thompson considered the meeting a good omen. Accordingly, the *Mirror* hired him as a rewrite man. He immediately
took up residence at the Los Angeles Press Club's Case Hotel
on South Broadway, then moved to a Wilshire boarding house
belonging to silent screen actress Mary MacLaren. A thirteen-
year-old fashion model before becoming a fourteen-year-old
Broadway chorus girl, MacLaren had starred in over a dozen
films, playing the Queen of France in Douglas Fairbanks's
1921 version of *The Three Musketeers*, and appearing in films
alongside Wallace Beery and Lionel Barrymore. In 1948
MacLaren was living in a large house, renting rooms to a
variety of eccentric individuals, including a man who would
be arrested for lewd vagrancy and a self-proclaimed Catholic
bishop who used the house as a church and rescue mission
for young men. By the time Thompson arrived, MacLaren
was finishing her novel, *The Twisted Heart*, which was to be
published in 1952. Thompson, despite being drunk most of
the time, claimed to have helped prepare MacLaren's novel
for publication.

At the *Mirror*, Thompson worked as a rewrite man, turning
reporters' notes into publishable stories. It was a never-
ending, deadline-oriented task for which he was paid $85 a
week. Thompson could handle the work, but it quickly
became tedious. He not only began to drink on the job, but
also used the newspaper's time and typewriter to work on his
fiction. After four months at the *Mirror*, Thompson was fired.

It could have been that, since *Nothing More than Murder* had
just been published, Thompson preferred to be a struggling
novelist than a bored rewrite man. Written in the manner of
James M. Cain, *Nothing More than Murder* concerns a husband
and wife who plot a murder. The husband, Joe Wilmot, runs
the local movie house, which belongs to his wife's family. It

is a reflection of Thompson's position on the periphery of Hollywood's film culture, and indicative of the role that movies had played in his life. As a youth, Thompson had constructed a shrine to the actress Theda Bara above his bed, and had appeared in a Fort Worth two-reeler. Later, he had managed a cinema in Big Springs, which he would describe in the novel.

While writing *Recoil*, which would not be published until 1953, Thompson, on the strength of *Nothing More than Murder* and the recommendation of a woman he had helped while working at the *Mirror*, was hired to teach creative writing at the University of Southern California. Liked by his students, he had them read Willa Cather's *Coming, Aphrodite!*, Hemingway's *A Farewell to Arms*, Cain's *Double Indemnity*, William Carlos Williams's *In the American Grain*, and the poetry of Robinson Jeffers. It is a rare glimpse of the books that Thompson, at the time, deemed important.

But such work wasn't going to pay the bills. So, in 1950, Thompson landed a job as an assistant editor at *Saga* magazine. *Saga* was the kind of men's magazine that carried stories about athletes, cowboys, soldiers and all things masculine. Thompson was quickly promoted to associate editor, then managing editor, supplementing his income by ghosting many of the magazine's articles and letters. But matters came to a head when the editor, after supporting his employees' attempts to unionise, was sacked by the publisher. In solidarity with the editor, Thompson promptly resigned. The following year he was hired as managing editor of the *Police Gazette* in New York. Perhaps it was working as a magazine editor and writer that prepared Thompson for his spate of novels, published in pulp paperback editions by Lion, a New York publishing company run by Arthur Hano, who would always have a high regard for Thompson's work.

When Hano decided, in the late 1950s, that Lion should cease publishing paperback originals, Thompson was left high but hardly dry. Burnt out but drinking more than ever, he began freelancing for various magazines, ending up as a copy-editor at the New York *Daily News*. He was not destined to last at that job either. Once again in financial difficulty, Thompson was rescued by a twenty-six-year-old *Look* magazine photographer named Stanley Kubrick. A fan of Thompson's fiction and with one low-budget film noir, *The Killer's Kiss*, under his belt, Kubrick sent his producer James B. Harris to ask Thompson if he would adapt Lionel White's heist novel *Clean Break*, which, in Kubrick's hands, would be called *The Killing*.

Kubrick had been impressed by Thompson's ear for dialogue, picked up during the 1920s while working as a roustabout in the Texas oil fields and as a night-shift bellhop at the Hotel Texas in Fort Worth (where JFK would stay on the eve of his assassination). Seeing a possible path to the film industry, Thompson signed on with Kubrick. Together, they mapped out the film, with Kubrick structuring the narrative and outlining the scenes and Thompson working on the dialogue. In return for Thompson's effort, Kubrick and Harris introduced him to their New York agent, advanced money to the writer, and supported him through 1959. Afterwards, Harris commissioned Thompson to write a short novel, *Lunatic at Large*, which Kubrick intended to develop into a movie. The story concerned an American soldier and a female psychopath, but the film was never be made, nor would the novel be published. According to Thompson's biographer, Robert Polito, all that survives of *Lunatic at Large* are the final three pages.

The Killing, however, remains a brilliantly plotted film with excellent performances from Sterling Hayden, Jay C. Flippen, Elisha Cook Jr. and Timothy Carey. As a heist movie, it prefigures such films as *Point Blank* and *Pulp Fiction*. But it would be Kubrick who scooped the screenwriting credits, with Thompson's name placed under the heading 'additional dialogue'.

An enraged Thompson believed that, at the very least, he

should have received co-writer status. Even then a self-styled *auteur*, Kubrick was notorious for his cavalier use of writers. Some authors would buy into the Kubrick myth to such a degree that they would come to thank the director for mistreating them. But there would be an assortment of complaints about Kubrick's treatment, not only from Thompson, but from the likes of Calder Willingham and Terry Southern. In this instance, the Writers Guild decided in Thompson's favour, and, by way of compensation, Kubrick agreed to hire Thompson to work on his next film, *Paths of Glory*, at $750 a week.

With the prospect of working on another picture, Thompson moved to Hollywood in June 1956 with Alberta. Arriving in Los Angeles by train, the couple were taken by Kubrick to their new residence, an apartment on Sunset Boulevard. It was the suite Thompson later described in *The Grifters* as belonging to Lily Dillon. When Kubrick visited the apartment for script sessions, it was Thompson who did the writing while Kubrick argued about details. For his work, Thompson would be paid $500 a week, $250 short of the agreed figure. Still, he had a contract that guaranteed co-screen credits.

Paths of Glory is set during World War I, and is an eloquent anti-war statement. For his part, Thompson did well in adapting what is, at best, a mediocre novel. In the summer of 1957, Kubrick handed Thompson's script to Calder Willingham, the celebrated author of *End as a Man*, for polishing. All three names – Kubrick, Thompson and Willingham – appeared on the cover of the second and third drafts of the script. When Kirk Douglas, who had been impressed by *The Killing*, met Kubrick, he was given a copy of the script, which he liked. But when he arrived on the set, Kubrick gave the actor a different script, which turned out to be Thompson's first draft. Douglas hated it. It was a typical Kubrick ego game. Not that Douglas disliked the writing, it was just that his part, compared to the draft he had originally read, had been considerably reduced. Willingham would claim that his script contained none of Thompson's original dialogue. Yet Polito maintains that Thompson's contributions account for nearly half the film's running time.

Though credits were to have been arranged in advance, the Writers Guild had to intervene, ruling that writing credits should go to Kubrick, Willingham and Thompson, in that order. While the film would consolidate the reputations of Kirk Douglas and Kubrick, and make them a great deal of money, Thompson would come out of the film only marginally better off than when he went into it. That Thompson felt slighted did not stop him from attending an awards banquet at the Moulin Rouge, where the film was nominated as the best-written American Drama of 1957, but lost out to Reginald Rose's script for *12 Angry Men*.

Hoping to cash in on the success of *Paths of Glory*, Thompson was once again circulating his stories around studio story departments. Again, they were uniformly rejected, as were his television proposals. According to Polito, part of the problem was Thompson's chronic shyness with strangers in an industry where charm, affability and insincerity are necessary attributes. Nor was Thompson capable of pitching his stories to executives. Story meetings made him nervous; he hated writing by committee; and he thought a handshake could seal a deal. In a town where everything is for sale, Thompson was unable to sell himself. As he put it in his abandoned late 1950s Hollywood novel, *Sunset and Cienega*:

> If you were lucky, you only have to do your selling to . . . the producer and/or the story editor – and that could be tough going enough with guys who yawned in your face, talked over the telephone while you were talking and assured visitors that they would be through with you 'in just a minute.' Sometimes, however, you might have an audience of as many as four . . . All of them poisonously critical, pitching

curved-ball questions at you, doing everything they could
to rip your story apart.

In November 1957, after the Thompsons moved to a water-
front cottage in San Clemente, New American Library bought
The Getaway, paying the writer a $2,500 advance and the
promise of a further $1,500 on delivery of the manuscript.
Between signing the contract and publication, Thompson was
hired as a rewrite man for the TV western, *Tales of Wells Fargo*,
after which he joined Ziv Television Programs to write for
another TV western, *Mackenzie's Raiders*, for which he would
receive four author's credits. But Thompson had yet to get
over his dislike of the medium. There were too many people
to please. He would watch the programmes – he received
$1,300 per teleplay and $297.50 for each repeat – and complain about the changes made to his scripts. Meanwhile, the
commute between San Clemente and Hollywood was
becoming tiresome. Once again Thompson's writing began
to take a back seat to his drinking.

Originally, Kubrick had wanted to direct *The Getaway*
himself. But the director, who had also considered making
The Killer Inside Me, passed on the project. Instead, he asked
Thompson to adapt the memoirs of 1920s safe-cracker
Herbert Emerson Wilson, entitled *I Stole $16,000,000*.
Thompson agreed, and on 7 May 1959, he signed with Harris-
Kubrick Pictures to deliver a screenplay in not more than
twenty weeks for a flat figure of $6,000, payable in weekly
increments of $300 per week, with an additional $9,000 to be
paid on the first principal day of photography. With a treat-
ment for the film having already been put to paper by *Clean
Break* author Lionel White, Thompson, three weeks after
signing the contract, delivered a 135–page script.

Within days of handing in the script, Thompson, not yet
fifty-three years old, suffered his first collapse, a mild stroke
exacerbated by a period of intense work, a cigarette addiction
of more than two packs a day, binge drinking and the amphet-

amine cocktails that he had been injecting for over ten years. Thompson had been a patient of the notorious Dr. Max Jacobson. 'Dr. Feelgood', as he was known, would have his medical licence revoked in 1975, but not before administering his cocktail – a melange of vitamins, steroids, hormones, placenta, animal organ cells, and speed – to John F. Kennedy, Judy Garland, Truman Capote, Cecil B. DeMille and Van Cliburn. Though Thompson's ability to walk and his speech were unaffected, his writing hand was temporarily paralysed. Despite his stroke and the work he had done on the script, Kubrick decided against making the movie.

When he regained his health, Thompson worked on a novelisation of a *Twilight Zone* episode, 'Cloudburst', but sold it to New American Library, for which he received $4,000. Although Thompson had written the novel, there was considerable dispute over who owned the rights and the title. Eventually Thompson changed the title and, in the following year, sold the book to Signet as *The Transgressors*.

Come Christmas 1960, Thompson was again sidelined, this time by a case of bleeding ulcers. Lacking health insurance, he was unable to receive immediate hospital attention. While waiting in the hospital lobby, he collapsed, then languished in intensive care for three weeks. Upon his release, he and Alberta moved into the Hollywood Continental Apartments on Hollywood Boulevard. While living there, Thompson began to hear about his popularity in France. Wanting to get out of Hollywood and hoping to capitalise on his reputation in Europe, he wrote to his friend R.V. Cassill about the possibility of teaching at the University of Iowa. But Cassill, an academic who had published pulp novels like *Dormitory Women* with Gold Medal, and who would, a few years later, pen a ground-breaking essay on Thompson, was unable to convince the university that Thompson would make an useful addition to the department. For the next two years, foreign rights money would account for a good portion of Thompson's income.

Though he was again nearly destitute, Thompson, in 1961, found a new agent, Robert Mills, a one-time editor at *Ellery Queen's Mystery Magazine* and *Mercury Mystery Magazine*. Mills, whose clients included James Baldwin, Walter Tevis and Harlan Ellison, would represent Thompson's literary interests for the rest of the writer's life. In 1962, with money borrowed from his daughter, Thompson bought a train ticket for New York, and personally delivered the manuscript of *The Grifters* to Mills, who sent it on to Ellison, who was at the time supplementing his science fiction by working as an editor at Regency Books.

After Ellison convinced Regency to publish *The Grifters*, the Thompsons moved into an apartment four blocks from Musso and Frank's and the Writers Guild. But it was not upward mobility that prompted their move. They needed a larger apartment because their twenty-five-year-old son, Michael, had attempted to kill himself, and the couple wanted an extra bedroom so that their son could live with them. Thompson channelled his distress over his son's condition into *Pop. 1280*, a nightmarish monologue narrated by Nick Corey, a small-town Southern lawman, and published by Gold Medal. It would be one of Thompson's final triumphs, for which he was paid $4,000.

By the mid-1960s Jerry Bick had become Thompson's television and film agent. Though he still had financial, family and drinking problems, Thompson, through Bick, was able to sell a script to the TV programme *Dr. Kildare* and an episode of the World War II series *Convoy*. In 1965, he was working in films again, this time assisting Sam Peckinpah, who was co-writing a screenplay, *Ready for the Tiger*, from a suspense novel by one-time Lion author Sam Ross. It was Sam Fuller who introduced Thompson to Peckinpah. Fuller was to recall that David Goodis was also present at that meeting. If this is so, it is the only recorded meeting of the two writers. It is uncertain, however, what Goodis, who quit Hollywood in 1950, would have been doing in town, unless it was to gather evidence for his plagiarism case against ABC-TV. Although Peckinpah loved Thompson's work, the future director would be unable to turn *Ready for the Tiger* into a finished product. It would be one more Thompson project that would never see the light of day.

Next, it was Sal Mineo's turn to discover Thompson. Not long before he was fatally shot in a Hollywood garage, Mineo asked Thompson to write a screenplay about the Hell's Angels. Thompson did a treatment and a first draft, but had to go to the Writers Guild to obtain his $5,255.25, which, at the time, was Guild minimum. By December, Thompson was back in the hospital complaining of abdominal pains, culminating in the removal of his gallbladder and half of an ulcerated stomach. He was released three weeks later, thousands of dollars in debt.

Part of Thompson's problem with the studios was that he could not come to grips with the art of writing screenplays. Some of his offerings, like the *Dr. Kildare* script, were not even written in screenplay form. As Jerry Bick said, 'Jim could write a novel in ten days, but he couldn't write a screenplay on his own in ten years.' Returning to fiction, Thompson wrote *South of Heaven*, a novel about his experiences as a 'powder monkey' for the Texas Company's construction of the Port Arthur pipeline in 1927. He also received an advance from Avon of $1,700 for the novel *King Blood*.

Despite having hardly any stomach left, Thompson was still drinking heavily when he was asked to do an episode and a novelisation of the TV programme *Ironside*. It would be the closest he would come to a straightforward detective novel. This was followed by a novelisation of Victor V. McLaglen's post-Civil War film, *The Undefeated*. Considering Thompson's past work, both efforts were well below par.

Then came the lopsided *White Mother, Black Son*, which attempted to cash in on the era's black power movement. The novel would be promptly rejected by Popular Library, and would not be published until Lancer brought it out in

1972, retitling it *Child of Rage*. Reading it one can see why Popular Library didn't want to put their name to it. It is not the subject matter but the language – both author and narrator seem to suffer from a kind of literary Tourette's – that makes the novel so extreme, even for the early 1970s.

Next up for membership in the Thompson adulation society was Tony Bill of Bi-Plane Cinematograph. Bill had become interested in Thompson's writing while at Stanford. At a local bookshop in Los Angeles, he discovered where Thompson lived. He tracked him down and asked if he would be interested in writing a screenplay about hoboes. It was a subject Thompson knew well. As their project gained momentum, Thompson, with Bill and director Vernon Zimmerman in attendance, would drunkenly hold forth at Musso and Frank's. For hours on end, he would ramble on about hoboes and the Depression. Thompson's drinking had become so excessive that, according to Bill, he at one point offered to sell the rights to everything he had ever written to Bill for anything from $500 to $1,000. To his credit, Bill refused the offer.

Given an office on the Columbia lot, Thompson saw his hobo project mutate from an original screenplay to an adaptation of *South of Heaven*, whose rights he had sold to Bi-Plane. Thompson was to receive $1,500 upon signing, $4,500 upon completion of a first draft, $2,000 for any revisions, and a final $2,000 for the shooting script. Bi-Plane supposedly took possession of the film and TV rights for a token $10. In July, Robert Redford joined the project as co-producer and star. Meanwhile, the title changed from *South of Heaven* to *Hard Times* to *Bo*. But in Redford's opinion, Thompson's script was not good enough. Though they paid Thompson his full $10,000, Bill and Redford scuppered the project and went on to make *The Sting*.

The last of Thompson's novelisations – again, barely mediocre – was *Nothing But a Man*, which was published in 1970 and was based on Michael Roemer's 1964 deserving black and white film about a struggling African-American couple in the American south. This was, for Thompson, still hack work. When Pierre Rissient came from Paris to secure the rights to *White Mother, Black Son*, Thompson told him he blamed his problems in the film and publishing world on the blacklist. While that is a possibility for someone so radical in terms of literary style and social perspective (and it is strange that no one has investigated the effect of Thompson's politics on his lack of success in Hollywood), Thompson's failure probably had more to do with the author's unreliability, his drinking and his literary extremism. Be that as it may, Rissient paid Thompson $5,000 to finish *White Mother, Black Son*, and flew the author to Paris. Thompson arrived drunk, only to receive a telegram from Alberta saying that Michael had tried to kill himself again, whereupon Thompson left France. According to Alberta, though Michael had threatened to kill himself, the telegram had been a ruse concocted by the couple to get Thompson back to California. However, Thompson's arthritis now made it difficult for him to type. When, in 1972, Lancer Books finally issued *White Mother, Black Son* under the title *Child of Rage*, the author must have sensed it would be his last novel.

In the final years of his life, Thompson handed over his affairs to future Orion and TriStar executive Michael Medavoy. It was an odd pairing, for Medavoy's clients included Hollywood heavyweights Steven Spielberg, George Lucas, Terrence Malick and John Milius. Thompson was the only novelist on his books, and probably the only one not making a six-figure salary. The two men first got together in 1970 after Tony Bill showed Medavoy a copy of *The Getaway*, which the latter immediately sold to David Foster, a publicist for Steve McQueen, who wanted to play a Bogart-styled gangster. Thompson's novel seemed perfect for the actor. A week after Foster mailed him a photocopy of the script, McQueen gave the project the go-ahead. Peter Bogdanovich, who had just finished shooting *The Last Picture Show*, was lined up as director. Thompson was paid $1,500 for the option and $20,000 for the motion picture rights. The contract stipulated that he should be paid $15,000 for the screenplay and a bonus of $25,000 if he merited a screen credit. The total amount, which came to a possible $61,500, was as much money as Thompson had made over the previous ten years.

Sam Fuller once called *The Getaway* 'the most original gangster story ever written. I could film it without a script.' But that was not quite the case as far as the McQueen project was concerned. After Thompson delivered a ninety-page first draft, Foster sent it back with as many pages of recommendations. For sixteen weeks, Thompson worked on the screenplay, only to receive one ten-by-thirteen envelope after another filled with suggestions. By June, Thompson was replaced by Walter Hill, who went on to make *Southern Comfort* and *The Driver*. Par for the course, Hill received sole credit for the script.

Foster would insist that Thompson's script had too much dialogue in it, but Medavoy maintained that Thompson's version was simply too dark for them. Foster also claimed that the second half of the novel was another movie altogether. Certainly Hill's script lacks the novel's bleak and surreal finale set in the Kingdom of El Rey. Just after Thompson was fired, Bogdanovich left to make *What's Up, Doc?* Transferring the script of *The Getaway* to his own company, McQueen hired Sam Peckinpah. Though Peckinpah had worked with Thompson and was familiar with the novel, the director opted for Hill's script. Outlaw he might have been, but Peckinpah realised that Hollywood was not going to allow Thompson's extremism to run rampant and unsettle a project that was, with the bankable Ali McGraw on board, potentially lucrative. McQueen's contract also gave the actor the final cut. In the end, as Thompson would later tell the Writers Guild, the film bore little relationship to his novel. However, McQueen's cut was too much even for the director. Viewing it in Mexico, an enraged Peckinpah walked up to the screen and, unzipping his trousers, pissed on it, screaming, 'This is not my film!' Later Peckinpah, hoping to recoup some credit, if not self-respect, claimed it had been his intention to make a satire. At the end of the day, Thompson received $36,500. Not a bad sum until one compares it to the $18 million the film would make domestically and $35 million worldwide – or realises that, at that time, it was the fifth highest grossing film ever made.

After Sphere books finally published *King Blood* – the last novel to be published in the author's lifetime – in 1973, Thompson and his wife, on Labor Day, moved into a penthouse apartment not far from the Hollywood Bowl. In less demand than ever, Thompson had become thoroughly embittered. Fortunately, Jerry Bick gave him a helping hand. Having just optioned *Farewell, My Lovely*, and remembering Thompson's role in that Fort Worth two-reeler, Bick, now representing Thompson again, asked director Dick Richards to consider the writer for the role of the judge in the latter's remake of Chandler's classic. Richards, who had read Thompson's novels, knew he would be perfect. It was not much of a part, but it allowed Thompson, thanks to the Screen Actors Guild, to receive medical coverage. In the film, Marlowe was played by Robert Mitchum, whom Thompson had interviewed in the late 1940s, after the actor had been arrested on his well-publicised marijuana charge. Remembering the interview and acknowledging Thompson's place in the noir pantheon, Mitchum, whenever they were on the set together, made a point of fetching sandwiches for the ailing writer.

Four years earlier, Warner Brothers had purchased the rights to *The Killer Inside Me* for only a thousand dollars. Directed by Burt Kennedy, it was released in 1975 and starred Stacy Keach and Susan Tyrrell. It was a mediocre venture. When Thompson saw the film, he said to his daughter, 'Sharon, it was a bad deal.'

To everyone's surprise, the stalwart Alberta suffered a heart attack in 1975. Thompson dropped everything and spent his time caring for her. While doing so, he was approached by the French writer and director Alain Corneau, who wanted to adapt *Pop. 1280*. However, Corneau dropped out of the project, and the film would not be made until 1981, when Bertrand Tavernier turned it into *Coup de torchon*, inventively switching the film's locale from the American South to West Africa, but without using Thompson's screenplay. Two years after Thompson's death, Corneau adapted *A Hell of a Woman* (Série Noire), with a script by, of all people, French Oulipo writer Georges Perec.

On Thanksgiving 1975, Thompson was back in the hospital for cataract surgery. It failed to improve the vision in his right eye, which prompted him to cancel an operation intended for his other eye. Robert Mulligan (who directed *To Kill a Mockingbird, Summer of '42*) inquired about purchasing the rights to *South of Heaven*, only to find that Thompson had sold them years before to Bi-Plane for $10. Thompson, however, was surprised that he no longer owned his novel, saying that he could not recollect signing away the rights. This prompted him to sue Tony Bill and Vernon Zimmerman of Bi-Plane for $100,000 in compensatory damages and $5,000,000 in exemplary damages. He claimed that Bill and Zimmerman had instructed him to sign the papers after plying him with alcohol, and that *Hard Times* was a distinct entity from *South of Heaven*. Bill said that he had no recollection of Thompson signing over the rights to *South of Heaven*, and could only conclude that the author must have made a separate deal with Columbia.

In 1976, while reading a newspaper in his apartment, Thompson suffered another stroke. This time he lost his power of speech. Even when it returned, his speech tended to lag far behind his thoughts. Three weeks after the stroke, Thompson began to have seizures. For ten months Thompson was in and out of the hospital. Too ill to give a deposition against Bill and Zimmerman, he was now contemplating another lawsuit, this time against Robert Redford. Thompson was certain that *The Sting* had been stolen from *The Grifters* – unlikely since the film is apparently based on David W. Maurer's *The Big Con*, a semi-academic study of the confidence trickster in 1940s America.

Not long after this stroke, Vietnam veteran Gary Graver, looking for a novel that he and Orson Welles could adapt, contacted Thompson, who gave him photocopied versions of a number of his books. Graver and Welles decided on *A Hell of a Woman*, and optioned it for $2,000. Though a script was written, no film was made. In November, Thompson suffered another stroke, and spent a month in intensive care before being transferred to a nursing facility. When he got home, he made Alberta promise that, no matter what happened, he would not be hospitalised again. Unable to write, Thompson began to starve himself. In April 1977, at the age of seventy, he died. As his sister, Freddie, said, 'Hollywood basically killed him off.' Sadly, Thompson's death was of no great concern to Hollywood or its literary community. Only a handful of people showed up for the funeral, though some say this had to do with a misprint in his obituary. Thompson's daughter said that when she was a child her father used to say to her, 'Life doesn't have a happy ending.' It looked like he had been right. Before he died Thompson had told his wife that his time had yet to come, that eventually he would be appreciated. At the time of his death, none of his books was in print. Two years later, the Thompson revival would begin.

David Goodis

Though he worked on various films, David Goodis would gain few screenwriting credits. It was not that he was bad at his job. It was just that he was one more slightly-above-average Hollywood writer. What he had in his favour was a sense, gained from working for the pulps, of what the public wanted.

On the other hand, his temperament rarely allowed him to translate that knowledge to the screen. Had Goodis possessed a different character, and not been so enamoured with the myth of Hollywood, his career might well have been more successful.

What was Goodis like? Director Sam Fuller, who got to know him during the 1945 writers' strike, called Goodis a mild person, not the kind who mixed easily with others: 'Sensitive. Isolated. A healthy guy who wanted to live his life his way . . . He harmed no one, and wanted never to be harmed by anyone.' Others have said that Goodis was something of a chameleon, adapting to any situation or social milieu. Screenwriter Catherine Turney, who befriended Goodis's collaborator James Gunn, was unable to place him. Neither could W.R. Burnett. Others remember Goodis's bizarre behaviour, behind which lay the desperation one finds in his fiction, a desperation that was part and parcel of Goodis's nature, the result of the various misfortunes he had suffered. No matter how he was regarded, Goodis, during this period, was marking time, making the best of a good contract, which, in the long run, was just another bad deal.

Goodis arrived in Hollywood in 1942, three years after the publication of his first novel, *Retreat from Oblivion*, which had appeared when he was just twenty-two years of age. It wasn't long before Goodis found work at Universal, where his first job was to put together a treatment for John Meehan Jr.'s adaptation of *Destination Unknown*. This would be followed by a treatment for *The Vicious Circle*. During that year he met and married his own personal *femme fatale*, Elaine. Together they returned to Philadelphia, then New York. Buxom, beautiful and, like Goodis, Jewish, Elaine soon concluded that her husband was not cultured enough for her. After leaving him, Elaine found work in a fashionable Manhattan clothing shop. Their relationship, partially described in *Behold This Woman* (1947), irrevocably scarred Goodis and partly accounts for the hard, devouring women that populate his fiction. Just as his fictional women taunt their men, so Elaine taunted Goodis. In future years Goodis would continue to speak bitterly about her. After her departure, Goodis went on to write *Dark Passage*, a novel in which Gert, whose death has led to Parry's imprisonment, assumes some of Elaine's worst qualities.

In January 1946, though *Dark Passage* had not yet been published, Goodis sold the story rights to Warner Brothers for $23,500. At the time, studios were desperate for original narratives, and *Dark Passage* was, if nothing else, original. But the story did not appear in print until the summer, when it was serialised in the *Saturday Evening Post*. Come the autumn, Julian Messner published it in hardback. Eight months after selling the story to the studio, Goodis signed a six-year contract with Warner. It was a surprisingly good deal. Written into the contract was a clause to the effect that the writer need only spend six months of each year working at the studio and the remaining months at home, writing fiction or film. Of course, *home*, to Goodis, meant Philadelphia. Not a bad contract for someone whose first novel had already retreated into oblivion and whose second novel had just seen the light of day.

The contract also meant that Goodis could bid farewell to the pulp magazines for which he had been writing. In periodicals like *Battle Birds*, *Daredevil Aces*, *Popular Sports* and *Detective Fiction*, he had written stories about baseball players, aviators, boxers, criminals and cops (he had also penned scripts for radio shows like *Superman* and *Hap Harrigan of the Airwaves*). Goodis is said to have cranked out some half-million words for such publications, sometimes contributing five or six stories in the same issue under various pseudonyms. His final magazine story was 'Caravan to Tarim', in the more respectable *Colliers* in 1946. In that same year he also published an article in the *San Francisco Chronicle* about the murder in Los Angeles of Elizabeth Short, the Black Dahlia, whose butchered body was left in a vacant lot. It was a crime that would obsess future writers like James Ellroy, Michael Connelly and John Gregory Dunne, but the Black Dahlia is not a subject one associates with Goodis, who, for the most part, preferred grand gesture to gritty realism.

The year 1946 would be a good one for Goodis. Within a six-month period he had received $23,500 for *Dark Passage*, placed the novel with Julian Messner for a further $2,500, and found a publisher (Curtis) for *Behold This Woman* and *Nightfall*. Making $750 a week at Warner Brothers, Goodis moved into the Oban, a rundown hotel on Yucca Street. While the Oban had the advantage of being close to Burbank, where Goodis was working, his choice of residence was typically Goodis. Most newly arrived writers making such money would have opted for more respectable Hollywood quarters, like the Roosevelt or the Knickerbocker. Whether tightwad or eccentric, Goodis was either seeking something befitting a writer of pulp fiction or serving notice that he considered himself a temporary resident, preferring to test Hollywood's waters before plunging into its depths.

His first assignment was to work with James Gunn (according to Turney, the two men may never have actually met) on *The Unfaithful*, an adaptation of W. Somerset Maugham's play *The Letter*, coincidentally about a failed marriage, which had already been filmed in 1929, directed by Jean de Limur, and in 1940, directed by William Wyler and starring Bette Davis. Goodis would spend his first six months in Hollywood writing and rewriting the script. Also working on the screenplay were novelists John Collier and Jo Pagano, though their contributions would go uncredited.

The combination of Goodis, Gunn and Maugham was hardly a recipe for success. Seen through contemporary eyes, *The Unfaithful* has few redeeming features. Badly directed with wooden performances, it does none of the writers justice. Yet *The Unfaithful* was a commercial success and remains, along with *The Burglar*, the only real evidence of Goodis's ability as a screenwriter. Unfortunately, in this instance, Goodis's script was painfully mediocre. Perhaps his mind was on the imminent publication of *Behold This Woman* and *Nightfall*. Whatever the film's failings, Goodis had impressed the studio enough to be given the short-lived opportunity to adapt Chandler's *The Lady in the Lake*. But the studio quickly realised that translating Chandler to the screen was better suited to someone with more workmanlike habits, such as the film's eventual writer, Steve Fisher. However, Goodis's involvement in *The Lady in the Lake* is interesting, if only for its subjective camera, a technique that connects the latter with *Dark Passage*.

Despite the commercial success of *The Unforgiven*, by the time *Dark Passage* was released in 1947 Goodis was already disillusioned with screenwriting. When Jerry Wald and Delmer Daves visited the writer in Philadelphia, he was talking about writing a film entitled *Brotherly Love*, but when he returned to Hollywood he was back slogging away on a series of aborted projects. First there was a thirty-nine-page treatment for B producer William Jacobs's *The Persian Cat*, based on a novel by John Flagg. Then there was a script for *Within These Gates*, based on Irving Shulman's *The Big Break*, about a doctor sent to prison on a murder charge. Inside, he performs an operation on a fellow inmate which leads to his release. Then Goodis worked uncredited on *Backfire*, directed by Vincent Sherman with Edmund O'Brien, Ed Begley and Virginia Mayo. In April and May 1948, Goodis wrote eleven treatments for Warner Brothers, all of them for Lou Edelman's *Of Missing Persons*. In June, Goodis would take two weeks out to turn the treatments into a novel that would be published by Morrow.

During this time, Goodis liked playing the role of town eccentric. Despite his salary, he had quit his hotel and moved in with his old Philadelphia friend, the lawyer Allan Norkin, renting his sofa for $4 a week. Norkin was married to Ruth, the great love of Goodis's life. It could be said that Goodis's attraction to Ruth and Elaine – apparent opposites – mirrors, to a degree, the situation found in his novels, where the protagonist is torn between two women, one voluptuous and devouring like Elaine, the other vulnerable and unattainable. Ruth would eventually divorce Norkin, only to marry another Philadelphian, Paul Wendkos, who would direct Goodis's *The Burglar.*

While other screenwriters gravitated towards Cadillacs or sports cars, Goodis owned a battered Chrysler, a vehicle that would end up in Edwin Gilbert's Hollywood novel *The Squirrel Cage* ('The canvas top was studded with big patches, one of which dangled over the side. Other sections of the mangled top had small splotches that looked green and decayed. Only half of the front bumper remained.'). Some have a better recollection of the car than of the driver. And if clothes make the man, Goodis was definitely *unmade*, opting, as he did, for threadbare suits, which he dyed blue, and secondhand clothes – he had a weakness for shopping in surplus stores – in which he sewed fashionable labels. Despite his stinginess, Goodis would occasionally give his friends presents selected from catalogues from up-market jewellers and tailors. It was his way of demonstrating his sophistication and taste. Though he was apparently not sophisticated or tasteful enough to wash on a regular basis, nor deliver the goods when it came to his self-professed cooking prowess. When he finally got around to preparing a long-promised meal for Norkin, Goodis, his eccentricity and humour rising to the occasion, placed a lone Kaiser roll and a plate of assorted jelly beans in front of his famished friend.

At the cinema – his favourite film was Luis Buñuel's *L'Age d'or* – Goodis would insist on sitting in the balcony, where he would talk throughout the performance. On his way out of the theatre, to frighten friends, onlookers and theatre managers, he would take an intentional but fatal-looking dive down the stairs. This was on the same order of prank as stuffing the red paper found inside a pack of cigarettes up his nostrils to feign a nosebleed, or, at parties, wearing a turban and a bathrobe and passing himself off as a white Russian prince.

At Norkin's, Goodis sometimes received phone calls from starlets like Lizabeth Scott, Lauren Bacall and Ann Sheridan, requesting that he accompany them to various social functions. But Goodis insisted that Norkin tell them he was indisposed. For Goodis preferred spending his evenings going, as he put it, 'to the Congo', by which he meant driving to South Central LA, where he would frequent clubs and dance halls and seek out large African-American women, whom he paid to abuse him verbally and sexually.

To locate these venues, Goodis would peruse the Communist Party journal, the *Daily Worker*. In South Central, Goodis would have heard a cross-section of jazz musicians – Duke Ellington, Charlie Parker, Count Basie – who were playing in the area at the time, whether at dances, regularly held at the Vogue Ballroom or the Shrine Auditorium, or clubs like the Chicken Shack and the Club Alabam.

Though a reputed jazz fan, Goodis, in fact, preferred classical music, particularly Sibelius and Bruckner. But he also knew Basie's music, which plays an important role in *Dark Passage* – Parry thumbs through Irene's 78s, finding such sides as 'Texas Shuffle', 'Lester Leaps In', 'Every Tub', establishing the atmosphere and common ground between the couple. Surprising, given his concern with style, Goodis preferred the Basie band featuring the solid Texas saxophonist Hershel Evans, rather than the more influential, avant-garde and mellow-toned Lester Young.

Despite a photograph showing him playing the piano, Goodis was not very adept on the ivories. Though he did teach himself the first bars of a Shostakovich piano concerto, which he would play at parties, invariably stopping after the first few measures, whereupon he would wait for his fellow revellers to urge him on, only to indicate that he was too sensitive to finish the piece. Complementing this soft-guy approach, Goodis liked frequenting bullfights in Tijuana and boxing matches at the Hollywood Legion Stadium and the Olympic Auditorium, followed by a late-night meal either at Du-Par's, a cheap but popular restaurant in the area, or at a rib joint in Watts, where he could eat barbecue ribs and sweet-potato pie.

While working on a typewriter he had owned since his teenage years in Philadelphia, Goodis chain-smoked and consumed mint pastilles. One day he entered Norkin's house and announced that the price of mints had gone up to six cents a pack. But it was an argument over sofa rent money that led Goodis to take up residence in the Hollywood Tower on Franklin, the street where Chandler had placed Philip Marlowe's residence.

Despite his new address, socialising with movie people at watering holes like Musso and Frank's held little attraction for Goodis. Likewise, conversations about books and writers. Though he did make an exception in an interview following the screen adaptation of *Dark Passage*, when he confessed his admiration for Steinbeck, Wolfe and Hemingway. However, he was quick to point out that it was the social importance of these writers, rather than their literary talent, that he found commendable. Less reserved would be Goodis's later praise for Henry Miller. One might be excused for thinking his adulation was meant merely to shock; after all, some, at the time, considered the author of *The Tropic of Cancer* barely more than a pornographer. But Goodis appreciated Miller enough to make a pilgrimage to Big Sur to visit the writer, who would entertain visitors while ensconced in his outdoor bathtub. Goodis claimed to have got on well with Miller. In turn, Miller wrote a blurb for the cover of the Grove Press edition of *Shoot the Piano Player*.

Goodis was obsessed by an imagined resemblance to Tyrone Power. Although he had been classified 4-F (disqualified from military service for medical reasons), he liked to tell women about his war experiences, which turned out to be those of his faux lookalike in the film *The Sun Also Rises*. As for his politics, Goodis once told Philadelphia jazz musician and friend Dick Levy that he 'couldn't understand a world that tolerated racism; a world like that doesn't have a future'. According to Levy, when he spoke to Philippe Garnier, 'It was the only time . . . I saw him serious.' Though he chastised Goodis for not participating in the civil rights movement, Levy thought his friend, like Bogart in *Casablanca*, would at some point become political. But it never happened. 'He practised a personal politics,' said Levy, 'not social or political.' But this was the era of Norman Mailer's *The White Negro*, and the hip existential individualist who observes the culture from the outside but, more often than not, refrains from involving himself in it. Certainly this is the attitude and voice that Goodis assumes in his fiction. Despite his tendencies, Goodis, a creature of the 1950s, would be unable to make the transition to the more politically conscious 1960s.

Even though he was making $1,250 a week, Goodis's studio career was at an impasse. Though he had worked hard, Goodis had not exactly carved out a brilliant career. It was as though Goodis's goal had been to become another second-rate screenwriter, indistinguishable from scores of others who dotted the studio landscape. So in 1950, aged thirty-two, Goodis quit Hollywood. His departure coincided with the end of his career, if not as a scriptwriter, then certainly as a mainstream hard-cover novelist. While living and working in Tinseltown – a period of eight years – Goodis had published three novels. After his departure, he would enter the world of pulp culture with a vengeance, writing classics like *Of Missing Persons, Cassidy's Girl, Of Tender Sin, Street of the Lost, The Burglar, The Moon in the Gutter, Black Friday, Street of No Return, The Blonde on the Street Corner, The Wounded and the Slain* and *Fire in the Flesh*. Suddenly Goodis was a down-in-the-dirt writer of paperback fiction, whose work bore the imprint of lowbrow companies like Lion and Gold Medal.

Returning to Philadelphia, Goodis moved back to the family home, sharing it with his ageing parents and mentally retarded brother. He had the occasional girlfriend and managed to travel to the Caribbean as well as to the more accessible Atlantic City. After his initial run of novels, including *Cassidy's Girl*, which sold millions of copies, Goodis's output would tail off. In the last ten years of his life, he was able to complete only a 1963 teleplay for *The Alfred Hitchcock Hour*, entitled 'An Out for Oscar', and arguably inferior novels like *Night Squad* (1961), *Raving Beauty* (1966) and the posthumous *Somebody's Done For* (1967).

His meagre output during those years might have been a case of writer's burnout. But he was also spending inordinate amounts of time and energy caring for his brother and ailing parents, as well as pursuing his long-running lawsuit against ABC-TV. Up to the time of his death, Goodis maintained that the idea for *The Fugitive*, which had recently hit the nation's television screens, had been plagiarised from *Dark Passage*. It was an accusation that Goodis would have found difficult to prove, since it is now common knowledge that the TV programme was based on a true case. At the same time, however, the idea that it would make a successful TV programme might well have been based on the success of Goodis's novel or its screen adaptation.

After the death of his parents, Goodis placed his brother in a home. In 1966, with the strain getting the better of him, Goodis admitted himself to a psychiatric hospital, where he probably received electroshock treatment. The following year, at the age of forty-nine, he suffered a brain haemorrhage and died in the Albert Einstein Medical Center, leaving behind a series of pulp paperback classics, none of which was in print at the time of his death.

One would have thought that directors would still be falling over one another to put Goodis's work on the screen. But, as of this writing, there have been no Goodis adaptations since 1989. Before that there had been many: Delmer Daves's 1947 *Dark Passage*; Pierre Chenal's 1956 *Section des disparus*, based on Goodis's *Of Missing Persons*; the same year, Jacques

Tourneur's *Nightfall*, starring Aldo Ray, Brian Keith and Anne Bancroft; and Paul Wendkos's 1957 *The Burglar*, a poetic if self-conscious portrayal of a desperate group of criminals, starring Dan Duryea and Jayne Mansfield.

Of course, the film that gained Goodis the greatest amount of notoriety was François Truffaut's 1960 *nouvelle vague* classic, *Tirez sur le pianiste*, based on the novel *Down There*. (The novel was retitled *Shoot the Piano Player* by Grove Press to coincide with the American success of Truffaut's film.) Truffaut said he made the film because he felt that Goodis's novel encapsulated the poetic spirit of Série Noire – the black and yellow series of mostly American hardboiled paperbacks published in France. At the time of the film's release, Goodis had already become reticent regarding public attention. When, in New York for the première of Truffaut's film, the media sought to interview him, Goodis disliked fielding questions so much that he decided to take the earliest possible train back to Philadelphia.

Starring Charles Aznavour, *Tirez sur le pianiste* was the last Goodis adaptation to be made in the author's lifetime. But Goodismania would not hit its apogee until the 1980s. After Henri Verneuil's *Le Casse*, a 1971 French-Italian remake of *The Burglar*, starring Omar Sharif and Jean-Paul Belmondo, and René Clément's 1972 *La Course du lièvre à travers les champs*, based on *Black Friday, Raving Beauty* and *Somebody's Done For*, starring Robert Ryan and Jean-Louis Trintignant, there would be Jean-Jacques Beineix's *The Moon in the Gutter* (1983); Gilles Béhat's *Rue Barbare* (1983), based on *Street of the Lost*; Francis Girod's *Descente aux enfers* (1986), based on *The Wounded and the Slain*, starring Claude Brasseur and a young Sophie Marceau; and Samuel Fuller's adaptation of *Street of No Return*, a French-Portuguese production starring Keith Carradine.

In 1956 Goodis would briefly return to the world of film to work with Paul Wendkos on an adaptation of his novel *The Burglar*. Wendkos, who had known Goodis in Philadelphia, considered himself a director of art films. Unfortunately, he was to fulfil neither his ambition nor his potential. Beginning as a documentary film-maker for the State Department, Wendkos ended up working for television, cranking out episodes of *Dr. Kildare*, *Mr. Novack*, *Naked City* and, ironically, *The Fugitive*. Prior to his small-screen career, Wendkos directed not only *The Burglar* but also the underrated *Angel Baby*, a 1960 low-budget effort that rode the coattails of Richard Brooks's arguably inferior *Elmer Gantry*, released to much acclaim earlier that year. Grittier and more evocative, *Angel Baby* is the story of a mute girl, played by Salome Jens, who renounces her sins after evangelist George Hamilton restores her power of speech. It also features the weirdly marvellous Mercedes McCambridge (Joan Crawford's twisted *alter ego* in *Johnny Guitar*), Joan Blondell and a young Burt Reynolds.

Not only was *The Burglar* written and directed by Philadelphians, and for much of the film shot in Philadelphia, but it was financed by a Philadelphia advertising merchant. Even the overblown music was performed by the Philadelphia Symphony Orchestra. Influenced by Orson Welles's *The Lady from Shanghai*, *The Burglar*, with its self-conscious close-ups and a convincing script, comes close to capturing Goodis's fatalistic world. In an interview with Garnier, Wendkos called the film 'experimental, ambitious and complicated to make'. Perhaps that was because some 150,000 feet of film had been shot, which meant that it would take a year to edit. After seeing the film, Columbia's Harry Cohn was impressed enough to bring Wendkos to California and put him under contract, where, for the burgeoning teen market, he would make a trio of *Gidget* films, as well as *Guns of the Magnificent Seven* (1969). He did try to redeem himself in 1971 when, aided by Ben Maddow's script, he directed a watchable but contrived piece of middle-class horror, *The Mephisto Waltz*.

For hard-core film noir enthusiasts, two Goodis adaptations stand out: *Dark Passage* and *Nightfall*. While the latter best captures Goodis's tone and atmosphere, the former is the film noir most associated with Goodis, memorable not just for Bogart's performance but for its use of the subjective camera which, for the first third of the film, requires that viewer see the world through Bogart's eyes. The technique relates to the main problem regarding the novel's adaptation: namely, that the lead actor, Bogart, must acquire a new face after undergoing plastic surgery at the end of the first act.

Jerry Wald would maintain that it was his idea to use a subjective camera in *Dark Passage*. Certainly, Wald was responsible for paying a substantial amount of money for a novel by a relatively unknown author. Immortalised as Sammy Glick in Budd Schulberg's *What Makes Sammy Run*, Wald, often an intermediary between directors and studio bosses, fought to get *Dark Passage* onto the screen. This was not unusual, for Wald, once bitten, would push hard to get a project realised. He wielded so much power that Goodis called him 'The Great White Father'.

Dark Passage was to rekindle the Bogart–Bacall spark of *To Have and Have Not* and *The Big Sleep*. However, Jack Warner was not all that enthusiastic about the project. Nor was he interested in using a camera technique that had just been deployed by Robert Montgomery in *Lady in the Lake*, on which Goodis had briefly worked. In fact, the two films were separated by only eight months. Shooting on Montgomery's film terminated on 5 July 1946, and MGM released it on 23 January 1947. The filming of *Dark Passage* concluded seven days later, on 30 January, and it was released nine months later, in September 1947.

What was it about the subjective camera that attracted Montgomery, Wald and Daves? Beyond concealing the visage of the film's star, the technique could have denoted a particular postwar malaise: an example of existentialism hitherto unseen in Hollywood, in which existence – the eye of the camera – precedes essence – the unnatural objectivity of the camera eye. Or it could simply have been a technique that approximated a first-person narrative. If the latter, it might have been more applicable to Chandler, who at least was an authentic first-person writer, than Goodis, who wrote, more often than not, in the third person. Meanwhile, according to Jon Tuska in *The Detective in Hollywood*, it was Montgomery who had first sought to use the subjective camera for a proposed adaptation of John Galsworthy's story, 'Escape', about a convict on the run, but the studio rejected the idea, offering Chandler's novel in its place. Yet Daves, who would be the one who ended up making a film about a convict on the run, always claimed that he had given the subjective camera idea to Montgomery. Wald's input notwithstanding, it might even have been that Jack Warner, having heard about Montgomery's plan, did not want to be outdone by his arch rival Louis B. Mayer.

In making *Dark Passage*, Daves shot some 7,200 feet of film, making the editing a time-consuming and complicated process. Certainly, editor David Weisbart should be given partial credit for the film's success. In an interview in the New York *Sun* to coincide with the film's release, Goodis declared himself reasonably satisfied with the finished product, though he said he would have liked to have adapted the film himself. His sole criticism was that Daves, who wrote the screenplay, had stuck *too* close to the novel. Said Goodis, 'I am not Dashiell Hammett, and *Dark Passage* is far from being *The Maltese Falcon*, which in my opinion is the best melodrama ever made in Hollywood.' In a rare moment of public introspection, Goodis went on to say that he had not been more successful in Hollywood because 'I spent several years writing for the pulps and for radio serials and I'm afraid that the things in my scripts are too simple. When one writes for the radio, it is necessary to constantly explain things, because there isn't any visual support. When you write for the pulps you acquire other bad habits: staying too long with a particular person, confining oneself to him, telling the story from his point of view. It is difficult to write subjectively, and finally it is very constraining.'

Jacques Tourneur's 1956 *Nightfall* is the other noteworthy

film noir adapted from a Goodis novel. Not that Goodis had any input on the project. Instead it was scripted by Stirling Silliphant, who, along with Reginald Rose, was one of the few writers in Hollywood to move comfortably between film and television. Writing episodes of *Route 66*, *Naked City* and *Perry Mason*, Silliphant's scripts would kick-start the careers of directors like Sam Peckinpah, who started out in television. Silliphant was able to make Goodis's novel cinematically realisable by changing certain scenes, yet retaining the book's sense of voyeurism and unease. Released a year after *The Burglar*, *Nightfall* is not only less contrived, but looks like it could have been made ten years earlier, around the time of Tourneur's *Out of the Past* (1947), with which it is often compared. While *Nightfall* centres on a protagonist, Vanning, who lurks in the shadows, *Out of the Past* focuses on Bailey, who toils in the outdoor light of a Hopperesque rural service station. Unlike Robert Mitchum's Bailey, Aldo Ray's Vanning is innocent in every sense of the word. The latter's paranoia, caused by the possibility that he might have been responsible for the doctor's death, makes *Nightfall* the more deterministic film. Unlike most film noir, the mean streets, rather than representing danger, offer Vanning a degree of protection, while the snow-covered Sierras become for him an infinitely more perilous landscape.

Excellent though they might be, neither *Nightfall* nor *The Burglar* totally succeeds in translating Goodis's sense of doom to the screen, nor gives one the feeling that their fictional representations inhabit a landscape both fanciful and real. While the two films border on the operatic, the novels are populated by simulations of those portraying their screen equivalents, their gestures dictated by malcontent, abuse and the history of noir literature and film.

At least Wald recognised Goodis's talent. Goodis realised this, and in 1947, three years before quitting Hollywood, he felt confident enough to send Wald a thirty-eight-page memo outlining his plan for a screenplay about America's entry into the atomic era, entitled *Up Till Now*. In the memo, Goodis informed Wald that he envisioned the film taking place in Philadelphia, that it would be a broad-canvassed project depicting American society, an uplifting film with a positive message. The story was to centre on a young man confronted with insurmountable obstacles, who finds the solution to his problems in the guise of a woman. Though bordering on the bathetic, and expressing ideas worthy of Barton Fink, Goodis's memo went on to say that the film's narrative would be told in a stream-of-consciousness style, with flashbacks that would not necessarily follow a linear progression.

Given Goodis's sense of humour, one might be forgiven for thinking *Up Till Now* a joke, the butt of which was Wald. Though it is more likely that, having become entangled in the dream factory, Goodis decided to go for broke and reveal his more serious, if sentimental, side. At any rate, Wald took the project seriously, suggesting that John Garfield might star in the film, or even Ronald Reagan. Three months before the scheduled shoot and six months before the project was finally abandoned, Wald said in an interview that he was going to make a film about the way democracy had overwhelmed communism and fascism. He insisted that it would encapsulate an era. Though, in the proposed film, now said to star Jane Wyman, Claude Rains and Broderick Crawford, the young protagonist is initially fed up with democracy, it was democracy that would triumph in the end. Wald was so taken with the idea that he, in turn, deluged Goodis with his own memos. By the end of 1947 Goodis was making $1,000 a week, and had written several versions of the script.

By the end of 1948, however, Goodis would no longer be connected with the project. Wald was now searching for a screenwriter with a more relevant track record, like Arthur Miller, Abe Polonsky or Lillian Hellman. But he must also have realised that it was not the most propitious moment to make the film. With McCarthyism in full stride, any talk about communism, or even liberal democratic ideals, had become suspect. Besides, Jack Warner, who had never been convinced of the project, was about to testify before the House Un-American Activities Committee. 'Combining good picture-making with good citizenship' was his studio's new motto. And Warner, who had once been the most progressive of moguls, did not want to leave himself open to any criticism. In fact, he had always moved in whatever direction the wind happened to be blowing. Upon America's entry into the war, he became, at his own behest, an army lieutenant-general in charge of Los Angeles public relations. After getting a well-known Hollywood tailor to fit him for a uniform, which he wore for the duration of the war, he insisted that others address him as 'General', even though his claim to the title was, at best, tenuous. When Warner appeared in front of the Committee, a young California Congressman, Richard Nixon, asked if he was making any anti-communist films comparable to the anti-Nazi films of the early war years. The only film Warner could come up with was *Up Till Now.* Needless to say, Nixon was not satisfied. Was *Up Till Now* really to have been an anti-communist film? Or was that merely Warner's fantasy? Whatever, the film remained one of Wald's unfulfilled dreams, and a project about which he was still speaking in the mid-1950s. As for Goodis, he revived the story to some extent, albeit on a reduced canvas, in his 1954 novel *The Blonde on the Street Corner.*

According to Wendkos, Goodis's problem was that he could not take Hollywood seriously. While the director considered him 'one of the most eccentric people I've ever known', he was nevertheless astonished that Warner Brothers did not have a higher opinion of him. As for his reputation in France, Wendkos believed that it was due to Goodis's 'melancholy existentialism', comprising 'An attitude stripped of all judgment toward people touched by destiny in a way that overcomes them completely, but who nevertheless do not lose their dignity, or certain ethical values, or their capacity to feel things'. More to the point, Wendkos pointed out that Goodis's characters 'never lose their humanity, even if they seem always superficially consumed by despair . . . It's a sensibility all but incomprehensible to Americans, who are forever consumed by optimism . . . I wonder if David didn't write these things completely unconsciously; I am certain that he never thought in such terms.'

Since Sam Fuller's 1989 film *Street of No Return* – a homage to his friend – the heat has gone out of the Goodis revival. Could it be that Goodis's stevedores, bus drivers, cheap crooks, waifs and devouring women had, by the end of the 1980s, reached their sell-by date, replaced by narratives and protagonists more extreme and warped than Goodis could have imagined? Or perhaps Goodis's characters and plots are too romantic for contemporary audiences. With a thin line separating parody, pastiche and poetry, producers and directors no longer seem so eager to investigate Goodis's downbeat urban opera.

In the end, Goodis was too much an outsider to make it in Hollywood. Though he loved the romance of film, he had little time for the unsavoury aspects of the industry. Besides, his talent lay not in screenplays, but in a type of fiction that, as Wendkos said, most Americans find difficult to appreciate. Maybe Tinseltown drove Goodis back to Philadelphia, maybe he wanted to return to his family, or maybe he simply wanted to concentrate on writing fiction. Unlike other Hollywood refugees, Goodis, once he managed to extricate himself, was for a short period able to produce some of his best work. At the same time, perhaps Hollywood provided him with a visual sense that helped him write those novels, many of which, despite their simplicity, remain beyond Hollywood's ability to fully exploit.

Unable to hustle themselves and their work sufficiently, Goodis and Thompson had only their writing to trade on. Of course, Goodis deluded himself and others into thinking he was a mere hack, but one realises from reading him that this was just a means of protecting himself against failure. He wanted to give the impression that he was churning out stories on the cheap, and when he wrote for the pulps he had been doing just that. However, he and Thompson were to pay a price for their various delusions. Finding the collaboration process difficult, neither could tolerate the way studios – unable to understand their work or way of looking at the world – patronised them. For both writers, Hollywood was more a prison sentence than a way of freeing them from the exigencies that the obsession of writing demands.

6

IN THE THIEVES' MARKET

**A.I. Bezzerides, Daniel Mainwaring, Jonathan Latimer,
Leigh Brackett**

The attitude of some writers regarding Hollywood was so
professional that they willingly abandoned, permanently in
some cases, their careers as novelists. This they had to do if
they were to succeed in what was becoming an increasingly
competitive field. In 1946, the year that saw the publication
of Daniel Mainwaring's *Build My Gallows High* and the
release of *The Big Sleep* with a script by Leigh Brackett and
William Faulkner, there were some 1,200 writers attached to
Hollywood studios. But out of these only 350 were employed
throughout the year. The rest were part-timers or not working
at all. To make matters even more difficult, there was the
amorphous 'morality clause', which gave studios the right to
terminate a writer's contract on the flimsiest of grounds. The
likes of Mainwaring, Brackett, A.I. Bezzerides and Jonathan
Latimer worked hard to respond to the demands of the
market, and an industry powerful enough to form and
manipulate public opinion. In 1945, 95 million went to the
movies each week compared to 18 million who attended
weekly church services and 19 million who went to public
school each day. Because of their attitude, the following
writers, exploited though they might have been, would not
only flourish in Hollywood but would refuse to be destroyed
by their experience.

A.I. 'Buzz' Bezzerides

With its hardboiled dialogue, tough-guy violence and helter-skelter atmosphere, Robert Aldrich's 1955 adaption of Mickey Spillane's novel *Kiss Me Deadly* has been called 'the apotheosis' of the classic noir style by film encyclopaedist Steven H. Scheuer. Nicholas Christopher, author of *Somewhere in the Night*, believes it to be 'perhaps the most perfectly realized film noir ever made'. However highly critics rate it, most agree that the real genius behind the film is not Spillane but writer A.I. Bezzerides, whose screenplay, combined with Aldrich's oeuvre, drags Spillane's novel and film noir as a genre kicking and screaming into the post-McCarthy era.

Spillane has gone on record about how much he dislikes Bezzerides's script. And no wonder. For Bezzerides, who trained as a communications engineer, disassembles the novel, only to put it back together as an instrument of subversion rather than, as Spillane intended, a reductionist artefact supporting the dubious values of 1950s America.

After reading the novel Bezzerides told the director, 'This is lousy. Let me see what I can do with it.' Three weeks later the script was finished. Bezzerides said to Lee Server in the mid-1980s, 'I wrote it fast because I had contempt for it. It was automatic writing. You get into a kind of stream and you can't stop.' Obviously he enjoyed the task. For Bezzerides puts macho tough-guy Mike Hammer through the wringer, making him chase the 'Great Whatsit' – not money or drugs as in the novel, but an atomic Pandora's Box – and, in doing so, turns Spillane's novel into a warped quest that ends in nuclear oblivion.

Yet Bezzerides makes no great claim regarding the film's relationship to McCarthyism and the atomic bomb, saying, 'I didn't think about it when I wrote it. These things were in the air at the time . . . I was having fun with it. I wanted to make every scene, every character, interesting.' Accordingly, Bezzerides populates his adaptation with an assortment of corrupt and crazy characters, including a dim-witted murderess, a scientist who cannot stop talking about ancient myths, a thieving autopsy surgeon, an escaped lunatic and a nymphomaniac ('Whatever it is, the answer's yes'). So well organised is Bezzerides's script that Aldrich was able to shoot the film in three weeks.

So who is A.I. Bezzerides? He was born in 1908 in Turkey. His parents – an Armenian mother and a Turkish-speaking Greek father – moved to Fresno, California, while Albert Issok – later to be known as Al or 'Buzz' – was an infant. Influenced by Chekhov, Dostoevsky, Isaac Babel and, later, Sherwood Anderson, Bezzerides began writing while studying communications engineering at the University of California at Berkeley. Like fellow Armenian and childhood acquaintance William Saroyan, Bezzerides would be drawn to writing about first-generation families eking out a living in the fields and towns of Central California.

After a string of jobs in the communications industry, Bezzerides found employment as a researcher at the Department of Water and Power in Los Angeles. While there he wrote and published his first novel, *The Long Haul*, better known as *They Drive by Night*. Eventually, Bezzerides would go on to publish two other excellent novels: *There Is a Happy Land* and *Thieves' Market*. The former is the story of an indolent and irresponsible Okie who, along with his wife and children, moves in on a respectable farming family in the San Joaquin Valley. *There Is a Happy Land* was published by Henry Holt in 1942, after Bezzerides's career as a screenwriter was well established, and has been out of print for many years – a copy will currently set you back something like $450. Like Tom Kromer's *Waiting for Nothing*, it has become a forgotten Depression classic.

Better known are Bezzerides's trucker-noir novels, *The Long Haul*, first published in 1938 by Carrick & Evans, and *Thieves' Market*, published in 1949 by Scribner. Both are based on personal experience and stories heard from his father about independent truckers and their life on the road, or in the fields, packing houses, and markets of Stockton, Oakland and San Francisco, where, according to Bezzerides, cheating and brutality were a regular occurrence. Some of these sites are shown on the back cover of a 1950 Dell paperback edition of *They Drive by Night*, as it became known after the film's release. Below the heading WHERE WILDCAT TRUCKERS FIGHT THE LONG HIGHWAYS is a map – typical of Dell paperbacks during the era – on which the journey of the book's protagonist along Highway 99, from Holland's Summit Cafe in the Tejon Pass to Red Bluff in Northern California, can be traced. Four decades later, Bezzerides would link those early experiences to *Kiss Me Deadly*'s hardboiled perspective, saying, 'When I saw what the produce dealers did, and what the engineers with their swindle sheets were doing, I knew that the world was going to end.'

Both novels would be snatched up and, in Bezzerides's opinion, ruined by Hollywood. *The Long Haul* would be adapted for the screen by Warner Brothers in 1940 under the title *They Drive by Night*. Directed by Raoul Walsh, it stars George Raft and Humphrey Bogart. At least Bezzerides was allowed to write the screenplay for *Thieves' Market*, which would be purchased by Twentieth Century Fox in 1949 and renamed *Thieves' Highway*. Directed by Jules Dassin, the film stars Richard Conte and Lee J. Cobb.

Bezzerides is right: neither film does its novel justice. Yet both films, however flawed, have much to offer and, like a handful of other films during the 1940s, come as close as Hollywood would dare to a proletarian cinema. This was an era just prior to the hysteria engendered by McCarthyism, which would affect Bezzerides as it did so many others. Though a member of the leftwing Writers Guild, Bezzerides, unlike many of his friends, never joined the Communist Party – probably for the simple reason that he was too independent and unable to follow anyone's party line. Nevertheless, he taught writing at the Little Red Schoolhouse, where many communists worked, and because of this his name was temporarily placed on the blacklist.

Bezzerides has a low opinion of producers – 'the goddamnedest crooks you ever saw' – from having experienced a veritable catalogue of movie rip-offs. For example, shortly after *The Long Haul* was published, an agent phoned and asked if he'd be interested in selling the novel to Warner Brothers, saying he'd be able to get $1,500 for it. When Bezzerides balked at the figure, the agent said, 'We'll see if we can get more.' He phoned back and said the studio was willing to go up to $2,500. Bezzerides reluctantly agreed to the offer. When he went to the studio he noticed on Jack Warner's desk a copy of a script adapted from his novel by Jerry Wald. The story goes that George Raft had gained too much weight to make his next film, which was supposed to be a boxing movie. To keep him at the studio, Warner Brothers decided that *The Long Haul* would be perfect for him. Later, when Bezzerides told another studio writer about what had happened, the latter said, 'You could have asked for $100,000 and they would have given it to you.' In the end, Bezzerides received $2,000, while George Raft was paid $55,000, Bogart $11,200, screenwriter Jerry Wald $11,167, and director Raoul Walsh $17,500.

By the time *Thieves' Market* was published in 1949, Bezzerides was a highly paid freelance scriptwriter who had already worked for most of the major studios, including five years at Warner Brothers. The latter had offered Bezzerides $100,000 for the rights to *Thieves' Market*, but his agent had already agreed to sell it to Twentieth Century Fox for $80,000, still a substantial amount of money in 1949. In the end, Bezzerides was less than satisfied with the film. For one thing, Fox decided not to use the original title because 'San Francisco objects to it' – whether that means San Francisco's city fathers or the unions is unclear. Then Dassin insisted on casting his then girlfriend, Valentina Cortese, as the prostitute, a role that Bezzerides felt would be perfect for an actress like Shelley

Winters. Worst of all, the studio altered the story. In the novel, the father is dead from the outset. To validate his father's life, the kid decides to take up trucking. But executive producer Darryl Zanuck insisted that in the film the father should be alive, albeit crippled, and the young protagonist motivated by his father's inability to work.

Bezzerides ended up writing some fifteen screenplays and numerous television dramas. His first screen credit was Curtis Bernhardt's 1942 *Juke Girl*, starring Ann Sheridan and Ronald Reagan, in which the latter, still a real-life liberal, plays a Florida drifter who sides with striking growers against packing-plant owner Gene Lockhart. In a scene that prefigures the truck crash in Dassin's *Thieves' Highway*, Bezzerides represents wasted labour and the savagery of capitalism in *Juke Girl* by depicting packing-plant scabs in the act of destroying tons of tomatoes. But the film is not without its faults, owing, to some extent, to the strained relationship between Bezzerides and co-writer Ken Gamet, who found it hard to accept that his inexperienced writing partner not only knew about the world of itinerant crop pickers but could write realistically about it. After *Juke Girl*, Bezzerides went on to write *Action in the North Atlantic* (1943) and *Desert Fury* (1947), as well as *Thieves Highway* (1949); Nicholas Ray's 1951 noir classic, *On Dangerous Ground* (another example of Bezzerides's fascination with the psychology of male violence); Bernhardt's 1951 *Sirocco* at Columbia; Gerald Mayer's 1952 *Holiday for Sinners* at Metro (which, like *On Dangerous Ground*, was produced by John Houseman); Robert Webb's 1953 *Beneath the 12-Mile Reef* at Twentieth Century Fox; William Wellman's 1954 *Track of the Cat* at Warner Brothers (Bezzerides always regretted that Wellman did not allow him to make some vital changes in the script); Lewis Allen's 1955 *A Bullet for Joey* at United Artists; Robert Aldrich's 1959 *The Angry Hills* at MGM; and Melvin Frank's 1959 *The Jayhawkers* at Paramount. His television work included episodes of *Sunset Strip, Wells Fargo, The Virginian, Rawhide, Bonanza* and *DuPont Theater*. He also worked uncredited on a number of films, including André de Toth's *Slattery's Hurricane* (1949). What typifies Bezzerides's various contributions is his ability, despite working in the impersonal world of Hollywood, to put his individual stamp on a screenplay.

In the mid-1960s Bezzerides was responsible for creating *The Big Valley*, a TV series, meant to be an antidote to *Bonanza*, about immigrant families in Central Valley. It proved one of the most popular syndicated programmes of the era, yet those producing it made sure that it never showed a profit on paper, thus denying Bezzerides a share in its four-year run. Its star, Barbara Stanwyck, sued for her portion of the profits, but Bezzerides hadn't the means to follow her example, and had to settle out of court for a fraction of what should have been coming to him.

While working at the studios during the war, Bezzerides befriended William Faulkner. Bezzerides was to say of Faulkner, 'The screenplay form was alien to him.' Fifty years later, anecdotes about their relationship would figure in the Coen brothers' film *Barton Fink*. While the writer in that film, played by John Turturro, was based primarily on Clifford Odets, one might be excused for thinking that the film's portrayal of the relationship between Barton and the Faulkner-like southern writer might have been based on John Fante's, as much as on Bezzerides's, friendship with the notorious southerner. In fact, Fante and Bezzerides were something of a double act, their friendship having been established in 1939 when the young wannabe writer Fante walked by Stanley Rose's Hollywood bookstore and saw Bezzerides staring at his newly published book, *The Long Haul*, which was on display in the window. According to Bezzerides, Fante noticed the author's photograph on the book jacket and asked how much of an advance he had received. When Bezzerides told him, Fante asked if he would loan him the money. A trusting and generous person, Bezzerides claims to have surprised Fante by signing over the cheque to him. Apocryphal, perhaps, but an often-cited incident. Stephen Cooper, for instance, in his biography of Fante, *Full of Life*, claims that 'the silver-tongued Fante talked Bezzerides into loaning him his publisher's advance'. A year after the incident, Fante, in a letter to his mother, would write that he and Bezzerides were working on a story that they hoped to sell to one of the studios. It was about farming. Says Bezzerides, 'It would have made a hell of a picture.'

In the early 1950s Bezzerides met, and soon married, Silvia Richards, who had worked alongside King Vidor and Fritz Lang and written such screenplays as *Possessed, Ruby Gentry* and *Rancho Notorious*, and who had, for a time, been Lang's mistress. Before meeting Bezzerides, Silvia had been married to Robert L. Richards, writer of a handful of films including Fred Zinnemann's 1949 *Act of Violence*. According to Philippe Garnier, Silvia, after an acrimonious separation, appeared before the House Un-American Activities Committee and named, among others, her ex-husband. Silvia, like many other Hollywood personalities, was seeing Tinseltown shrink Phil Cohen, who at the time was advising his patients to comply with the HUAC, and allegedly gave information to the FBI. Blacklisted, Robert Richards, like writers such as Alvah Bessie and John Bright, and director Cy Endfield, found work with ex-Bowery boy Hal E. Chester on a series of Joe Palooka films. Sadly, Silvia died in 1999, after suffering from Alzheimer's for a number of years.

These days, Bezzerides, cantankerous as ever, is still writing. Among his plans is a book concerning the various swindles he has witnessed over the years, a book 'that will point like a long finger toward the sky-scratching high-rises that cluster in the hearts of all big cities . . . in the world, towers destined to metamorphose into tombstones that will mark the end of MAN-CONCOCTED CIVILISATION'. An interesting prospect from a formidable writer who sacrificed his career as a novelist for the glitter and gold of Hollywood.

WH: How did Thieves' Market *come about?*

AB: The idea of *Thieves' Market* was that you would haul produce to San Francisco and get gypped by produce thieves who would take it on assignment and sell it for a lot of money, telling you that they hadn't. They did that to my father several times. They did it to me. The guy who did it used his sense of humour and friendliness to cover up what he was doing. I got so angry that I got a whole truckload of empty boxes, took them back to Fresno and went to an orange-packing house. I said, 'Do you have any oranges that are on the verge of rotting?' 'Oh, yeah,' he said, 'I've got around four hundred boxes of them.' They *looked* perfect. 'But,' he said, 'in four days they're going to go.' I said, 'I want to buy those.' He said, 'You do? Why?' I said, 'I got to get even with a guy.' He said, 'When you get near San Francisco, go through the boxes and throw out the ones that are rotting.' So, along with my brother, we changed the four hundred boxes to three hundred boxes and I delivered them, and they were beautiful. This guy who had swindled me was delighted. Boy, was he going to give me a grand fucking! I unloaded them and drove away as fast as I could. When I finally went back, he said, 'Well, you got me, didn't you?' He wasn't angry. Yeah, I got him for a couple thousand dollars.

I didn't sell *Thieves' Market*. An agent sold it. She screwed me out of $20,000. She made a deal to sell it to Fox even though I got a $100,000 offer from Warner Brothers. They felt guilty because of what they did with *The Long Haul*. She said, 'Oh, no, I've already sold it.' 'What do you mean, you've already sold it? I got a $100,000 offer.' She said, 'Fox offered $80,000 and I accepted.' Well, she was trying to make a hit. Because Fox was thinking of doing the same thing that Warner Brothers did with my novel. See, I didn't write the screenplay to *They Drive By Night*. They stole it from the book.

WH: When did you first come across Faulkner?

AB: My first wife, Yvonne, gave me a copy of William Faulkner's book *As I Lay Dying*. First I was annoyed and threw the book away, but picked it up again because I wanted to know where it went. Then *The Sound and the Fury*. What a picture that could be! Then I found out that he'd written two books before that. Later, when I was working at Warner Brothers, the door opened and in an easy chair with his legs crossed was this little man. I went over and said, 'Bill! Remember me?' He said, 'I certainly do.' Because years before I had gone to a restaurant in Hollywood and Faulkner was there with a girl. He already had a job with a studio. The girl he was with was his secretary. He was very much in love with her, although he was married. He kept going home and coming back to her. But he never wrote pictures that were made. Although one director [*Howard Hawks*] was very fond of him and would use what he did. My wife and I saw him in this restaurant. I said, 'There's Faulkner!' I walked over to him and said, 'Mr. Faulkner!' And he said, 'Suh.' I said, 'I've read all your books, everything I could get my hands on, and I think you're a wonderful writer.' He said, 'Thank you, suh.' He got up and we shook hands. At that time I was working as an engineer. Then I'm at Warner Brothers and I said, 'Remember me?' And he said, 'I certainly do. Yes, suh.' I was just a beginning scriptwriter, but little by little we began to work together, and became very good friends. They had us polish a picture [*Escape in the Desert*]. But he couldn't write scripts. A script has limitations. You can't write three pages of endless dialogue and expect audiences to sit there on their asses listening to it. I'd read it and say, 'Bill, do it in three or four lines. Maybe ten, but not three pages.' He never could do it. It wasn't that he had an ego. His writing just couldn't be changed to the active writing that's required in making a picture. In a picture things have to happen. We had a scene in which a bunch of German prisoners were in a tent with a bunch of people they'd taken hold of, and they were going to butcher them all if they weren't shipped back to Germany. I thought of a scene where one of the guys sees a snake. And Faulkner was awed by what I'd done. They were going to shoot the film, but Jack Warner thought it would make pregnant women watching the film miscarry. In all the time I knew him, Faulkner never did a script. But Warner boasted, 'I've got the best writer in the world, and I pay him peanuts.'

WH: You also knew John Fante quite well, didn't you?

AB: Very well. *The Long Haul* had been sold and was in the goddamn bookstores. I'm standing there looking at it and thinking it's not selling and what the hell did I write that for, although I was working at the studio then. The guy standing next to me says, 'You wrote that, didn't you?' I guess my picture was on the book cover. I said, 'Yeah.' He said, 'Did you get much of an advance?' I said, 'Yes.' He said, 'How much?' I said, '$350.' He said, 'Can I borrow it?' I said, 'What for?' He said, 'I need some money. I'll pay it back.' I don't know why I did it. He had such a personality. A little fellow. Fierce. So I endorsed the cheque and gave it to him. Weeks went by and he never paid me back. He kept saying, 'Next week. Next week.' He was living out on Wilshire Boulevard in a big twenty-storey building. They were kicking him out of his place because he didn't have enough money to pay his rent. I went over there to see his wife. I knew that his wife had money. She said, 'I've heard about you.' I said, 'I loaned your husband $350.' She said, 'I gave him the money to pay you four different times.' She said, 'This time I'll give it to you.' She gave it to me, and when he heard about it later he was furious.

WH: He worked on a lot of pictures.

AB: He worked on a lot of pictures but with very little success. He was a wonderful writer. He knew about reality, but he couldn't do it in pictures. Those were two people I related to, and neither of them could write a script. But Faulkner admitted it. Fante didn't. We liked each other, yet we were always fighting like brothers. I saw him in the Motion Picture hospital with one leg cut off on the verge of dying. I said, 'John!' He'd gained weight because he couldn't exercise or anything. He was sitting there in the wheelchair. Then going to the hospital again, seeing my wife in a wheelchair, it was very upsetting, I can tell you.

WH: Do you wish you could have written more novels?

AB: Oh yeah. I remember this secretary – Jewish girl from New York – coming into the room with a sheaf of papers in her hand that I'd given her to type. She had a funny look on her face. I said, 'What's the matter? Can't you read what I wrote?' She said, 'No, before I type anything I read it first.' She said, 'You shouldn't be writing screenplays; you should be writing novels.' I said, 'You might be right, but books don't sell.' There's no guarantee that anything you write is going to be a best seller. But, when it comes to screenplays, there was a guarantee that I was going to make money. There was no point in writing books when I was making the money I was making. From forty dollars that I was making as a communications engineer with various companies, I went, as a screenwriter, from $300 up to a couple thousand dollars a week.

WH: So did you get involved in the Hollywood lifestyle?

AB: I was never really involved with Hollywood people. Because they were living in a world I didn't want to be in. So when a guy says he wants to do a film noir character, my nature is do what's real, to do reality. Scripts about trucking were about reality. Then my book *There is a Happy Land* was about reality. I think that's a helluva book. It's about Oklahomans. This guy is a real shit, because he's got a little boy. And his wife's got another child and it's a little girl. From that point on, he moves into an abandoned farm and begins to treat his family like a family. Because he looks at the girl and he knows that girl is going to be somebody's wife, like his wife is to him. That's all in that book. And no studio wanted to buy it. They weren't aware of what it was about. Now I want to do a book called *The Big Valley – A Century in Decades*, about what happened to the Big Valley. Because what happened to it is a tragedy, and now the same thing is happening throughout the world.

The Long Haul was my reality. The same with *Thieves' Market*. The odd thing is that when they gave me a job at Warners, because they had a guilty conscience about what they did with that script, I wrote *Juke Girl*. One of the goddamnedest pictures. Pure film noir! The story they gave me was about a farmer. I junked it. Some guy wrote to me and said I'd stolen his story. I said I didn't steal your story, I threw it away. Sue me! You can't sue me because I'm not writing your story any more. I wrote about what I knew. I knew about crop workers, and I did a lot of research. I saw this tiny beautiful girl playing the guitar and singing in a juke joint. So I called it *Juke Girl* and wrote a story about the crop workers. All I remember about that film is the girl.

WH: What was it like working with John Houseman?

AB: I did a lot of writing for him. And always got into trouble. I wrote a thing about a doctor who dies and his son takes over his father's practice [*Holiday for Sinners*]. In that film there was a punch-drunk fighter who keeps borrowing money from these gangsters. He's too punch-drunk to pay them back. He goes to a priest, a prostitute and a doctor for help. They all turn him down. They shoot him, and as he's laying on the ground dying, he looks up and sees all these people, and he says, 'Where were you? I've been looking for you.' Houseman thought the story was about a young doctor who took over his father's profession. But people came out after the preview and said they were more interested in the punch-drunk fighter. I had said that to begin with. I wasn't interested in the doctor story. I was more interested in the punch-drunk fighter story and how people won't help him. Houseman said, 'Do what you got!' I said, 'Well, I like to improve what I've got, if I can.' He said, 'Do what you got.' So I wrote it. Then this handful of opinions came from the theatres that had seen the preview. When the punch-drunk fighter was lying on the ground and said what he said, the audience just knew. When we came out of the place, and read what the audience had written, Houseman said, 'So how do we change it?' And I said, 'It's too late. John, it's too late. You have to shoot the whole picture all over again.'

WH: I've always liked On Dangerous Ground.

AB: Yeah, but look at that director, Nicolas Ray. He was very much involved with Houseman. I had a scene where they sent the tough cop out of town because he killed another prisoner. I liked that story – this boy has killed a girl – because the idea came, in a peculiar way, from an experience I'd had. There were two girls living right near this cheap house where we lived. They were doctor's daughters and they lived in a large house near the playground. I thought these two girls were wonderful. Well, these two girls were walking down the alley. I was in the alley and I knew they were going to be upset about me. Because they would run away every time they saw me. I decided I wasn't going to frighten them, so I went into the yard. They ran to their house, and then they were at the window looking out from behind the curtain to see if I was there. I looked over and there they were, ogling me. The boy in the film killed the girl because he couldn't talk to her. He says this to the cop, who suddenly understands. All the people the cop had killed had stories like he did. But this time he was hearing it from a kid. 'I didn't want to kill her,' said the kid. 'I was just hugging her. I didn't mean for her to get hurt. Why was she always running from me? When I let her go she was dead.' The cops says, 'When you tell that to the judge, he might listen to you. You might have to serve some kind of time, but it won't be bad; it'll be good, and you'll be able to think about what happened and why you did it.' So he's walking towards the boy and the boy's backing up. And there's a cliff. Four hundred feet down. He says, 'You're going to fall.' And, what do you know, the boy falls down the cliff. And the cop almost falls as well, because he's leaning over. Nick Ray changed it. He arranged a pile of rocks. And guess what? The boy climbs up to the top of the pile, and something happens and he slips back down to the vicious cop's feet. Stupid! They shot my scene. And Nick Ray didn't like it. And that shithead John Houseman listened to his fuckin' director instead of to the writer who thought of the story in the first place.

WH: And what about Kiss Me, Deadly?

AB: That's a hell of a picture. Though I thought it was shit. The book was shit. So I changed it. In the book, the locker in the Athletic Club had an open cardboard box with dope in envelopes in it. I didn't want that. In the fifties they were doing dope, but they were also doing something else. They were building shelters to protect people against nuclear devices. I looked at that scene and didn't know what to do. So I went to the Los Angeles Athletic Club to confront myself with these lockers. So I'm standing there and the guy gave me a key and he went with me and showed me an empty locker and I opened the door. I looked at the bottom and all that crap about nuclear devices came to me. And I looked down and I thought, there's one down there in a box. I mentally visualised an oak box with brass on the corners and a nice lock on it. I told the guy what I thought. He said, 'That's wonderful.'

In the book, there was a detective with a girlfriend who was his secretary, and he adored her. The girlfriend screwed husbands so the wives could get a divorce. The detective screwed wives so husbands could get a divorce. I thought that was shit. In the opening there was a girl in a raincoat who tried to get a ride in a car. That was done badly in the book. I'll tell you about distortions. Robert Aldrich who directed the film was dying in 1980 and he said, 'I got the script to *Kiss Me Deadly* out of the files.' I said, 'What do you want to read that damn thing for?' He said, 'It wasn't a "damn thing", it was a hell of script.' He said, 'I couldn't understand how I could direct it in twenty-one days.' That was fast, man. I didn't know that was remarkable, but when he said that I realised it was. I said, 'How could you direct it in twenty-one days?' He said in a kind of awed voice, 'Buzz, it was all there.' I know why he said it. Because he was dying and he was going to release it to his family and his kids and retain the rights of the whole thing. Back when he assigned me to write it, he gave me $80,000. It was peanuts. At the time, I said, 'Bob, I read the book and don't like it. I'm going to fix it. Just leave me alone and I'll write it and give it to you.' I sat in that house and I wrote it and I gave it to him. He never called me or anything. He shot it. And I was on the picture when he was shooting it, and if I wanted to polish something, he'd let me. Then years later he said, 'It was all there.'

But it wasn't all there. There's a scene in which the mysterious guy who wants to get the nuclear device back is following the detective. And the detective knows it. As he's walking down the street, he senses that he's being followed. The guy's got tennis shoes on. So he crosses to the edge of the street where there's a cliff. This is in downtown Los Angeles. Because I changed the location from New York to Los Angeles. He's walking near the cliff. Suddenly he senses the guy's going to grab him, and he steps to one side and the guy goes past him, and he grabs him and shoves him. Then he goes to the edge and watches and watches and watches him as he falls. Aldrich shot that – watching and watching – then a close shot over his head of the guy slipping down and then another shot. I said, 'Bob, take those shots out.' He says, 'Why?' I said, 'Because I want the audience to topple over the side of the cliff like the character in the film is doing. The way you're shooting, they won't.' Aldrich said, 'I'm trying to satisfy them.' I said, 'Don't try to satisfy them. Let them be anxious about what they're *not* seeing.' I also wanted the audience to just see his shoe sticking out in the bushes down below. But Aldrich wouldn't listen. Then they had some doubts about my ending, so they shot another one. Now that picture has two endings. I asked an audience in Paris which ending they wanted, and it was my ending they chose. They don't listen to writers! You write something with feeling. Maybe some writers don't, but I do. After the picture came out, I was in France with Aldrich, waiting to do another picture in Greece, and I got a phone call from Truffaut. He said, 'I want to know about the different scenes in *Kiss Me Deadly*. Did you do them or did the director do them?' I said, 'Tell me what the scenes are.' Every one of them was what I had in the script. Truffaut said, 'Aldrich isn't one of the first film noir directors. You are.'

Daniel Mainwaring

Exploiting Hollywood as much as Hollywood exploited him, Daniel Mainwaring, through a single novel and a handful of groundbreaking screenplays, would exert a considerable influence on future noir fiction and film. With a flair for evoking the dialogue and reality of small-town California, this former journalist and press agent also penned some forty non-noir screenplays as well as a series of mild-mannered 'whodunits'. Born in 1902 in Oakland, California, Mainwaring came from a well-to-do family headed by his English father. After attending Fresno State College, he took a variety of jobs – office boy, itinerant fruit picker, salesman, teacher and private detective – before finding work as a reporter for a series of newspapers – the *San Francisco Chronicle*, *Herald Examiner, Daily News* and *Evening Express* – covering the Los Angeles area.

As for his physical appearance, John Fante's wife, Joyce, when interviewed by Philippe Garnier, described Mainwaring as a large man with blue eyes, and chestnut hair cut in a military style. With his penchant for tweeds and pipes, he must have looked less like a native Californian than a member of the local British expatriate community. Despite their different approaches to writing, Mainwaring and John Fante would become friends. Mainwaring was one of the first to read Fante's *Ask the Dust* – at least, the first seventeen pages of it, after which Mainwaring stopped and told Fante he thought the book was terrible. He suggested a different opening and a more linear and accessible style. A week later Fante had rewritten the novel according to Mainwaring's specifications.

Like Thompson and Bezzerides, Mainwaring's first novel, the 1933 *One Against the Earth*, was in the proletarian tradition. About a widow raising three children on a Californian farm, it would be Mainwaring's only such novel, but the first of a number of narratives set in small Californian towns. According to director Joseph Losey, Mainwaring was able to evoke the 'good things about small towns'. Yet Mainwaring was no rural romantic. He told a seminar on gangster films at Northwestern University in 1972, 'Small towns are miserable places. Farmers I know in the San Joaquin Valley have been trying to put out a contract on [Cesar] Chavez (head of the United Farm Workers) . . . for organising migrant workers. They're sweet people.' After the publication of *One Against the Earth*, Mainwaring was hired as a publicist at Warner Brothers at a salary of $85 a week. Three years later, Mainwaring quit Warner to become a full-time writer. He wanted to try his hand at writing mysteries. The result would be a series of clever 'whodunits'. Though these novels were moderately successful, they made little impact on the literary world, even though Mainwaring, to provoke the interest of the reading public, deployed a series of protagonists, ranging from the relatively conventional to the moderately bizarre.

His first whodunit novel, published in 1936, was *The Doctor Died at Dusk*. Written under an English-sounding and, in the future, often used *nom de plume*, Geoffrey Homes, it featured journalist Robin Bishop. In his 1938 *Then There Were Three*, Mainwaring summoned up a new investigator, the milk-drinking, accordion-playing private detective Humphrey Campbell. Four years later, in *The Street of Crying Women*, he introduced Hispanic cop, José Manuel Madero, a Zapotec Indian who knits socks and smokes cigarettes after flipping them in the air and catching them between his lips. Robin Bishop would go on to feature in *The Man Who Murdered*

Himself (1936), *The Man Who Didn't Exist* (1937) and *The Man Who Murdered Goliath* (1938). Humphrey Campbell became the protagonist in *No Hands on the Clock* (1939, and adapted for the screen in 1941 by Frank McDonald), *Finders Keepers* (1940), *Forty Whacks* (1941, and adapted for the screen as *Crime By Night* by William Clemens in 1944) and *Six Silver Handles* (1944). The sock-knitting Madero would make a final appearance in *The Hill of the Terrified Monk* (1943).

To supplement his mystery writing, Mainwaring, in 1941, began working for Pine-Thomas at Paramount. William Pine and William Thomas – known as 'The Dollar Bills' – specialised in war and detective films. It was Bill Thomas who saw Mainwaring's potential as a scriptwriter and gave him his start. Mainwaring worked at Paramount until 1945. In one year alone, he churned out six screenplays. Except for William Thomas's *Big Town*, the story of a crusading editor of a metropolitan newspaper, all of them were, by Mainwaring's admission, mediocre. By 1947, he had notched up ten credits, all-important in an industry where having one's name on the screen is the key to further recognition, work and financial reward.

In the ten years he spent writing fiction and films, Mainwaring became a regular at Stanley Rose's bookshop on Hollywood Boulevard (before it was busted for pornography and immortalised as Bennett's Bookstore in *The Big Sleep*, the likes of Hammett, McCoy, Burnett, Faulkner, Tully, Milburn, Pagano and Fante would gather there). But by the mid-1940s he had grown bored with writing whodunits. He disliked having to come up with the necessary twists and endings. At that 1972 seminar, he'd said, '[Detective] stories are a bore to write . . . I'd get to the end and have to say, Whodunit? and be so mixed up I couldn't decide myself.' Mainwaring wanted to write another kind of novel. But to do so he had to get away from Hollywood. So in the final weeks of 1945, Mainwaring moved to Bridgeport, near Lake Tahoe, very much like the town described in the novel he was about to write. Once settled, Mainwaring began work on a book rooted in the Hammett school of hardboiled fiction. It even had traces of the proletarian effort that had kick-started his career. Like his previous books, *Build My Gallows High* would be published by William Morrow. Appearing in bookstores in 1946, it was quickly bought by RKO, who also wanted Mainwaring to adapt it for the screen.

Not only was *Build My Gallows High* Mainwaring's best novel, it would also be his last. In the following years, Mainwaring would concentrate on film work, contributing stories and scripts to such critiques of American culture as Don Siegel's *The Big Steal* (1949) and *Invasion of the Body Snatchers* (1956), Losey's *The Lawless* (1950), Ida Lupino's *The Hitch-Hiker* (1953), and Phil Karlson's *The Phenix City Story* (1955). But this was less a case of Hollywood adversely affecting the career of a promising hardboiler than of Mainwaring realising that there was little reason to struggle in the competitive world of fledgling novelists when he could derive greater satisfaction and make more money writing screenplays.

RKO's Bill Dozier was responsible for purchasing Mainwaring's novel. He, in turn, put ex-Warner, Paramount and RKO writer Warren Duff in charge of production. Duff would write *Appointment with Danger* and *Chicago Deadline*, both directed by Lewis Allen, as well as William Dieterle's *The Turning Point*. According to Mainwaring, Duff was only attracted to *Build My Gallows High* because of 'the part about the kid at the lake using a casting rod to pull the guy off the cliff'. Nevertheless, the film helped reinforce various elements of film noir, from its thematic density to the presence of the proverbial *femme fatale* (Jane Greer joining the likes of Barbara Stanwyck in *Double Indemnity*, Ava Gardner in *The Killers* and Yvonne DeCarlo in *Criss Cross*). However, the script's finalisation was, as often the case, anything but a straightforward matter.

Firstly, Duff, to cover his bases, gave Mainwaring's draft to James M. Cain, who put together an entirely new screenplay. Cain's sensibility – stuck in the urban muck of his own fiction

– was diametrically opposed to Mainwaring's. Placing the film in the city, Cain nullified the tension between small town and city life that permeates the novel. Realising that all was not right with Cain's version, Duff took the script to Frank Fenton. Author of the Los Angeles novel, *A Place in the Sun*, Fenton was an expert at polishing screenplays. After ironing out some of the rough spots, Duff took the screenplay back to Mainwaring. Though he believed Cain's script excessively brutal and the characters unpleasant, Mainwaring retained Cain's two-part structure in the final draft.

While the novel is set in New York, the film takes place in San Francisco. It was an alteration that had little to do with artistic interpretation; it was simply that the company preferred shooting in San Francisco. Another difference is that in the novel the police kill Jeff Bailey, while in the film it is Whit Sterling (Kirk Douglas) who kills Bailey (Robert Mitchum). Either Mainwaring had no problem with such changes or he had no say in the matter. On the other hand, it was Mainwaring's idea to use a voice-over for the flashbacks into Bailey's past, which provides a context for Mitchum's predicament.

Moving a script between writers was no more unusual then than now – a surfeit of cooks might spoil the broth, but they calm the nerves of studio executives who doubt whether the broth can be cooked at all. 'You'd turn around and spit and some other writer would be on your project,' said Mainwaring, who finished his final draft in a matter of days. In later years, Mainwaring would play down Cain's and Fenton's contributions, just as he would Sam Peckinpah's contribution to *Invasion of the Body Snatchers* (Peckinpah not only polished that script but rewrote several scenes, worked as dialogue director and acted in the film). Concerned about advancing in the industry, Mainwaring, unlike Cain, sought to protect his reputation. In the end, Cain received a little over $16,000, Fenton $8,000 and Mainwaring $11,000, plus $20,000 for the rights to the novel.

Once the script was finalised, RKO hired Jacques Tourneur to direct the film. The son of French director Maurice Tourneur and a protégé of producer Val Lewton, Tourneur had already made *Cat People, I Walked With a Zombie* and *The Leopard Man*, each treading a thin line between schlock-horror and expressionist poetry. Tourneur's only other film noir would be his 1957 adaptation of David Goodis's *Nightfall*. It wasn't Tourneur but the marketing department who changed Mainwaring's title, taken from an African-American poem, to the more pertinent *Out of the Past*. While the film is superbly directed, its convoluted story-line troubled some critics. On its release in 1947, *New York Times* film reviewer Bosley Crowther commented, 'If only we had some way of knowing what's going on in the last half of the film, we might get more pleasure from it.'

Mainwaring would always maintain that Tourneur's film was superior to his novel. He would also admit that, in writing the novel, he had stolen mercilessly from Hammett. So it's hardly surprising that the author would have initially wanted Bogart, so memorable in Huston's adaptation of Hammett's *The Maltese Falcon*, to play Jeff Bailey. Bogart, who had known Mainwaring back in the days when the latter was a publicist, was keen to play the role, but Warner Brothers vetoed the idea. Seen with hindsight, the perfectly cast Mitchum personifies the movie's juxtaposition of urban and small-town ethics. At the time Mitchum's reputation as Hollywood's bad boy was reaching its peak. According to Mainwaring, Mitchum did his best to live up to that reputation, openly smoking marijuana on the set. The following year Mitchum would be arrested for possession and sentenced to sixty days in jail. Instead of ruining his career, the notoriety only increased Mitchum's box-office appeal.

Mainwaring was himself something of a Hollywood bad boy – at least according to Howard Hughes, who considered Mainwaring a dangerous leftist because he had failed Hughes's absurd *I Married a Communist* test. The eccentric producer would ask those he suspected of leftwing sympathies to contribute to his film, a rabid paean to morbid rightwing Americanism. If they refused, Hughes, convinced of their politics, promptly fired them. In the producer's warped mind, it was a perfect trap, as tight-fitting as the brassière he had designed to contain Jane Russell's voluptuous breasts in *The Outlaw*. He would apply his political litmus test to numerous writers and directors, beginning with Joseph Losey. A man of principle who relocated to England during the McCarthy era, Losey 'refused it categorically'. In 1948, Hughes assigned the film to Nicholas Ray, who excused himself because, luckily, he was set to direct *Knock on Any Door* at Columbia. In all, the film would be offered to thirteen directors, before landing, like a hot potato, in the hands of Robert Stevenson, more famous for directing *The Absent-Minded Professor, Mary Poppins* and *Herbie Rides Again*. Much to the delight of anti-communist fundamentalists and the chagrin of everyone else, the film (also known as *The Woman on Pier 13*) would be one of the most blatant examples of political propaganda to come out of Tinseltown. Hughes's concern about leftwing infiltration would eventually all but halt film production at RKO. This seems at odds with the fact that he had phoned John Huston in 1947, offering the use of one of his planes – at a reduced rate – to transport the Committee for the First Amendment (Huston, Bogart, Bacall, Garfield, etc.) to Washington where they were to witness the House Un-American Activities Committee's investigation into communist subversion in Hollywood. Five years later, with film production at a stand-still, Hughes, worried that he too might be seen as a red, would close down his studio.

Having refused the chance to work on Hughes's film, Mainwaring became *persona non grata* at RKO. In spite of this and the climate of fear created by the blacklist, Mainwaring continued to write scripts for the next nineteen years. In 1951, he managed to contribute the story for RKO's *Roadblock*. With a script by Steve Fisher and George Bricker, and directed by Harold Daniels, this is a tale of middle-class malaise concerning an insurance investigator and a money-loving woman who poses as his wife. In the same year Mainwaring furnished the story (uncredited) that would become *The Tall Target*. Directed by Anthony Mann at MGM, it revolved around a discredited police officer who, on a train to Washington, attempts to stop the assassination of President Lincoln. The following year, at Warner Brothers, Mainwaring wrote the screenplay for *This Woman is Dangerous*, about a gun moll, played by Joan Crawford, who learns that she is going blind, and falls in love with her eye surgeon. Directed by Felix Feist, it's a decent enough gangster weepie, though not a patch on Feist's 1947 noir classic *The Devil Thumbs a Ride*. In 1955, Mainwaring wrote *A Bullet for Joey* for Lewis Allen at United Artists. The film, which would star Edward G. Robinson and George Raft, was about a policeman preventing the murder of an atomic scientist. After Mainwaring finished the script, Buzz Bezzerides was called in to spruce up the dialogue, first for Robinson, for which Bezzerides was paid $5,000, then for Raft, for which he was paid a second time. Despite the quality of its writers and actors, the film failed to live up to its promise. In 1957, Mainwaring and Irving Schulman put together the script for Don Siegel's *Baby Face Nelson*, with Mickey Rooney. While these are among Mainwaring's better efforts, the likes of *The George Raft Story* and *Space Master X-7* are best forgotten.

Some of Mainwaring's better contributions, however, are as good as film noir gets. Take, for instance, the story that became the 1953 film *The Hitch-Hiker*. Directed by the underrated Ida Lupino and made during the final days of McCarthyism, the film is less about the dangers of stopping for anyone with an outstretched thumb than about the fear of strangers, lest they be serial killers or dangerous communists. Because he'd been banned by Hughes, Mainwaring's contribution would go uncredited.

Lupino's film was based on a true incident. In 1950, while

hitchhiking in the Southwest, a twenty-two-year-old ex-convict from Missouri, William Edward Cook Jr., killed a family of five and a travelling salesman. He was caught in Baja California where he was holding two El Centro prospectors hostage, and was eventually executed. Accordingly, *The Hitch-Hiker* centres on two men who, on a fishing trip, offer a man a ride, unaware that he's a mass murderer. Beginning innocently enough, Lupino's film turns into the darkest of road movies, and depicts an era when postwar values were in flux and the nation was distinctly ill at ease.

The Hitch-Hiker would be Ida Lupino's fourth film as a director, and her only film noir. It's a rare example of a film noir from that era directed by a woman. In fact, since Dorothy Arzner, whose final film, *First Comes Courage*, came out in 1943, there had been few, if any, female directors working in Hollywood. With his politics and perspective, Mainwaring fitted comfortably into Lupino's socially oriented perspective. For their efforts, Mainwaring and Lupino would be air-brushed from Hollywood history, the victims of the very paranoia depicted in *The Hitch-Hiker*.

Generous tax advantages following the 1949 antitrust decision to break up the studios' monopoly had given independent production companies an opportunity to flourish. Consequently, the number of independent productions would rise from ninety in 1947 to 165 in 1950. Having starred in such films as *High Sierra*, *They Drive by Night* and *On Dangerous Ground*, Lupino grew tired of being a poor man's Bette Davis and formed a production company with her second husband, Collier Young. At first Lupino and Young bankrolled their own films, but Howard Hughes – noting the advantages, including tax breaks and the use of non-union labour – wanted a piece of the action. Hughes's involvement is ironic when one considers that Lupino, between 1949 and 1954, would resuscitate the low-budget social conscience film, something Hughes was never noted for supporting, and which might have had something to do with his political paranoia and the closure of his studio.

For some five years Lupino was a force to be reckoned with. The first independent production in which she was directly involved was *Not Wanted*, about the plight of an unmarried mother. This was followed by *Outrage*, which deals with rape and its after-effects. She went on to make *Hard, Fast and Beautiful* (1951), about a mother who pushes her daughter into the world of competitive tennis, and *The Bigamist* (1953), which focuses on a man who juggles two separate existences. She also had a hand in writing, acting and, according to some, producing the excellent film noir *Private Hell 36* (1954), directed by Don Siegel. As Lizzie Franck points out, Lupino's world was marked by a concern for ordinary people and their plight. One might add that her films also illustrate the thin line separating film noir and a certain type of melodrama. Unfortunately, when Lupino and Young were divorced, the company chose to focus on distribution, and, apart from her 1966 convent comedy *The Trouble with Angels*, Lupino directed no more films. She was left to find work as an actress and director on television programmes like *Have Gun Will Travel*, *The Fugitive*, *The Untouchables* and *The Twilight Zone*.

Meanwhile, Mainwaring's career continued – apparently, it was easier to revive the career of a discredited leftist than to resurrect that of an independent female director. In the following years he would work on half a dozen films, including four westerns and a crime film, *Alaska Seas* (1954), but his next significant film would be *The Phenix City Story* (1955). Directed by Phil Karlson, the film mixes *verité* with fiction, following, in pseudo-documentary style, the government's attempt to break the gambling, vice and dope ring in Phenix City, Alabama, a town founded by runaway slaves, renegade whites and Civil War deserters (as a pleasure town for Fort Benning soldiers, it also had the highest venereal disease rate in the country). A typical Karlson low-budget affair, the film follows events in the wake of the State Attorney-elect's murder and the occupation of the city by the National Guard. Karlson, who began filming while the murder trial was in progress, was able to uncover evidence that helped convict the suspects. Mainwaring's background as a journalist was to stand him in good stead. His script, which he wrote with Crane Wilbur, crackles with tabloid certainty. Combining hard facts with hardboiled dialogue, it highlights the historical moment while creating scenes that underscore the town's corrupt and violent nature.

Though the McCarthy era was all but over, Karlson's hiring of Mainwaring still took some courage. Born in Chicago in 1908 of Jewish-Irish parents, Karlson began his career at Universal Studios, moving from props man to second assistant director to film editor, associate producer, short feature director and, finally, director. As a king of the Bs, he directed scores of films, among them *Scandal Sheet, Five Against the House, The Brothers Rico, The Silencers* and *Walking Tall,* which he made in 1973. Like Mainwaring, he was fascinated by Hammett's *Maltese Falcon,* and admitted that his 1955 *Hell's Island* was simply his version of Huston's famous film, reset on a Caribbean island.

The Phenix City Story may have been a low-budget success, but the apogee of Mainwaring's career would be his screenplay for *Invasion of the Body Snatchers.* Closer to *The Hitch-Hiker* than *The Phenix City Story,* Don Siegel's film places film noir paranoia within the framework of a science-fiction narrative. For most, the film is a dark but entertaining critique of small-town values and anti-communist hysteria, while some read it as a critique of collectivism. Critic Peter Biskind provides a third view, believing the film 'attacked extremism in the guise of attacking the Red menace, to suggest that, like Communism, extremism was subversive'.

Regardless of how the film is interpreted, Mainwaring and director Don Siegel would deny that *Invasion of the Body Snatchers* is a political critique of any kind, saying instead that they had simply wanted to make an entertaining movie. Meanwhile, inhabitants of Sierra Madre, California, where the film – whose original title was *Sleep No More* – was made, believed the movie to be an accurate depiction of their middle-class community, a town so boring at the time that, as one citizen put it, 'it could have put an insomniac to sleep'. And once asleep there would be no way, as the film attests, to wake up again or be conscious enough to criticise the culture.

Made in 1956 and adapted from Jack Finney's novel, Siegel's film cost Allied Artists (formerly low-budget specialists Monogram) a mere $416,911. Previous Allied successes had been limited to Bowery Boys films and a version of *Jungle Boy*. Consequently, when it came to theatre dates, it was assumed that Siegel's film would be just another Allied B effort, even though the film's producer was Walter Wanger, who had already notched up such successes as *Queen Christina*, *Stagecoach* and *Scarlet Street*, and would later make *I Want to Live!* *Invasion of the Body Snatchers* was Wanger's chance to repair a reputation that was on a downward spiral, having been damaged by a disastrous production of *Joan of Arc* in 1948, followed by a period when he'd been red-baited by McCarthyites. Still, Wanger had been relatively successful with his previous Allied outing, Don Siegel's *Riot in Cell Block Eleven*, and it was the writer of that film, Richard Collins, who suggested to Siegel that Mainwaring collaborate with him on *Invasion of the Body Snatchers*. Collins had worked with Mainwaring on three earlier films and he gave the latter control of the script. Once the film was in production, Mainwaring worked closely with Siegel, while Collins came in later to work on various scenes. In all, Mainwaring wrote five films for Siegel, prompting the director to name him as his favourite scriptwriter.

Even a small studio like Allied was concerned about the film's content, and would insist that a prologue and epilogue regarding totalitarianism in America be added – so much for this not being a political film. In the prologue a police car carries the protagonist to a hospital where he tries to convince the psychiatrist that pods are taking over the planet, while the epilogue depicts an ambulance bringing an emergency case to the hospital, where the driver explains that the man has been injured in a crash with a truck loaded with seed pods, after which the psychiatrist phones the FBI. Though both prologue and epilogue were written by Mainwaring, they have the effect of reducing the film's immediacy and diluting the subject matter, and Siegel objected to them on the grounds that they were unnecessary to the content and structure of the film.

Despite the framing device, the movie touched a nerve, particularly among young audiences. When something approaching the director's cut – or at least a version that stopped before the concluding portion of the framing device – was shown at the Cinema Theater on Western Boulevard in Los Angeles in 1964, a near riot ensued. Clearly it was a case of hysteria surrounding a film about hysteria. In the same year as that controversial screening, Mainwaring was to contribute his final scripts, first for Gordon Hessler, entitled *The Woman Who Wouldn't Die* (1964), followed a year later by a western at Twentieth Century Fox, directed by Lesley Selander, entitled *Convict Stage*.

When Mainwaring died in Los Angeles in 1977, his obituary in *Variety* said, 'in recent years he had collaborated in Europe with producer-director-author Hardy Krueger'. Though it's difficult to find any evidence of this, Mainwaring had been in Europe during the previous decade, writing screenplays for *Atlantis, The Lost Continent, The Minotaur* and *The Revolt of the Slaves*. Such productions were a long way stylistically and geographically from the hardboiled *Build My Gallows High*, which would be tediously recycled at Columbia in 1984 and retitled *Against All Odds*, or *Invasion of the Body Snatchers*, which would be remade on two occasions.

Under different conditions, Mainwaring might have gone on to write other hardboiled novels. But unlike his friend

John Fante, he wasn't obsessive enough to be a successful novelist. Like a number of other screenwriters, Mainwaring carried the work ethic of journalism into the world of film. Nevertheless, in the space of one novel and a few thought-provoking screenplays, Mainwaring was able to investigate some of the darkest corners of postwar America.

Jonathan Latimer

Not an innovator like Hammett, nor a master like Burnett, Jonathan Wyatt Latimer was a consummate professional capable of producing convincing hardboiled novels and screenplays. One of the last to be associated with the golden age of tough-guy fiction, his writing is notable for its corrosive humour, off-the-wall perspective, bizarre settings and protagonists who solve classical crime puzzles through a woozy but instinctive grasp of the deductive process.

Latimer was born in Chicago in 1906, his father a legal councillor, his mother a violinist. Named after an ancestor who served under George Washington, Latimer studied at Knox College in Galesburg, Illinois. From 1929 to 1935 he worked as a crime-beat reporter in Chicago. There he met Al Capone, Bugsy Moran and other Windy City gangsters. He was still a newspaperman when he wrote his first two novels, *Murder in the Madhouse* and *Headed for a Hearse*. Motivated by the success of those two books, Latimer moved to Florida in 1935. There he cultivated the friendship of Hemingway. When *Studs Lonigan* author James T. Farrell came to visit Hemingway, he stayed with Latimer. While there, Farrell was said to have accused his host of putting on literary airs. Hemingway took Farrell's side, saying, 'These fellows have nothing but their writing. Take that away from them and they'll commit suicide.' To Hemingway and Farrell, Latimer was just a hack writer, in it purely for the money it brought him. Latimer responded by telling the two writers that his, Latimer's, literary career had been validated by a London *Sunday Times* compilation listing *The Lady in the Morgue* as one of the world's greatest crime stories.

Three years later, and married to Grosse Point debutante Ellen Peabody, Latimer moved to La Jolla, California, where he befriended Raymond Chandler. The two men became drinking companions, frequenting the El Toro bar, along with their mutual friend Theodore Geisel, better known as Dr. Seuss. Once settled in La Jolla, Latimer was contacted by Joseph Sistrom, at the time working at Columbia. Sistrom liked Latimer's work and asked if he'd be interested in putting together a treatment for Joseph Vance's *The Lone Wolf's Daughter* – part of the *Lone Wolf* series about a thief turned sleuth. It led to a new career, one that would be momentarily interrupted when, in 1943, Latimer joined the Marines, his tour of duty lasting for the duration of the war.

In all, Latimer authored ten crime novels, eight of which were hardboilers. The first, *Murder in the Madhouse*, appeared in 1934, and featured the wisecracking Bill Crane, who would appear in Latimer's four following books. Employed by a New York private detective agency run by the notorious Colonel Black, Crane reads *Black Mask* – whether as entertainment or trade journal is unclear – and fears no one. Known for never turning away a client, Crane, like a bull in a bar room, launches his investigations through a series of misdeeds and reckless alcohol-stimulated behaviour. This is exemplified by *Murder in the Madhouse* – a novel that reads as though Chandler had rewritten Michael Avallone's *Shock Corridor* – in which Crane finagles his way into a lunatic asylum to uncover valuables stolen from a wealthy patient.

Latimer's classic *Headed for a Hearse* was published in 1935, followed by *The Lady in the Morgue* (1936), *The Search for My Great-Uncle's Head* (1937, under the name Peter Coffin), *The Dead Don't Care* (1938) and *Red Gardenias* (1939). These five iconoclastic novels, if not totally original, helped further define and popularise the private eye genre. By 1940, Latimer had also published a non-Crane novel, *Dark Memory*, by which time the author was, at thirty-four, ghost-writing for US Secretary of the Interior Harold Ickes, penning screenplays, and working on his scandalous cult novel, *Solomon's Vineyard*.

The novel was first published in Britain, in 1941. Featuring tough-guy Karl Craven, it is a demented tale of murder, perverse sexuality and small-town religion. It proved too hot for US publishers, and would only appear in the US in 1950 – even then in a severely edited version, and retitled *The Fifth Grave*. This was nothing unusual for Latimer, whose *Headed for a Hearse* had also been censored. The first unexpurgated US version of *Solomon's Vineyard* would not appear until 1988, some forty years after its British publication.

Solomon's Vineyard is Latimer's homage – evidently unconscious – to Hammett. As in *The Maltese Falcon*, the detective, Craven, must solve the murder of his partner, even though he never really liked the man. But when asked if either his editor or Hammett had ever pointed out the similarity between his book and Hammett's, Latimer is reported to have said, 'No, I didn't know I'd lifted the idea until someone mentioned it years later.' As for Hammett himself, '[The] only time I ever saw him,' said Latimer, 'was one morning around 3 a.m., at the Beverly Wilshire Hotel. He was being lugged across the lobby by an assistant manager and two bellhops. They wrestled him into the night elevator and ran him upstairs, where I suppose they put him to bed. Hell of a fine writer, though, drunk or sober.'

As down-in-the-dirt, tough-guy writing, *Solomon's Vineyard* goes beyond Hammett into the nightmare world of Mickey Spillane. What separates Latimer from Spillane is that, despite the violence, Latimer's fiction contains an element of humour, if not satire. In *Solomon's Vineyard*, Latimer prepares the reader for what's to come in the following way: 'Listen. This is a wild one. Maybe the wildest yet. It's got everything but an abortion and a tornado. I ain't saying it's true. Neither of us, brother, is asking you to believe it.' Critic James

Naremore misses the point when he says that *Solomon's Vine-yard* 'deserves to be placed alongside Paul Cain's *Fast One* as one of the toughest, most sadomasochistic Hammett imitations of all time'.

In Hollywood, Latimer contributed scripts to numerous films. He was particularly adept at creating lively, true-sounding dialogue. One of a handful of crime writers to forge a successful career out of scriptwriting, Latimer specialised in film noir, working on such films as *The Glass Key*, *The Big Clock*, *The Lady in the Morgue*, *Nocturne* (from an unpublished story by Fenton and Rowland Brown), *Night Has a Thousand Eyes*, *The Accused* (uncredited) and *They Won't Believe Me*.

After *Solomon's Vineyard* and its 1950 expurgated version, Latimer would publish two other novels, *Sinners and Shrouds* (1956) and *Black is the Fashion for Dying* (1959). The latter, Latimer's revenge on Tinseltown, is the story of the murder of an unpleasant Hollywood star. The former concerns reporter Sam Clay, who wakes up with a hangover and a beautiful dead woman – a fashion reporter and colleague of Sam's – in his bed. Both novels demonstrate Latimer's ear for language and Hammett's influence. But whereas *Headed for a Hearse* was a comedy in the style of *The Thin Man*, which had been published a year previously, Latimer's later fiction moved in the direction of Hammett's earlier novel, *Red Harvest*.

Beneath the surface, Latimer's writing reflects the era's anxieties about crime and gangsters, tensions concerning ethnicity, class and gender, and a fear of the outsider. In negotiating these undercurrents, Latimer's detectives seek the margins of society, where they act out their love–hate relationship with the elitist culture they unwillingly serve. In the postwar years, Latimer's detectives visit the powerful only to find that they, the investigators, are tainted by their need to compromise, and the realisation that they are convenient scapegoats for crimes committed in the name of preserving the status quo. While Naremore has accused Latimer of racism in his treatment of African-Americans, it is a charge that, seen with hindsight, might be better levelled at the era than at a single writer who, it could be argued, has chosen to reflect that era.

One of the first hardboiled detectives who did not initially appear in pulp periodicals, Bill Crane is a tough guy who can also solve traditional locked-door mysteries. Mixing elements of the classic whodunit with a sharp satirical sense, Latimer was able to push, if to a limited degree, the parameters of the genre. By 1935, in *Headed for a Hearse*, he was already parodying a literary style that had, in his opinion, grown too serious. According to Latimer, not even Hammett's Sam Spade seemed to have much fun. When it comes to humour, only Chandler would be Latimer's equal. While Crane and Marlowe are spiritual brothers, Latimer's satire, which centres on content rather than on language or cultural perceptions, is not as subtle as Chandler's. Still, it might have been Latimer who influenced Chandler, for *Headed for a Hearse* appeared at least four years before Chandler's first novel, *The Big Sleep*.

Certainly Crane can outdrink Marlowe. In fact, alcohol drives his investigations. Consequently, he'll drink anything, particularly if mixed with whiskey. When necessity demands it, he'll even imbibe embalming fluid. But unlike many private eyes, when Crane drinks he actually gets drunk, a condition that leads to much of his humour, perceptions and plot resolutions. In fact, Crane might well be considered the precursor of Lawrence Block's Matt Scudder before the latter began searching for AA meetings. Like early Scudder, Crane enjoys drinking with friends and fellow detectives. And as in the early Scudder novels, he tries, often in vain, to maintain his equilibrium, if not his sobriety, only to end up bumping into furniture and stumbling over words. Yet his narrative remains sober. Says Latimer of Crane in *Murder in the Madhouse*, 'He felt very pleased he had fooled them into thinking he was drunk . . . He carried out his role so thoroughly he had to be helped into the phone booth.'

So Latimer helped deflate the overblown image of the detective at a time when it was in danger of being taken too seriously. The banter between Crane and Ann Fortune in *Red Gardenias* parodies the combative dialogue between Nick and Nora Charles in Hammett's *The Thin Man*, a revisionist text published five years earlier. But Latimer was not just a satirist. He could also turn a phrase and write with chilling truthfulness, as in the death-row scene in *Headed for a Hearse*. Despite his relative popularity, Latimer realised he was repeating himself, and so abandoned his prize protagonist after five novels. In what had become an increasingly competitive genre, Latimer's humour would become both the basis of his popularity and a stumbling block to future progress.

Nevertheless, his work was cinematic enough for three of his first four books to be adapted for the screen, beginning with *The Westland Case*, based on *Headed for a Hearse*. Directed by Christy Cabanne at Universal in 1937, it stars former professional wrestler and ex-singer for the Pennsylvania Grand Opera Company, Preston Foster, as Bill Crane. Cutting a commanding figure at six foot two and 200 pounds, Foster figured in more than a hundred films, including *Kansas City Confidential* and *I Shot Jesse James*, while Cabanne, who had once been an assistant to D.W. Griffith, had written and directed scores of films, working, in the process, with the Gish sisters, Francis X. Bushman and Douglas Fairbanks. The following year saw two other Latimer novels adapted for the screen. Both were made at Universal and once again starred Preston Foster: *The Lady in the Morgue*, directed by Otis Garrett at Universal, and *The Last Warning*, adapted from *The Dead Don't Care*, directed by Albert S. Rogell at Universal. A hack director, Rogell began his career making Ken Maynard westerns and progressed to second features, including *Li'l Abner* and *Song of India*. Though better than average private-eye outings, none of these Latimer adaptations was about to set the cinematic world alight.

Having handed in his treatment for the *Lone Wolf's Daughter*,

Latimer, in 1939, was given the chance to write a script for Peter Godfrey's *The Lone Wolf Spy Hunt*. Further *Lone Wolf* films were to launch the careers of such distinguished directors as Edward Dmytryk and André de Toth. For this film, Latimer showed an astuteness regarding the dialogue, in this case spoken by two young actresses, Ida Lupino and Rita Hayworth. There would be two other efforts for Latimer as a journeyman scriptwriter: *Phantom Raiders* (1940) for Jacques Tourneur and the spoof supernatural *Topper Returns* for Roy Del Ruth (1941).

Latimer's first major film would be Stuart Heisler's *The Glass Key* (1942), made at Paramount and starring Alan Ladd and Veronica Lake. It remains one of the best adaptations of a Hammett story and one of Latimer's better efforts, even though the writer would stray from the spirit and plot of the novel. This was the second attempt at filming Hammett's novel, the original version, directed by Frank Tuttle and written by Harry Ruskin, Kathryn Scola and Kubec Glasmon, having appeared in 1935. Heisler's version was much better. Inspired by the success of *The Maltese Falcon*, which had appeared a year earlier, it is notable for William Bendix's demented performance, Theodor Sparkuhl's low-key photographic effects, and a script that spits out a range of colloquialisms while retaining the sexual chemistry between the two main characters that had been missing from the earlier version.

At RKO, Latimer wrote the script for Edwin Marin's *Nocturne* (1946). It stars George Raft as a detective hunting the killer of a composer, who was shot while playing the piano. Latimer's script is interesting in its investigation of the composer's lifestyle. Along with Allen Rivkin and Barré Lyndon, he also contributed (uncredited) to Ketti Frings's script on *The Accused*, directed by William Dieterle for Hal Wallis at Paramount in 1948. A glimpse into the sexual politics of the era, and starring Loretta Young and Robert Cummings, it's about a female professor who kills one of her students in self-defence after the latter sexually assaults her.

Latimer's next three films are, artistically, among his most successful. The most renowned is the tense whodunit *The Big Clock*. Directed by John Farrow at Paramount in 1948, it stars Ray Milland, Charles Laughton and Maureen O'Sullivan. Adapted from Kenneth Fearing's nail-biting novel, the plot revolves around a publisher who murders his mistress and assigns one of his editors to investigate the crime. Highlighting the novel's slow-building paranoia, Latimer's script is an impressive example of soft-core noir. At the same time, Farrow established the film's ambience with his opening shot, a pan of the city, and voice-over. An Australian who arrived in Hollywood in the late 1920s, Farrow began his career filming sea sequences. He then worked on scripts for *A Woman of Experience* (1931) before making his directorial debut in 1934 on the film *The Spectacle Maker*. After working on a series of B features, he moved on to full budget productions, hitting his peak in the late 1940s and early 1950s with films like *His Kind of Woman* (1951) with Robert Mitchum and Jane Russell; *Where Danger Lives* (1950) with Mitchum and Faith Domergue, the plot of which bears an uncanny resemblance to Charles Willeford's novel *Wild Wives*; as well as *Night Has a Thousand Eyes* (1948), made at Paramount and starring Edward G. Robinson and Gail Russell. Taken from a novel by Cornell Woolrich, the last film was written with Barré Lyndon. Latimer said of it, 'My intention was to establish a real sense of terror.' He came close to succeeding. However, even though Latimer is able to convey the notion that the night is the film's true antagonist, his script and the film are neither as bleak nor as doom-ridden as Woolrich's novel.

In the 1960s and early 1970s, having fallen out of favour in Hollywood, Latimer slid sideways into television, contributing scripts to *Checkmate*, *Hong Kong*, *Perry Mason* and *Columbo*. At the time of his death in 1983, he was all but forgotten as a hardboiled novelist and scriptwriter. Though not in the first rank of hardboiled writers, Latimer remains an important figure in noir fiction and film, despite the fact that from 1941 until 1951, the years corresponding with his most important work in Tinseltown, his career as a fiction writer had been at a standstill, only recommencing – *Sinners and Shrouds, Black is the Fashion for Dying* – as his screenwriting career declined. Though somewhat dated and unoriginal, Latimer's fiction remains entertaining and evocative. As with so many writers who emerged from the world of journalism, his concept of writing related more to making a living than achieving literary immortality. Yet, given the state of society, his novels are appealing examples of how the private eye fits into the cultural patterns of both the prewar and postwar eras.

Leigh Brackett

No less professional than Jonathan Latimer was Leigh Brackett, whose first novel, the Chandler-influenced *No Good from a Corpse*, appeared in 1944. Howard Hawks was so impressed by it that he told his secretary, 'Call in this guy Brackett. He'd be good to write the screenplay of *The Big Sleep* with Bill Faulkner.' Hawks was surprised when Brackett entered his office: 'In walked a rather attractive girl who looked like she had just come in from a tennis match. She looked as if she wrote poetry. But she wrote like a man.' Brackett was high-spirited, energetic, stubborn, self-sufficient and self-deprecating – not dissimilar from such Hawks favourites as Katherine Hepburn, Carole Lombard and Lauren Bacall. Despite his macho perspective, Hawks had never been averse to employing women writers. Seven years earlier he'd hired the young Hagar Wilde to work on a script for her novel, which would become *Bringing Up Baby*. Not only would Brackett write *The Big Sleep*, but she'd soon rank among Hawks's favourite screenwriters.

Before *No Good from a Corpse*, Brackett had contributed to

an assortment of pulp magazines. Yet it wasn't hardboiled writing that initially attracted her, but science fiction. An avid reader of Edgar Rice Burroughs's Martian tales, she published her first story, 'Martian Quest', in a 1940 issue of *Astounding Science Fiction*. Following the publication of *No Good from a Corpse*, Brackett would go on to ghost-write *Stranger at Home* (1946) for actor George Sanders, followed, under her own name, by *An Eye for an Eye* (1957) and *The Tiger Among Us* (1957), as well as such science fiction novels as *Shadow Over Mars* (1951), *The Starmen* (1952), *The Sword of Rhiannon* (1953), *The Long Tomorrow* (1955), *The Galactic Breed* (1955) and *The Big Jump* (1955). Most of her stories and scripts are set in a violent, male-dominated world. As Hawks crudely observed, there is little in Brackett's fiction to indicate her gender.

The war had enabled many female novelist-scriptwriters to find studio employment, and for a greater number of films oriented towards the female market to be made. Said Catherine Turney, 'One of the reasons they hired me is that the men were off at the war, and they had all these big female stars. The stars had to have roles that served them well. They themselves wanted something in which they weren't just sitting around being a simpering nobody.' Most female writers were put to work on 'women's films', a term that Turney, for one, was more than willing to embrace. A substantial number of such films were melodramas with a strong psychological angle (a Hollywood obsession since the 1930s when Samuel Goldwyn asked Sigmund Freud to write a script for him – Freud declined), making them distant cousins to film noir, which were, at the time, referred to as psychological melodramas. Not surprising, then, that many noir-oriented films were based on stories by women writers: Charlotte Armstrong (*The Unsuspected*), Dorothy B. Hughes (*Ride the Pink Horse; In a Lonely Place*), Gertrude Walker (*The Damned Don't Cry*) and Vera Caspary (*Laura; The Blue Gardenia*). Likewise, a number of film noir scripts were written by women: Lenore Coffee

(*Sudden Fear*), Joan Harrison (*Dark Waters, Nocturne*), Adele Comandini (*Strange Illusion*), Ida Lupino (*The Hitch-Hiker*), Marguerite Roberts (*Undercurrent*), Catherine Turney (*Mildred Pierce, No Man of Her Own*), Virginia Kellogg (*White Heat*). However, Brackett would be one of the few female writers to pen both noir fiction *and* film.

Brackett's 1957 *The Tiger Among Us* – which would be adapted for the screen in 1962 and retitled *13 West Street*, starring Alan Ladd and Dolores Dorn, and directed by Philip Leacock – is a hardboiled thriller, one of many in the 1950s that examined the theme of juvenile delinquency, the rise of suburbia, and attempts by upstanding citizens to maintain a sense of community. While *The Tiger Among Us* strains for hard-core status, its wafer-thin social awareness is a throwback to liberal narratives like Thomas B. Dewey's 1954 novel *The Mean Streets* and a precursor to 1970s vigilante films like *Death Wish*. While the protagonist's desire for revenge reveals the nature of his politics, Brackett attempts to reach a mass readership and indemnify herself in an era when McCarthyism was on the wane but liberalism was still suspect.

What differentiates Brackett from others who have ventured into this territory is her willingness to empathise with victims of violence, and her detailed exploration of suburban life. The theme of *The Tiger Among Us* is that, if a person is not vigilant, those tranquil suburban streets will become as dangerous as the mean streets associated with urban-oriented hardboiled literature. Like William McGivern's *The Big Heat*, Brackett's novel depicts a couple, Walter and Tracey, as suburban settlers. But unlike cop and wife in the former, or the misguided duo in Lionel White's *The Big Caper*, Brackett's couple are committed front-yardists who probably voted for Eisenhower rather than Stevenson, but Kennedy rather than Nixon. Brackett's portrayal of Walter as a patronising citizen of a barbecueville and Tracey as a militant housewife is not so much tongue-in-cheek as an attempt to out-step the author's male counterparts, making *The Tiger Among Us* less a satire than a condemnation of the era's sexual politics and consumerist obsessions.

Born in Los Angeles in 1915, Brackett grew up in Santa Monica. After her father died in the 1918 flu epidemic, she was raised by her mother and maiden aunt. Attending an all-girls high school, Brackett gravitated towards the theatrical arts, but realised her talent lay in writing. Through Laurence D'Orsay's literary agency, which, for her, functioned as a de facto school of creative writing, her work came to the attention of a literary agent, Julius Schwartz, who sold her first story in 1939 and, four years later, her first novel.

In 1946 Brackett married sci-fi writer Edmond Hamilton, and together they would come to divide their time between Southern California and rural Ohio, where Brackett would set up her typewriter beneath the eaves of their farmhouse and pound out science fiction and crime stories. By the time of her death in 1980 she had notched up eleven film credits – including not only *The Big Sleep* but also *Rio Bravo*, *Hatari!*, *Man's Favorite Sport*, *El Dorado*, *Rio Lobo*, *The Long Goodbye* and *Star Wars: The Empire Strikes Back*. In addition to her four crime novels, she published fourteen science-fiction novels and two westerns, and contributed scripts to such television programmes as *The Rockford Files*, *Archer*, *Checkmate* and *Alfred Hitchcock Presents*.

Hawks had been able to secure the services of Brackett and Faulkner for *The Big Sleep* after Jack Warner had enquired, on the way back from the première of *To Have and Have Not*, if the director had another story for Bogart and Bacall. Hawks said he had something less like *To Have and Have Not* than *The Maltese Falcon*, called *The Big Sleep*. Warner immediately gave Hawks $50,000 to buy the novel. Aided by the author's naïveté, Hawks paid Chandler $5,000 for the rights. It's not clear what became of the remaining $45,000, though it wouldn't be surprising if Hawks had simply pocketed the leftovers.

Because Chandler was under contract at Paramount, Hawks

opted for Faulkner, followed by Brackett. Before contributing to *The Big Sleep*, Brackett had been involved in two B films: *The Vampire's Ghost* (1945), a ten-day wonder at Republic, and *Crime Doctor's Man Hunt* (1946) at Columbia. Consequently, she was relatively inexperienced when she began working with Hawks. She was new to the genre of hardboiled fiction, her single novel being *No Good from a Corpse*, and that written only after seeing *The Maltese Falcon*. Under the spell of Hammett and Chandler, Brackett could not help but be intimidated by the thought of adapting Chandler, much less working alongside a writer of Faulkner's stature.

On Brackett's first day at the studio, Faulkner walked into her office and announced how they would write the script: they would simply alternate chapters. Before she could say anything, Faulkner had disappeared and Brackett never saw him again. This was par for the course for Faulkner, who hated Hollywood even more than Chandler and Hammett had. 'They don't worship money here,' he would say. 'They worship death.'

Unlike many screenwriters, Faulkner was no pulpist. By the time he arrived in Hollywood in 1932, his first four novels, including *Soldiers' Pay* and *The Sound and the Fury*, had sold, on average, fewer than 2,000 copies each. When he attempted to pen a best seller, *Sanctuary*, his publisher went bankrupt. Even *As I Lay Dying* and *Light in August* had sold poorly. Needing money, he managed to find employment at MGM – always willing to co-opt literary writers – at $500 a week. When asked what movies he wanted to work on, Faulkner replied 'I want to write for Mickey Mouse.' When he was told the studio did not own the rights to Mickey, Faulkner said he wanted to write newsreels. So they showed him a wrestling movie. Faulkner was so depressed he ran from the studio. When he returned, they put him to work patching up scripts and cut his salary to $250 per week. Eventually he was fired, went back to Mississippi, and wrote *Absalom, Absalom*. When that novel didn't sell, he went back to Hollywood and was hired by Darryl Zanuck at Fox, at $1,000 a week. A year later Fox fired him, and Faulkner returned to Mississippi where he wrote *Wild Palms* and *The Hamlet*. His royalty statement from Random House for 1942 came to a grand total of $300. By the following year, all his books, with the exception of *Sanctuary*, were out of print. Back in Hollywood, he was given a seven-year contract at Warner Brothers at $300 a week. When he asked Hal Wallis if he could work at home, the producer agreed, not realising that, to Faulkner, home meant Oxford, Mississippi. Eventually, he was dragged back to Tinseltown. Constantly drunk and in poor health, Faulkner would only quit Hollywood after winning the Nobel Prize. Fortunately, Hawks, who admired his writing, purchased the film rights to *Soldiers' Pay*. Though the movie was never made, he managed to get Faulkner to work on *Today We Live*, starring Gary Cooper and Joan Crawford, followed by *The Road to Glory* and *To Have and Have Not*.

Miraculously, the Brackett–Faulkner partnership worked, even though neither saw what the other had written. They would simply hand in their work to Hawks, whose only further chore regarding the script was to call in Jules Furthman to shorten some of the later scenes. When it came to filming, however, Hawks decided against using a final script, preferring to hand the actors their pages moments before shooting a particular scene.

Furthman had been the right person to call. Not only was he adept at rewrites, but in Hawks's opinion he was, as a writer, the equal of Hecht, Hemingway, MacArthur and Faulkner. Having worked on films since 1915, Furthman had been von Sternberg's main writer. Among his credits were gems like *Morocco*, *Shanghai Express*, *Blonde Venus*, *Only Angels Have Wings* and *Nightmare Alley*. It was Furthman who, on Hawks's urging, wrote Bacall's now famous insolence into *The Big Sleep*. In fact, Bacall's presence in Hollywood, and her screen debut opposite Bogart in *To Have and Have Not*, had been the result of another Hawks error. The director had only wanted to get some information about a young woman whose face had appeared on the cover of *Harper's Bazaar*, but his secretary had misunderstood and sent the teenage actress a plane ticket and an invitation for a screen test.

Brackett, Faulkner and Furthman's playful script is almost impossible to follow. Yet the dialogue, the staging of scenes, the characters and the acting are so superb that few mind the plot's incomprehensibility. Like the book, the film moves from scene to scene with a fluidity that makes the process by which one arrives at the final plot point more interesting than understanding the end result. Even the actors and writers were perplexed. When Bogart asked who had killed the chauffeur, Brackett said she wasn't sure. They asked Faulkner, who said he didn't know either. So they telegrammed Chandler, who wired back saying he hadn't a clue.

Brackett had considered Chandler's novel something of a hardboiled bible, and was initially reluctant to alter it. Gradually her awed attitude changed. When he saw the end result, Chandler admitted that he liked Brackett's ending, which Hawks would have to eventually shorten. There were two reasons for this change. Not only did Jack Warner want to put more emphasis on the Bogart–Bacall romance, which was the talk of Hollywood at the time, but according to Hawks the Production Code office had demanded a different ending. According to them, no one in the movie had been sufficiently punished. So Hawks asked the Production Code office if they'd provide an acceptable ending. Hawks would always say their version was more violent than his own. However, Bogart's portrayal of Marlowe was basically Brackett's doing. Since seeing him in *The Maltese Falcon*, he had been her favourite actor. Not only had she written the part with Bogart in mind, but she was surprised to find, on the set, that he was well trained in the theatrical arts and able to learn his lines and perfect his timing within minutes.

By Brackett's admission, it took a bit of time to learn how to write screenplays. But she realised that from doing so she learned a great deal about story construction. So long as she could write a script straight through, from beginning to end, Brackett seldom had difficulties. Problems only occurred if she happened to write herself into a corner, at which point she would have to stop and figure out where she'd gone wrong. A more immediate problem faced her in writing *The Big Sleep*: Hawks terrified her. He had a reputation for telling writers what he wanted, then going away, not to be seen for a number of weeks. Brackett was afraid she might do the same at her first story conference. But she managed to get through it and gradually gain confidence as a scriptwriter. About screenwriting, she would say, in an interview with Steve Swires, 'If I sit down to write a novel, I am God at my own typewriter, and there's nobody in between. But if I'm doing a screenplay, it has to be a compromise because there are so many things outside a writer's province.'

Brackett would also team up with Robert Altman, another director who liked to leave actors in the dark regarding the final script. Brackett's ex-agent Elliott Kastner, having set up a project with United Artists to do a film with Elliott Gould, remembered Brackett's script to *The Big Sleep*, and asked if she'd be interested in adapting *The Long Goodbye*. Though she never considered Gould a full-fledged Marlowe, and he was hardly a typical tough guy, she came to the conclusion that Gould was more than adequate in the role. As far as Brackett was concerned, twenty years had passed since the novel had been written and the private eye was now a cliché. Altman felt the same. He wanted to create an antihero, saying, 'I think Marlowe's dead. I think *that* was "the long goodbye." I think it's a goodbye to that genre – a genre that I don't think is going to be acceptable any more.' Consequently, there was a point to be made regarding Gould's whimsical take on the role.

But Brackett knew that *The Long Goodbye* would be more difficult than *The Big Sleep* to adapt. If filmed as Chandler had written it, audiences would have been required to sit in movie theatres for some five hours. So Brackett set out to condense the novel, a process that necessitated changing sections of the story. First of all, the idea that the morally ambiguous Terry Lennox had planned everything from the start was too contrived. So much so that at first Brackett found she was spending her time writing people out of the boxes in which they had been trapped by this particular artifice. When she visited Altman in London, where he was editing *Images*, Brackett found that she and the director were in agreement regarding her take on the film. She was also encouraged that Altman wanted to change the setting, moving the Chandler conventions and mores of the 1940s to the context and reality of the 1970s. In Altman's opinion, the Los Angeles that Chandler had written about no longer existed. 'In a sense,' said Brackett, 'it never existed except in [Chandler's] imagination.' So Brackett, who liked Edward Dmytryk's *Murder, My Sweet* with Dick Powell but had reservations about Robert Montgomery, and his subjective camera, in *Lady in the Lake*, was able to solve the problem of the plot by removing the moral ambiguity, and making Terry Lennox a clear-cut villain. According to Brackett, 'it seemed the only satisfactory ending was for the cruelly diddled Marlowe to blow Terry's guts out'.

In the end, Gould's version of Marlowe, though something of a parody, demythologises the character. After killing his friend, Gould walks off into the sunset whistling 'Hooray for Hollywood'. It is a jarring and cynical moment, but one that brings the viewer back to reality. As Brackett told Jon Tuska in *The Detective in Hollywood*, the ending illustrates that Chandler's characters are not real, but are movie conceptions of people. As far as Brackett is concerned, Marlowe kills his friend because he is an honest man in a world that has kicked him in the teeth once too often. In Brackett's opinion, Marlowe was 'a real loser, not the fake winner that Chandler made out of him'. Consequently, her ending seems logical. Had the censors allowed her to do so, she would, on her own admission, have ended *The Big Sleep* in a similar way. Having turned Marlowe into a powerless observer, and making society's indifference – crimes are observed but more often than not ignored – the cornerstone of the film, Brackett, Altman and Gould were able to update the role and the genre. Some years later a young Michael Connelly would see the film, prompting him to quit the building trade and become a crime writer.

According to Brackett, writing is often more technical than creative: 'What you have to be is a very good journeyman plumber and put the parts together. And then, if you can still inject a little bit of something worth while, you've done as much as can be expected.' She proved her point on more than one occasion, subtly injecting new ideas into noir fiction and film at a time when both genres appeared to have already written their own epitaphs.

7

LIFE SENTENCES

Edward Bunker

There is no one better at depicting the criminal world and the ease with which society can draw someone into that world than Edward Bunker. Concerning his own criminal past, Bunker, born and raised in Los Angeles, and having served sentences in San Quentin and Folsom prisons, has said, 'If God weighed what was done to me against what I did, I'm not sure how the scales would tip.' These days, with ever-increasing numbers being placed behind bars, Bunker's stories have become more relevant than ever. The downside is that, having spent much of his life locked up, and writing about it with such urgency and accuracy, Bunker not only risks narrative repetition but invites prurient interest and a pseudo-hip voyeurism. Nevertheless, Bunker, increasingly in demand as a screenwriter, can hardly be blamed for how he is perceived by others.

When not incarcerated, Bunker has maintained a special relationship with Hollywood. Born in 1933, the son of a stage-hand and a chorus girl, Bunker saw his parents split up when he was four years old, from which time he was sent to a series of foster homes. It wasn't long before he was involved in a life of petty crime. Each time he was apprehended, the more difficult it was for his father to find a foster home or military academy prepared to take him. Despite the fact that he was still committing what amounted to petty crimes, Bunker, after stabbing a prison guard, became, at the age of seventeen, the youngest inmate to walk through the doors of San Quentin. It was there that he met the 'Red Light Bandit', Caryl

Chessman, perpetrator – Bunker believed him innocent – of a series of sexual assaults and robberies on Mulholland Drive (also known as Lovers' Lane, or, in homage to the excitable wrestling announcer of the 1950s, Dick Lane). Even though he hadn't murdered anyone, Chessman would be controversially executed in the late 1950s. (Bunker on the death penalty: 'No doubt some deserve to die . . . How do we decide? I refer you to Camus's monumental essay: "Reflections on the Guillotine." ') While in prison Chessman had written four books: *Cell 2455 Death Row*, *Trial by Ordeal* and *The Face of Justice*, and a novel about a boxer, *The Kid Was a Killer*. Apart from an alcoholic ex-newspaperman he had met in Camarillo State Hospital, Chessman was the first writer Bunker had ever come across. Chessman would lend him Jack London's *The Sea Wolf* and George Santayana's *The Last Puritan*. From there the young inmate moved on to Dreiser, Wolfe, Fitzgerald, Hemingway, Dos Passos and Faulkner. More than anyone else, Chessman would be responsible for Bunker joining the ranks of such prison writers as Chester Himes, Jean Genet, London, O'Henry, Clarence Cooper Jr. and Malcolm Braly, as well as those, like Robert Tasker, Ernest Booth and Jim Tully, who, upon their release, would write screenplays in Hollywood.

Between sentences, Bunker, thanks to his lawyer, was befriended by Louise Fazenda Wallis, the former actress and wife of producer Hal Wallis. Though her friendship would not keep Bunker out of prison, Fazenda did have a positive effect on Bunker. Arriving in Hollywood during the silent era, Fazenda appeared in her first film in 1913. Two years later she was working with Mack Sennett in his *Joker* and *Keystone Cop* films. Not particularly beautiful, Fazenda specialised in playing rural types, appearing in *Tillie's Punctured Romance*, in which she played Tillie opposite W.C. Fields, and Norman McLeod's *Alice in Wonderland*, in which she appeared as the White Queen alongside Fields, Gary Cooper, Charles Ruggles, Cary Grant and Edward Everett Horton. Her last film was

Edmund Goulding's 1939 women's film, *The Old Maid*, along-side Bette Davis and Miriam Hopkins.

By the time he met Fazenda, Bunker was already acquainted with her husband's name, having seen a number of Wallis productions, particularly gangster films featuring Edward G. Robinson, Bogart and Raft. One of Hollywood's top pro-ducers, Wallis had by that time already had such successes as *Little Caesar* and *I Am a Fugitive from a Chain Gang*. After Darryl Zanuck left Warner Brothers in 1933, Wallis became head of production and would soon equal Thalberg's remarkable output at MGM, with films like *They Drive by Night*, *The Maltese Falcon*, *High Sierra* and *Casablanca*. So enraged was Wallis when studio boss Jack Warner beat him to the stage to collect an Oscar for *Casablanca* that he quit the studio and formed his own company, producing films like *The Strange Love of Martha Ivers*, *The File on Thelma Jordan* and *Dark City*, which came close to equalling the standard he had set at Warner.

Fazenda was so free with her money that at first Bunker thought he was about to become another Hollywood gigolo. But Fazenda had more humanitarian intentions, and the two quickly became close friends. However, it was neither her humanitarianism nor her money but her library that first impressed Bunker. For the first time anywhere he found rows of books by a variety of authors, including two of his prison favourites, Teilhard de Chardin and Karen Horney. Through Fazenda, Bunker would meet an assortment of Hollywood personalities. He accompanied her to William Randolph Hearst's castle in San Simeon, where he met Marion Davies, Greta Garbo, John Gilbert, Charlie Chaplin ('a good tennis player'), Zazu Pitts and Hearst himself, who by then had only a short time to live.

It wasn't long before Bunker, having been convicted of theft, was back in prison, moving from juvenile facilities to Vacaville and, finally, San Quentin, which would be his resi-dence throughout the early 1950s. After consulting her friend, California state politician Jesse 'Big Daddy' Unrah,

Fazenda hired a lawyer. Thanks to his efforts, Bunker was paroled in 1956, and moved into an apartment over a four-car garage attached to the Wallises' home in Hancock Park. Though he tried to remain on good terms with Hal Wallis, the latter would view him with suspicion, even blocking his attempt during this period to find employment as a Hollywood script-doctor. Unable to get studio work, Bunker returned to a world of crime. Less comfortable with Hollywood film people than with the city's *demimonde*, Bunker began frequenting nightclubs and associating with criminals, prostitutes and drug dealers. After taking part in another robbery, Bunker became a fugitive from justice, crisscrossing the nation as one of the FBI's most wanted. Once apprehended, and judged criminally insane, he was sent to Atascadero State Hospital, and then to Folsom Prison.

It was in Folsom that he began writing his novel *No Beast So Fierce*. In 1972, while still behind bars, Bunker learned that the book was to be published. Seven years later it would be adapted for the screen by the former diamond-cutter Ulu Grosbard and retitled *Straight Time*. The book follows a Bunker-like protagonist as he attempts to adjust to life outside prison, only to be forced back into a life of crime. The film stars Dustin Hoffman, who mimics Bunker's mannerisms to perfection. But in the end, Bunker was disappointed with the film, and still hopes it will be remade, because, he says, 'the truths of the book were not in the first movie'.

The script to Grosbard's film was written by Alvin Sargent, who encouraged Bunker to contribute to the screenplay. It would mark the beginning of Bunker's career as a scriptwriter. He was already familiar with the form, having written a script entitled *Slick Willy*, about a man in his fifties who breaks out of a Los Angeles jail, which he sent to a New York fellowship award competition. Bunker's script, out of 600 entries, was judged the best. Nevertheless, it was Sargent who was to teach Bunker the art of scriptwriting. By the time he and Bunker worked together, Sargent was already a veteran writer with a career stretching back to the mid-1960s. Among his credits were screenplays for Peter Bogdanovich's *Paper Moon*, for which he received an Oscar nomination, and Fred Zinnemann's *Julia*, for which he received an Academy Award.

As for Bunker, he would go on to receive credit, along with Djordje Milicevic and Paul Zindel, for the nail-biting action film *Runaway Train* (1985). Adapted from an original screenplay by Akira Kurosawa, the story concerns two escapees from prison, Manny and Buck, who find themselves in the Alaskan wilderness, having commandeered a train that literally cannot be stopped. The film was directed by Andrei Konchalovsky ('The best director I've ever worked for'), and starred Jon Voight as Manny ('Based on somebody I'd known') and Eric Roberts as Buck ('There were a lot of kids in prison like Buck, who were wannabes').

While his services as a writer or adviser have often been sought by directors in search of a touch of realism regarding prison life or crime, Bunker would eventually be asked to appear in an assortment of crime movies. Though he tends to be typecast, Bunker has now appeared in some twenty films. He usually plays a professional criminal, the most notable of which is his portrayal of Mr. Blue in Quentin Tarantino's *Reservoir Dogs* – a film influenced by *Straight Time*, which Tarantino studied before embarking on the project. Besides *Reservoir Dogs* and small parts in *Straight Time* and *Runaway Train*, Bunker has appeared in the likes of *The Long Riders*, *The Running Man*, *Tango & Cash* and *Animal Factory*.

Bunker's most recent film adaptation is *Animal Factory* (2000). A follow up to *No Beast So Fierce*, Bunker's 1977 novel and the film that is based on it concern Ron Decker, a middle-class twenty-five-year-old, sentenced to San Quentin for what he thought would be a minor drugs charge. The sordid reality of everyday life in prison comes as a shock, and Decker, if he wants to survive, must come to terms with it. At the heart of the story is the relationship – essentially, a platonic love affair – between Decker and Earl, a long-term convict, who takes it upon himself to instruct the younger man on the brutal protocol of prison life and the strategies essential for survival. Directed by Steve Buscemi, with Bunker and John Steppling sharing the screenwriting credits, the film, which stars Willem Dafoe, Edward Furlong and Mickey Rourke, was shot outside Philadelphia at Holmsburg Prison in a mere twenty-nine days. With one film (*Trees Lounge*) and TV episodes of *Oz* and *Homicide: Life on the Street* under his belt, Buscemi proves himself adept at depicting the vulnerabilities of inmates (including Rourke, who plays Decker's transvestite cell mate) and the claustrophobic environment in which they must live. Surprisingly low-keyed, the film is a timely critique of the modern penal system and, at the same time, a throwback to the social-problem dramas of the late 1940s.

Bunker's next novel, *Little Boy Blue* (1981), focuses on an eleven-year-old boy who rebels against the system. To protect himself from society, he resorts to violence, which escalates until he's finally incarcerated. He escapes, is rearrested and once again put behind bars. There he finds his only means of liberating himself from the mental confines of prison life is through literature. This book, like *Animal Factory*, contains autobiographical elements, and is arguably his most personal novel. After *Little Boy Blue*, fifteen years would pass before Bunker's next novel, *Dog Eat Dog*, which might have gone unpublished had not Bunker found a new agent through fellow writer James Ellroy (Bunker had written a script for a yet-to-be-made film of Ellroy's *Suicide Hill*). About a group of ex-cons in search of one last score, *Dog Eat Dog* articulates the tension between going straight and returning to a life of crime, while examining the difference between old-style gang-sters and more recent coke-inspired hoodlums. Here the friendship that exists between the ex-cons is put to the test as they plan an armed robbery that eventually goes wrong. The novel reads like a modern-day *High Sierra*. But Bunker is not about to become another W.R. Burnett, not so long as he writes fiction that is self-referential and so openly critical of

society. Following *Dog Eat Dog* came Bunker's long-awaited
1999 autobiography, *Mr. Blue: Memoirs of a Renegade* (entitled
Education of a Felon in the United States), which provides the
reader with the lowdown on the writer's notorious past.

Like George V. Higgins, Bunker does not consider himself
a crime writer, unless, as he says, 'Dreiser, Dostoyevksy and
Truman Capote are crime writers.' Crime is simply the milieu
Bunker knows best. As he puts it, 'I write novels that happen
to be about crime and criminals because I know crime and
criminals better than anyone else. At least better than anyone
else who can write.'

Courted as the person who understands not only prison
life but the criminal mind, Bunker occupies a special place in
Hollywood. Consequently, film people treat him with cautious
respect. Some even fear him. But Bunker takes a realistic
approach to his work: 'Writers are well paid . . . I am treated
well. I have always had directors who I respected and who
respected me. Again, I am not just a screen writer. I'm essentially a book writer.' With Hollywood capable of sinking to
criminal-like depths, Bunker maintains that most thieves have
more honour than the average Hollywood agent.

These days Bunker has influenced various directors and
writers. When making *Heat*, director Michael Mann gave the
entire crew a copy of *No Beast So Fierce* to read. Mann's 1995
film reflects Bunker's professional attitude to crime – except,
as Bunker says, for the hiring of a fellow criminal whom no
one in the gang knows nor has worked with before. What's
more, Jon Voight goes beyond Hoffman's performance in
Straight Time, playing a character that closely resembles the
writer. Says Bunker, 'They had my picture in the make-up
room. If you look at Jon Voight in the movie, he looks just
like me, so much so that when I go with Danny Trejo, a friend
of mine who was in the film, to a restaurant, people say, "Oh,
you guys were great." They know it's him and they just assume
that I'm Jon Voight.'

In pursuing verisimilitude, Bunker challenges his audience

to reach an understanding with the world he once inhabited. While his fiction remains evocative, informative, interesting and entertaining, his approach to the business of screenwriting is never less than straightforward. Attempting to make a living without compromising himself any more than necessary, Bunker stakes out his own ground, saying, 'I'm not going to do a script for free. I'll do it for minimum, but you can't ask me to do it for nothing. They always want to fuck the writer. It really is true.'

WH: *Why are some writers successful at doing screenplays, and others aren't?*

EB: To write a screenplay you have to be able to think visually. And you have to be able to write visually. One of the first books I read about writing – way back, about forty, fifty years ago when I first started – by some guy called Jack Woodford, said, 'Imagine you're watching what you're writing.' That wasn't relative to writing screenplays; that was relative to writing anything. Novels, stories, whatever. But it put me in that paradigm, that in my mind I'm watching the scene and describing what's going on in the scene. I go a little deeper. I describe the scene and then go into the mind of those who are in the scene. In the end, I hold a mirror up to it. So it's on two different levels. With a screenplay you don't deal with that second level. You just deal with the first level. And some people are just natural screenwriters. Like Quentin Tarantino. I don't think he's a great director, but he's a great screenwriter. He's just an average director, but, as a screenwriter, he's great at dialogue and structure.

WH: *Do you find it easy to write screenplays?*

EB: I found it easy to write *Animal Factory*. And, as a matter of fact, *Runaway Train* was the easiest thing I've ever written. When they gave it to me it wasn't a very good script. They already had all the train action, and the bridge that they were going to crash over. Those kind of things were already set. But what happened with the convicts, that was all mine. When

I got it, Manny was a wife-killer. But you can't be a wife-killer *and* a legend. And Manny was a legend. Being a wife-killer isn't quite as bad as being a child-molester, but it's almost as bad. So I had to change all that. So I totally rewrote the first twenty minutes until they get on the train, and I created the characters. In the original script, the characters – I'm not going to say the characters were shit, but they were close to it. And I had a great director working right with me, getting the best out of me. I'd tell him a story and he'd say, 'Oh, we'll use that!' He'd take a line, he'd literally snip one little fucking thing, take it, and paste it over here, right where it was supposed to go. And he'd get stories out of me. I don't know how well you remember the movie, but where they come in they're yelling, 'Man-ny, Man-ny, Man-ny!' Well, I had that happen to me in San Quentin. I'd been transferred from Vacaville and I came through the gate. And from the adjustment centre – which is now all Death Row, but was then part Death Row and part Hole – they could see out the gate. I hadn't been there in years. It was twilight and I came in and the guys knew me in there. They started yelling and, man, I didn't know if they were going to kill me or if they were praising me or what. I told the director about it, and he said, 'We'll use that.'

WH: It must make it a lot easier to work with a director like that.

EB: That's right. Directors. Fuck 'em. That's what my friend Alvin Sargent says. Goddamn directors. He's been lucky to have good directors who see the same thing he sees. In television it's not so. In television the writer is much more powerful.

WH: Why is that?

EB: Because they shoot to schedule, and they shoot tight. The director mostly just directs traffic. The writer is the real boss in television.

WH: You wrote Straight Time *with Alvin Sargent, didn't you?*

EB: Yeah. Actually, I didn't do that much of it. He more or less just gave me a credit. But I learned an awful lot from him. Actually, the opposite of what I learned from Quentin. If you look through Quentin's shit, everything comes from another movie. He's never had an original thought. Yet he often does it better than the original. But still it's not original. Whereas Alvin has the opposite attitude. He tells me, 'If you've seen it in a movie before, get rid of it. Always avoid what you've seen before.' Whereas Quentin does the exact opposite.

WH: Do you rank Quentin and Sargent amongst the best screen-writers?

EB: Yeah, but there're others. There's Frank Pierson who wrote *Cool Hand Luke*. There's Lorenzo Semple who wrote *Three Days of the Condor*. And some of the old-timers like Rafelson. Quentin hasn't written that much, so you don't know how big his chest is. From working with Quentin I've learned about being loose with dialogue. I used to write much tighter, to always move the story, and to make the point and make it good. But I learned from Quentin to make it a little bit frivolous sometimes, and to hang loose. I adapted an Ellroy book, *Suicide Hill*, for a French-Algerian who's had it for eight, nine years. A great script, one of the best I ever wrote, maybe the best script I ever wrote. And he won't make it. And he knows he's got directors. He showed me letters from directors who've said, 'This is great. Let's do it.' It was very hard to adapt. Ellroy's really hard to adapt.

WH: I thought that was the thing with L.A. *Confidential. I didn't think it was that great a film, but what a script.*

EB: Because Ellroy's all over the place. His strength is in his characters and he has great scenes. But his weakness is in his structure. His structure is hard to fucking adapt.

WH: Then there were all those writers who came here in the 1940s and never wrote another novel.

EB: Like Faulkner. They had to leave. And when all the intelligentsia left blue-eyed Europe during World War II – Bertolt Brecht, Aldous Huxley, Christopher Isherwood – they all came out to the Santa Monica Canyon. They would meet at Leon Feuchtwanger's place in Pacific Palisades. They came to one spot. They had a little enclave down there. Tim Zinnemann – Fred Zinnemann's son – was hanging out on the fringe of that.

WH: Has writing for films affected the way you write novels?

EB: No, I don't think so. Though I do think film writing has affected the novel. It's become a much more visual medium. I'm a kind of stripped-down novelist anyway. I didn't study great literature and how to do things that way. I'm a storyteller. I'm a pretty good storyteller. But I'm not fancy. I tell a story from beginning to end. There's very little flashbacks, which, to me, in most instances, slow things down. In *Animal Factory* I switched viewpoints back and forth between the older convict and the younger convict. That's the only novel in which I did that. But I don't think screenplay writing has affected my novels. I hope not. Though when I wrote the novel, *Animal Factory,* I wrote it so it could be made into a movie. I deliberately wrote in a James M. Cain fashion with stripped-down scenes consisting of action and dialogue, and deliberately made it very easy to adapt.

WH: So besides the films you're credited with, what other films have you worked on?

EB: I worked on *Johnny Handsome*. I didn't get any credit for it. But then probably nobody deserved credit for that one. There are others that I can't remember. They call me in. I love it when they have a *go* picture and the studio's throwing money around. Oh, man, they pay you. But when you're negotiating with them for something, they're really tight with their money. They'll kill a deal over twenty grand.

WH: I guess that's the attraction. The money.

EB: Yeah, but I don't like the collaboration. Though I've written a couple scripts on spec, just because I've needed to. I've got a couple good ones, but I won't do that any more. Somebody asked me if I'd write *Little Boy Blue*. They wanted to produce it. But they wanted to know if I'd take a shot at it. Why should I take a spec shot when I can take a spec shot at a novel and I know I'm going to be published in nine countries? You know what I mean? In the movies, there's thousands and thousands of fucking scripts written on spec, so what are the chances of getting it made?

WH: Would you rather write the script for one of your own books, or would you rather have someone else write it?

EB: I would rather write the script. But I'd rather get paid. I don't want to do it for nothing. I may do it for a little bit at the front end, or at the back end, but I'd much prefer to control my own material. That's the idea. Somebody options one of my books, they've got to pay, not much, but the Guild minimum, and whatever the overs are.

WH: Would you rather deal with book publishers or producers?

EB: That's a hard question. I've had bad luck with both. American publishers especially. My European publishers are beautiful. I get great reviews. *Dog Eat Dog* was huge in France. All of my books do well there. But especially *Dog Eat Dog*. There's American writers who can't get published here, who get published in France. Like Dan Fante, whose father was John Fante. He's a good writer. I just discovered John Fante a couple years ago. I thought I'd read everything in the fucking world. Somebody gave me a book – *Dreams from Bunker Hill* – I read it and said, 'Man, that's great.'

WH: What about directors? Have you had any bad experiences with them?

EB: Not really. I thought Ulu Grosbard could have done a better job on *Straight Time*. I don't think he liked the gangster character. I felt that, the way he handled it. Still I like him, and I think he's a great director of actors.

WH: So on the three films with which you're credited, were you the only writer, or did they call in other writers?

EB: I was the last writer on *Animal Factory* and *Straight Time*. On *Animal Factory*, I just went through arbitration and lost. I've got to share a credit, and I don't think I should have had to do that. I wrote the book twenty years ago to be a movie, then about twelve years ago I wrote a spec script. Christopher

Lambert optioned it, made a deal to pay me to write the script, then reneged. He gave me some of the money and then he let the option lapse and it reverted to me. So I had this script and I was always thinking, it's a good script, it's a prison script, and who else can write about prison as well as I can? So when I adapted it on my own, I made some changes from my book, which is my prerogative since it's my book. When Steve Buscemi came in to direct he looked at the script and he wanted some of the things I'd left out from the book put into the script. So he hired John Steppling (*52 Pick Up*) and told him what to do. Essentially, what he did was go back to *my* book, and took scenes that Steve told him to take and put them back into the script. We put in for credits and I get a single credit, and John Steppling files a protest that he deserves a credit, and he wins. Now the Writers Guild have weird rules. Because I'm a co-producer I have to write seventy-five percent of the script. If he proves he only wrote twenty-five percent, he's entitled to co-credit. Not only that, but you don't know who the judges are. All they consider are three scripts and they take a vote. Man, I want witnesses. I want to be able to cross-examine. If I had taken my name off as co-producer, he would have had to prove he had written fifty-one percent and he couldn't have done that.

WH: I read something you said about your average criminal being more trustworthy than your average Hollywood agent.

EB: It's a really sleazy town. There's a lot of sleazy shit, because there's so much money involved. The people around the talent are the ones who are sleazy. Because that's all they've got going for them.

WH: Do you think you intimidate movie people?

EB: Sometimes I do. When I want to I do. On the other hand, I don't like to do it too much because they get scared. Then there are the ones who want me to validate their manhood. Actors especially. They always want to know, 'What would happen to me inside? Would I get along?' If I accept them as a man it validates their manhood, their macho-ness.

You'd be surprised how many actors have sociopathic traits. They do. They have criminal attitudes. They're antisocial. Their attitudes don't conform with the attitudes of normal society.

8

PRIME SUSPECTS

Elmore Leonard and James Ellroy

With a greater awareness of the relationship between noir fiction and film, recent crime writers tend to assume a more hardboiled attitude towards Hollywood. At the same time, most, though voicing the usual concerns about the industry, remain willing to be co-opted. After all, the lure of money and mingling with the famous often proves irresistible.

With so much at stake, an industry has been built that panders to Hollywood hopefuls, crime writers or otherwise. These days, with film schools churning out screenwriters and weekend workshops charging exorbitant amounts to disseminate information and expertise, most consider writing fiction only as something they might try once they've established themselves as screenwriters. Consequently, a new type of Hollywood writer has emerged, homogeneous, competent and mediocre. At the same, Hollywood, more competitive than ever, and seeking writers with an edge to their work, continues to court novelists, invariably on an *ad hoc* basis.

Linked to the screenwriter's place in the industry is the seemingly contrary notion propagated by the likes of Richard Corliss and Pauline Kael that writers are, in their own way, *auteurs*. Though containing a grain of truth, this view ignores the economics of film-making and the dynamics of corporate politics. Lacking power when it comes to production or negotiation, not even the best scriptwriters can be considered *auteurs*. Yet neither are they, as Jack Warner once called them, 'schmucks with Underwoods'. Often overpaid and always under-appreciated, with little or no say when it comes to the final product, writers remain an essential part of the film-making process.

Clearly, Hollywood, despite its resources, has rarely been kind to writers. They are, and always have been, on the sharp end of the industry's artistic switchblade. As always, working in Tinseltown is a high-risk occupation. To engage with it, one would be advised at least to have an inkling of its history. Only then is it possible to assume the appropriate attitude. Celebrated though they might be, the following two writers, conversant with the destructive aspects of Hollywood, represent different approaches to the film industry. While Elmore Leonard is fairly laid-back, James Ellroy takes a more circumspect position regarding Tinseltown.

Elmore Leonard

Though his novels appear to be ready-made for the screen, Elmore Leonard, for the past decade, has refused to write screenplays for Hollywood. He's learned from experience. From 1972 to 1987 he wrote a number of scripts, none of which led to a film that equalled the book from which it was derived. His experience was to lead him to the conclusion that he'd stick to writing novels and let others worry about adapting them for the screen. Thanks to his success as a novelist, he was able to do this without any undue financial suffering.

In fact, Leonard had been publishing for ten years when, in 1961, in a deal brokered by H.N. Swanson, Twentieth Century Fox paid him $10,000 for *Hombre*, at which point Leonard decided to quit his advertising job. Though he was not quite the struggling novelist he once was, he was still not able to support himself by his writing. For the next two years, he would supplement his income by writing scripts for industrial and cultural films put together by his old ad agency.

Hombre, directed by Martin Ritt and starring Paul Newman, would finally be released in 1967.

Leonard's publishing career begins back in 1951, when he sold his first story – a western, 'Trail of the Apache' – to *Argosy*. Two years later his first novel, *The Bounty Hunters*, appeared, as did Leonard's other well-known story of the West, '3:10 to Yuma', which would be adapted by Delmer Daves in 1957, with a screenplay written by Halsted Welles. One of a handful of psychological westerns that appeared in the wake of *High Noon*, *3:10 to Yuma* stars Van Heflin as a rancher who, to collect the bounty money that will save his drought-stricken ranch, escorts outlaw Glenn Ford to the state penitentiary. Daves had the right background to do justice to the film, having worked, as a student, as a prop boy on the 1923 epic *The Covered Wagon*, and having lived on a Navajo reservation prior to beginning his forty-year Hollywood career.

It was in 1957 that one of Leonard's favourite films was released: Budd Boetticher's *The Tall T*. Scripted by Burt Kennedy from a Leonard story, it stars Randolph Scott and Richard Boone. If any old-school director was to do justice to Leonard it surely would have been Boetticher, whose low-budget bleak westerns are invariably set in the hot desert sun, and are concerned with such perennial themes as death, courage and cruelty. *The Tall T*, in focusing on such mythic values, remains one of the more underrated films to be adapted from Leonard's body of work. Though Leonard's westerns can be extremely violent, they are psychologically well conceived and, more often than not, anti-racist in their treatment of the non-white population. At least that's the case with *The Tall T*, *Hombre*, which was published in 1961 and adapted for the screen in 1967, and *Valdez Is Coming*, published in 1970 and filmed in 1971. The latter film was directed by Edwin Sherin and stars Burt Lancaster as a Mexican double-crossed by a rancher. Though perhaps not the classic it appeared to be, *Valdez Is Coming* remains one of the better westerns of that era.

As the 1960s ended, so did the paperback market for westerns. It was then that Leonard switched to crime novels. His first effort was *The Big Bounce* in 1969. Though his westerns may have been anti-racist, his first crime novels, such as *The Big Bounce* and *The Moonshine War*, were, true to the spirit of pulp crime writers like Day Keene and Gil Brewer, misogynistic in tone and anarchistic in spirit. Leonard would, over the years, refine the latter tendency and correct the former. From 1985 and the publication of *La Brava*, women would play an ever-increasing role in his work.

Throughout the 1970s, Leonard's scripts would be turned every which way but loose by a series of lackadaisical directors and penny-pinching producers. The first such disaster was *The Big Bounce* (1969), directed by Alex March and starring Ryan O'Neal. Unlike other directors, such as Fleischer and Sturges, March was a TV director without any movie success to his name. Leonard would later call *The Big Bounce* 'the worst movie ever made'. The following year, at MGM, Richard Quine would direct *The Moonshine War*, featuring Patrick McGoohan. Fresh from the groundbreaking TV series *The Prisoner*, McGoohan is said to have asked Leonard, who was on the set, 'What's it like to stand there and hear all your lines fucked up?' One imagines Leonard shrugging his shoulders, knowing that, as a writer, he had little control over the end result. A couple of years after *The Moonshine War*, Leonard was writing *Joe Kidd* (1972) – bounty-hunter tracks down Mexican bandits – for John Sturges at Universal. Starring Clint Eastwood and Robert Duvall, this film, like Quine's, is not only unnecessarily violent but also morally dubious. Though these two offerings are not complete disasters, neither is comparable to their directors' best work, nor to Leonard's subsequent fiction.

In 1974, *Mr. Majestyk*, made at United Artists, harks back to the anti-racist westerns that Leonard once wrote. Directed by Richard Fleischer, it stars Charles Bronson as a melon grower who confronts the local mafia. Like Quine and Sturges, Fleischer was a Hollywood veteran with a good track record. Having made films since 1946, including such noir classics as *The Narrow Margin*, *Violent Saturday* and *Compulsion*, he was past his prime and unable to handle the subtleties of Leonard's offhand manner, non-literary literariness and libertarian perspective, qualities that can be easily misinterpreted. Quine's directorial career had begun in 1948, and his work included *Drive a Crooked Road* and *Pushover*. Sturges had directed a series of underrated westerns, such as *The Capture*, *Gunfight at the O.K. Corral*, *Last Train from Gun Hill* and the modern-day western *Bad Day at Black Rock*. All three directors were searching for material that would allow them to repeat past successes. Unfortunately they were more inclined to recycle clichés than to reinterpret their chosen genres.

Leonard fared no better during the 1980s. In 1985 Burt Reynolds did his best to butcher *Stick*, an otherwise perfectly decent novel. And in the late 1980s, Whiskers Productions gave Leonard $20,000 to rewrite the first twenty pages of a script to his novel *Cat Chaser*. Once started, Leonard was unable to stop until he had rewritten the entire script. After all, it was his novel. But the studio had their own ideas about the movie, and promptly fired Leonard. Abel Ferrara would say of his 1989 film, 'Even I couldn't understand it. And I directed it.' At least Leonard received a writing credit for it. As he would for *52 Pick-Up* (1986) and *The Rosary Murders* (1987). Ironically, it was at this time, when Leonard's screenwriting career was practically over, that he became a hot Hollywood property. By the late 1990s, Leonard would be increasingly influenced by film. One can see this in recent novels and adaptations of *Get Shorty* (1995), *Jackie Brown* (1997, originally published as *Rum Punch*) and *Out of Sight* (1998). Not only are his novels now replete with references to Hollywood movies, but his characters react as if they were playing their favourite film characters. After all, Leonard's comedy of manners comes straight from the heart and soul of popular culture.

WH: Why does Hollywood seem to destroy so many writers, but leaves others untouched?

EL: First of all, you can't take Hollywood too seriously. Or worry that your story is going to be destroyed or altered. Thirty out of thirty-two of my novels have been optioned or bought outright. The reason they buy them is because they read the manuscript and it reads like a movie. There are scenes and there is some good dialogue. The problem is that what's left after the adaptation is just the dialogue, and it's not always my dialogue. Up to *Get Shorty* the problem was that, when you take one of my 360-page manuscripts and get it down to 120 pages, a lot of the good stuff is gone. You also realise my books are not just about dialogue. Nor are they just about plot. It has more to do with the characters. So the screenplay is just the plot. An unusual plot, but it's still just a plot. When Barry Sonnenfeld did *Get Shorty*, he realised the book is about character. I told him before he started shooting, when one of the characters says something funny, don't cut to another character to get a reaction or a laugh. Treating them that way is horrible. Treat them seriously and let the audience decide. When I wrote screenplays, I would stay at home and plot out adaptations straight from the books because I thought that's what they wanted. And I just assumed that they liked the style, and that there's an ironical element running throughout the story, which is not exactly comedy. I said to Barry Sonnenfeld when I saw that they were advertising *Get Shorty* as a comedy. I said, no, it isn't a comedy. Sure, the characters say funny things, but, ultimately, the characters aren't trying to be funny.

WH: What about the other adaptations of your work?

EL: Quentin Tarantino has always been a fan of mine. Ever since as a teenager when he stole *Switch*, and got caught doing it. Then he went back and stole the book again. When, thirteen years later, *Rum Punch* was published, and he realised that some of the same characters are in that book as were in *Switch*, he wanted to buy it right away. This was right after *Reservoir Dogs*. But he didn't have the money. Then a few years later Miramax bought the option on it. I thought *3:10 to Yuma* and *Hombre* were also fairly successful adaptations. There were only a couple things in those films that I didn't like. Mainly, it had to do with using expressions that weren't quite right for the 1880s. But I liked both films. And there was a film called *The Tall T* with Richard Boone. Almost all of the dialogue of that film came right out of the novel. You know, the only difference between my westerns and my crime novels is the language. Especially when it comes to profanities. But I never worried too much about accuracy.

WH: Does it help to be cynical when it comes to Hollywood?

EL: There's no need to be cynical about Hollywood and what they might or not do with your work. It won't help. You just have to accept. Accept what's going to happen. It's never bothered me all that much. Because there's not much you can do about it. I try not to get involved, though I was on the set of *Get Shorty* for three or four days. And I got to be friends with Scott Frank, who wrote *Get Shorty* and *Out of Sight*, and who is an excellent scriptwriter. He would consult me every now and then. For instance, I was asked about who I thought should be cast in *Out of Sight*. I suggested Elizabeth Shue because *Leaving Las Vegas* had just come out. And also Ashley Judd. Then Jennifer Lopez came along, and I liked her immediately.

WH: Do you think in terms of the cinema when you write your novels, or is that you approach your work cinematically?

EL: I write cinematically because I write in terms of scenes. But I don't write with the idea of how this will look on the screen. When I see my scenes, I see real life. And I see situations from the point of view of my characters. I sometimes wonder if screenwriters see things that way.

WH: What problems have you encountered in the adaptations of your work?

EL: Sometimes when I get to know them, directors and screenwriters will ask me about certain things. In *Out of Sight* Scott Frank and I talked a lot about the film and we only disagreed when it came to two major changes. He wanted to put the escape artist in the van and use the character that was referred to in an earlier scene. And he wanted a more upbeat ending. I said to him, 'You've got to remember it's *her* story.' But Scott Frank said, 'No, it's *her* book, but it's *his* film.' When I saw the picture, I realised he was right.

WH: What about adapting your own work?

EL: I prefer to let others adapt my work. It's difficult. You've put all your energy and thought into the book, and then you've got to redo it in a script. It's hard to work yourself up for it. You've got to take out your plot, rewrite it and get your novel down to 120 pages. So you've done that first draft and it might be good, but then you've got to rewrite it a number of times. I like to add scenes, but then when you come to the transitions you're in big trouble. You can't just stick a scene in because you feel like it. In the end you get sick to death of the whole thing.

WH: What scriptwriters do you like?

EL: I don't know a lot about scriptwriters, but among those I like are Robert Towne and David Mamet. Don Westlake's *The Grifters* was excellent.

WH: Do you think a lot of crime writing will become pastiche, or do you see an endless set of permutations in the genre?

EL: George Higgins really started it all with *The Friends of Eddie Coyle*. When *The Friends of Eddie Coyle* came out my agent in Hollywood rang me up and said, 'Get a copy of that book, because he's doing what you're doing.' Even though I was writing in terms of scene and dialogue, Higgins loosened me up, got me to think in terms of composition, and he got me to let my characters drive the novel. George Higgins made me aware of language, especially when it comes to using profanities. And that you don't need to describe everything. Or worry too much about plot. All you have to do is let your characters do the talking, and the important things in the book, including the plot, will emerge. Because you get a lot of ideas while you're writing. For instance, some minor character will suddenly become interesting. It might be something about the way he or she talks or looks, and then that person will take over the novel. So I don't plot out my novels. You can waste four weeks doing that. I let my characters create the plot. I learned a great deal from Higgins. Now my agent tells me, 'You wouldn't believe all the novels that come to me that are written in the style of Elmore Leonard.' Eventually, from that something else is going to develop. And I think, in the future, film will affect writing more and more.

James Ellroy

Unlike many noirists, James Ellroy, who now prefers to call himself a historical novelist, was once known for his antipathy towards the film industry. Nevertheless, much of his work, particularly his much acclaimed L.A. Quartet (*The Black Dahlia, The Big Nowhere, L.A. Confidential* and *White Jazz*), is not only eminently filmable but dominated by the sleazier aspects of Tinseltown culture.

Ellroy writes about a world that illustrates the adage *crime follows money*. In fact, gangsters since the days of Bugsy Siegel, Johnny Rosselli, Mickey Cohen and Frank Nitti have sought to carve out a place in Hollywood, not only by associating with actors (from George Raft and Jean Harlow to Frank Sinatra, Lana Turner and Ronald Reagan) but also by buying into film production (Budd Boetticher claimed to have made his 1969 *A Time for Dying* with money from the Mob) and extorting money from studio bosses in exchange for controlling Tinseltown unions. They were also to influence the Production Code office and trade journals like the *Hollywood*

Reporter. For they were buying into an industry that, according to Gerald Horne, in his book, *Class Struggle in Hollywood,* has been essential to the economic health of numerous financial institutions (Chase Manhattan and Bank of America have been underwriting Hollywood for some seventy years). Citing a report by Los Angeles Economic Development Corporation, Horne reports that in 1997, when *L.A. Confidential* and 412 other films were released, a quarter more than a decade earlier, 500,000 people were working in the movie industry, 4,400 firms were connected with the making of films, $25.6 billion was being generated in economic activity, and industry profits stood at $6.42 billion, compared with $5.7 billion a year earlier. With so much at stake, the industry remained the perfect fodder for organised crime, as well as for Ellroy's investigations of late twentieth-century American culture.

Aware of Hollywood's history, Ellroy was once known to zealously proclaim his position: take Hollywood's option money but have nothing to do with the adaptation. Then came the critical and box-office success of *L.A. Confidential,* after which Ellroy, to some extent, changed his tune. Now he has not only softened, saying, 'I don't want to bite the hand that feeds me,' but he has even begun to dabble in the art of screenplay writing. He has not only written a script from his novel *White Jazz,* updating it to a more contemporary Los Angeles, but has written at least four other scripts, none of which has yet made it to the screen: *The Plague Season,* set against the backdrop of the Rodney King verdict and the 1992 L.A. riots; *The Night Watchman,* concerning police corruption around the time of the O.J. Simpson trial; a TV pilot (since rejected) entitled *L.A. Sheriff's Homicide,* about Ellroy's deal-ings with the Homicide Division while researching *My Dark Places,* the book about his mother's murder; and *77,* about the unsolved murder of an LAPD officer and the South Central shoot-out between the LAPD and the Symbionese Liberation Front. Accordingly, his revised position seems to contradict his view of Tinseltown as the epicentre of corruption and public manipulation – a position that has only served to make Ellroy's work all the more attractive to Hollywood producers.

Other than *American Tabloid* and *The Cold Six Thousand*, all of Ellroy's novels have, at one time or another, been optioned to production companies. But putting these stories onto the screen is another matter. Adapting an Ellroy novel can be a tricky process, particularly when it comes to condensing his sprawling fiction into a two-hour mass-market product. It's ironical that adapting his novels should be, for many writers and directors, so problematical when one considers the degree to which Ellroy relies on stylisations – editing techniques and fractured dialogue – derived from past Hollywood movies.

Whatever one's opinion of Curtis Hanson's *L.A. Confidential* – a film that, for some, has become so overrated that it is now underrated – the script was able to chisel away various narrative elements, making Ellroy accessible to cinema audiences. Others have not been so successful. While *Brown's Requiem* (directed and written by Jason Freeland, 1998), and *Blood on the Moon* (*Cop*, directed and written by former Kubrick assistant James B. Harris, 1987), have made it to the screen, neither is able to translate Ellroy's lopsided view of the world. As of this writing, there are various Ellroy adaptations in the pipeline: Edward Bunker's script to *Suicide Hill* remains in the hands of French producer Samuel Hadida, who produced *True Romance*, *Killing Zoë*, *Le Pacte des loups* and *Resident Evil*; David Fincher (*Fight Club*) is contemplating a black and white version of *The Black Dhalia*; Ron Shelton (*White Men Can't Jump*) is set to direct *The Plague Season*, now titled *Dark Blue*, starring Kurt Russell, with a revised script by David Ayer (*Training Day*, *U-571*); former Oliver Stone cinematographer Robert Richardson is about to take *White Jazz*, starring John Cusack and Nick Nolte, into production (release date 2002); Robert Greenwald is to produce and direct *My Dark Places: An L.A. Crime Memoir*, starring David Duchovny as Ellroy (release date 2003); and in France, Benoit Cohen and François Guérif are adapting *Because the Night*.

It remains to be seen how Ellroy's forays into Scriptland will affect his fiction, or compromise his vision of Los Angeles. Since becoming involved with Hollywood, Ellroy has, to this date, produced two novels, *American Tabloid* and *The Cold Six Thousand*, which move beyond Hollywood, and constitute two-thirds of a proposed trilogy regarding late-twentieth century America. These two historical, but no less criminally obsessed, novels – the first is about the Kennedys, the second about the aftermath of JFK's assassination, the killing of Martin Luther King, Vietnam, Howard Hughes's take-over of Las Vegas – are arguably the most significant political reworkings of the genre since Hammett's *Red Harvest*. Though not without their faults, the two novels, in dealing with complex conspiracies enacted by armies of stooges, occupy a territory in which crime, placed within a historical context, assumes greater meaning.

As one notes from the following interview, Ellroy remains cautious about Hollywood and his involvement with it. Whatever the result of future collaborations, Ellroy will remain in demand so long as he holds a mirror up to the industry. It hardly matters that he criticises Hollywood. For there is nothing Tinseltown likes more than to present itself as part and parcel of the American grain. At the same time, Ellroy's range and protean literary nature should never be underestimated.

WH: I remember you saying some ten years ago that you were never going to get involved in Hollywood, then along came L.A. Confidential. *Is that what changed your perspective?*

JE: No, I just got lucky on that. And all of the other books except *Cold Six Thousand* and one other have been optioned to various screenwriters, film-makers, studios or production companies. I'm just assuming that none of them will ever get made.

WH: What's happening with the film adaptation of White Jazz?

JE: It's out there in the ether. Since in Hollywood dysfunction rules, I would be extremely surprised if it will ever get made.

WH: But I notice there's even a web site for it which mentions the production company and the actors. Richardson, Nolte and Cusack are all mentioned.

JE: Really! Well, I know that was the general plan.

WH: But you prefer to stay outside the project.

JE: Well, I adapted it. So let's see what happens.

WH: What do you think it is about Hollywood that makes it such a destructive place? Is it the power, the money, or what?

JE: It's all of those things. It's the confluence of neurotic people. It's the fact that motion pictures, in order to be popular, have to pander to a wide range of tastes, and thus it's about the vulgarisation of your source material. Also it's a collaborative art form, and the more people you have involved in something the greater the chances that it's going to be fucked up.

WH: Do you have to have a fairly laid-back attitude regarding your books being made into films?

JE: Well, you know what you can control and what you can't. I would never criticise any film made from one of my books for retribution. Because no one has forced me to take the money. You have to know what you're getting into from the start. A) It's extremely unlikely that they'll ever make the film, B) they'll screw it up if they do make it. But since you took the money and no one forced you to do so, be quiet.

WH: I suppose it comes down to a case of who you sell the movie rights to.

JE: No, I don't think so. I think a bad movie can't hurt you, a good movie can help you. And the books remain inviolate.

WH: What would a film of American Tabloid *or* Cold Six Thousand *be like?*

JE: They would be very long. I don't see them being made into feature films.

WH: No question about it, they'd be very difficult to adapt, but then I thought L.A. Confidential *would be difficult to adapt. Yet it was amazing how Helgeland and Hanson condensed your novel into a two-hour film.*

JE: It was two hours and sixteen minutes. It's really only 20 per cent of the story.

WH: Do you have any favourite Hollywood screenwriters?

JE: I don't think about it much. I like film noir from 1946 to 1960, but I don't think about it much.

WH: You've been influenced by film noir, haven't you?

JE: Not really. I didn't even start watching film noir, except for the few that I saw accidentally, until I was well into my literary career. When I realised I could see movies that were occasionally similarly themed that were shot in LA in the years I was writing about, I started renting whatever was available, just to physically touch the fabric of my books. I saw a couple heist-gone-bad movies like *The Killing* and *The Asphalt Jungle*, and I saw *Sunset Boulevard* and *Double Indemnity* as a kid but that was about it. I think I was forty years old when I saw *Out of the Past*. I went to a lot of crime movies when I was a kid, but by that time film noir had passed, and it was another era of film.

WH: With all these neo-noir films, do you think film noir is in danger of becoming a parody of itself?

JE: You know, I don't know. I don't read at all in the genre. And since I've become a historical novelist, I go to some pains to mark that distinction. I care even less. It's just one of those things. I'm my own frame of reference now. I've got a dense fifteen-book career. I've written twelve novels, I've changed, I've grown as a stylist, and I've written a book of short stories, a book of journalism, and a memoir. So I'm my own frame of reference now. I don't care what anyone else has done.

WH: But your relationship with the L.A. Confidential *people must have been fairly good.*

JE: Oh, yeah. Curtis Hanson and I are good friends. Brian Helgeland, the co-screenwriter, and I are good friends. It was a good experience.

WH: What do you read these days?

JE: Nothing. The last two novels I read and admired were DeLillo's *Libra* and *Underworld*. These days, when I'm not working, I just like to brood and spend time with my wife and be quiet in Kansas City.

9

TO LIVE AND DIE IN HOLLYWOOD

Gerald Petievich

Neither as prolific nor as successful as Elmore Leonard, Gerald Petievich is best known for his script to William Friedkin's *To Live and Die in L.A.* Based on his own novel *To Die in Beverly Hills,* and filmed in San Pedro (*To Live and Die in San Pedro* doesn't sound quite so alluring), it's one of the better examples of 1980s film noir. Petievich has also written such novels as *Money Men, One-Shot Deal, Shakedown, The Quality of the Informant* and *Earth Angels.* Though his novels may not be as incisive as James Ellroy's, they remain more than mere workmanlike. After *To Live and Die in L.A.,* Petievich became a much sought-after screenwriter, which led to an unintended secondment from writing fiction. Petievich has recently completed a political thriller, his first novel in eleven years. Given his unique perspective, one can't help but think that Petievich's best work is yet to come.

WH: Why do you think Hollywood destroys some writers but leaves others untouched?

GP: I've never subscribed to the argument of 'what they did to my work', because movies are not art. Movies are entertainment. They're a medium that requires lots of people and lots of money. Writing a novel is pure art. It's like sculpture or painting. But movies are something else. They're a technological invention. So it's a business. It's nice if they can take your book, which is art, and turn it into some form of entertainment, from which you can make a lot of money. What changes writers is the money. Because there are about twenty writers who make a million dollars a book, and after that the list gets short. The money alters people and causes the problems. It alters the way you look at things. Sometimes it can affect what you do in your writing. Because the money is enormous. Suddenly you're rich. Maybe writers aren't supposed to be rich.

When I was a US Secret Service agent, I started writing as a hobby. Eventually I published one novel, then another novel. *To Live and Die in L.A.* was my fourth novel. I've had another movie made from one of my books, *Boiling Point*, made by Jimmy Harris, which is a bad movie because it was a bad script. I didn't have anything to do with the script. For instance, I could tell you *To Live and Die in L.A.* could have been a better movie if they would have gone along with what I wanted to do with the script rather than what the director did. But there's no way to prove that. But *To Live and Die in L.A.* was pretty close to the story that was in the book. It wasn't as good as the best film noir made in the fifties, which were all made for $50,000. But as far as what's being made now, it was pretty good. But I had no control over the script. The director insisted on changing scenes and doing things with it so he could get in on the money for the writing of the script, which is what directors do. The reason they want to write the script is they make money from writing the script. They make an extra three, four, five hundred thousand dollars. That's the reason they do it. It has nothing to do with them wanting to have their input. You see, the *auteur* theory is bullshit. That was created by some kind of reviewer that doesn't know anything about the business. It's like believing a Frank Lloyd Wright house was made great by the general contractor rather than the architect. And in the film business, it's the writer who is the architect. No one else really creates anything. Most Academy Award-winning directors go to other films and copy scenes. They actually bring the video tape machine to the set, and they watch the movie. In fact, it's not a bad way to make movies. Because movies are not art. When you see something done that's really great in a movie, it's usually a mistake.

WH: So you have to be fairly cynical to work as a writer in the movies . . .

GP: Granted, I am a cynical person. I write cynical books. I write cynical movies. Out of all the people I've met in the movie business, I've never met anyone who has any creative ability whatsoever. I've met business people. The directors that I know, if it wasn't for the money, they would be in another business. It's about the money. It's not that they want to be in film or in something they think is art. There's more money in film than there is in cars. Where have you heard about someone in the automobile industry making $2 million for six weeks' work. So you find people who come in who are very aggressive and who know a lot about other movies that have been made. But they are not really artists. It's about 'the deal'. The reason people don't like to go to the movies any more is because the stories don't make sense. And that's because there are no writers. If you look at who was writing film noir – Faulkner and James Cain – these guys aren't around any more, and they wouldn't be working here because the studio system no longer exists.

WH: Of course, they were imprisoned in factory-like conditions.

GP: Well everybody's in prison. It's a business. It's the same thing if you worked for an advertising agency. They'd say, 'Sit here for eight hours a day and write.' They don't care if it's artistic. They just want a certain product. Nobody talked about film noir in the fifties. Nobody talked about the philosophy of film. They were just copying from one another crime movies based on pulp magazines of the thirties and forties. So it was just a fluke. You may not agree with me, but I don't see it as any kind of artistic statement. It just happened. I know all the films and watch them over and over again. I love those films. There's some great writing there. And that's what made them great. It certainly wasn't the cinematography, because most of them were made on a stage set. There are two things that make a movie. One is a good story. Two is the acting. Even a good story will fail if you don't have good acting. And vice versa. The rest of it is window dressing. Nobody has said, I really love this movie because of the cinematographer. Or I really loved it because of the way the shots were directed.

WH: Do you think writing for films affects the way you write novels?

GP: Yeah, in a certain way it hurts you. What happens is you can get confused. Because there's nothing extra in a screenplay. You can't venture off, even for one second. Because it's a visual medium. Character development has to be done with one action and one scene. It's a very different medium. And when you write a book, you can't really think about anything else. You can't think about what kind of movie it would make. It's a big mistake to do that. The way a writer gets treated in Hollywood, it's usually an accident. If you've got a director who's a nice guy, he'll treat the writer nice. They might even let you write a draft of the screenplay rather than steal the credit. But it's not very common, because it's a very competitive business.

WH: So what's the usual process of writing a film?

GP: The director may say, 'You write this scene, and I'll write that scene.' But I don't really believe in collaboration in art. An artist has one idea. It's either your idea or it's someone else's idea. And the amalgam seldom works. It works best in TV shows. Because TV shows are just the grind of two-page scenes. There's a few words in each one and a little story. But to actually sit down and do a major motion picture with two people writing it, it's usually one person who helps and someone who does all the writing. And it's usually the writer who does all the writing. And then somebody sits there and changes a word in each sentence or changes the names to try and horn in on the credit. Because in a big movie there's lots of money involved. And there's lots of money in the residuals.

WH: What happens if you try to take that kind of practice to the Writers Guild?

GP: The Guild's rules generally favour the person who does the original screenplay. But it's so Machiavellian it's difficult to explain. Whenever there's a movie, because the people who make the movies don't know how to develop it artistically, because most of them don't know about art, what they do is, if you are the writer of the novel and they want you to write the screenplay, they hire two or three other people at the same time to write the screenplay, and they just pick what they want from each one. If it was for real, writers would be the directors. But it's not like that. It's all a bunch of people who don't know anything about art trying to figure out how to do it. It would be like me going to work in the shoe industry, and I'd say, 'Develop a new shoe.' I wouldn't know what to do, so I'd say, 'You develop a shoe, you develop a shoe, and you develop another shoe.' And I'd get all the shoes and see which one I liked best.

WH: What screenwriters do you admire?

GP: William Goldman is about as good as it gets. Robert Towne was great at one time. The only perfect screenplay I ever read was *Bring Me the Head of Alfredo Garcia* [Gordon Dawson and Sam Peckinpah]. Then there was Ben Hecht. This guy made one film after another with stories so tight they could not be altered. That's screenwriting. Did you ever see *Paths of Glory*? The screenplay was by Jim Thompson. The book was sort of boring, but it was a perfect screenplay. And done by a great director. Thompson is another example of a guy who had the ability to create these unique stories. Talk about a cynical guy. There's a real cynic, but a real writer.

WH: Have you ever seen Cockfighter?

GP: You know I've read the book. Charles Willeford is my favourite author of all. But I've never seen the movie. But he's the best when it comes to crime novels. There's nothing out of place in his novels. I remember when I was making *To Live and Die in L.A.*, I was having lunch with the director, I happened to mention to him that the Secret Service, who I worked for at the time, which is in charge of investigating counterfeit money and such, was also in charge of protecting the President. Immediately he wants to film a scene about protecting the President, which has nothing to do with the movie or the story, and so I sat down and wrote out a scene. Then he got a motorcade and rented a motel and filmed this whole thing. Reviewers, when they saw the film, said, 'What is this all about?' It had nothing to do with anything.

WH: The thinking is, if the writer knows something about anything, then use it?

GP: The general contractor would say the same thing. 'I've got this great idea for a patio. Even though you're not building a patio, let's build one anyway.' But an architect would know that's not what you do, because it doesn't all go together. They don't really understand. When a movie is popular, most directors look at it superstitiously. Like, 'Why did they come?' Because they are not like the people who go to the movies. They like different things. They have different values. Most of them are rich people. But most people who go to movies are not rich people. So they don't really know what people want to see. The biggest preview house in the country is on Sunset Boulevard. Do you think the people who live near Sunset Boulevard and who go to the previews are indicative of the way people are who live in Missouri?

WH: When you write a novel, do you think about it cinematically?

GP: Having been involved in the motion picture business, I have a tendency to think cinematically. At least subconsciously. I don't really want to do that. I believe, like Balzac, above all else write clearly. I don't find that in a lot of literature these days. Even though I have a college degree, I don't know what a lot of novels are talking about. I can sit there and read the first twenty-five pages of two or three books on the best-seller list, and I have no idea of what the story's about. It's because somebody hasn't spent enough time figuring out how to make the story clear. My books have always been pretty clear. My stories progress chronologically. So nobody has ever said, 'I didn't understand what the first chapter's about.' I think that's the reason I've had two of them made into movies.

WH: Do you think there are endless permutations to the genre, or do you think noir fiction and film will eventually become a parody of itself?

GP: There will always be crime novels, because all art, all movies, all novels are about good and evil. You can go back to every classic that's ever been written, and it's about good and evil. The crime novel is just the simple form of that. What's better as a moral and dramatic question than somebody who decides to murder someone? But the permutations in movies are permutations of whatever happens to make money at the box office. I remember having a meeting with a major producer. I had an idea for a movie and I pitched it to him. He cut me off and said, 'Let me explain something to you. The only crime movies that can do well are buddy movies.' And he named the movies. I said, 'OK, thanks a lot,' and that was it. He was right, by the way. But what he didn't realise was the only reason that those movies have been successful was because they were OK movies. When you say that, does that mean that all the people in the United States wouldn't want to see a good film noir, that they wouldn't want to see a straight caper movie? No, all he knows is the business. That's all he's concerned about. But in his perception, what was successful last week at the box office is what we make this week. Remember the movie *One False Move*? You take an unknown director, you get a decent story, and he makes this great movie on the cheap. That could be done today. But when you make a movie like that, you can't get it distributed. So it's destined to be a small movie. It's a self-fulfilling prophecy. If you spent $60 million making the same movie, it wouldn't have any problem getting distributed.

WH: It's incredible when you think that someone like Samuel Fuller made movies in ten days on barely no budget at all. A film like Pickup on South Street . . .

GP: That's a great movie. In today's money that would be made for $400,000. Maybe more because they did have actors. So it would cost maybe a million dollars. But, still, that's absolutely nothing. They make documentaries with budgets of $4 million. Television movies have budgets of $5 million. That was a great movie because of the acting and the story. I would love nothing more than to go out and write my own script and then direct it myself. You see, anyone can direct. People think it's like an art. I mean, what do you have to do, invent a camera? They have the camera. They have the crew. They have the guy who aims the camera. And he'll even give you suggestions about what the best shots are. So if you can't film a scene, there has to be something wrong with you.

WH: *Now you have writers just out of film school with no literary background.*

GP: Nothing is harder than writing a novel or a screenplay. If you copy some other movie, that's one thing, but creating an entire hour-and-a-half drama of three acts out of whole-cloth, nobody out of film school is going to be able to do that. They're going to have to copy someone else. That's OK, because that's what films are. I mean the guy that has the new body style for Chevrolets, he copied from the last one. He didn't just sit down and invent a car. But nothing's more difficult than writing a story. Because writing a story for a movie is a long-term project. I love it when someone says, 'Yeah, I really knocked myself out. I just wrote this movie. It took me three and a half weeks.' Three and a half weeks? It should take three or four months just to come up with the outline.

WH: *Do you get the same satisfaction from writing a screenplay as you would from writing a novel?*

GP: Nothing is like the satisfaction of writing a novel. Because that's my work. And for the two movies that were made, if anyone wants to find out what they were about, they have to read the book. The movie, what comes with that, is glory. Suddenly, after I became involved in *To Live and Die in*

L.A., I became a great writer. I'm writing the same stuff I've been writing for years, but now everyone loved me. Everyone wanted to meet me. Everyone wanted me to write movies for them. But it's all meaningless. It's a throw-off of the market-place, and it has nothing to do with my talent as a writer. I never really got any thrill from it. I loved the money. You can buy a new car, and people listen to you. But so what? Writers aren't in it for that, unless you're like Norman Mailer, and you want to be a caricature of yourself. Well, I'm not interested in that. I'm just some guy who likes to write. I'm not interested in dealing with a lot of people every day, so what I do is I write. That's why I chose it. I don't want to sell shoes. I want to write. But people in the movie business, they want to sell shoes. I remember I was doing a movie in Canada with NBC which Billy Friedkin directed. One morning he said, 'Last night I met this fascinating guy while I was taking a steam bath.' He said, 'He could only breathe air from an ioniser.' I said, 'What do you mean, an ioniser?' He said, 'It filters the air into ions. And this guy won't go anywhere without this ioniser. So I want the villain to have this ioniser.' The screen-play had already been written and we were actually filming the movie. So I wrote a scene. And if you get this film on video, you'll see a scene in which they go to the villain's house and they search it, and somebody walks outside holding this machine, and somebody says, 'What's that?', and somebody says, 'Oh, that's an ioniser.' It doesn't fit with anything else in the movie. But you can't agonise over things like that. That's just the way it is. I mean, first I was a civil servant, then I was a writer making what people make when they write mystery novels. Suddenly you write a scene about an ioniser and you get paid a lot of money.

WH: You'd think Hollywood would have some understanding of what the writing process entails.

GP: I have never seen anyone in Hollywood who has any understanding at all, *at all*, of the creative process entailed in writing. It's like they've never even read a magazine article on it. Because a writer is concerned with the total work – as an artist you have to be concerned with the whole thing. Not just the hands but the entire statue. The second thing they don't understand is that you can't hurry it up. Speed kills all art. And the third thing they don't understand is rewriting. As you know, all things that are written must be rewritten many times to make them good. There's been a couple times when I've had directors beg me, 'Please show me your work in progress.' I'd say, 'Look, you've got to understand, this is a work in progress and it will change fifteen times within the next two or three months.' And they'd say, 'Please! If you'll just let me see it.' I remember showing a work in progress to this one producer and you know what she said? She said, 'There's a misspelling on the first page.' Another time a director looked at it and said, 'Oh, I don't like this. This just doesn't cut it.' I said, 'Didn't you hear what I said? This is the first draft.' But they don't understand that. There are jokes about this among screenwriters. It's like the sign in the studio that says 'Write faster'. Because that's all they can tell you. They think you're just going to make some changes, and they'll tell you what to do, and then they're going to go out with it. They don't understand that isn't the way creative things work. It takes time. And, you know, writers are willing to spend the time, but no one allows you to make the time. It's a business, so there's always a production schedule. The mistake that screenwriters make is they take it too seriously. So you'll find that many screenwriters now have three or four friends to help write the script. They'll have a secretary. They turn it in. They get the notes back. And they have their friends work on it again. And they turn in a mediocre or crummy screenplay, and go on to the next project for another million dollars. Because they realise it's nothing more than a business and they don't strain themselves. The problems occur when you start taking things seriously in Hollywood. You go to Hollywood and you think you're going to make your story the way you want your story to be told. But they're going to make it the way *they* want it told. If you want to put up $20 million, you can make it your way. Though, because of the distribution system, nobody loses in the movies any more. You make a movie for $20 million, you are not going to lose money. You'll recoup your money through world-wide rights. There's a lot of money to be made there. Every country in the world buys nearly every movie. So the rights are sold ahead of time. The more the movie costs, the more a foreign country will pay for it. It's a sure-fire business. It's no different than making soap. You go into a store, there's a certain kind of soap there. Why is it in every store? Because someone bought the distribution rights. Is it better than other soap? No. There may even be a better soap. But the other soaps don't get in there. It's a product. It's a video store product, that's what movies are.

WH: Most writers seem fairly embittered about Hollywood.

GP: I have never met any writer in television or movies who likes their job. They love the money. But they hate every day of what they have to do. Because whatever you write, someone is going to come along and rewrite it. That's the kind of medium it is. Maybe it has to be that way. But since it is that way, none of them like it, they all complain, they all feel put upon, they all go to psychiatrists, and feel out of control and question their abilities about whether they'll ever be able to write again. When I'm writing a movie I feel the same way. You feel like a second-class citizen, and you know when you walk out of the room the producer is talking behind your back. They just want you to hurry up and write your draft so they can get in and get some other guy to write it. You know, writers take all this too seriously. You think the guy that works for Tide's soap agonises over whether he's going to get his soap into Ralph's Market? It's the same thing in movies. 'That's another movie. We got six others coming out this week.' And here's some writer who's worried about whether the villain is going to be killed in scene three. In that way, it's absurd. And like I've told writers who've asked me about it, who say, 'What should I do? Should I get a lawyer to sue to keep the story my way?' You know what I tell them? 'Don't sell it! That way you can keep it perfect.' And, by the way, I know writers who do that. I know writers who will not sell. For any amount. Why? Because they know what will happen, that someone else will do a bad movie, a horrible movie, a movie so bad that it will be embarrassing to watch, and their name will be on it. And everyone will say, 'That was a terrible book you wrote, because it was a terrible movie.'

10

FORCE MAJEURE

**James Crumley, James Lee Burke, Walter Mosley, Sara
Paretsky, Tony Hillerman, James Hall, Joseph
Wambaugh, Donald Westlake**

According to novelist and screenwriter John Gregory Dunne
(*True Confessions, The Panic in Needle Park, A Star Is Born*),
succeeding in Tinseltown has less to do with talent than with
making connections. Certainly Dunne, along with his wife,
Joan Didion, have over the years cultivated their own set of
contacts, allowing them to put together deals, sometimes
based on next to nothing, like the package derived from
photographs depicting oil wells that had appeared in a report
of a drilling company in which they had once owned shares.
Meanwhile, other screenwriters make hundreds of thousands
of dollars without ever seeing a script go before the cameras.

Though writers occupy the lowest point on the 'above the
line' pyramid (camera operators, painters, carpenters, etc.,
are considered 'below the line'), no picture could be made
without them. As Dunne says in his book *Monster,* having such
power, *and* being in a position to transmit ideas, explains why
producers have such antipathy for them, and why there have
been so many strikes. Since 1969, the Writers Guild of
America have sanctioned five stoppages. The last strike was
in 1988, lasting twenty-two weeks, which cost the industry
$500 million, roughly two and a half times the cost of making
the *fin de siècle* extravaganza, *Titanic.*

Yet that strike was not a total disaster for those studios
able to offset a proportion of their losses by cutting back on
commitments, while at the same time exercising greater

control over writers. They were able to accomplish this because, during the 1988 strike, the only scripts they could legitimately consider were those written on spec. Consequently, under the usual *force majeure* contract clause, which relates to unforeseen disruptions, studios were able to cancel numerous projects, and get around the Writers Guild requirement that screenwriters be paid a significant portion of their salary upon signing a contract. Once the strike was over, any scripts in development – a majority of which would never have made it to the screen – could be written off, saving the studios money that would otherwise have gone to writers for unrealised projects. Furthermore, they could now increase their profits by giving screenwriters only piecemeal employment. With speculative scripts the rage, and adaptations subject to cost-cutting, a few writers were to make large amounts of money, while others were to find the going tougher than ever. As for the studios, they had finished scripts in front of them, and, under no obligation, could either discard them or quickly take them into production.

As Dunne says, '[The] screenwriter has been regarded at best as an anomalous necessity, at worst a curse to be borne.' Screenwriters measure their worth in dollars because, with little control over what they produce, that's the only form of measurement at their disposal. Dunne maintains that a screenwriter is 'neither a writer in the sense that a script is not meant to be read but seen, and its quality only then to be judged', nor a film-maker in the sense that he has any say over the final product: '[Style], mood, pace, rhythm, texture, and point of view . . . [are] manufactured in the cutting room, where the director is sovereign.' What's more, a writer's skill is often compromised by the perceived wisdom that the more writers on a project the better. Not only is more always better in Hollywood, but employing numerous writers means attention can be focused on the director. Dunne concludes that, because studios regard a writer's time as intrinsically less valuable than that of a director, producer and actor, business attorneys believe that, if they stall long enough, the writer will eventually cave in to their demands. All to appease the shareholders and locate the lowest common denominator. This is why the writer, according to Dunne, must understand the negotiation process and the way competing parties try to insert a breach-of-contract into every clause.

The following noirists appear to confirm Dunne's comments. Each, in his or her own way, has fallen prey to Hollywood. This is hardly unusual, for the experiences of James Crumley, James Lee Burke, Walter Mosley, Tony Hillerman, Sara Paretsky, Joseph Wambaugh, James Hall and Donald Westlake constitute the rule rather than the exception. Even though all have written cutting-edge novels, their work has been, more often than not, butchered by Hollywood, and their scriptwriting talents exploited. Though such is the nature of Hollywood, one might be excused for naively wishing their plight might one day constitute the exception rather than the rule.

James Crumley

James Crumley's early fiction – *The Wrong Case, The Last Good Kiss, Dancing Bear* – exerted a considerable influence on contemporary crime writers, while creating a new readership for noir fiction. However, none of his novels has made it to the screen, despite the fact that most of them, at one time or another, have been optioned to studios and production companies. Not surprisingly, Crumley, having helped redefine modern noir fiction, has often been courted by Hollywood.

While his first novel, *One to Count Cadence*, published in 1969, was not a crime novel but part of the tradition of Vietnam writing that was to become popular in the following decade, it exhibits signs of the kind of honky-tonk bravado that, in 1975, would mark his first crime novel, *The Wrong Case*. Caught between a desire to write a hardboiled novel and creating an anti-genre, Crumley, in *The Wrong Case*, managed to filter Chandler and Ross Macdonald through the bar room libertarianism of Willie Nelson. In doing so, he made what was, up to that time, one of the most significant revisions of private-eye fiction since Chandler's cynical parodies of Hammett and the *Black Mask* school of writing. Few writers or serious readers of noir fiction have not read this novel, which features the hard-drinking, ageing veteran and private eye Milo Chester Milodragovitch. Managing to retain a political as well as personal edge, the novel, with its references to the Vietnam war, reinvents the process and meaning of private investigation. Meanwhile, the novel's opening two sentences – 'There's no accounting for laws. Or the changes wrought by men and time' – state a theme common to Crumley and future noir writers: the inevitable confrontation between personal morality and crime.

The Last Good Kiss, published in 1978, centres on another Crumley *alter ego*, Texas Vietnam veteran C.W. Sughrue. Moving between private investigation work and bartending, Sughrue – the rawer half of Crumley's tag-team of investigators – searches the Pacific northwest for a missing woman. At the heart of the novel is the drunken poet Trahearne, loosely based on Richard Hugo, the well-known Montana poet who was responsible for introducing Crumley to the work of Raymond Chandler.

In 1983, Crumley's *Dancing Bear* recycles Milo Milodragovitch. Older and more cynical, Milo, despite having inherited family money, still works as a private investigator. Despite its subject matter and laudable viewpoint, *Dancing Bear* does not quite carry the same impact as his previous two novels. Yet it is superior to Crumley's next two outings, both of which would appear in the 1990s, *The Mexican Duck Tree*, which is the most dispersed of his novels, and *Bordersnakes*, featuring both Milo and Sughrue, which lacks the immediacy of his earlier work. However, Crumley would return with a vengeance in his 2001 *The Final Country*, a Texas-based novel featuring an ageing Milo Milodragovitch and a plot that, like Chandler's *The Big Sleep,* flirts with incomprehensibility.

WH: One thing I'm interested in is how Hollywood affects novelists, specifically of the hardboiled variety. Does a screenwriter have to be particularly cynical about his work to be successful, or stay sane, and survive in Hollywood?

JC: I suspect I went to Hollywood like any number of novelists, full of the notion that screenplays are a bunch of white space, and anybody can write one. Well, I was half right. Which half I'm no longer sure. The screenplay is an entirely different form than the novel, and I had to sit down to study the form before I was even vaguely competent. I was lucky because the first director I worked with, Tim Hunter, became my lifelong friend, and my writing partner on several screenplays. Some years later I also worked with Robert Towne.

My early cynicism was wrong. It's just a different form of work. My later cynicism is based on studio executives and producers who can't write anything but a cheque, and then only under the threat of gunfire or a lawsuit. Or it could be based on the fact that nothing I've ever written has ever made it to the screen. It's just another way of telling a story, and everybody does it differently. Some of the dullest minds I've ever met are tremendously successful screenwriters, as are some of the sharpest. Making a movie is like starting a small war: win or die. There are many ways to survive Hollywood: madness is one; maturity another; luck works, too; a good lawyer is essential. It seems to me that if one goes to Hollywood, one has to get involved, and not become insulated.

WH: What films have you worked on? Have you worked in collaboration with other writers? Have you had your own work adapted for the screen by another writer?

JC: I've worked on *The Last Good Kiss, Dancing Bear, The Tunnels of Chu Chi, Judge Dread, The Big Nowhere* and half a dozen unfilmed low budgets. I've seen people all the way from Walter Hill to the producer's son adapt my work.

Uniformly dog shit. *The Tunnels of Cu Chi*, which came from a book by two Brits who worked for *Panorama*, seemed to fizzle out either when they figured out how expensive it would be or when the star decided his part wasn't big enough. I'm not quite sure what happened to *The Big Nowhere* – leftwing politics, I'd guess, either the lack or the inclusion, I don't exactly remember – but it also came to nothing. And *Dancing Bear*? The first time around, Tim Hunter (*River's Edge*) and I wrote the script for Tim to direct. During the project, the studio head got fired, and although he and Sidney Pollack picked up the option, nobody could ever agree on an actor to play Milo, then the project drifted into turnaround hell back in '86. Only to be revived several years later at another studio. As often happens, the director never had a clear idea what he wanted to do with the book. He just knew what he didn't want me to do. Studio executives changed, people forgot why they got involved in the project, and it died. It is yet again being revived by an independent producer, so the story's not over, but it's certainly taken a long time to tell.

WH: Which, if any, screenplay has given you the most satisfaction, either as a script or as a finished film?

JC: *The Tunnels of Cu Chi*, without a doubt, was the best, the most fun, and the most soundly thrashed by everybody from studio to star. The most fun I've ever had writing a script was perhaps the first time, when Tim Hunter and I wrote the first draft of *Dancing Bear*. Or maybe the last time, when I did a low-budget original for an independent producer – my idea, my version of this reality. Then, as it always does, it got Hollywood. I don't like people standing over my shoulder when I write, and I sometimes wonder why producers hire writers at all, since producers obviously know more about writing than any writer does. I'm happy to write from any source – my book, somebody else's book, a comic book – but there's not much call for a sixty-year-old white guy these days.

WH: What skills does it take to be a good screenwriter as opposed to being a good novelist?

JC: Screenwriters need to know something about the process of making a movie.

WH: What's the main thing you learned from writing film scripts?

JC: Directors are always right.

WH: Are there any screenwriters you particularly admire?

JC: The guys who fixed James Ellroy's *L.A. Confidential.* Of course, Robert Towne is one of the best. He's smart, quick and driven. He works very hard and always finds a new way to look at old stories. Except for the fact that he never much liked anything I wrote for him, he was easy to work with. We had some good times along the way.

WH: What problems have you encountered in writing screenplays?

JC: It's always the same problem: tell the story.

WH: Do you think there's a danger that noir film and fiction will become mere pastiche and a parody of itself? Or do you think the relationship between film and fiction throws up a series of endless permutations?

JC: Film noir began as a parody of itself. How are we supposed to take Poe and Conan Doyle and Agatha Christie seriously. It's supposed to be fun.

James Lee Burke

At the time of their publication, in the late 1980s, James Lee Burke's *The Neon Rain* and *Heaven's Prisoners* represented a significant marriage of public and private investigation. They also helped reinvigorate investigatory fiction. Burke was no newcomer. Prior to these books, the Texas-born author had published such promising novels as *The Lost Get-Back Boogie, Lay Down My Sword and Shield* and *Two for Texas,* as well as two collections of stories.

One of the first contemporary crime novels to investigate and criticise the politics of the Reagan era, *The Neon Rain* introduced Burke's protagonist, Vietnam veteran Dave Robicheaux, a character whose analysis of his situation and the world around him depends on his sobriety. Moving between New Orleans and the bayous, *The Neon Rain* makes good use of Louisiana's rich cultural traditions. Thus Burke, by adding his name to a list of writers that includes James Ross, Charles Williams and Jim Thompson, all of whom set much of their work in the South, revives the genre's links with regionalism.

With strong populist literary leanings, Burke encloses his politics within well-structured plots. Though his examination of CIA excesses, Latin American drug dealing and Nicaraguan Contras predates public knowledge of the Irangate scandal, *The Neon Rain*, published in 1987, is as concerned as much with personal as with national redemption. Battling those carrying out covert activities as much as the bottle, Robicheaux, who, as a Nicaraguan Somocista gangster puts it, 'talks like a Marxist', falls back on lessons learned in Vietnam, specifically, 'Never trust authority. But because I had come to feel that authority should always be treated as suspect and self-serving, I had also learned that it was predictable and vulnerable.'

With his fiction, until recently, on auto-control, Burke can sometimes become entangled in his own narrowing narrative web, and the exigencies of having to produce a novel per year. By the fifth Robicheaux novel, *A Stained White Radiance*, his investigative technique had threatened to become a parody of itself. Though making a partial recovery, neither *Dixie City Jam* nor *Burning Angel* had the urgency or political incisiveness that marked his earlier work. Burke must have realised as much, for he has recently returned to form in his *Cadillac Jukebox* (1996), *Cimarron Rose* (1997), *Purple Cane Road* (2000) and *Bitterroot* (2001).

In *Cadillac Jukebox*, Robicheaux, once again employed as a cop, this time in the very heart of Cajun country, extrapolates on politics during the Clinton era, when pseudo-liberalism, corruption and blow-dry charisma were the order of the day. He finds that the new Southern Democrats, though educated and liberal, are as corrupt as their predecessors. In *Cimarron*

Rose, Burke forsakes Robicheaux for a Texas lawyer, Billy Bob Holland. In one of his best efforts, *Purple Cane Road*, Robicheaux finds himself investigating his mother's death. And *Bitterroot* takes the reader to Montana with lawyer Billy Bob Holland. These four novels demonstrate that Burke is still more than capable of producing relevant and often subtle critiques.

It's been some forty years since Burke's first novel appeared. As of this writing, only *Heaven's Prisoners* and *Two for Texas* have been adapted for the screen. Unfortunately, neither film does justice to the novel from which it derives. It must be said, however, that, while Burke writes fiction that appears perfectly suited for the cinema, his reliance on references and descriptive elements can pose problems for those trying to negotiate the complex road that takes a novel from the page to the screen.

WH: You've had two films – Two for Texas *and* Heaven's Prisoners. *But you didn't write the scripts to either of them . . .*

JLB: I wrote an earlier screenplay for *A Morning for Flamingos* with the producer of *Heaven's Prisoners*. But you'll notice it's not playing in the theatres.

WH: Any particular reason why it didn't make it to the screen?

JLB: I can't say, but I can tell you what my difficulty was in doing the screenplay. It was in encapsulating the three previous novels into the screenplay. Because it's the fourth novel in the series. So the producers decided to shift gears and start with an earlier book, *Heaven's Prisoners*, which is my second novel. The second consideration is they hired a guy who knew what he was doing. In fact, they hired a couple good scriptwriters. The other problem I had was that in the novel *A Morning for Flamingos*, Dave Robicheaux becomes an undercover operative inside the Mafia. So his thoughts are not externalised. Without using a voice-over it's very difficult – it was for me – to convey what Dave is really thinking without seeming heavy-handed. I had a heck of a time with it.

WH: Was it an experience you'd like to repeat?

JLB: There are two scripts that I would like to write. I'd like to write the screenplay for *Purple Cane Road* and *The Lost Get-Back Boogie*. Those are two that I would really like to have a run at.

WH: Do you like to be involved when someone else adapts one of your books?

JLB: I discovered that screenwriting is a different art form. It's a collective venture. You meet interesting people, and you have a good time. But at a certain point you have to let go of it. You can't try to impose your way. They're professionals. In other words, a choice is made at a certain juncture. The author has to decide if these people are going to treat your work with respect. Are these good actors, writers and directors? Then once you make that choice, you have to detach yourself.

WH: Why do you think some writers can write novels and screenplays while others are destroyed by it? Is it just a matter of temperament?

JLB: I think the answer may have less to do with the nature of Hollywood than the nature of any experience. In other words, for what reasons are we attracted to any activity? If we're attracted to an activity for the wrong reasons, the consequences are going to be appalling. But my experience in Hollywood was the following: the creative people I met were, by and large, nice people. They like writers. Everyone treated us well. But when you get on the business end of things, you meet some very rough people. But that's true of virtually any kind of business. Publishing has changed dramatically over the years. I submitted my first novel in 1960 and forty years later there have been dramatic changes. The nature of business is that people and money are a very bad combination. I think Hollywood is a fairly easy target. I don't think it's any different from any other kind of corporate business. It's like anything. When you meet people whose positions are earned because of their talent and their hard work, you usually meet pretty decent people. When you encounter those who are there in an opportunistic way, whose careers are characterised by mediocrity, who live off the abilities of others, you come across some pretty sordid types. And I think it's this that gives Hollywood a bad name.

WH: Do you have to be fairly cynical about it, or just accept what goes on?

JLB: You do as well as you can with something, up to a certain extent, and then you have to let go of it. But you meet some good, decent folk. I remember when I wrote the screenplay for *A Morning for Flamingos*. It didn't work and the producer at Orion Motion Pictures – his name was Hutch Parker – phoned me. Hutch is such a gentleman. He paid me a fair amount of money for the script. He had to tell me there was a problem in the script. He was a very genteel sort, a bright decent fellow. He came out and spent a week with us trout-fishing. I don't think a writer could ask for more. They were very gracious and I had a good experience working for them.

WH: Is there a separate art to writing screenplays than to writing novels?

JLB: Certainly. Writing screenplays is a very disciplined form. It's like putting an elephant inside a telephone booth. Or playing a guitar with handcuffs on. It's a very tight form. You don't have much latitude. You have 120 pages and three acts and things have to happen within those three acts in the same way that events progress in the five acts of Elizabethan drama. You have to have a visual concept. Ideally every line should be emblematic of the character. A person has to bring some knowledge of music or an affinity for music, and seeing the world through a lens. You know, it's a really interesting world. The set is filled with some very unusual people. People whose names are not well known. You know, they build a set out of nothing. There are people who do illusions on camera that are absolutely mystifying. And they work very hard. They work a twelve-hour day. And the conditions are often terrible.

In *Heaven's Prisoners* it was so hot in August that everyone lost about twenty pounds.

WH: Can you think of any screenwriters or screenplays that you admire?

JLB: Sure. You know one of the best screenplays I ever saw was a television screenplay for *The Glass House*. I think it was the best film ever made about prisons. It was written by Truman Capote and then rewritten by Keenan Wynn's son [Tracy Keenan Wynn]. But it starred Vic Morrow. You remember Vic Morrow? Boy, he was a great actor. Morrow played a convict by the name of Hugo Slocum. Clu Gulager played a prison guard. It was a great film, and a perfect script. Like *The Treasure of the Sierra Madre*, which was another perfect script, and one of the best films ever made. Look at the great dialogue in there and it's all from the book. You remember when the Mexican thieves are digging their own grave and one of them says, 'Boy, it's hot in here. I hope they get this over with soon.' Shakespeare would take off his hat and bow to a line like that. It's a line right out of Chaucer. The best screenplays are the films that contain lines that we never forget. Like *For Whom the Bell Tolls* or even *Gone with the Wind*. You know F. Scott Fitzgerald did the polish on that film. Selznick hired him not for his great talent as a writer, but for his knowledge of Southern protocol. Because no one else knew what Southern men would have been like in the antebellum era. But there are still some good guys around today. Like the guy who wrote *The Usual Suspects* [Christopher McQuarrie]. And the two guys who adapted *L.A. Confidential* – Curtis Hanson and Brian Helgeland. To my mind that's also one of the best crime films ever made. It was a great book as well. There are a lot of good scriptwriters around. The fellow who's interesting to listen to and read is William Goldman. His books on screenwriting are probably the most helpful for someone who wants to enter that world. He tells novices, you might make a lot of money, but you're not going to have much creative control.

WH: Have any of your other novels been optioned?

JLB: John Kent Harrison did the adaptation of my novel *Cimarron Rose*. He's the person who directed William Faulkner's *Old Man*, *What the Deaf Man Heard* and *You Know My Name*. And *To the Bright and Shining Sun* has been optioned by the fellows who produced Mario Puzo's *The Last Don*. Evidently they already have a screenplay for it.

WH: Do you think crime fiction and film noir are in danger of becoming pastiche or do you think there are endless permutations on the genre?

JLB: I guess it depends on what you consider crime fiction. It's like anything else. Like fiction about the expatriate. There's never too much of it, but there's always too little of quality within the experience that's being treated. If a writer finds himself deliberately writing in a generic fashion, it's not art, it's something else. I'm not denigrating it. But it's not art. It serves some other kind of function. The stuff of real crime stories is the stuff of Elizabethan theatre. Or *Everyman* and morality plays. It's like the American western is really the stuff of the nineteenth-century Natty Bumpo novel. But it really all goes back to the *Song of Roland*, and all the great epics. And the epic story has its origin somewhere in the collective unconscious. Great art always goes back to the same source. In Elizabethan theatre the play was emblematic of the universe they moved in. That's why Dave Robicheaux says again and again, 'Only the names of the players change.' A crime story sometimes tells us more about what we are than any other kind of writing.

WH: So yours are not crime stories per se, but are part of another kind of tradition which includes crime fiction?

JLB: That's the intention. Writing about a region, the author hopes the region is somehow emblematic of a larger topography.

Walter Mosley, Sara Paretsky, Tony Hillerman, James Hall

No less subtle, and seemingly better suited for the screen, is Walter Mosley's fiction, portraying as it does a world that has been, at best, romanticised by Hollywood and, at worst, ignored or denigrated. Interestingly, the first Easy Rawlins novel, *Devil in a Blue Dress*, was written after Mosley came across Graham Greene's novelisation of *The Third Man*, and realised that, by eliminating any extraneous literary detail and highlighting the dialogue and visual nature of his story, he could make his narrative more direct and accessible. In other words, in a film-dominated world, he chose to write as though he were adapting a film script, or writing a novelisation to a film that did not yet exist. In doing so, Mosley was not appealing to the lowest common denominator but courting a process wherein he could be both obvious and subtle, while at the same time ensure that his work would remain open to interpretation. Adopting the trappings of a book based on a film does not mean that Mosley lacked literary acumen, but suggests the visual nature of the genre, and the influence of film on contemporary literary tastes.

Mosley's narratives have yet to be adequately captured on the screen, however. Carl Franklin's evocative adaptation of *Devil in a Blue Dress* only highlights the fact that Mosley is less interested in plot than in character, and as concerned with circumstances described by a specific place and time as he is with investigating the crimes of the culture. This is equally apparent in Mosley's lone screenwriting credit, his adaptation of his novel *Always Outnumbered, Always Outgunned*, which he wrote for director Michael Apted (1999) for US TV. Known for films such as *Coal Miner's Daughter* and *Gorillas in the Mist*, the British-born Apted is not exactly the first director one would associate with Mosley's fiction. Yet the film remains an effective and understated character study, which with its excellent portrayals – particularly Laurence Fishburne in the lead role – deserved more than its TV-straight-to-video release. At the same time, the film narrowed Mosley's narrative to such a degree that it takes on the appearance of a morality tale for young adults. Not that there is anything wrong with that, but it short-changes Mosley as a novelist of substance. Hopefully, Mosley will not succumb to either the worst or best aspects of Hollywood.

Other noirists have not even fared as well as Mosley. Sara Paretsky has been particularly unfortunate. *V.I. Warshawski*, the 1991 film based on her novels, starring Kathleen Turner, directed by Jeff Kanew and written by Edward Taylor, turns Paretsky's politically astute protagonist into a lame-brain comic figure. But Paretsky's writing deserves better treatment. After all, her depiction of Chicago's geography, demographics and politics, in novels like *Killing Orders* (1985), *Toxic Shock* (1988, US title: *Blood Shot*), *Burn Marks* (1990), and *Tunnel Vision* (1994), stands alongside the work of Windy City novelists Nelson Algren, James T. Farrell, Willard Motley and Eugene Izzi. However, Paretsky, for better or worse, has, as of this writing, shown little interest in writing screenplays, or controlling the way her protagonist is portrayed on the screen. Without any character flaws or a dark side to her personality, Warshawski can be all too easily manipulated when it comes to the way others depict her. In the proper hands, however, there is no reason why her working-class, feminist perspective should not, at some point, be successfully portrayed on the screen.

Better, but still missing the mark, is Errol Morris's adaptation of Tony Hillerman's 1991 *The Dark Wind*. With a screenplay by Neal Jimenez and Eric Bergren, and starring Lou Diamond Phillips, Gary Farmer and Fred Ward, this Robert Redford production was meant to be the first in a series of films based on Hillerman's reservation crime novels. Unfortunately, this is the only one to reach the screen. In it, Hillerman's Navaho cop, Jim Chee, investigates a drugs-related murder, and finds himself at odds with local FBI agents. Interesting in terms of setting and characterisation, *The Dark Wind* remains a worthy but uninspired effort. One might have expected more from Morris, who directed the docu-thriller *The Thin Blue Line*. Nevertheless, it is worth seeing for Stefan Czapsky's sympathetic cinematography, and solid performances by Phillips, Farmer and Ward. It makes one wonder, however, if modern film noir might not have some way to go before catching up with noir fiction. Or perhaps it's just that noir fiction loses its political impact when translated to the screen.

But Hillerman met a slightly better fate than James Hall. After publishing his first novel, *Under Cover of Daylight*, in 1986, Hall went on to write *Tropical Freeze, Bones of Coral, Hard Aground, Mean High Tide, Gone Wild, Buzz Cut, Red Sky at Night, Body Language, Rough Draft* and *Blackwater Sound*, as well as screenplays for *Under Cover of Daylight* and *Bones of Coral*, and a television series loosely based on his ever-present protagonist, Thorn. Hall's screenwriting success has been minimal. Neither *Under Cover of Daylight* nor *Bones of Coral* would reach the screen. Nevertheless, Hall is fond of recalling his trials and tribulations, particularly when it comes to *Bones of Coral*. After Hall contributed two drafts of a screenplay for the movie, MGM fired Hall because his script was too close to the book. A second writer produced a script that director Hugh Hudson and producer Alan Ladd Jr. found satisfactory. At the last moment, however, Ladd put the project in turn-around because, according to Hall, 'He decided it wasn't the same story they'd told him about earlier.' *Bones of Coral* is about a young man who has to come to terms with his abandonment by his father. Said Hall, 'This is roughly Alan Ladd's story, so I'm assuming that's what drew him to the project to begin with.' Unfortunately the new screenwriter and director didn't care much for that aspect of the story, so left it out of the screenplay, not knowing how much Alan Ladd wanted to tell his own story.

'Screenplays,' says Hall, a former poet from Kentucky,

'aren't about language, but are about images. The dumber the better. I hate doing them.' Accordingly, he prefers to have as little contact with Hollywood as possible: 'When I'm forced to sit in a story meeting or pitch an idea to a studio exec, I keep my eyes open for the absurd moment, so I can retell the story in one of the keynote speeches I frequently give. So I see every humiliation, every slight, every goofy moment as material for my stand-up routine. But I know writers who take it all too seriously and get in an eager-to-please frame of mind which can absolutely milk their soul right out of them.'

Joseph Wambaugh

One of James Ellroy's favourite writers, Joseph Wambaugh has also had his problems with Hollywood. These days this former LA cop seems to have fallen out of fashion. Though he is considered by some to be more rightwing than many of his contemporaries, much of his writing – *The Onion Field, The Choirboys, The Black Marble* – goes out of its way to be politically correct. Not only has Wambaugh written screenplays for *The Onion Field* and *The Black Marble*, but he's also adapted two of his novels, *Fugitive Nights* and *Echoes in the Darkness*, for television. Some twenty-five years ago he also wrote a screenplay for *The Choirboys*, but was eventually fired by director Robert Aldrich. Less than pleased with the film, Wambaugh still talks about remaking it. Regarding Hollywood, Wambaugh says, 'Ultimately you know you don't have any power whatsoever. So you pretty much have to submit to them if you want to be a screenwriter.' This is why Wambaugh and some friends decided to finance *The Onion Field* and *The Black Marble* themselves. 'We raised the money, and when you have the money, you have the power. That also meant I did something extraordinarily risky. Because if we hadn't been able to find a distributor, we simply would have had the world's most expensive home movie.'

Both films were directed by Harold Becker, who, as well as being a photographer, had worked on television commercials with Ridley Scott. Says Wambaugh, 'With his background, Becker didn't want me telling him how to direct. So I had to let the dialogue carry the story. The stage directions were minimal. That's what he insisted on. I see some of these screenplays today and they're full of prose narrative and lyrical poetry that can't possibly be translated to the screen. I write screenplays the old-fashioned way.'

When asked what's wrong with Hollywood, Wambaugh says, 'It's the so-called *creative process* in which all the businessmen associated with the project – by which I mean the producers and those connected with the distribution company – have to put their fingerprints on the project. That's their idea of being *creative*. Because they don't have the power to deal with a star or a star director. But the writer, being the low man on the totem pole, is the person they can boss around and be *creative* with.' Wambaugh has figured out how to get around this. 'I've had situations where I've written a screenplay in the length of time it takes business people to negotiate with my agent for a contract. But we don't dare present that screenplay because that would fly in the face of their creative input. Far from being happy about a writer who's so fast that he can give them a screenplay before they pay for it, they are, in fact, unhappy about it. Because you've written it without their creative input. I'm convinced that the most perfect screenplay imaginable could be presented to these gentlemen – and they are almost always men – and they would find a way to insert their creative input at the expense of destroying the best writing in the screenplay. So I think it's wise to insert a few things in the screenplay that you know they will want to change, and then go to your first meeting, and let them say, "Oh, this should go out in the light of the story arc" – they love clichés like *story arc* – and let them have the idea that the obvious changes you're going to make are their idea.'

Not that Wambaugh gets much satisfaction from writing

screenplays. 'I've never known a successful book writer who sat around longing to be a screenwriter. These days screenwriters are more worried about obscure things like "rack focus" than where the story's going. Also, you can present the best screenplay in the world, and if there is a major star – an actor or director – involved in the project, I guarantee you what's going to get up there on the screen is what the star wants, not what you want. That's not the kind of business a successful writer of books would aspire to.'

Donald Westlake

Veteran screenwriter and novelist Donald Westlake would undoubtedly agree with Wambaugh. Combining humour, snappy dialogue and a hardboiled perspective, Westlake, born in 1933, has written numerous crime novels over the years, including those penned under such pseudonyms as Tucker Coe, Samuel Holt, Allan Marshall and, best known of all, Richard Stark. It was under this last name that Westlake wrote *The Hunter*, which would be adapted for the screen by John Boorman and retitled *Point Blank*, a film that was to kick-start the era of neo-noir, and *The Outfit*, the film version of which, directed by John Flynn, proved to be equally hardboiled. Among Westlake's screenwriting credits is *The Grifters*, one of the best adaptations of a Jim Thompson novel.

Westlake attributes whatever good fortune he has had to having worked with Europeans and New Yorkers rather than directors from Hollywood. While his first screenwriting credit was for Aram Avakian's 1973 *Cops and Robbers*, Westlake, when I spoke to him, made no mention of that film, implying, for whatever reason, that his entry into the medium was *The Stepfather* – a mediocre 1987 horror film. In any case, the latter was not a particularly auspicious project: 'I felt like a girl on a first date: this guy [Joseph Ruben] doesn't care about me, what I think, what I want to talk about, who I really am, he just wants to get into my pants. That was a Hollywood director.' But Stephen Frears [*The Grifters*] was different. 'It was a real collaboration, except that, during filming, obviously there can only be one captain of the ship.'

Westlake also worked with Volker Schlöndorff on an adaptation of Eric Ambler's *Passage of Arms*, which never reached the screen. 'But our relationship led me to believe Volker would have been similar to Stephen Frears.' Regarding the two adaptations, Westlake says, 'The Ambler and the Thompson novels were both written around 1960, and had to be updated. Ambler was always so aware of the politics and the societies and the nuances of his settings that moving his Southeast Asia from before Vietnam to after was absolute hell. Thompson, on the other hand, never gave a damn about anything except his characters' emotional relationships with one another. To update him, all I had to do was take the hats off the men. Well, not quite. He had a nurse who was a concentration camp survivor. All I could do was drop that element, which further showed Roy's shallow nastiness, because there's no equivalent for a concentration camp.' Interestingly, Westlake was not required to make Thompson's protagonist more palatable for a cinema audience. 'At the very first meeting, with Stephen, Marty Scorsese (our producer), and a woman from Universal, I said, "You know, we can't change the ending. Without that ending, there's no story." And they all said, "Good! You understand." '

When asked whether it was Tinseltown's nature to destroy writers, Westlake said, 'Hollywood has a natural tendency to destroy everybody, actresses worst, then directors, then writers, then actors. I don't think many writers do it for artistic challenge. To quote myself: "When I write a novel, I'm God. When I write a screenplay, I'm cupbearer to the gods." Why the cupbearer gets paid better than God, I'll never know.'

As far as the difference between screenplays and novels, Westlake maintains the former are easier to write because 'it isn't the thing itself, it's the blueprint for the thing'. So one merely gets the surface: 'Three-quarters of what the novelist does in a movie is done by the actors, the director, the set designer, the costume designer, the location scout, and half a dozen other specialists.'

But Westlake is dubious about others adapting his work. 'A couple of times, principally Bill Goldman on *The Hot Rock*, the writer has wanted to consult me, which is nice. As James M. Cain said, when asked what he thought of what the movies had done to his books, he said, "They didn't do anything to my books; there they are on the shelf." A couple of times I've been talked into adapting something of mine myself, a mistake I won't make again, and my relationship with the movie becomes complicated by my feeling that directors feel I conceal a spy for the author somewhere about my person. Surgeons don't operate on close family members and neither should writers. Having been on both ends of the process, I've come to believe the screenwriter's job is to bend the material ruthlessly to fit this new shape, without losing the emotion or philosophy or truth that informed the original material.'

On the subject of noir fiction and film becoming a parody of itself, Westlake says: 'Pastiche and parody long ago pervaded the noir field. When SF writer Cyril Kornbluth was asked by an also-ran, "I work as hard as anybody else, why don't you think my stuff is any good?" Kornbluth answered, "A writer is somebody who lives his life, whatever that life may be, and from time to time he sits in a room and writes a story based on the life he's lived, so his story is one remove from reality. You read his story, and you write a story based on his story, so your story is two removes from reality, and that's why you're no good and you'll never be any good." '

Though the aforementioned noirists are hardly *pastichistes*, the process by which Hollywood adapts a story or idea – taking it to yet another remove from reality – can, unless done with the utmost care, turn even the best material into a parody of itself. But that, as has been pointed out, must be considered an occupational hazard for which there is only a limited form of indemnification.

11

SMART GUYS

Barry Gifford, Michael Connelly, Dennis Lehane, George P. Pelecanos

In a corporate enterprise with budgets approaching the gross domestic products of small nations, failing to make money in Hollywood is a punishable offence. Consequently, some writers make millions while others struggle to gain a foothold on the industry's slippery ladder. To further complicate matters, it's increasingly the case that the corporations who own the studios also own publishing houses, video companies, distributors and movie theatres. For example, as of this writing, AOL Time Warner has money in Warner Brothers, Castle Rock Entertainments, New Line Cinema, the libraries of MGM, RKO and pre-1950 Warner films, as well as in publishers Warner Books and Little, Brown & Company. Viacom owns a share of Paramount Pictures, as well as publishers Simon & Schuster (Scribner, Fireside, The Free Press, etc.) and Pocket Books. Pearson plc has money in Phoenix Pictures and also owns the Penguin Group, which includes Penguin Putnam Inc. – which in turn includes imprints Ace, Dutton, New American Library, Penguin, Plume, G. P. Putnam's Sons and Viking – as well as UK publishers Allen Lane, Hamish Hamilton and Michael Joseph. News Corporation owns HarperCollins, as well as Twentieth Century Fox, Fox 2000, Fox Searchlight and Fox Family Films. The Walt Disney Company owns Hyperion Books, Buena Vista Home Video, as well as Walt Disney Pictures, Touchstone Pictures, Miramax, and Buena Vista Pictures. While these constitute clear examples of corporate centralisation, it's equally true to say that considerably more money goes into the production and distribution of a film than into the production and distribution of a novel. Consequently, only the most daring producer or director would give a writer the same autonomy, much less respect, that they receive in the world of publishing.

These days, many noirists are familiar with the politics surrounding the two media. Such writers, influenced as much by film as by fiction and knowing the history of both, tend to be more realistic in their attitude regarding the film industry. It should be obvious by now that Hollywood is caught within a contradiction: on the one hand, it distrusts writers and what they produce; on the other hand, it must rely on them. Not that this guarantees a writer's success. Among the following, only Barry Gifford can be said, at this point, to have carved out a place in the world of fiction and film. However, all four – Gifford, Pelecanos, Lehane and Connelly – are familiar with the dynamics of the industry and are unafraid to tackle it on their own terms.

Another feature that the following writers have in common is their willingness not only to investigate particular cultures but often to cross cultural lines. Romancing marginality, Barry Gifford works hard to extend the pulp tradition of David Goodis. In doing so, he delves into Latino culture, if from an odd, even surreal, angle. More dedicated to realism, George Pelecanos examines working-class and African-American culture. Likewise, Dennis Lehane, who focuses on Irish-Americans but also writes convincingly about a cross-section of inner-city inhabitants. Michael Connelly, meanwhile, investigates the large melting-pot that is Los Angeles. It is their ability to navigate the culture, their knowledge of the genre in which they work, their depictions of those on the margins of the culture, and the authenticity of their vision that makes their work interesting and offers a degree of hope regarding the future direction of noir fiction and film.

Barry Gifford

Coming from the world of poetry and literary fiction, Barry Gifford has written novels – *Wild at Heart: The Story of Sailor and Lula, 59 Degrees and Raining: The Story of Perdita Durango, Sailor's Holiday, Consuelo's Kiss, Sultans of Africa, Bad Day for the Leopard Man* – that link surrealism with the pulp tradition. As influenced by film as by fiction, Gifford has also authored an idiosyncratic book on film noir, *The Devil Thumbs a Ride and Other Unforgettable Films* (reprinted as *Out of the Past: Adventures in Film Noir*). Though too literary and self-conscious to be an authentic noir writer, Gifford's work inhabits a category of its own, typified by a noirish sense of danger, nostalgia and a dark humour. Having worked for the likes of David Lynch, Francis Ford Coppola and Gus Van Sant, Gifford has already carved out his own place in the world of film.

WH: Does Hollywood have a natural tendency to eat up outsiders?

BG: And *insiders*. As a writer yourself you know that the only thing the writing of a screenplay and the writing of literary fiction have in common is that they both necessitate the use of words. They are entirely different disciplines. To be good at one certainly does not qualify you to write in the other. And many writers have found this out, from Scott Fitzgerald to Faulkner. Then there are directors who look at scripts as blueprints and there are others who take them as gospel. I've worked with David Lynch, Coppola, Gus Van Sant and so on. The best directors to work with are the ones who are visionaries. By that I mean those who have a vision. The screenwriter's job is to help directors create that vision. We've all done our time. But I only work on projects that mean something to me. I've been privileged to work with directors whose work I respect. With most directors I've had very good experiences. There have been some disappointments. *On the Road* was all set to be made at Columbia. Gus was going to direct it. But because of internal politics and things beyond our control, it was never made. These things happen. Recently my novel *Perdita Durango* was made into a film. It played in forty-two countries. It was made in English. It was not the movie that I would have made but, in any case, it couldn't be released here because of permission problems regarding the Burt Lancaster estate and the use of footage from one of his films [*Vera Cruz*]. It's a crazy film. Some people loved it. It was finally released under the title *Dance with the Devil*. I asked Unipix why they changed the title, and they said, 'It was too Hispanic.' These are the two disappointing things that have happened to me. But they were beyond my control. As long as you've made the movie you wanted to make. Like Lynch and I with *Lost Highway*. Some people loved it. Some people didn't understand it. It doesn't matter. Because that's the movie we wanted to make. And down the line people will begin to appreciate that movie even more. So I think we accomplished what we intended to do. And I think that's the best you can hope for. You don't want to be accepted for the wrong reasons. I've recently written three movies, and I hope to make one of them, but you never know. The ratio is not good.

WH: You don't sound too cynical about it?

BG: I hope it hasn't made me cynical. I talked to some people in the beginning of all this. I was first asked to write screenplays back in the early 1980s. I wrote a screenplay for my novel *Port Tropique*, which was never made. That's a more typical Hollywood experience. Back then I didn't know anything about writing screenplays. So I talked to people like Buzz Bezzerides, Coppola and people who really know the business, and some contemporary people like Jim Harrison, who's one of the few people who do what I do, who go back and forth between film and literary work. There aren't too many people who have that kind of range. Both Jim Harrison and Tom McGuane said, 'Don't write more than one screenplay a year. Because if you do, it's going to affect your literary voice.' I think that's sound advice. You know, if you have a family, and you've got children, the money is awfully good, and isn't easy to ignore.

WH: Have other people adapted your work?

BG: Sure. David Lynch adapted *Wild at Heart*. I was the creative consultant. But I was busy writing the Sailor and Lula novels which followed *Wild at Heart*. I didn't have time to do the script. So Lynch would show me the script. He wrote it in six days. Basically it was very close to the book, then he added the Oz stuff. Then Álex de la Iglesia and his partner did the rewrite of *Perdita*. When Lynch and I did *Hotel Room* for HBO, I wrote the film and he just directed it. On *Lost Highway*, it was our collective brainchild. We wrote it together. I think it's generally a good idea to work with the director. I wrote a film about Arthur Cravan called *Disappearing Man* for an Italian director called Giovanni Veronesi, who just made a film with Harvey Keitel. I don't know what's going to happen to it. And I'm about to begin writing a film for Gianni Amelio, who directed *Stolen Children* and *Lamerica*. He's one of the great directors. This is the kind of project that will not be in the Hollywood style, but this is a director who I admire, and to help him achieve his vision is a great thing.

WH: Do you think of a screenwriter as an author of the film?

BG: He can't be. Some directors use the screenplay as a blueprint. But a director like Lynch depends heavily on the writer for the dialogue. You have to know who you're working with. Now, if you're directing the film yourself, it's different. When Gus Van Sant wrote *My Own Private Idaho* it was barely eighty pages long. It was in the form of notations more than anything else. So unless, as an actor, you trusted that director, you didn't know what you were going to get.

WH: What screenwriters do you admire, past and present?

BG: The top of the list has to be Herman Mankiewicz. Certainly Pauline Kael, in her essay, gave him too much credit for *Citizen Kane*. Then his younger brother, Joseph Mankiewicz wrote *All About Eve*. What's better than that? I admire Robert Riskin who wrote with Capra. There's almost too many to mention. Curt Siodmak who wrote *The Wolf Man*. And who was better for a while than Billy Wilder and I.A.L. Diamond? The thing is, I can name a lot of people, but I'll leave out a lot of people. Look at John Huston's screenplay *The Treasure of the Sierra Madre*. It's brilliant. It's a perfect screenplay. He was a director doing his own screenplay, adapting Traven's novel. And there it is. But I will say this: to this day the only screenplay I've ever read that reads like a novel is Robert Towne's screenplay for *Chinatown*. I've also read a lot of oddball screenplays that have never been produced that have just been wonderful. When I began to write screenplays I had to go and find out how it was done. I never read a book about how to write screenplays. But I did read a lot of screenplays. And then when I saw what they were doing, I realised that you could develop your own language and your own style, and all you have to do is allow people reading the screenplays to see the movie. The funny thing is I had always assumed that the only reason anyone would ask me to write screenplays is because they thought the dialogue was true. But some highly placed person once said, 'You know Barry: he's particularly good when it comes to structure.' I had to bite my tongue. Because I've never thought about structure for a second. I have it, I guess, by osmosis.

WH: So when you write a screenplay, do you approach it as you would a novel?

BG: You have to plan it out ahead of time. Richard Price has talked about this. He's a terrific writer. And a great screenwriter who can really write dialogue. He's another guy who made the transition from literary novelist to screenwriter. There are moments when he regrets it. But you've got to do what you're good at. And he became very adept at writing screenplays. It's a not a transition that I would choose for myself. But there are different types of writers. Writing is not a competitive sport. All the same, I don't think they're going to call me to write the next Julia Roberts film. It's not what I do. I'm interested in using cinema. Which is why I like working with Lynch. Because he uses cinema, he stretches the language. I can't stand these movies that are formulaic, that have a woman and a kid, a man and a kid, or these imitations of Italian realism. When someone does something for the first time, it's a revelation, and it's recognised for what it is. But when you start putting these pieces together, and start saying, 'We need a poor kid, and we need this guy, and then they steal a bicycle.' You put these things together, and it's like pressing a button to make people cry or laugh.

WH: Do you think there's a danger that film noir and fiction will become mere pastiche?

BG: It was parody and pastiche to begin with. Guys like Leonard and George V. Higgins write great dialogue. When Higgins tried to become literary, he wasn't so successful. But those early novels, there's nothing like them. Leonard never deluded himself into thinking he was writing literature. So his antecedents are different than mine. But we're both thrown into this thing called Hollywood. This is why the Coen brothers' *Barton Fink* was so beautiful. It was based on Odets, who was a great example of a serious writer, a good writer, highly thought of, who came to Hollywood and ended up writing *Wild in the Country* for Elvis. 'We need a man to go to hell with' is the epigraph of *Wild at Heart*, which was taken from the film *Wild in the Country*. In any case, Hollywood is a great leveller. Remember *The Killers* – the one directed by Robert Siodmak? It's wonderful. The first fifteen minutes is Hemingway's short story. Then comes the movie and the backstory. Then Edmund O'Brien comes into the picture. It's one of the most well-done adaptations of a literary short story, done in an intelligent style with great touches all the way through. This is an example of what can be done with literary fiction translated to the screen. But these were great guys, coming out of Europe. These guys, I'm sorry they're gone. It's such a shame. Going to the movies now is like television with a bigger screen. That's why I'm not holier than thou at all. Something's missing, and it's called intelligence. They're giving people what they want, which is what they were always doing, but you really have to work at it now to try to do something that's unique. And, God forbid if anyone with an original thought is allowed to make a movie or given access to money and distribution. But sometimes movies do get made that are interesting. And sometimes good movies are made but can't get the distribution. It's always a gamble.

Michael Connelly

It was seeing Robert Altman's *The Long Goodbye* and reading Raymond Chandler that prompted Michael Connelly to pursue a career as a crime novelist. After studying with Harry Crews at the University of Florida, Connelly worked as a journalist, including three years on the *Los Angeles Times* crime beat. There he began his carefully constructed novel, *The Black Echo*, based partly on a true LA crime, featuring LAPD Detective Hieronymus Bosch. Published in 1992, it won the Edgar Award for best first novel. Three Bosch books followed: *The Black Ice*, *The Concrete Blonde* and *The Last Coyote*. Then, in 1996, came *The Poet*, this time with a newspaper reporter as the protagonist. In 1997 Connelly returned to Bosch with *Trunk Music*, and in 1998 another non-series thriller, *Blood Work*, inspired by a friend's heart transplant and the attendant 'survivor's guilt', came out. Bosch reappeared in *Angels Flight*, published in 1999, while *Void Moon*, which appeared in 2000, introduced a new character, the high-stakes Las Vegas thief, Cassie Black. Connelly's most recent novel, *A Darkness More than Night*, unites Harry Bosch with Terry McCaleb from *Blood Work*. The title comes from Raymond Chandler, who, when asked why his early hardboiled stories were so popular, said it was because in the stories the 'streets were alive with a darkness that was more than night'. Connelly takes that concept to another level, saying, 'The philosopher Friedrich Nietzsche wrote that when you look into the darkness of the abyss the abyss looks into you. Probably no other line or thought more inspires or informs my work.' It should come as no surprise that Connelly, having written novels that read like movies, also writes screenplays. At the time of the interview, he was working on a television film.

WH: What is it about Hollywood that destroys some writers and leaves other unscathed?

MC: I guess I have a novice's opinion because I'm entering that world where I'll either be destroyed or saved, or something like that. I've had some good experiences writing screenplays that have so far *not* been produced. And I've had some bad experiences. I've had some experiences where my sense of storytelling and what is important has been ignored because I haven't come from that world. So that the people in that world have an opinion of me that's more or less something along the lines of, 'That's nice, but let us do it. This is what we do for a living.' It hasn't worked and I think they've wrecked some of my stories. In some cases, they've come back and said, 'You know, you were right, let's do it your way.' I think as far as what can hurt a writer is if – especially if you're talking about people who have written books and have then gone into the movie world – if you leave one for the other, which is not something you should ever do. I've probably increased my workload and increased my stress level and so forth by trying to always be in the middle of writing a book. I think that keeps you grounded and it can make what happens in this world more acceptable. It's a cliché that it's a collaborative thing, but, as clichés go, it's true. Like this TV show I'm working on has had so many fingers in the pie, from producers to directors and actors. Everyone has their thoughts. Some of them have been good. Some of them not so good. But I think it's benefited from everyone being involved. I think I'm more open to listening to what anyone has to say about my stories because I have other things going on. I just finished a book about three weeks ago. And I've been working on this film project for almost a year, so I was balancing both at once, and I could always go to my private world where no one tells me a thing about what to write and what makes a good story, to almost a day job where I was always getting that kind of input about whether it was good or not. When I was hired to write the screenplay to *Void Moon*, it turned out to be one of the better processes I've been through. They didn't even hire a writer to rewrite me. So that made me feel I'd hit whatever they needed. Because it's a female lead, Warner Brothers felt we should start with the actress and then go for a director. Early on, they were talking to directors, but Warner Brothers felt they didn't want to change the story, they wanted to stay close to the book. It's a long process. You start at the top and wait a long time.

WH: Do you have to be somewhat cynical about the process of making a film or should you just accept whatever happens?

MC: I think it's both. I think it's healthy to be cynical about this process because it seems like 80 per cent of what comes out is not very good. And so I've always gone into it with the idea that things are possibly going to go wrong. That way you set up the element of surprise. Like on this show I've been seeing dailies and what they've been filming and I'm suddenly surprised because I had a low threshold or a cynical view of what was going to happen. But so far that hasn't happened. So to be pleasantly surprised is a good position to be in.

WH: Has anyone tried to adapt your work for the screen?

MC: Yeah, I've tried to adapt some of my stuff, and there have been three other writers who have worked on adapting Harry Bosch books, each with a completely different take. Someone was hired about seven years ago to adapt my second book. He did a script. Then about four years ago I was hired to rewrite that person's script. Then a couple months ago that same person was hired to rewrite both of our scripts. That's kind of like Hollywood in a nutshell.

WH: It must be strange to have to rewrite your own book.

MC: Yeah. In fact, I'm rewriting someone else's take on my own book. It's interesting but I always feel that the main thing for me is my book. If they ever make a film of one of my books, how it comes out will probably change my opinion of this whole process. But until that happens I'm kind of labouring with this sense of cynicism and hope and so forth.

WH: Would you rather be involved in the adaptation of your books or not?

MC: I would like to be kept informed. I have different books with different studios, and various degrees of involvement, from being fully informed and knowing what's going on from week to week, to one project – *Blood Work* – with Warner Brothers and Clint Eastwood, which, other than meeting him for about an hour three years ago when I sold it to him, I have no idea what's going on with it. I know a script was written, but I wasn't invited to look at the script or anything like that. I'm not saying that's good or bad. I'm furious about it, but that's how he makes movies, and I kind of accepted it when I sold him the book. So that's his choice, not mine. Someone like Elmore Leonard has the right attitude, which comes from the experience of having dozens of his books made into good and bad movies. But I really think a movie is someone else's turn to tell the story. So the only place you have any sense of control is when you pick who buys it. Hopefully you have a number of people to choose from. For me, that's the extent of what control you have. After that, you can be involved and be told what's going on, but you're not going to make any of the decisions.

WH: And what about the satisfaction level of writing a screenplay as opposed to writing a novel?

MC: Since I've never had a screenplay made, I can say there's almost no satisfaction. Writers have egos. I have an ego that's probably healthier than most and a lot of it is fed by the response to my books. So to me it would be very hard to be a screenwriter who has only a very small percentage of my work seeing the light of day or getting on a screen. I've been writing screenplays part-time for about five years, but I've always had these books coming out every year, and that has kind of served as my creative fulfilment. Because it hasn't come from my screenplays. Now that might just be a personal thing. I'm a writer who wants to see some reaction to what I write, as opposed to someone who writes a good page or a good sentence or a good piece of dialogue and can just sit and be happy with it all by themselves in a kind of vacuum.

WH: A lot of older guys, once they got to Hollywood, their fiction writing just dried up.

MC: Because I'm a writer of books first, that makes me feel bad. I think we lost a lot of stuff. I have a couple friends – one in particular that I thought wrote some great books, but then started writing screenplays, and hasn't written a book in ten years. His movies have been good, but there seems two routes you can take. You leave one world for the other, or you take one with you. And taking one with you is the best thing to do. To me, it's a touchy subject.

WH: So is it the money and the Hollywood myth and lifestyle that's the main attraction with writing for the screen?

MC: I think it's the myth. For some it's the money. But on this project I'm actually taking a pay cut. To me, especially people around my age, I'm as equally influenced by books as by good movies. Maybe, in some cases, movies are even more influential. I want to try to write something as good as my favourite movies, as well as my writing heroes. It's not that I can sell a screenplay for a million dollars. Probably every writer will probably tell you that. Because I got in it late, and got into it because of the success of my books, studios came to me to see if I wanted to do it. I was already doing, on a financial level, pretty well before I ventured into this world, so it wasn't like I went into it to make a lot of money.

WH: Who are the screenwriters that you admire?

MC: I'm not as schooled as most people as to who's a good screenwriter. I think more in terms of movies. *Chinatown* is probably my favourite movie of all time. That's something that would be a benchmark for me. It's a screenplay that I've read several times. There's an art to reading screenplays, and I don't know if I've captured it yet. I just don't get enthralled by screenplays. I've met Scott Frank a few times, and he's done the two best Elmore Leonard movies. On a more current level, he'd be someone I would look to and try to learn from.

WH: Do you think the genre of noir fiction and film is in danger of becoming mere pastiche? Or do you think there's endless permutations you can do in noir fiction and film?

MC: Because I'm in it, I would hope that there would be endless permutations of it. Whether it's film or books, that's the way I look at it. Within the setting of a crime novel or movie you can do whatever you want. You can explore whatever you want. So to me it doesn't seem like it's a tired genre or something that's going to lapse into parody or something like that. I'm not well schooled on this kind of stuff. But the best way for me is not to be too schooled on the past. To a similar extent, I've only read the most well-known crime writers. Like Raymond Chandler and Ross Macdonald.

WH: Since you've been influenced by film, do you think cinematically when you write your novels?

MC: I don't write in terms of when they make this a movie, this will make a neat scene. But I do write in terms of putting words together that will trigger the movie projector everyone has in their head. I want people to visually see the story. So it's similar, but I'm not writing in terms of this is going to be a movie.

WH: But you obviously write cinematically?

MC: I hope so. The only book that came close to writing a novel as though it were a movie was *Void Moon*. Because I was writing a female protagonist for the first time, I wanted the book to be more plot-driven than my previous books. Because it was plot-driven, it was designed from the start to be sleek and fast. I wanted the book to move like her car. Also, because I was venturing into new territory with a female protagonist, I did an outline, which I don't usually do. But I did a bare-bones outline so I knew where the story was going and how I'd be able to cut between her and the guy who was chasing her. I'd written a good portion of it and an outline for the rest, and sold it to Warner Brothers based on that. Before I even finished it I was having meetings with producers and so forth. So I think that influenced whether or not this was written as a movie or not.

Dennis Lehane

Combining an intelligent political perspective with a Chandleresque sense of humour, Dennis Lehane's fiction examines the underbelly of contemporary society. Influenced by Westlake writing as Richard Stark, Leonard, Burke and Crumley, Lehane published his first novel, *A Drink Before the War*, in 1994, at the age of twenty-eight. This was followed by *Darkness, Take My Hand* (1996), *Sacred* (1997), *Gone, Baby, Gone* (1998) and *Prayers for Rain* (1999). All feature Boston private investigators Angie Gennaro and Patrick Kenzie, and take place in blue-collar Boston. In *Mystic River* (2001), Lehane temporarily abandoned his private investigators in favour of a south Boston-set story about the loss of innocence, the deterioration of urban life, and the effect of a girl's death on a tightly knit community. As well as having an ability to evoke a particular time and place, Lehane, like Pelecanos, manages to create characters who seem to have stepped right off the street. As Lehane says, 'Character is action. It's the oldest law of writing . . . Plot is just a vehicle in which you see them act.' Three of his most cinematic novels, *Prayers for Rain, Gone, Baby, Gone* and *Mystic River*, have been optioned, the first two by Paramount and the third by Clint Eastwood.

Regarding screenwriters, Lehane isn't sure that Hollywood deserves all the blame it gets. He has worked with independent companies and occasionally in Hollywood, and sees no substantial difference between the two. According to Lehane, whom I contacted by email, it comes down to money, and the fear of losing it: 'Several people have invested and/or raised substantial amounts of money in a project and they're scared. But I've also seen the crass stupidity by committee that can destroy a good script when producers forget why they hired the writer in the first place, and second-guess all the writer's instincts.' On one occasion, Lehane had to threaten a lawsuit to have his name removed from a film: 'I had been hired to "class up" the film only to have to sit back and watch as the producers then dumbed it back down again and filled it with the most egregiously idiotic smut in order to please foreign markets where they believed "sex sells".' However, he blames himself: 'I sensed the main producer was a scumbag when I met him, but I enlisted on the project anyway. Writers who whine about such situations remind me of the guy who leaves a whore complaining he didn't feel loved.'

Surviving Hollywood is, according to Lehane, a matter of being realistic: 'If you believe you're going to write a script so great no one will touch a line and they'll go along with all your casting ideas and hire the perfect director and spend whatever it takes to translate your vision to the screen, and, oh yes, pay you seven figures for the privilege – well, good luck and God help you. If, however, you have the attitude of Richard Price or Elmore Leonard – both of whom seem to feel that once writers are paid Hollywood can (and will) do whatever it wants – then I think you're much less likely to be destroyed by it.'

As far as his own film experience, Lehane wrote, produced and directed *Neighborhoods* on a shoestring budget, has an original script in development with a Boston independent film company, and has worked on an adaptation of his novel *Prayers for Rain*. Yet he has reservations about others adapting his work. Says Lehane, 'I'm pretty sure I wouldn't be real happy about such a scenario, but I'd try to take the Elmore Leonard attitude.' However, he's recently conceded that he's more than willing to let Eastwood hire his own scriptwriter for *Mystic River*.

Making *Neighborhoods* gave Lehane an insight into the difference between writing fiction and film. 'There were moments that came out as good or even better than I'd envisioned in the script. Unfortunately, there were a lot that came out worse, and I discovered something through that process that showed me a lot about the difference between the page and the screen: what often plays quite nicely on the page doesn't necessarily work on the screen. Once, I cut three pages of a scene on the day we shot it, and it was a smart move because the camera conveyed far more in a matter of seconds than the dialogue had over the course of three minutes.'

The only director, other than himself, with whom Lehane has worked 'was the guy who directed the film I had my name removed from, and he was an amiable hack. The conversations we had about the film were moronic and revealed the mind of a guy who didn't know dick about narrative, character or structure, so I wouldn't say it was a positive introduction to the process.' However, Lehane is no less hard on himself: 'I seem to remember that, as a director, I chopped half my best lines on the set and was, in general, a pain in the ass.'

At the same time, Lehane, who counts among his favourite screenwriters Richard Price, Paul Attanasio (*Quiz Show, Donnie Brasco*) and Scott Frank, gets little satisfaction from writing screenplays. 'A novel is so much about language and the interior lives of the characters. A screenplay is a blueprint; it's quite technical, really, and the quality of the prose – except in dialogue – is largely irrelevant.'

George P. Pelecanos

Having written ten novels – *A Firing Offense, Nick's Trip, Down by the River Where the Dead Men Go, Shoedog, The Big Blowdown, King Suckerman, The Sweet Forever, Shame the Devil, Right as Rain,*

Hell to Pay – set in working-class Washington DC, George P. Pelecanos has created a body of work typified by an ear for urban speech rhythms, and an assortment of characters that reach across the cultural divide. Particularly noteworthy are his private investigators, whether former TV and stereo salesman Nick Stefanos or one-time cop Derek Strange. Dennis Lehane compares Pelecanos's work with Elmore Leonard's, in that his characters 'act on impulse and affect things'.

Unafraid to tackle prickly contemporary issues like racism and the effect of trickle-down economics, the largely self-taught Pelecanos has been as influenced by film and music (1970s soul, 1980s punk rock) as by hardboilers such as Hammett, Goodis, Willeford and Himes. As well as writing fiction, Pelecanos has worked in film, as a screenwriter and executive producer (he managed Circle Films, an independent production company responsible for such films as the Coen brothers' *Raising Arizona, Miller's Crossing* and *Barton Fink*). He cites two reasons why he writes scripts: 'It was a dream of mine to write movies . . . And . . . I want to send my kids to college . . . Screenplays are for my family; the novels are for me.'

But any novelist wanting to pursue a career as a screenwriter, must, in Pelecanos's opinion, delineate the two professions. 'The novelist already has his art. If creating art is his only goal, then he needs to stick with writing novels. Because writing for the screen (on the studio level) is more about commerce than it is about art. Once you understand this, and admit this to yourself, it gets much easier to do the job.' Differences between fiction and film come down to the amount of money at stake: 'A literary novel, or a genre novel that attempts to be something more than formula fiction, often draws a modest advance. The publisher is not on the hook for much money, so the author can be expected to fight for his manuscript and go "to the wall" if necessary to keep his manuscript intact. A screenwriter, on the other hand, is paid a lot of money for his work. On top of this are the production costs and marketing costs that drive the budget of most features into the tens of millions of dollars. Naturally, investors and producers feel they have the right to alter the content of a film script, as they try to ensure it is more commercial for the masses. Even if they're wrong, and they are wrong most of the time, they have this right – it's their money which is at risk. The writers who get eaten up are the ones who can't accept this.'

Though not one to underestimate the role of the script-writer, Pelecanos does not believe the writer can be considered the author of any given film: 'Any writer, and any director who's not delusional, will tell you that the "A Film By" credit at the head of a movie is a lie. The nature of cinema precludes any one individual from "authoring" a film. That includes the screenwriter. But all good films, without exception, come from fully realised screenplays. You can't "fix" a film on the set or in the editing room if the film wasn't already complete on the page.'

As for his screenwriting experience, Pelecanos wrote two drafts for *King Suckerman*, but Dimension Films, a division of Miramax, which had bought the rights, weren't satisfied with the results. According to Pelecanos, 'The plot of my screen-play, apparently, followed too closely the plot of my book. A rewrite man came on and turned in something with which they were even more unsatisfied. Now they have reoptioned the book and have hired Michael Imperioli, who co-wrote Spike Lee's *Summer of Sam* and who plays Christopher in *The Sopranos*, to rewrite my script. Dimension has treated me with respect and kept me in the loop throughout this process.'

Pelecanos has also rewritten a script for Dimension. Set in Harlem in the early 1980s, it's 'about some kids who get into the drug game at the dawn of hip-hop'. It was a good experi-ence for Pelecanos: 'I worked closely with the director during the writing process, and the feeling I had throughout was that we were all trying to make a good film. Also, every time you write a script you learn something new, and I felt like I came away from this one a better screenwriter.' Since then Pelecanos has written a screenplay for HBO Films, based on the true story of the Spirits of St. Louis, a team in the old American Basketball Association (ABA) of the 1970s.

But his experience on *King Suckerman* has made him wary about adapting his own work. 'I found I was not very willing to lose characters and themes for the sake of the adaptation, which of course must be done. Still, I'd like to be consulted. My books are very specific to Washington, DC. I want to make sure that the slang, speech patterns and geography are correct. And I'd always like to have that last shot at the polish before the film goes to production.'

As an independent producer, Pelecanos has been involved with a handful of directors: Robert M. Young on *Caught*, Susan Skoog on *Whatever*, and George and Mike Baluzy on *Blackmale*. Being on the other side of the table was to prepare Pelecanos for the compromises he would later have to make as a screenwriter. However, because he was already a novelist, Pelecanos says he tended to be 'more hands-off as a producer than I should have been out of respect for the screenwriters. But I found that this attitude often doesn't serve the film.' Nevertheless, he believes Young was able to elevate the material and turn *Caught* into a 'pretty good film'. Realising that Skoog's vision was complete from the very beginning, he had the sense to leave her alone. 'Consequently,' says Pelecanos, '*Whatever* is the film I am most proud of being involved with as a producer.'

When I asked him whether noir fiction and film is in danger of becoming a parody of itself, Pelecanos replied, 'First of all, most producers don't even understand what noir is. Sure, they know the signs: Venetian blind shadows, cigarette smoke, etc. But they don't understand the core psychological aspects, the undercurrents of claustrophobia and anxiety which drive noir. Contemporary noir tends to be a parody, and it has been for some time. Look at the last of the original film noir cycles in the 1950s – *Kiss Me Deadly* and *Touch of Evil* are outsized comments on the genre. So now what we often get is a parody of a parody. The best noirs of the last few years have come to us in disguise: urban dramas, like *Menace II Society*, or westerns, like Clint Eastwood's *Unforgiven* or western literature, like Cormac McCarthy's *Blood Meridian*, James Carlos Blake's *In the Rogue Blood* and Daniel Woodrell's *Woe to Live On*. As long as we have these permutations, then the tradition is alive.'

As the writers in this chapter – novelists first, screenwriters second – demonstrate, to inhabit both worlds – fiction and film – one should have a working knowledge of the politics involved, maintain a realistic approach and accept that Hollywood rip-offs are the rule rather than the exception. Gone are the days when a novelist like Dashiell Hammett or Raymond Chandler could entertain notions of single-handedly manipulating the film industry. It would be ridiculous to believe that one person can fight a global empire or change the laws of market capitalism. Though it might be possible to subvert the industry through one's work and attitude, Tinseltown, up to now, has either destroyed or co-opted just about everything thrown in its path. While Hollywood's fate depends on economic factors and its status as a corporate entity, the future for writers belongs to those who can read the culture and articulate the history of the media in which they work.

Filmography

Dashiell Hammett

Roadhouse Nights, a.k.a. *The River Inn*, 1930 (uncredited, based on novel *Red Harvest*); *City Streets*, 1931 (story 'After School'); *The Maltese Falcon*, a.k.a. *Dangerous Female*, 1931 (uncredited, also novel); *The Thin Man*, 1934 (novel); *Woman in the Dark*, a.k.a. *Woman in the Shadows*, 1934 (story); *Mister Dynamite*, 1935 (story 'On the Make'); *The Glass Key*, 1935 (novel); *Satan Met a Lady*, 1936 (based on novel *The Maltese Falcon* and story 'Money Man'); *After the Thin Man*, 1936 (story based on unpublished manuscript of *The Thin Man*); *Secret Agent X-9*, 1937 (serial, comic strip); *Another Thin Man*, 1939 (story); *The Maltese Falcon*, 1941 (novel); *Shadow of the Thin Man*, 1941 (characters); *The Glass Key*, 1942 (novel); *Watch on the Rhine*, 1943; *The Thin Man Goes Home*, 1944 (characters); *Secret Agent X-9*, 1945 (serial, comic strip); *Song of the Thin Man*, 1947 (characters); *Yojimbo*, a.k.a. *The Bodyguard*, 1961 (said to be based on novel *Red Harvest*); *Miller's Crossing*, 1996 (uncredited, said to be based on novels *Red Harvest* and *Glass Key*); *Last Man Standing*, 1996 (based on novel *Red Harvest*).

Raymond Chandler

The Falcon Takes Over, 1942 (based on novel *Farewell, My Lovely*); *Time to Kill*, 1942 (based on novel *The High Window*); *Double Indemnity*, 1944; *Murder, My Sweet*, 1944 (based on novel *Farewell My Lovely*); *And Now Tomorrow*, 1944; *The Unseen*, 1945; *The Blue Dahlia*, 1946; *The Big Sleep*, 1946 (novel); *Lady in the*

Lake, 1947 (co-scriptwriter, also novel *The Lady in the Lake*); *The High Window,* a.k.a. *The Brasher Dubloon,* 1947 (novel); *Strangers on a Train,* 1951; *Marlowe,* 1969 (based on novel *The Little Sister*); *The Long Goodbye,* 1973 (novel); *Double Indemnity,* 1973 (TV, based on script by Chandler/Wilder); *Farewell, My Lovely,* 1975 (novel); *The Big Sleep,* 1978 (novel); *Blackmailers Don't Shoot,* 1989 (TV, story); *Once You Meet a Stranger,* 1996 (TV, based on screenplay for *Strangers on a Train*); *Poodle Springs,* 1998 (TV, unfinished novel).

Horace McCoy

Dangerous Crossroads, 1933 (story); *Soldiers of the Storm,* 1933; *Man of Action,* 1933 (uncredited); *Hold the Press,* 1933; *Speed Wings,* 1934 (also story); *Fury of the Jungle,* 1934 (story); *The Trail of the Lonesome Pine,* 1936; *Spendthrift,* 1936 (uncredited); *Postal Inspector,* 1936; *Parole,* 1936; *Fatal Lady,* 1936; *King of the Newsboys,* 1938 (story); *Prison Farm,* 1938 (uncredited); *Hunted Men,* a.k.a. *Crime Gives Orders,* 1938; *Dangerous to Know,* 1938; *Persons in Hiding,* 1939; *Undercover Doctor,* 1939; *Television Spy,* 1939; *Island of Lost Men,* 1939; *Parole Fixer,* 1940; *Texas Rangers Ride Again,* 1940; *Women Without Names,* 1940; *Queen of the Mob,* 1940; *Texas,* 1941; *Wild Geese Calling,* 1941; *Gentleman Jim,* 1942; *Valley of the Sun,* 1942; *Flight for Freedom,* 1943 (story); *Appointment in Berlin,* 1943; *There's Something About a Soldier,* 1943; *The Fabulous Texan,* a.k.a. *The Texas Uprising,* 1947; *Kiss Tomorrow Goodbye,* 1950 (novel); *The Fireball,* a.k.a. *The Challenge,* 1950; *The Turning Point,* 1951 (story); *Montana Belle,* 1952; *The World in his Arms,* 1952 (additional dialogue); *The Lusty Men,* 1952; *Bad for Each Other,* 1953 (also story); *El Alaméin,* a.k.a. *Desert Patrol,* 1953; *Destinées,* a.k.a. *Daughters of Destiny,* a.k.a. *Love, Soldiers and Women,* 1953; *Dangerous Mission,* a.k.a. *Rangers of the North,* 1954 (also story); *Rage at Dawn,* a.k.a. *Seven Bad Men,* 1955; *The Road to Denver,* 1955; *Texas Lady,* 1955; *They Shoot Horses, Don't They?,* 1969 (novel); *Un linceul n'a pas de poche,* 1974 (novel *No Pockets in a Shroud*).

W.R. Burnett

Little Caesar, 1930 (novel); *The Finger Points*, 1931 (co-story); *Iron Man*, 1931 (novel); *Law and Order*, a.k.a. *Guns A'Blazing*, 1932 (uncredited, novel *Saint Johnson*); *The Beast of the City*, 1932 (story); *Scarface*, a.k.a. *Scarface: The Shame of the Nation*, 1932; *Dark Hazard*, 1934 (novel); *The Whole Town's Talking*, a.k.a. *Passport to Fame*, 1935 (uncredited, story 'Jail Breaker'); *Dr. Socrates*, 1935 (story); *36 Hours to Kill*, a.k.a. *Thirty-six Hours to Live*, 1936 (story 'Across the Aisle'); *Wine, Women and Horses*, 1937 (novel *Dark Hazard*); *Wild West Days*, 1937 (serial, based on *Saint Johnson*); *Some Blondes are Dangerous*, 1937 (novel *Iron Man*); *King of the Underworld*, 1939 (story 'Dr. Socrates'); *The Westerner*, 1940 (uncredited); *The Dark Command*, 1940 (novel); *Law and Order*, a.k.a. *Lucky Ralston*, 1940 (novel *Saint Johnson*); *High Sierra*, 1941 (also novel); *The Get-Away*, 1941; *Dance Hall*, 1941 (novel *The Giant Swing*); *This Gun for Hire*, 1942; *Bullet Scars*, 1942 (uncredited, remake of 'Dr. Socrates'); *Wake Island*, 1942 (also story); *Crash Dive*, 1943 (story); *Action in the North Atlantic*, 1943 (additional dialogue); *Background to Danger*, 1943; *San Antonio*, 1945 (also story); *Nobody Lives Forever*, 1946 (also novel); *The Man I Love*, 1946 (uncredited); *The Walls of Jericho*, 1948 (uncredited); *Belle Starr's Daughter*, 1948 (also story); *Yellow Sky*, 1948 (novel); *Colorado Territory*, 1949 (uncredited, novel *High Sierra*); *The Asphalt Jungle*, 1950 (uncredited, also novel); *Vendetta*, 1950; *Iron Man*, 1951 (novel); *The Racket*, 1951; *Law and Order*, 1953 (novel *Saint Johnson*); *Arrowhead*, 1953 (novel *Adobe Walls*); *Dangerous Mission*, 1954; *Night People*, 1954 (uncredited); *Captain Lightfoot*, 1955 (also novel); *Illegal*, 1955; *I Died a Thousand Times*, 1955 (also novel *High Sierra*); *Accused of Murder*, 1956 (also novel *Vanity Row*); *Short Cut to Hell*, 1957 (remake of *This Gun for Hire*); *The Badlanders*, 1958 (novel *The Asphalt Jungle*); *The Hangman*, 1959 (uncredited); *September Storm*, 1960; *The Lawbreakers*, 1960 (uncredited); *Sergeants Three*, 1962 (also story); *Cairo*, 1963 (novel *The Asphalt Jungle*); *The Great Escape*, 1963;

Four for Texas, 1963 (uncredited); *The Jackals*, 1967 (remake of *Yellow Sky*); *Ice Station Zebra*, 1968 (uncredited); *Stiletto*, 1969 (uncredited); *Cool Breeze*, 1972 (novel *The Asphalt Jungle*); *Thunderbolt and Lightfoot*, 1974 (uncredited, remake of *Captain Lightfoot*).

Paul Cain

Gambling Ship, 1933 (story); *Affairs of a Gentleman*, 1934; *The Black Cat*, a.k.a. *The House of Doom*, 1934; *The Vanishing Body*, 1934 (also story); *Jericho*, a.k.a. *Dark Sands*, 1937; *Twelve Crowded Hours*, 1939 (story); *Grand Central Murder*, 1942; *Mademoiselle Fifi*, 1944; *The Night of January 16th*, 1941 (uncredited); *Alias a Gentleman*, 1948 (story).

James M. Cain

She Made Her Bed, 1934, a.k.a. *The Baby in the Icebox* (story); *Algiers*, 1938 (additional dialogue); *Blockade*, 1938 (additional dialogue); *Stand Up and Fight*, 1939; *When Tomorrow Comes*, 1939 (story 'A Modern Cinderella'); *Le Dernier Tournant*, a.k.a. *The Last Turn*, France, 1939 (novel *The Postman Always Rings Twice*); *Wife, Husband and Friend*, 1939 (story, 'Career in C Major'); *Money and the Woman*, 1940 (screenplay construction contributor, uncredited, also story 'The Embezzler'); *The Shanghai Gesture*, 1941 (uncredited); *Ossessione*, 1943 (novel *The Postman Always Rings Twice*); *Gypsy Wildcat*, 1944; *Double Indemnity*, 1944 (novel); *Mildred Pierce*, 1945 (novel); *The Postman Always Rings Twice*, 1946 (novel); *Everybody Does It*, 1949 (story 'Career in C Major'); *Serenade*, 1956 (novel); *Slightly Scarlet*, 1956 (novel *Love's Lovely Counterfeit*); *Interlude*, 1957 (story); *Double Indemnity*, 1973, (TV, novel); *The Postman Always Rings Twice*, 1981 (novel); *Butterfly*, 1981 (novel); *Girl in the Cadillac*, 1995 (novel *The Enchanted Isle*); *Szenvédély*, Hungary, 1998 (novel *The Postman Always Rings Twice*).

Cornell Woolrich

The Haunted House, 1928 (titles); *Seven Footprints to Satan*, 1929 (titles); *The House of Horror*, 1929 (dialogue); *Children of the Ritz*, 1929 (novel); *Manhattan Love Song*, 1934 (novel); *Convicted*, 1938 (story 'Face Work'); *Street of Chance*, 1942 (novel *The Black Curtain*); *The Leopard Man*, 1943 (novel *Black Alibi*); *Phantom Lady*, 1944 (novel); *Mark of the Whistler*, a.k.a. *The Marked Man*, 1944 (story 'Dormant Account'); *Deadline at Dawn*, 1946 (novel); *Black Angel*, 1946 (novel); *The Chase*, 1946 (novel *The Black Path of Fear*); *Fall Guy*, 1947 (story 'C-Jag'); *The Guilty*, 1947 (story 'He Looked Like Murder'); *Fear in the Night*, 1947 (story 'And So to Death'); *The Return of the Whistler*, 1948 (story 'All at Once, No Alice'); *I Wouldn't Be in Your Shoes*, 1948 (story); *Night Has a Thousand Eyes*, 1948 (novel); *The Window*, 1949 (story 'The Boy Cried Murder'); *No Man of Her Own*, 1950 (novel *I Married a Dead Man*, from story 'They Call Me Patrice'); *El Pendiente*, Argentina, 1951 (story 'The Death Stone'); *Si meuro antes de despertar*, Argentina, 1952, (story 'If I Should Die Before I Wake'); *No abras nunca esa puerta* (1952, from stories 'Somebody on the Phone' and 'Hummingbird Comes Home'); *Obsession*, France, 1954 (stories 'If the Dead Could Talk' and 'Silent as the Grave'); *Rear Window*, 1954 (story 'It Had to Be Murder'); *El ojo de cristal*, Spain, 1956 (story 'The Eye of Doom'); *Nightmare*, 1956 (story 'And So to Death'); *Escapade*, France, 1957 (story 'Cinderella and the Mob'); *Aa Bakudan*, Japan, 1964 (story 'Dipped in Blood'); *Dro itsureba gantiadisas*, a.k.a. *Time Enough for Next Morning*, Georgia, 1965 (novel, *Deadline at Dawn*); *The Boy Cried Murder*, 1966 (story); *Srok istekaet na rassvete*, USSR, 1966 (novel *Deadline at Dawn*); *Yoru No Wana*, Japan, 1967 (novel *The Black Angel*); *La Mariée était en noir*, a.k.a. *The Bride Wore Black*, France, 1967 (novel); *La Sirène du Mississippi*, a.k.a. *Mississippi Mermaid*, France, 1969 (novel *Waltz into Darkness*); *Martha*, West Germany, 1973 (TV, story 'For the Rest of Her Life'); *La pupa del gangster*, Italy, 1974 (story 'Collared'); *Union*

City, 1979 (story 'The Corpse Next Door'); *J'ai epousé une ombre*, France, 1982 (novel *I Married a Dead Man*); *Cloak & Dagger*, 1984 (story 'The Boy Cried Murder'); *I'm Dangerous Tonight*, 1990 (TV, story); *Corsa in discesa*, Italy, 1990 (story 'Debt of Honor'); *Mrs. Winterbourne*, 1996 (novel *I Married a Dead Man*); *Rear Window*, 1998 (TV, story 'It Had to Be Murder'); *Die Unschuld der Krähen*, 1998 (story 'Momentum'); *Original Sin*, a.k.a. *Péché originel*, 2001 (novel *Waltz into Darkness*).

Jim Thompson

The Killing, 1956; *Paths of Glory*, 1957; *The Getaway*, 1972 (novel); *The Killer Inside Me*, 1976 (novel); *Série noire*, 1979, France (novel *A Hell of a Woman*); *Coup de torchon*, a.k.a. *Clean Slate*, 1981, France (based on novel *Pop. 1280*); *Kill-Off*, 1989 (novel); *The Grifters*, 1990 (novel); *After Dark, My Sweet*, 1990 (novel); *The Getaway*, 1994 (novel); *Hit Me*, 1996 (novel *A Swell-Looking Babe*); *This World, Then the Fireworks*, 1997 (story).

David Goodis

The Unfaithful, 1947; *Dark Passage*, 1947 (novel); *Nightfall*, 1956 (novel); *Section des disparus*, France/Argentina, 1956 (novel *Of Missing Persons*); *The Burglar*, 1957 (also novel); *Tirez sur le pianiste*, a.k.a. *Shoot the Piano Player*, France, 1960 (novel *Down There*); *Le Casse*, a.k.a. *The Burglars*, France/Italy, 1971 (novel *The Burglar*); *La Course du lièvre à travers les champs*, a.k.a. *And Hope to Die*, France/Italy, 1972, (novels, *Black Friday* and *Somebody's Done For*); *Rue Barbare*, a.k.a. *Street of the Damned*, France, 1983 (novel *Street of the Lost*); *La Lune dans le caniveau*, a.k.a. *The Moon in the Gutter*, France/Italy, 1983 (novel); *Descente aux enfers*, France, 1986 (novel *The Wounded and the Slain*); *Street of No Return*, a.k.a. *Rua Sem Regresso, Sans espoir de retour*, France/Portugal, 1989 (novel).

A.I. Bezzerides

They Drive By Night, a.k.a. *The Road to Frisco*, 1940 (based on novel *The Long Haul*); *Juke Girl*, 1942; *Action in the North Atlantic*, 1943; *Desert Fury*, 1947; *Thieves' Highway*, a.k.a. *Collision*, 1949 (also novel *Thieves' Market*); *Sirocco*, 1951; *On Dangerous Ground*, 1951; *Holiday for Sinners*, 1952; *Beneath the 12-Mile Reef*, 1953; *Track of the Cat*, 1954; *Kiss Me Deadly*, 1955; *A Bullet for Joey*, 1955; *The Angry Hills*, 1959; *The Jayhawkers!*, 1959.

Daniel Mainwaring

No Hands on the Clock, 1941 (novel); *Secrets of the Underground*, 1942 (story); *Dangerous Passage*, 1944; *Crime by Night*, 1944 (novel *Forty Whacks*); *Scared Stiff*, a.k.a. *Treasure of Fear*, 1945; *They Made Me a Killer*, 1946; *Swamp Fire*, 1946 (also story); *Hot Cargo*, 1946; *Tokyo Rose*, 1946; *Big Town*, a.k.a. *Guilty Assignment*, 1947 (from radio programme); *Big Town After Dark*, a.k.a. *Underworld After Dark*, 1947 (from radio programme, *Big Town*); *Out of the Past*, a.k.a. *Build My Gallows High*, 1947 (also story); *Big Town Scandal*, a.k.a. *Underworld Scandal*, 1948 (also story, from radio programme, *Big Town*); *Roughshod*, 1949; *The Big Steal*, 1949; *The Lawless*, a.k.a. *The Dividing Line*, 1950 (also story 'The Voice of Stephen Wilder'); *The Eagle and the Hawk*, a.k.a. *Spread Eagle*, 1950; *The Tall Target*, 1951 (story); *Roadblock*, 1951 (story); *The Last Outpost*, a.k.a. *Cavalry Charge*, 1951; *This Woman is Dangerous*, 1952; *Bugles in the Afternoon*, 1952; *Powder River*, 1953; *The Hitch-Hiker*, 1953 (uncredited); *Those Redheads from Seattle*, 1953 (also story); *The Desperado*, 1954; *Black Horse Canyon*, a.k.a. *Echo Canyon*, 1954; *Wild Horse Canyon*, 1954; *Southwest Passage*, a.k.a. *Camels West*, 1954; *Alaska Seas*, 1954; *Tormenta*, Spain, 1955 (also story), *The Phenix City Story*, 1955; *A Bullet for Joey*, 1955; *An Annapolis Story*, a.k.a. *The Blue and the Gold*, 1955; *Invasion of the Body Snatchers*, a.k.a. *Sleep No More*, 1956; *Thunderstorm*, 1956; *Baby Face Nelson*, 1957; *Space Master X-7*, a.k.a. *Mutiny in Outer Space*, a.k.a. *Blood Rust,* 1958 (also story); *The Gun Runners,* a.k.a. *Gunrunners,* 1958; *Cole Younger, Gunfighter,* 1958; *Walk Like a Dragon,* 1960 (also story); *Teseo contro il minotauro,* a.k.a. *The Minotaur: Wild Beast of Crete,* a.k.a. *The Minotaur,* Italy, 1961 (also story); *The George Raft Story,* a.k.a. *Spin of a Coin,* 1961; *Atlantis, the Lost Continent,* 1961 (also story); *La rivolta degli schiavi,* a.k.a. *The Revolt of the Slaves,* Spain/Italy/West Germany, 1961; *The Woman Who Wouldn't Die,* a.k.a. *Catacombs,* 1964; *Convict Stage,* 1965; *Against All Odds,* 1984 (remake of *Out of the Past,* using original screenplay).

Jonathan Latimer

The Westland Case, 1937 (novel *Headed for a Hearse*); *The Lady in the Morgue,* a.k.a. *The Case of the Missing Blonde,* 1938 (novel); *The Last Warning,* 1938 (novel *The Dead Don't Care*); *Lone Wolf Spy Hunt,* a.k.a. *The Lone Wolf's Daughter,* 1939; *Phantom Raiders,* a.k.a. *Nick Carter in Panama,* 1940 (story); *Topper Returns,* 1941; *Night in New Orleans,* 1942; *The Glass Key,* 1942; *Nocturne,* 1946; *They Won't Believe Me,* 1947; *Sealed Verdict,* 1948; *The Accused,* 1948 (uncredited); *Night Has a Thousand Eyes,* 1948; *The Big Clock,* 1948; *Beyond Glory,* 1948; *Alias Nick Beal,* a.k.a. *The Contact Man,* 1949; *The Redhead and the Cowboy,* 1950; *Copper Canyon,* 1950; *Submarine Command,* a.k.a. *The Submarine Story,* 1951; *Botany Bay,* 1953; *Plunder of the Sun,* 1953; *Back from Eternity,* 1956; *The Unholy Wife,* a.k.a. *The Lady and the Prowler,* 1957; *The Whole Truth,* 1958.

Leigh Brackett

The Vampire's Ghost, 1945 (story); *The Crime Doctor's Man Hunt,* 1946 (based on radio programme); *The Big Sleep,* 1946; *Rio Bravo,* 1959; *Gold of the Seven Saints,* 1961; *Hatari!,* 1961; *13 West Street,* 1962 (novel *The Tiger Among Us*); *Man's Favorite Sport,* 1964 (uncredited); *El Dorado,* 1967; *Rio Lobo,* a.k.a. *San Timoteo,* 1970; *The Long Goodbye,* 1973; *Star Wars: Episode V: The Empire Strikes Back,* 1980.

Edward Bunker

Straight Time, 1978 (also novel *No Beast So Fierce*); *Runaway Train*, 1985; *Johnny Handsome*, 1989 (uncredited); *Maximum Bob*, 1998 (TV series, novel); *The Animal Factory*, 2000 (also novel).

Elmore Leonard

3:10 to Yuma, 1957 (story); *The Tall T*, 1957 (story); *Hombre*, 1967 (novel); *The Big Bounce*, 1969 (novel); *The Moonshine War*, 1970 (also novel); *Valdez Is Coming*, 1971 (novel); *Joe Kidd*, 1972; *Mr. Majestyk*, 1974 (also novel); *High Noon, Part II: The Return of Will Kane*, 1980 (TV); *The Ambassador*, a.k.a. *Peacemaker*, 1982 (novel *52 Pick-Up*); *Stick*, 1985 (novel); *52 Pick-Up*, 1986 (novel); *The Rosary Murders*, 1987; *Glitz*, 1988 (TV, novel); *Cat Chaser*, 1989 (also novel); *Border Shootout*, 1990 (story); *Split Images*, 1992 (TV, novel); *Get Shorty*, 1995 (novel); *Last Stand at Saber River*, 1997 (TV, novel); *Touch*, 1997 (novel); *Pronto*, 1997 (TV, novel); *Gold Coast*, a.k.a. *Elmore Leonard's Gold Coast*, 1997 (TV, novel); *Jackie Brown*, 1997 (based on novel *Rum Punch*); *Out of Sight*, 1998 (novel), *Tishomingo Blues*, 2003 (novel); *The Big Bounce*, 2003 (novel).

James Ellroy

Cop, 1987 (novel *Blood on the Moon*); *L.A. Confidential*, 1997 (novel); 'Since I Don't Have You', 1997 (TV series *Fallen Angels*, story); *Brown's Requiem*, 1998 (novel), *L.A. Sheriff's Homicide*, 2000; *Dark Blue*, 2002 (novel *The Plague Season*); *My Dark Places: An L.A. Crime Memoir*, 2003 (book).

Gerald Petievich

To Live and Die in L.A., 1985 (novel), *C.A.T. Squad*, a.k.a. *Stalking Danger*, 1986 (TV), *C.A.T. Squad: Python Wolf*, 1988 (TV, story), *Boiling Point*, 1993 (novel *Money Man*).

James Lee Burke

Heaven's Prisoners, 1996 (novel); *Two for Texas*, 1998 (TV, novel).

Walter Mosley

Devil in a Blues Dress, 1995 (novel); *Always Outnumbered, Always Outgunned*, 1998 (TV, novel).

Sara Paretsky

V.I. Warshawski, 1991 (novels); *Where Danger Follows You Home*, 1997 (story).

Tony Hillerman

The Dark Wind, 1991 (novel); *The Skinwalkers*, 2003 (TV, novel).

Joseph Wambaugh

The New Centurions, a.k.a. *Precinct 45: Los Angeles Police*, 1972 (novel); *The Blue Knight*, 1973 (TV, novel); *The Blue Knight*, 1975 (TV, novel); *The Choirboys*, 1977 (uncredited, also novel); *The Onion Field*, 1979 (also novel); *The Black Marble*, 1980 (also novel); *The Glitter Dome*, 1984 (TV, novel); *Echoes in the Darkness*, 1987 (TV, also novel); *Fugitive Nights: Danger in the Desert*, 1993 (TV, also book).

Donald E. Westlake (a.k.a. Richard Stark)

Made in U.S.A., 1966 (novel *The Jugger*); *The Busy Body*, 1967 (novel); *Point Blank*, 1967 (novel *The Hunter*); *Mise à sac*, a.k.a. *Pillaged*, France, 1967 (novel *The Score*); *The Split*, 1968 (novel *The Seventh*); *The Hot Rock*, a.k.a. *How to Steal a Diamond in Four Uneasy Lessons*, 1972 (novel); *Cops and Robbers*, 1973 (also novel); *The Outfit*, 1974 (novel); *Bank Shot*, 1974 (novel); *Cinque furbastri, un furbacchione*, Italy, 1977 (novel); *Hot Stuff*,

1979; *Jimmy the Kid*, 1983 (novel); *Le Jumeau*, a.k.a. *The Twin*, France, 1984 (novel *Two Much*); *Slayground*, 1983 (novel); *Fatal Confession: A Father Dowling Mystery*, 1987 (TV); *The Stepfather*, a.k.a. *Stepfather I*, 1987; *Stepfather II*, a.k.a. *Stepfather II: Make Room for Daddy*, 1989 (characters); *Why Me?*, 1990 (also book); *The Grifters*, 1990; *Stepfather III: Father's Day*, 1992 (TV, characters); *Two Much*, 1996 (novel); *La Divine Poursuite*, France, 1997 (novel *Dancing Aztecs*); *Payback*, 1999 (novel *The Hunter*); *Jimmy the Kid*, 1999 (novel); *A Slight Case of Murder*, a.k.a. *A Travesty*, 1999 (TV, book); *What's the Worst That Could Happen?*, 2001 (novel); *The Hook*, 2001 (novel).

Barry Gifford

Wild at Heart, 1990 (novel); *Hotel Room*, 1993 (TV series); *Perdita Durango*, a.k.a. *Dance with the Devil*, 1997 (novel *59 Degrees and Raining: The Story of Perdita Durango*); *Lost Highway*, 1997; *Sultans of Africa*, 2001 (also directed); *City of Ghosts*, 2002.

Michael Connelly

Blood Work, 2002 (novel); *A Darkness More than Night*, 2003 (novel).

Dennis Lehane

Neighborhoods, 1996 (also producer, director).

Sources

Anger, Kenneth, *Hollywood Babylon*, Dell Publishing Co., New York, 1983.

Bassett, Mark T., 'Preface', *Blues of a Lifetime – The Autobiography of Cornell Woolrich*, Popular Press, Bowling Green, Ohio, 1991.

Bezzerides, A.I., 'Afterword', *Thieves' Market*, University of California Press, Berkeley, reprint edition, 1997.

Biskind, Peter, *Seeing Is Believing: How Hollywood Taught Us to Stop Worrying and Love the Fifties*, Pantheon Books, New York, 1983.

Brubaker, Bill, *Stewards of the House: The Detective Fiction of Jonathan Latimer*, Popular Press, Bowling Green, Ohio, 1993.

Brunette, Peter, and Gerald Peary, 'James M. Cain: Tough Guy', in Patrick McGilligan (ed.) *Backstory: Interviews with Screenwriters of Hollywood's Golden Age*, University of California Press, Berkeley, 1986.

Bunker, Edward, *Mr. Blue: Memoirs of a Renegade*, No Exit Press, Harpenden, 1999.

Cassill, R.V., 'The Killer Inside Me: Fear, Purgation, and the Sophoclean Light', in David Madden (ed.) *Tough Guy Writers of the Thirties*, Southern Illinois University Press, Carbondale, 1968.

Caute, David, *Joseph Losey: A Revenge on Life*, Faber & Faber, London, 1996.

Christopher, Nicholas, *Somewhere in the Night: Film Noir and the American City*, Free Press, New York, 1997.

Clarens, Carlos, *Crime Movies: An Illustrated History of the Gangster*

Genre from D.W. Griffith to Pulp Fiction, updated by Foster Hirsch, Da Capo Press, New York, 1997.

Connelly, Michael, 'Looking into the Abyss', Time Warner Bookmark, http://www.twbookmark.com/, 2 January 2001.

Cooper, Stephen, *Full of Life: A Biography of John Fante,* Canongate Books, Edinburgh, 2000.

Corliss, Richard (ed.), *The Hollywood Screenwriters,* Avon, New York, 1972.

Coursodon, Jean-Pierre, and Bertrand Tavernier, *50 ans de cinéma américain,* Editions Nathan, Paris, 1995.

Crowe, Cameron, *Conversations with Wilder,* Faber & Faber, London, 1999.

Davis, Mike, *Ecology of Fear: Los Angeles and the Imagination of Disaster,* Vintage Books, New York, 1999.

— *City of Quartz: Excavating the Future of Los Angeles,* Verso, London and New York, 1990.

Duggan, Eddie, 'Writing in the Darkness: Cornell Woolrich', *Crime Time* 2.6, Harpenden, 1999.

Duncan, Paul (ed.), *The Third Degree: Crime Writers in Conversation,* No Exit Press, Harpenden, 1997.

Dunne, John Gregory, *Monster: Living off the Big Screen,* Random House, New York, 1997.

Durham, Philip, 'The Black Mask School', in David Madden (ed.) *Tough Guy Writers of the Thirties,* Southern Illinois University Press, Carbondale, 1968.

Eisenschitz, Bernard, *Nicholas Ray: An American Journey,* Faber & Faber, London, 1993.

Fisher, Steve, *I Wake Up Screaming,* Dodd, Mead & Co., New York, 1941.

Fitzgerald, F. Scott, *The Pat Hobby Stories,* Scribner, New York, 1995.

Flynn, Charles and Todd McCarthy (eds.), *King of the Bs*, Dutton, New York, 1975.

Francke, Lizzie, *Script Girls: Women Screenwriters in Hollywood*, British Film Institute, London, 1994.

Friedrich, Otto, *City of Nets: A Portrait of Hollywood in the 1940s*, University of California Press, Berkeley, 1997.

Garnier, Philippe, *Goodis: La Vie en noir et blanc*, Seuil, Paris, 1984.

— *Honni soit qui Malibu: quelques écrivains à Hollywood*, Grasset, Paris, 1996.

Geherin, David, *The American Private Eye: The Image in Fiction*, Ungar, New York, 1985.

Goldman, William, *Adventures in the Screen Trade: A Personal View of Hollywood and Screenwriting*, Macdonald, London, 1984.

Gorman, Ed, Lee Server and Martin H. Greenberg (eds.), *The Big Book of Noir*, Carroll & Graf, New York, 1998.

Govenar, Alan B., and Jay F. Brakefield, *Deep Ellum and Central Track: Where the Black and White Worlds of Dallas Converged*, University of North Texas Press, Denton, 1999.

Haut, Woody, *Pulp Culture: Hardboiled Fiction and the Cold War*, Serpent's Tail, London, 1995.

— *Neon Noir: Contemporary American Crime Fiction*, Serpent's Tail, London, 1999.

Hecht, Ben, *A Child of the Century*, Donald I. Fine, New York, 1983.

Himes, Chester, *My Life of Absurdity: The Later Years*, Paragon House, New York, 1990.

Hiney, Tom, *Raymond Chandler: A Biography*, Vintage, London, 1998.

Hoopes, Roy, *Cain*, Holt, Rinehart & Winston, New York, 1982.

Horne, Gerald, *Class Struggle in Hollywood, 1930–1950: Moguls,*

Mobsters, Stars, Reds, and Trade Unionists, University of Texas Press, Austin, 2001.

Hubin, Allen J., *Crime Fiction, 1749–1980: A Comprehensive Bibliography*, Garland, New York, 1984.

Internet Movie Database, www.imdb.com.

Johnson, Diane, *The Life of Dashiell Hammett*, Picador, London, 1985.

Katz, Ephraim, *The International Film Encyclopaedia*, Macmillan, London, 1982.

Kael, Pauline, *Raising Kane and Other Essays*, Marion Boyars, London, 1996.

Kuhn, Annette (ed.), *Queen of the 'B's: Ida Lupino Behind the Camera*, Flicks Books, Trowbridge, 1995.

Lardner, Ring Jr., *I'd Hate Myself in the Morning: A Memoir*, Nation Books, New York, 2000.

Latimer, Jonathan, 'Author's Introduction to the 1982 Edition', *Solomon's Vineyard*, Maurice Neville Rare Books, Santa Barbara, 1982.

LoBrutto, Vincent, *Stanley Kubrick: A Biography*, Donald I. Fine, New York, 1997; Faber & Faber, London, 1998.

Madden, David (ed.), *Tough Guy Writers of the Thirties*, Southern Illinois University Press, Carbondale, 1968.

McGilligan, Patrick (ed.), *Backstory: Interviews with Screenwriters of Hollywood's Golden Age*, University of California Press, Berkeley, 1986.

— *Backstory 2: Interview with Screenwriters of the 1940s and 1950s*, University of California Press, Berkeley, 1991.

— *Backstory 3: Interviews with Screenwriters of the 1960s*, University of California Press, Berkeley, 1997.

McGilligan, Patrick, and Paul Buhle (eds.), *Tender Comrades: A*

Backstory of the Hollywood Blacklist, St. Martin's Press, New York, 1997.

McWilliams, Carey, *Southern California Country: An Island on the Land*, 1946, reprinted Gibbs Smith, Salt Lake City, 1994.

Mate, Ken, and Patrick McGilligan, 'W.R. Burnett: The Outsider', in Pat McGilligan (ed.) *Backstory: Interviews with Screenwriters of Hollywood's Golden Age*, University of California Press, Berkeley, 1986.

Mellen, Joan, *Hellman and Hammett: The Legendary Passion of Lillian Hellman and Dashiell Hammett*, HarperCollins, New York, 1996.

Mesplède, Claude, and Jean-Jacques Schleret (eds.), *Les Auteurs de la Série Noire*, Joseph K., Paris, 1997.

Moreau, Michael (ed.), *John Fante and H.L. Mencken: A Personal Correspondence, 1930–1952*, Black Sparrow, Santa Rosa, 1989.

Muller, Eddie, *Dark City: The Lost World of Film Noir*, St. Martin's Press, New York, 1997.

Naremore, James, *More Than Night: Film Noir in Its Contexts*, University of California Press, Berkeley, 1998.

Nevins, Francis M. Jr., *Cornell Woolrich: First You Dream, Then You Die*, Mysterious Press, New York, 1988.

Nolan, William F., Introduction, *Nightmare Town: Stories*, by Dashiell Hammett, Knopf, New York, 1999.

Nolan, William F., *The Black Mask Boys: Masters in the Hard-Boiled School of Detective Fiction*, William Morrow, New York, 1985.

Oates, Joyce Carol, 'Man Under Sentence of Death: The Novels of James M. Cain', in David Madden (ed.) *Tough Guy Writers of the Thirties*, Southern Illinois University Press, Carbondale, 1968.

O'Brien, Geoffrey, *Hardboiled America: The Lurid Years of Paperbacks*, Van Nostrand Reinhold, New York, 1981.

Phelps, Donald, 'Cinema Gris: Woolrich/O'Neil's Black Angel', *Film Comment*, April, 2000, New York.

Polito, Robert, *Savage Art: The Life of Jim Thompson*, Knopf, New York, 1996; Serpent's Tail, London, 1998.

— 'Barbara Payton: A Memoir', in Luc Sante and Melissa Holbrook Pierson (eds.), *O.K. You Mugs: Writers on Movie Actors*, Granta, London, 2000.

Porfirio, Robert, 'Interview with Billy Wilder', in Robert Porfirio, Alain Silver and James Ursini (eds.), *Film Noir Reader 3: Interviews with Filmmakers of the Classic Noir Period*, Limelight Editions, New York, 2001.

Sallis, James, *Chester Himes: A Life*, Payback Press, Edinburgh, 2000.

— *Difficult Lives: Jim Thompson, David Goodis, Chester Himes*, Gryphon, Brooklyn, NY, 1993.

See, Carolyn, 'The Hollywood Novel: The American Dream Cheat', in David Madden (ed.) *Tough Guy Writers of the 1930s*, Southern Illinois University Press, Carbondale, 1968.

Server, Lee, *Screenwriter: Words Become Pictures*, Main Street Press, Pittstown, NJ, 1987.

Silver, Alain, and Elizabeth Ward (eds.), *Film Noir: An Encyclopaedic Reference Guide*, Bloomsbury, London, 1988.

Starr, Kevin, *Endangered Dreams: The Great Depression in California*, Oxford University Press, Oxford, 1996.

— *The Dream Endures: California Enters the 1940s*, Oxford University Press, Oxford, 1997.

Swires, Steve, 'Leigh Brackett: Journeyman Plumber', in Patrick McGilligan (ed.) *Backstory 2: Interviews with Screenwriters of the 1940s and 1950s*, University of California Press, Berkeley, 1991.

Thomson, David, *A Biographical Dictionary of Film*, Andre Deutsch, London, 1994.

Tully, Jim, *Shadows of Men*, Doubleday, Doran, Garden City, NY, 1930.

Tuska, Jon, *The Detective in Hollywood*, Doubleday, Garden City, NY, 1978.

Walker, John (ed.), *Halliwell's Film Guide*, 10th edition, Harper-Collins, London, 1994.

White, Garrett, 'Introduction', *Thieves' Highway*, by A.I. Bezzerides, University of California Press, Berkeley, 1997.

Willeford, Charles, 'Jim Tully: Holistic Barbarian', in *Writing and Other Blood Sports*, Dennis McMillan Publications, Tuscon, 2000.

Wilson, Edmund, 'The Boys in the Backroom', *Classics and Commercials: A Literary Chronicle of the Forties*, Farrar, Straus, New York, 1950.

Woolrich, Cornell, *Blues of a Lifetime – The Autobiography of Cornell Woolrich*, edited by Mark T. Bassett, Popular Press, Bowling Green, Ohio, 1991.

Wootton, Adrian, and Paul Taylor (eds.), *David Goodis: Pulps Pictured For Goodis' Sake*, BFI Publications, London, 1989.

Index

INDEX

Bronson, Charles 220
Brooks, Richard 148
Brower, Otto 48
Brown, Harry 54
Brown, Rowland 188
Brubaker, Bill 298
Brunette, Peter 87, 93, 298
Buhle, Paul 302
Bunker, Edward 203–16, 227, 294, 298
Burke, James Lee 246, 250–6, 279, 295
Burnett, W.R. 5, 9, 43, 55, 57–75, 90, 138, 174, 185, 208, 288, 302
Burnett, Whitney Forbes 72, 73, 74, 105
Burroughs, Edgar Rice 194
Buscemi, Steve 208, 215
Busch, Niven 2, 88–9, 99–100
Butler, Frank 31

Cabanne, Christy 190
Cagney, James 54
Cain, James M. 2, 5, 12, 27, 29, 31, 47, 50, 53, 73, 76, 78, 83–101, 104, 123, 124, 175–6, 213, 234, 264, 289, 298, 301
Cain, Paul (aka George Ruric, George Carrol Sims) 76–83, 88, 188, 289
Caldwell, Erskine 53
Campbell, Alan 51
Camus, Albert 51, 84, 204
Capone, Al 58, 61, 62, 64, 185
Capote, Truman 129, 209, 255
Capra, Frank 90, 97, 270
Carradine, Keith 147
Carey, Timothy 125
Carroll, Nancy 88
Caspary, Vera 194
Cassill, R.V. 129, 298
Cather, Willa 124
Caute, David 299
Cavett, Frank 31
Cerf, Bennet 21, 52
Chandler, Cissy 26, 28, 34, 35, 37, 38
Chandler, Norman 122
Chandler, Raymond 2, 3, 4, 8, 12, 17, 25–42, 43, 45, 51, 53, 56, 73, 77, 78–9, 83, 84, 94, 97, 122, 135, 141, 144, 149, 186, 189, 193, 196, 197, 199–201, 247, 248, 273, 278, 285, 286, 301
Chaplin, Charles 79, 205
Chenal, Pierre 99, 146
Chessman, Caryl 204
Chester, Hal E. 163

Christensen, Benjamin 103
Christie, Agatha 250
Christopher, Nicholas 157, 299
Cimino, Michael 73
Clarens, Carlos 299
Clemens, William 174
Clement, Rene 147
Clough, Mary Rebekah 85
Clurman, Harold 108–9
Cobb, Lee J. 159
Coen Brothers 4, 162, 272, 282
Coffee, Lenore 194
Cohen, Benoit 228
Cohen, Ernest Philip 163
Cohen, Mickey 225
Cohn, Harry 18, 61, 74, 90, 148
Collier, John 140
Collins, Richard 183
Comandini, Adele 194
Connelly, Michael 139, 202, 267, 273–9, 297, 299
Conte, Richard 159
Cook Jr., William Edward 180
Cook Jr., Elisha 108, 125
Cooper Jr., Clarence 204
Cooper, Gary 11, 198, 204
Cooper, Stephen 163, 299
Coppola, Francis, Ford 95, 268, 269
Corliss, Robert 217, 298
Cormack, Bartlett 70
Corneau, Alain 135–6
Cortese, Valentina 160
Cortez, Ricardo 48
Costello, Frank 29
Coursodon, Jean-Pierre 299
Crawford, Broderick 152
Crawford, Joan 68, 98, 101, 148, 179, 198
Crews, Harry 273
Cromwell, John 70
Crosby, Bing 31
Crowe, Cameron 299
Crowther, Bosley 177
Crumley, James 246–50, 279
Cukor, George 73, 90
Cummings, Robert 109, 191
Curtiz, Michael 98
Cusack, John 228, 229
Czapsky, Stefan 259

Dafoe, Willem 208
Dahl, Arlene 92
Dahlberg, Edward 122
Daniels, Harold 178

INDEX

Freeman, Y. Frank 36
Freud, Sigmund 194
Friedkin, William 232, 240
Friedrich, Otto 10, 300
Frings, Ketty 191
Fuller, Samuel 70, 74, 121, 130, 134,
    138, 147, 154, 238
Furlong, Edward 208
Furthman, Jules 198–9

Gable, Clark 45
Galsworthy, John 150
Gamet, Ken 161
Garbo, Greta 205
Gardner, Ava 175
Garfield, John 32, 67, 99, 152, 178
Garland, Judy 129
Garner, James 39
Garnett, Tay 54, 99
Garnier, Philippe 145, 148, 163, 172,
    300
Garrett, Otis 190
Geherin, David 300
Geisel, Theodore (aka Dr Seuss) 186
Gershwin, Ira 11
Giannini, A.P. 7
Gide, Andre 84
Gifford, Barry 267, 268–73, 297
Gilbert, Edwin 142
Gilbert, John 205
Girod, Francis 147
Glasmon, Kubec 191
Glover, Danny 39
Goldman, William 4, 6, 40, 236, 255,
    264, 300
Goldwyn, Samuel 35, 61, 94, 99, 194
Godfrey, Peter 191
Goodis, David 34, 118–19, 130,
    137–55, 177, 282, 291, 300, 304,
    305
Goodis, Elaine 138–9, 141
Goodrich, Frances 16
Gorman, Edward 300
Gould, Elliott 39, 200–2
Goulding, Edmund 205
Grant, Cary 32, 39, 81, 88, 204
Graver, Gary 137
Greene, Graham 58, 257
Greenberg, Martin 300
Greenwald, Robert 228
Greer, Jane 175
Grella, George 58
Griffith, D.W. 190
Grosbard, Ulu 206, 214

Guerif, Francois 228
Gulager, Clu 255
Gunn, James 95, 138, 140
Guthrie, Woody 120

Hackett, Albert 16, 20
Hadida, Samuel 227
Hall, James W. 246, 259–60
Halliday, Brett 28
Hamilton, Edmund 196
Hamilton, George 148
Hammett, Dashiell 4, 6–24, 25, 27,
    40–2, 43, 45, 51, 56, 77, 84, 85,
    104, 150, 174, 175, 177, 182, 185,
    187, 188, 189, 190, 191, 197, 228,
    247, 282, 285, 286, 301, 302, 303
Hano, Arthur 124
Hanson, Curtis 227, 230, 231, 255
Harlow, Jean 61, 225
Harrington, Curtis 104
Harris, James B. 125, 227, 233
Harrison, Jim 269
Harrison, Joan 194
Harrison, John Kent 256
Harry, Deborah 114
Hathaway, Henry 48
Haut, Woody 301
Hawks, Howard 32, 35, 62, 63, 73, 88,
    90, 165, 193, 194, 196–200
Hayden, Sterling 69, 125
Hays, Will 13
Hayward, Susan 54, 55, 109
Hayworth, Rita 107, 191
Hearst, William Randolph 205
Hecht, Ben 2, 11, 38, 50, 62, 63, 64,
    73, 198, 301
Heflin, Van 80, 81, 219
Helgeland, Brian 230, 231, 255
Heisler, Stuart 67, 71, 191
Hellinger, Mark 66, 67
Hellman, Lillian 12–16, 19–24, 152,
    302
Hemingway, Ernest 4, 124, 144, 185,
    198, 204, 272
Hepburn, Katherine 193
Hersholt, Jean 61, 62
Hessler, Gordon 184
Heston, Charlton 55
Higgins, George V. 209, 224–5, 272
Highsmith, Patricia 37
Hill, Walter 134, 248
Hillerman, Tony 246, 258–9, 296
Himes, Chester 18, 58, 82, 204, 282,
    301, 304

INDEX

INDEX